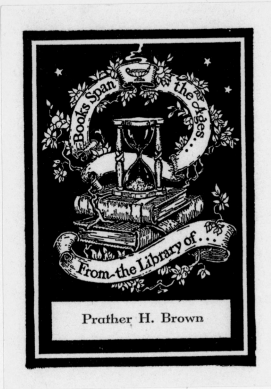

Books Span the Ages...

From the Library of...

Prather H. Brown

The Portuguese Escape

The Portuguese Escape

❧ A NOVEL BY ❧

ANN BRIDGE

THE MACMILLAN COMPANY
New York

With the exception of public figures, such as Dr. Salazar and Cardinal Mindszenty, who are mentioned by name, no reference is intended in this book to any living person.

The Portuguese Escape

Chapter One

Two young men were sitting under a gaily coloured sun-umbrella on the terrace of a restaurant, overlooking the Tagus between Lisbon and Estoril, a little detached from the crowd of people at the farther end, where a cocktail party was in progress. One was First Secretary at the American Embassy in Lisbon, the other his opposite number in the British Mission, and they were talking with the easy frankness which obtains between diplomats who are also friends.

"So she's really coming?" Richard Atherley, the Englishman, asked.

"She *is*—she's in Madrid at this instant, and arrives here tomorrow morning. I have to support the devoted Mama at the station at 9 A.M."

"We really have to hand it to the Countess for getting her out at last. *How* long has she been at it?"

"Well, it's ten years since she and old Count Páloczy came out themselves," Townsend Waller said, "and I suppose when they found there was no hope of getting back to Hungary they started in trying to get young Hetta out. Say nine years ago."

"Why did they leave her behind in the first place? It seems a mad thing to have done."

"She was down with scarlet fever at her convent school when the Russians came in—it wasn't very practical to move her. And I don't think anyone realised, at that stage, what the Russian occupation was going to amount to, nor how permanent it would be. Anyway it was really urgent to get the old Count out: the Communists had him as a top priority on their liquidation list, because he'd been a main opponent of Michael Károlyi and the Béla Kun Communist revolution in 1919."

"1919! He must have been very young then."

"Not all that young—he was a whole lot older than Dorothée. You never met him, did you?"

"No, he died just before I came."

"Pity. He was so nice, and a real *galant' uomo*," the Bostonian said thoughtfully. "And this child was the light of his eyes; I don't think he was ever *not* thinking of her for half-an-hour together—while he was awake, that is. He spent the last nine years of his life in hell. It was a damned shame, for a man like that."

"A damned shame for any man," Atherley agreed. But he had been doing sums in his head. "How old was the girl when they left?"

"Twelve, I think."

"So she'll be twenty-two now. Good Heavens!—a grown woman, who hasn't seen her mother since she was a child. What a strange situation."

"Strange enough—especially when you consider Dorothée," the American said, causing Atherley to give a short deep laugh rather like the brief bark of a big dog.

"Good God, yes." He continued to think it over. "Where's the girl been all this time?" he asked.

"I don't know—accurately. With the nuns, I suppose."

"I thought all the convents were washed up."

"No one knows that—no one really knows anything about actual conditions in Hungary. The child was traceable, and traced—because the Páloczys tried everything: Red Cross, Quakers, Hungarian Legation in Washington, American Legation in Budapest *and* in Vienna—with just precisely no result. At one point the Hungarian government tried to do a trade, the U.S.A. clamping down on the Voice of America broadcasts to Hungary in exchange for young Hetta: but of course the State Department couldn't agree to that. Then there was a round-about suggestion of money—so many thousand dollars to be made available for purchases of things they wanted. The Countess was advised against that, of course, but she wouldn't listen, and I believe she sprang half-a-million dollars. But still no Hetta."

"You don't say so!"

"It's exactly what I *do* say. Ask for money, get money, and don't carry out the bargain."

Atherley looked thoughtful.

"That is really horrible, when you think what tremendous 'gentlemen,' in the best sense of the word, the Hungarians used to be."

"Did you know them?" Townsend Waller asked.

"A little, yes. I was out there in 1939, shooting—only for a few weeks, but I stayed all the time in Hungarian houses, and got to know some of them rather well. It was a splendid way of life; it's hideous to think of it all being wrecked and ruined."

"Why was it so good? I thought it was pretty feudal."

"Feudalism *is* good—and pretty too!" the Englishman said roundly. "And just as nice for the peasant as for the prince! Don't go all bogus about the Common Man, Townsend; you know better in Boston." Then as his friend laughed, he reverted to the subject of Hetta Páloczy and her exit from Hungary. "Whose idea was the Press Conference? Yours?"

"Not on your life! It was Dorothée's own notion, and I know the Ambassador tried to shelve it; but of course she's an American citizen, and a free agent, and nobody could really stop her. Naturally Perce helped it along, once it was clear that Dorothée was determined to have it, and rounded up a good show of correspondents; but no one expected it to resound the way it did. I never remember anything like it, and nor does Perce; and he's been a Press Attaché for a long while, and a press-man for longer."

"Yes, it did resound," said Atherley. "I should rather like to have been there."

"Dorothée did it awfully well; I have to give her that. She's nobody's fool, whatever one may think of her social efforts, and she didn't over-play her hand at all; she kept very quiet, just gave all the facts, and what had been done, and promised, and the broken promises—and threw in the old Count's death with quite a neat quiet little implication that he'd died of a broken heart. I daresay he did, even if it was technically a grippe—I would imagine he felt he just couldn't go on living in that agony about the girl any more. Anyhow the world press the conference got must have shaken up Moscow quite considerably, for it was just forty-eight hours before the telegram came to say that the Countess Hetta Páloczy was being shipped out."

"A telegram from Moscow?"

"No, Budapest—but we all know where they take their orders from."

"Stinkers!" said the Englishman, without heat. "And what does your Ambassador say now?"

"Oh, he's as pleased as a dog with two tails!" said the American, with a wide agreeable grin.

"Well, here's to the poor little Countess." Raising his glass, he saw that it was empty. "*Mais dois,*" he said to a hovering waiter, who swept away their glasses, and returned almost instantly with two more. Atherley gave the toast again. When they had drunk it, "I suppose no one has any idea what the girl is like?" he said thoughtfully.

"I asked Johnson that, when he called me from Madrid to advise us that she was coming—all he said was 'Silent.'"

"Then she must be plain. Dorothée won't like that."

"She wouldn't like it so very much if she was a beauty," said the American.

"No. What the Countess would like is something in between— passably pretty, and chic. Can a woman from behind the Curtain be chic?"

"I wouldn't think so, by what I hear from our people in Moscow."

"Poor girl! It really *is* a situation," said Atherley thoughtfully—he never minded repeating himself. "You know, after all those years to come now, a grown woman, quite *fresh* to Dorothée—"

"Look out! Here she comes!" his friend adjured him hastily. The table at which they sat was just at the top of the flight of steps leading down from the restaurant to the broad roadway which runs along the north bank of the Tagus, now bordered with the dark shining shapes of parked cars, so that anyone descending the steps had to pass close by the two young men. Atherley glanced round. A tall woman, obviously middle-aged but still slender, was moving with rather deliberate grace-fulness towards them, accompanied by a man whose black garments, and still more the peculiar combination of urbanity, experience, and astute-ness of his expression unmistakably indicated a dignitary of the Roman Catholic Church.

"With her familiar spirit!" Atherley muttered irrepressibly.

"*Will* you shut up!" his companion repeated anxiously.

When she reached their table the Countess Páloczy paused.

"Are you two not at the party, or are you contracting out?" she asked, with a little smile.

The two young men sprang up.

"A little of both, Countess," Townsend Waller said. "We are at the party, but we had business to discuss."

"Practically in conference!" she said, with slight mockery. "You know Monsignor Subercaseaux, don't you?"

They both bowed.

"But naturally—I hope rather well," said Atherley, holding out his hand to the priest. In fact Atherley always enjoyed the company of the Monsignor—his high degree of intelligence, his subtlety, and his remarkably uninhibited freedom of speech were all most entertaining and refreshing, the young man felt, in the stereotyped and conventional society in which they both moved.

The Countess was speaking to Waller.

"You will be at the Rossio tomorrow morning? I—well, I shall be glad of support. It is so sad to be meeting the child alone." There was a slight stress on the last word.

"Yes indeed, Countess—I'll be there. I'm afraid your daughter will have an awful night, in those little coffins of sleepers they've put on now from Madrid."

"Are they bad?"

"Oh, ghastly! They've almost doubled the number of sleepers to a coach; you can hardly turn round, the washbowl's the size of a tea-cup, and there's no room for luggage—you can't fit in a hat-box!"

"I don't suppose Hetta has much luggage," the Countess said measuredly. "Very well—till tomorrow morning. Goodbye. Goodbye, Mr. Atherley." She moved away, still accompanied by the priest.

"I like Subercaseaux," Atherley said when the Countess Páloczy's Rolls-Royce, gliding noiselessly to the foot of the steps, had borne the pair off. "He can be such fun."

"He's entertaining all right; but do you think, Richard, that he's really a man of God?" the Bostonian asked, turning deep-set, suddenly serious eyes onto his friend. Atherley laughed out loud.

"You dear old Pilgrim Father! *I* don't know. If he is, it's too heavily overlaid with the wisdom of the serpent to be very obvious; but I don't exclude it. Nothing is ever obvious about R.C. priests, not even holiness —and there have been some very holy ones. Why does it worry you?"

"I don't think ministers of religion should get mixed up in politics," Waller said slowly.

"But Townsend, does he?"

"Oh Richard, be your age! None of these foreign royals and politicos here stir a foot without consulting him. I bet you he arranged this marriage between the King of Calabria's daughter and the Comte de Bretagne's son; and I shouldn't be a bit surprised to learn that it was he who tipped the Countess off to hold that press conference."

"He did a good job, if so. But if he does give advice—and I'm sure his would be good—it's as un-obvious as everything else about him."

Townsend Waller stared earnestly at his friend.

"Richard—forgive my asking—but you aren't thinking of becoming a Catholic, are you?"

At that question Mr. Atherley's laughter became like the baying of several bloodhounds, causing heads to turn at the more populated end of the terrace.

"Oh Townsend, you'll be the death of me," the young man said when he could speak. "NO! I'm only saying that a wise man, trained all his life to wisdom and self-abnegation—as well as being as clever as a sackful of monkeys anyhow—probably gives advice worth listening to when, if, he's asked for it. What's the worry?"

"I don't like Catholics," the American said slowly. "You mightn't, either, if you lived in Boston."

"Why not?"

"They run the city, and rackets—and anyway they're mostly Irish." Atherley laughed again, but less loudly.

"Subercaseaux isn't Irish, whatever other sins you may lay at his door," he said. "I don't know what his nationality is, as a matter of fact. But look, Townsend, I must leave in ten minutes—I'm dining with H.E., who keeps English time—and I think I had better mingle a little before I go. In fact you ought to mingle too." He rose, threw a note on the table, and walked off towards the throng of guests at the farther end of the terrace.

The Rossio Station is a curious place. In some ways it resembles the entrance to a rabbit-burrow, for the railway, tunnelling through one of Lisbon's seven hills, only emerges in the station itself, which is practically scooped out of the cliff of houses that overhangs it; it is cramped, gloomy, and awkward of access for cars.

Here, on the following morning, Townsend Waller stood beside Countess Páloczy on the platform, reluctantly inhaling the sulphurous fumes which always hang round the mouths of tunnels; these were also being inhaled by a group of reporters, several press-photographers, and a man with a television apparatus, who all stood as close to the two principals—Waller hated the realisation that he was, inescapably, a principal —as even press decency permitted, which was about seven feet away. The Countess was nervous; she tapped her foot on the ground, constantly uttered rather disconnected remarks, and snapped at one of the cameramen, who asked if he could take a picture of her "awaiting re-union with a beloved child"—he couldn't, she told him curtly. The train was late, it often is; the strain increased. Turning to her companion the Countess at last made a perfectly natural utterance, a thing not common with her—"Townsend, shall I *know* her? She was only a child when I saw her last."

Mr. Waller reassured her hastily. He had got Countess Hetta's coach and sleeper numbers from Madrid, and had caused the Wagons-Lits man to be instructed to contact the Station-Master as soon as the train arrived. This worthy was already on the platform, and Townsend went and spoke to him, glad to escape for a moment from the atmosphere of emotional disturbance generated by the Countess; a moment or so later the train steamed in, propelling fresh clouds of smoke and sulphur in front of it. Everything was managed with the unobtrusive skill and smoothness characteristic of the Portuguese. The Station-Master went over to stand beside Countess Páloczy, nodded at the Wagons-Lits attendant, standing by his half-open door, and when the train came to a halt said—"*That* is the young lady, Minha Senhora," as a dark pale girl, short but slender, climbed down out of the sleeping car.

Countess Páloczy went forward and put her arms round her daughter. While the cameras clicked, and the TV man cursed a correspondent and several porters who got in his way, Townsend stood by, assessing the new arrival. She too was clearly very nervous—her small ungloved hands were shaking. She was shabbily dressed—well, what could you expect?—and wore no make-up, and her hair was all wrong. But she had a pair of huge, splendid dark eyes under decisive brows, and that amusing and unmistakable structure of Central European faces, both lips and cheek-bones much more prominent than in western ones, and rather flaring nostrils; the whole thing was clean-cut, a good *strong* face—and her complexion was perfectly clear, pale but not dead. His instant private conclusion was that the Countess might have her hands full with this new acquisition; certainly she would not have the walk-over that she was accustomed to.

When he was introduced the girl spoke in good English, though with the pretty, rather full and plummy Hungarian accent. For something to say he complimented her on her English—"There used to be a nun from England at the convent," she answered, with what he noted as admirable self-possession.

The American Press Attaché now came up. Would she have just two words for the correspondents?—they were all keyed up, it would be very much appreciated. Before anyone else could speak Townsend intervened.

"Perce, I fancy the little Countess is starving—there's no restaurant-car on this wretched train. Let her get home and rest—the Press can go out to Estoril tomorrow." Perce Nixon tried to press it, while the correspondents crowded round. Townsend was prepared for a glance of enquiry from the girl to her mother, but nothing of the sort happened; courteously but quite decidedly, Hetta Páloczy said—"Not this morning. I am tired and, as Mr. Waller says, hungry; and not recollected. At another time." Mr. Nixon, his jaw dropping at this display of firmness, could do nothing but drive off his press-men, while the girl turned unconcernedly to the Countess.

"Mama, where is the car? Can we not go home? I should so much like to have breakfast."

"Well!" Nixon said, as he and Townsend drove off to the Chancery together, the ruffled feelings of the Press having been soothed by the promise of an interview the following day in the Countess's suite at the Castelo-Imperial in Estoril. "Well!" he repeated—he seemed unable to say anything else.

"That's some girl," said Townsend, with his gloomy chuckle. "She was one too many for you, Perce."

"I don't see why you had to put in your two-cents' worth," Mr. Nixon replied, not without irritation. "You gave her the tip—she might have talked, otherwise."

"I don't believe that young woman stands in any need of tips from anyone," said Townsend, thoughtfully.

"The Countess wouldn't have objected; in fact I know she wanted it."

"The Countess is a hard-baked, publicity-minded old So-and-So, with about as much consideration for other people as a sack of dried beans!" Townsend responded vigorously. "That train leaves Madrid at 10 P.M. and it's now"—he shot out his left wrist—"10:10. That unfortunate girl can't have had anything to eat for over twelve hours; she's coming into an unknown world, and you want to let these damned vultures drop on her with a lot of phoney questions! I'm ashamed of you, Perce."

"I don't see what difference two minutes would have made. You exaggerate, Townsend," Nixon said discontentedly. "You generally do. Anyway what did she mean by saying she 'wasn't recollected'? To recollect means to remember, but you can't remember yourself."

"I never heard the word used that way before," said Townsend, who had also been struck by the phrase. "I assume it's a Hungarian expression for not having pulled yourself together—if so, it makes sense." As the car pulled up outside one of the large bright modern buildings of which the newer parts of Lisbon are full—"Here we are," he said. "For mercy's sake leave the girl in peace till tomorrow, Perce. Will you?"

"All het up, aren't you?" his colleague said sourly, getting out of the car. "Yeah—I've fixed tomorrow morning for the boys. Don't you butt in on that!" he added, menacingly. "Don't forget it was the Press that got her out!"

In the other car, spinning over the grey-blue tarmac surface of the speed-way which leads along the estuary of the Tagus from Lisbon to Estoril, more reprehension of Hetta's refusal to speak to the Press was going on. The girl sat gazing out of the window, delighted by all she saw; the stately houses and black-and-white pavements in the Rossio Square and its adjoining streets—re-built by Pombal after the earthquake of 1755 had reduced most of Lisbon to rubble; then the shining river on her left, and to the right the heaped white houses with their coral-pink roofs, rising up against the brilliant blue sky. "Oh, but it is beautiful!" she exclaimed. "Lisbon is much more beautiful than Madrid, Mama."

"Lisbon is one of the most beautiful cities in the world," said her mother, rather repressively. "But listen, Hetti—of course you have everything to learn about life in the ordinary world, so I shall not hold it against you; but you should not have refused to speak to the correspondents. It was not gracious—they had all come to meet you, and waited a long time."

"Mama, how could I? I was quite unprepared for this request."

"You should have consulted me, instead of taking your own decision. I know the importance of these things."

The girl turned and looked at her mother.

"But you could not have told me what to say—and surely that was the important thing? I mean, that was what they wanted to hear?"

The Countess made a small rapid movement of impatience, quickly controlled.

"Dear child, you have a great deal to learn. Probably you don't realise that getting you out at all took some doing. I had to give a Press Conference."

"Did you, Mama? How good of you. But today I assure you that I am not equal to it. One should always be sure of saying the right thing, should one not? And this morning I am too tired and also too hungry, as this kind Mr. Waller understood."

It was the Countess's turn to stare at the pale face beside her in the Rolls-Royce—serious, calm, assured. Was that last remark, with its rather damaging implications, made innocently? Innocence gazed back at her from the immense dark eyes, but there was also that troubling assurance, that complete composure.

"Oh well, we'll leave it," she said rather shortly.

"Yes; and today when I have eaten, and rested, I will recollect myself, so that tomorrow I may be able to satisfy these journalists—and to please you, dear Mama, I hope." She turned to the window again. "Oh, how beautiful those white waves are, below that big round tower standing in the sea. What is it? I suppose that *is* the sea? Do you know that I have never seen it?"

"Why Hetti, you *have!* We went to Brioni, when you were little."

"How little?"

"Four or five, I suppose."

"Ah, well then I have forgotten. But what *is* the tower?"

"A lighthouse—it flashes at night," said the Countess rather absently. She was wondering which was likely to prove the more disconcerting—Hetta's tendency to take her own decisions, or her dutiful-daughter attitude. "Attitude" was the word she used in her own mind—she was not very familiar with spontaneity, in herself or in others; she did not, by choice, move in very spontaneous circles.

"And why do the waves break white just there?" Hetta asked. "Not above, not below—just at that point?"

"I have no idea."

It was a fact that Countess Páloczy had lived for ten years on the Tagus estuary without ever realising that a sand-bar stretches across it, and that the *raison d'être* of the two lighthouses, one on the great fort of São Julião da Barra, is to draw the attention of ships to this obstruction. How tiresome it was going to be if Hetti was always asking questions and demanding facts, she thought. Oh well, she would have to turn her over to the Monsignor, who knew everything.

The car presently turned inland past a public garden brilliant with flowers, and drew up before a large modern hotel. Porters and pages in uniform swarmed round the door; more porters and more pages stood bowing as they passed in through the big glass doors. The interior of the Castelo-Imperial is like that of any other super-luxury hotel, except that it is in rather better taste than most, the deep carpets and brocade upholstery of the hall and salons being mainly in a warm grey, with touches

of soft pinks and soft blues; the rooms of course vast, but with the un-
dignified low ceilings which hotel architects, forgetting the noise that
human voices in bulk make, always seem to design. Hetta's eyes grew
round as she glanced about her on the way to the lift—the enormous
spaces of floor, the masses of flowers, the numbers of people and still
more of those inclining uniformed attendants, who seemed to have no
other occupation. "Do they keep so many, just to bow to people?" she
murmured to her mother. The Countess gave a little laugh, not dis-
pleased; if Hetta could do an observant ingénue act it would not be at
all out of place. But here was the manager, washing his hands and also
bowing; she introduced him to Hetta, and he made an elegant little
speech of welcome and congratulation before they entered the lift and
were borne aloft. In fact, though Hetta did not realise it, most of the
occupants of the hotel and as many as possible of the staff had assembled
in the hall simply in order to catch a glimpse of the young lady who
had just come out, so romantically, from behind the Iron Curtain.

Countess Páloczy had a large suite in an upper corner of the big building, looking out on one side over the flowerbeds of the public garden,
on the other onto the sparkling estuary—it was even fuller of flowers
than the public rooms, and Hetta exclaimed at them in delight. "I like
flowers—I am glad you do too," her mother vouchsafed. The apartment
contained a dining-room and a salon, but they took breakfast in a small
pretty morning-room; Hetta tucked in thankfully to the omelette which
the Countess ordered for her, in addition to the normal coffee and rolls.
Then she was led to her own room, where a Portuguese maid had already unpacked her few possessions, and was putting a hot-water bottle
into the bed.

"I have ordered a cheval-glass for you, and a proper dressing-table at
which you can *sit* to do your face," said the Countess; the only mirror,
a small one, stood on a high chest of drawers. "This was your father's
room, so it is rather austere."

"Pappi's room? Oh then do leave it as it is—I should prefer it so.
Darling Pappi—how I wish he was not dead!" And to her mother's dismay Hetta Páloczy burst into tears.

Chapter Two

HETTA awoke from a long sleep to see Esperanza, her mother's Portuguese maid, setting down a huge vase of carnations on the businesslike writing-desk which stood under one of the windows. When she sat up and stretched the maid detached a small envelope from the flowers and brought it to the bed. On the card inside, below Townsend Waller's name, a few lines were scribbled—"I shall look in this evening about six-thirty to see how you are, if you are not too tired to see anyone. T.W."

"Oh, how kind! Please bring the flowers here," she said to the maid. Esperanza, who had been with the Countess for some years and had learned a modicum of English in the course of them, brought over the vase, and the girl smelled the strong scent. "Thank you. What is the time?" she asked. Like most dwellers behind the Iron Curtain she had no watch; the Russian troops, who had arrived in Europe with no watches either, had seen to that. The Portuguese servant, however, had a neat wrist-watch—"Five less a quarter," she said.

"So late! Can I have a bath?" She could, in a bathroom next door to her bedroom. "Only for the Menina," Esperanza explained; "the Condessa has her own"—from which Hetta guessed rightly that she herself was the Menina. While the bath was running she fingered the immense bath-towel and the fine linen face-towels, all with her mother's monogram, with astonishment—they seemed to her almost too beautiful to use. Esperanza meanwhile ran to and fro, bringing in freshly ironed underclothes—Hetta had only two sets, and neither had come up to the maid's standards of smoothness and cleanliness. Turning off the taps and dashing in bath essence—"And will the Menina wear her little suit, or the black dress? The dress is pressed." Hetta said she would wear the dress—this was in fact her only alternative to the suit. "I should like tea after my bath," she added.

"*Muito bem.* In the Menina's own room?"

"Yes please."

Bathed refreshingly in sweet-scented water, dressed in clean under-garments, Hetta, back in her room, lay on the freshly-made bed while she consumed a hearty tea of rusks, *marmelada*—a sort of quince cheese—and some very rich chocolatey creamy cakes. She was still hungry, and enjoyed it all hugely. As she was finishing the last cake her mother came in.

"Did you have a good sleep?" she asked kindly.

While Hetta slept the Countess had persuaded Monsignor Suber-caseaux to come round to luncheon, and had poured out her disappoint-ment over Hetta's refusal to say "even one word" to the journalists at the station, and her general concern about their future relationship. "She is so—so *independent,*" she said, in tones of dissatisfaction.

"But my dear Countess, how naturally! For ten years she has been without parents—how should she at once show a child's dependence on *your* judgement, when for so long she has been thrown on her own resources? You will have to be very patient, and let time, and your own affection and kindness, gradually develop what is usually a normal growth." Then he had asked what Hetta was like?

"Oh, small—small, and not pretty," the tall once-beautiful woman had replied. "But I think she *could* be made chic."

"You must be patient also with her lack of height and of beauty," the priest said, smiling. "Beginning *now*. These first days and weeks are crucial." Dorothée—whose real name was Dorothy, but who preferred to sign herself like a Frenchwoman—promised to be patient.

"Show affection," the priest further enjoined. "Neither of you can have much genuine affection for the other at present, since you are in effect strangers, and both grown women—but you can show it. Affec-tion, after all, is one aspect of charity."

The Countess had agreed to all this with suitable humility; later she asked Monsignor Subercaseaux if he had any news of "the invitation."

"Not so far. I understand that the lists are extremely long already—and as I told you before, dear lady, the Bretagnes are very anxious to keep it as far as possible a family affair—indeed so is the King."

"The Fonte Negras are going, and the Ericeiras."

"Ah, but Countess de Fonte Negra was a Lencastre, so in a way a relation; and in the case of the Duke of Ericeira there is his position in the Order of Malta—quite apart from the fact that he puts up so many of the guests, here and in his house in Lisbon. Last time I believe he accommodated forty!" said the priest, laughing cheerfully. "You will agree, Countess, that this gives him a certain claim!—though he is not doing so this year; his sister has not been well."

"Well, I rely on you to do what you can, Monsignor. You know that it means a great deal to me—and I am devoted to little Princess Maxine—she will make a charming bride."

However, sitting on a chair in her daughter's bedroom three hours later, the Countess was concentrating on showing affection, as her confessor had bidden her.

"I have made an appointment for you for 6:30 this evening with Alfred, the coiffeur," she said. "Esperanza will show you the way." Thoughtfully she studied her daughter's hair, which was dark, thick, straight, and at the moment merely a heavy mane. "Not a permanent wave, I think; but shaped to a rouleau at the back. I wish I could come with you, but I must go to a cocktail at the Belgian Embassy, so I shall have to leave soon after six. But Alfred is very clever about styling, and he will do you himself—so leave yourself entirely in his hands." She considered again. "Should you like a fringe?"

"Should *you* like me to have one, Mama?" Hetta also was anxious to be accommodating, up to a point.

"I am not sure—I should ask Alfred. He is a very good judge. And then we must see about getting you some clothes—of course you can't go anywhere until you have something to put on. But fortunately there is one really good tailor here, who was with Lanvin for years, and a wonderful woman for blouses; and for *petites robes* we can get you a few things off the hook in the Chiado."

For Countess Páloczy providing pretty clothes was one of the most genuine demonstrations of affection imaginable; Hetta, vaguely recognising this, took her mother's words in the spirit in which they were meant.

"That will be lovely, Mama. A person from the Government took me to get my suit and the black dress, but of course there was no time to get them altered and they are rather big and bunchy on me."

Dorothée opened her eyes wide.

"A person from the *Government* bought your clothes? What can you mean?"

"Oh yes—they wished me to look nice when I came out, so this woman came and took me to a shop, and bought the suit and jersey, and the dress. But it was all done in a great hurry; and the clothes are not as pretty as yours. I see that," said Hetta simply, little realising that her parent's exquisitely plain grey frock came from Balenciaga. Oh goodness, why couldn't she have told the Press that this morning, Dorothy Páloczy thought—*what* a story! Look *nice* indeed!—she must get that publicised somehow. But mindful of the Monsignor's exhortations, she said nothing for the moment.

"Well, we'll have fun together, getting you fitted out," she said.

"Oh yes, indeed. Mama, do you think I could have a watch or a clock? It is so tiresome not to know the time."

"Of course. But what became of the little Rolex your father gave you?"

"The Russians took it."

"Good gracious! Yes, we will get you one tomorrow—and for now"— she went to her own room and returned with a little travelling-clock. Glancing at it—"I must be off," the Countess said. "And you'll go along to Alfred this evening."

But at that point Hetta's spirit of accommodation stopped short. She was determined not to miss the nice American.

"No, Mama. I am too tired tonight. I will go to the coiffeur tomorrow, as early as you wish—but not today."

The Countess did her best not to show her vexation.

"You are sure? It is all arranged, and it is not so easy to get Monsieur Alfred himself."

"I am sorry, Mama, but I am quite sure." Oddly enough Hetta's conscience did not trouble her in the least about this white lie; people who live under Communist régimes soon develop callosities on the conscience.

The Countess, resignedly, took up the telephone beside Hetta's bed, cancelled the appointment in fluent French, and made one for the following afternoon. Then she kissed her daughter and went off to her party.

The moment she had gone Hetta sprang up, put on the government-provided black dress, which was indeed very bunchy, dragged a small cheap comb remorselessly through her thick mop of hair—hair-brushes are of rare occurrence in the People's Democracies—and then, standing in front of the small looking-glass on her father's tall chest of drawers, unskilfully applied a little powder to her pale face. The powder was of a rather tawny shade, and as cheap as the comb; like the black dress it had been provided by the female emissary of the Hungarian Government. About 1943 Moscow started a drive for cosmetics, but the quality was poor—Hetta, after looking at her face covered with Soviet powder ran to the bathroom for a towel, and rubbed it all off again. "It does not *match* me!" she muttered disgustedly.

So it was unpowdered and in all her Communist inelegance that she went through into the drawing-room. Besides the flowers, mostly hot-house white lilac, it was full of signed photographs of celebrities in silver frames, newspapers, and French, English, American and Spanish illustrated weeklies—there were no books. She had only been sniffing the cold delicate scent of the lilac for a few moments, and wondering vaguely about her father in such surroundings—as she remembered him he was always knee-deep in books, with a gun somewhere close at hand—when Esperanza ushered in Townsend Waller.

"Well!" he said, shaking her warmly by the hand—"You look better. Are you fed, and rested?"

"Yes—both, wonderfully. You were so *kind* this morning," she said, with an earnest sincerity which struck the young man as almost frightening in a girl of her age. "And the flowers are lovely—thank you so much." She paused.

"Mama is not here," she went on; "she had to go to a party."

"I know—the Belgians' cocktail. I cut it; I wanted to see how you were making out."

"Please?" "Making out" quite defeated Hetta.

"Well, getting along," he said laughing—in fact not helping her much. But the mention of the word cocktail caused him to glance round the room. The usual tray with bottles was not there.

"Don't you want a drink?" he asked.

"Thank you, I am not thirsty. I had tea not long ago."

He looked at her with incredulous amusement.

"I didn't mean tea, or real thirst; I meant *drinks,* what one has at this time of day."

"What does one have? You see I do not know. Do you want something?"

"Yes please. One has sherry, or cocktails, or whisky, before dinner, here," he said.

"Oh, I am sorry." She too looked round the room, rather helplessly. "I wish you could have what you like, but there does not seem to be anything here."

"One rings the bell for it," he said, doing so.

When Esperanza appeared he told her that the young Countess desired *as bebidas*—the maid smiled, said "Immediately, Minho Senhor," and disappeared in the direction of the dining-room. Waller looked at Hetta thoughtfully.

"Don't you have drinks before meals in Hungary?" he asked.

"I did not. You must forgive me for entertaining you so badly, but I have never drunk a cocktail in my life."

"Well, try one now," Townsend said, as Esperanza reappeared with the tray. He mixed two Martinis. "Only take a little—we mustn't make you tight!" he said.

"Please?"

Oh God, what will become of her? Townsend thought. He explained.

"But not *women?*" Hetta said, now as incredulous as he.

"Not often, no; and never nice women, unless they are inexperienced, and it happens by mistake. Do you like that?"

Hetta sipped, then wrinkled up her nose in a funny grimace.

"No. It has rather a disagreeable taste, I think; curious, but not agreeable. Wine is nicer."

"Then you'd better have some sherry." He poured her out a glass of Manzanilla.

Townsend, well-brought-up in the high Bostonian sense of the phrase, nevertheless had few or no qualms about thus organising drinks for himself in Countess Páloczy's apartment. She was always liberal with them, and would have hated a compatriot, or anyone else, to sit dry and miserable in her rooms; she was fundamentally quite a kind person, he reflected, if she did tend to attach a rather exaggerated importance to social success.

"So you do drink wine?" he said to Hetta, who was not making any faces over the sherry.

"At Detvan we did, even I—it was always on the table at meals. Our own wine—we made it at home. Pappi loved his vineyards, and was so proud of his wine."

"I bet it was good." The young man followed up this promising line; he asked questions, and listened with interest to the answers, which on this familiar and obviously well-loved subject came in an eager flow. He got a clear, even a vivid picture of a happy country childhood in patriarchal surroundings—the vast flat fields, intensively cultivated; the enormous herds of cows and oxen, the droves of pigs, the flocks of geese and turkeys being brought back to the village at night by the swineherds and goose-girls. "Of course the pigs and geese belonged mostly to the peasants, and when they came down the village street in the evening it was so funny, how each small flock knew its own homestead, and of its own accord turned in at the right gate—the geese stepping so sedately, the cows walking, the calves perhaps jumping a little, but the pigs *galloping*, kicking up their heels and squealing!" Her face was alight.

"But why were the pigs and the cows all mixed up together, so they had to find their own gates?" Townsend asked, rather puzzled.

"Oh, but of course the animals from the whole village went out to feed together; Pappi gave the grazing, and paid the wages of the cowherd and swineherd. It is always so—I mean it *was*," the girl said, rather sadly.

"Didn't the peasants have any land of their own, then?"

"Each house half a hectare, to grow what they liked—and of course the garden round the house. But one cannot graze five cows on half a hectare, especially with calves too."

"Did each peasant have five cows, then? For goodness sake! And how many peasants in the village?"

"In Detvan there were a hundred-and-fifty houses; in the other two villages perhaps a little fewer; about a hundred in each, I think. But each peasant could keep up to five cows, and as many as forty pigs—not more."

Townsend did sums in his head.

"And your father gave free grazing to sixteen hundred cows, *and* their calves? And paid the cowherds' wages with it? It's fantastic!"

"Why?" Hetta asked flatly. "With us it was always so."

"Fourteen thousand pigs too," Townsend mused. "Don't know what *they* eat. And your father just *gave* the people all this?"

"But naturally."

"Doesn't seem at all natural to me, in the twentieth century."

"I cannot see what the century has to do with it. They were our people; they worked for us."

"Did they get any wages?"

Hetta laughed at such ignorance.

"Of *course* they received wages—and some of the produce of the estate: maize, and wheat, and wine for each family."

"I begin to see what Atherley meant about feudalism," Townsend said thoughtfully, really to himself. "Yes—on those lines it *is* pretty good for the peasants too. He's quite right."

"Who is Atherley?" the girl asked, catching hold of something concrete in these rather puzzling utterances.

"A friend of mine in the British Embassy here—you must meet him; he's a grand person. And he knows Hungary."

"No! Oh, I should so much like to meet someone who knows Hungary."

"You'll meet him all right—your mother likes him. But tell me—I say, might I call you Hetta?"

"I had rather you called me Hetti—that is what friends used to call me."

"Fine—though I like Hetta better than Hetti. Anyway, what's become of all this free grazing and everything since the Russians came in? Weren't all the big estates broken up?"

"Yes, indeed; everything was taken, and the land divided up among the peasants—at first."

"Did they like that?"

"How should they like it?" the girl exclaimed vigorously. "Each family was given four-and-a-half hectares, and a pair of horses or oxen to plough. But what is this, compared with what they had? You cannot feed two cows, and make hay for them, on four-and-a-half hectares, and where were the bread-grains to come from?—and the land for the pigs to feed? Concerning the pigs, this was soon settled"—she gave an angry little laugh—"because the Russians took them nearly all away."

"Took them away?"

"Yes. Over five million pigs they sent to Russia in the first year, and nearly all the turkeys. The women loved their turkeys; they fed in the fields after the harvest, and so grew fat; when they were sold the money was for the housewife—the birds were hers."

Townsend was doing more mental arithmetic—American career diplomats are very well-informed.

"The hectare is nearly two-and-a-half acres," he said, thinking aloud. "No, you couldn't do even subsistence farming on eleven-and-a-quarter acres. But why was there enough for everyone before?"

Hetta had her answer pat.

"Because on a big estate, with huge fields and no divisions—fences, do you call them?—and with good manuring, much more was produced than simple peasants can do, on these silly little plots. Also everyone worked then *together* at the harvest, as my father and his—do you say manager?—directed; whereas now, except in the collectives, each man works alone, or tries to get his neighbours to help; and there are arguments and quarrels—all is without organisation."

In spite of the curious phrases she used, Townsend got a clear picture of the two different epochs; so clear that it rather surprised him. "How do you come to know so much?" he asked.

"Oh, before my parents went away I used to go with Pappi when he drove about the estate to overlook everything; the harvest, especially, was in the holidays, so that I was at home, and he liked to have someone with him. Mama did not care so much for the country things, she liked Pest better; so it was I who went."

I bet she liked Pest better, Townsend thought. Aloud he only said— "But how do you know what it's like now—were you in the country? Didn't you stay in your convent in Budapest?"

"Till the end of 1948, yes; then the Communists forced all convents to close. It became a crime to be a nun!" Hetta said, her dark eyes huge. "All had to put on civilian dress; they looked so strange without the habit!—in fact in ordinary clothes they looked *awful*."

Her tone made Townsend laugh. "Awful in what way?" he asked.

"Silly!" Hetta said crisply. "In the habit, and living their own life of work and prayer they looked as they felt—calm and full of purpose; therefore dignified. But thrown out into the world, which they had given up and forgotten, they felt utterly lost; and again they looked as they felt— lost, and very silly."

This time the young man did not laugh. Some strange ring, of a strangely objective compassion, in the young girl's voice as she pronounced the last four words precluded laughter.

"Were they always silly? One hears nuns get so," he said.

"But not in the least! Living the life they had vowed themselves to, of prayer and works of charity—or of education, like my nuns—they are perfectly competent; noble, heroic even. But suddenly obliged to take jobs as servants, or as waitresses in factory canteens, which is what most of them did, can you wonder if they were at a loss, and seemed foolish? *Oldish* women, please reflect. No Mass to begin the day, and Holy Communion; no times of meditation before the Blessed Sacrament. Instead, hustle and bustle among pots and pans, or handing plates of food to young Communists! This they willingly did for the love of our Lord, who blessed even a cup of cold water given in His name; but how should they be good cooks, or quick waitresses? Of course they seemed silly."

As Hetta poured this out—"She looks like a sybil"—the young man thought to himself. It was all surprisingly reasoned, too; she was no fool, if she did seem a bit ultra-religious.

"Yes, I get all that," he said. "Well, go on—where did you go when your convent broke up? You were—let's see—fifteen then, I suppose?"

"Nearly sixteen. Mother Scholastica—she was one of the nuns, who taught us Latin—took me with her; she went first to the house of a friend in Pest, as a cook, and I helped her. To strangers we had to pretend that I was her daughter—*imagine*, for a nun!—but I was accustomed to calling her 'Ma mère,' so it was not too difficult. Then after a time the deportations began, and the lady we were working for was threatened, so we had to leave."

"What deportations? To Russia?"

"No no—from Pest to the country; the May deportations. All who were not 'workers,' in industry or something the Communists thought useful were sent away, to make room, so they said, for the workers; but really it was just"—she hesitated—"animus. Should I say spite, or malice, perhaps?"

"Animus will do," Townsend, who had received a classical education, said smiling a little. "Where did these deportees go, in the country?"

"To peasants' houses—in a *good* room, if the peasants were friendly, as usually they were; but then often the village Commissars came, and said that they were 'enemies of the people,' and must sleep in the barn, on straw. Oh, the wickedness and cruelty! Shall I tell you what I have seen with my own eyes?"

"Please do," Townsend said, unable to repress a secret wish that Perce's press correspondents could hear what he was hearing.

"There was an old lady—over seventy—the widow of a former Prime Minister, the Countess X; this is a great name in Hungary, and he had done much for the people, and was beloved. She was sent to the same village where Mother Scholastica and I went, and naturally the peasants treated her like a queen, and gave her the best of whatever they had. But the Commissars came and said she must work for the nation, and since she was far too old to do any real work they took her out into the cornfields, and tied branches to her head and hands, and made her stand there in the burning sun, waving her hands to frighten the birds from the grain—she was to be a bird-scare."

"Scare-crow," Townsend muttered automatically. "Good God! You *saw* that?"

"Certainly I did. As often as I could, when no one was about, I went and changed places with her, so that she could go and rest in the shade —I put on her old hat with the branches, and she tied the other boughs to my hands, and so I stood, hour after hour. The heat is unbearable, in the Alföld in harvest time."

"Good for you. What's the Alföld?"

"The central plain of Hungary, down to the east of the Danube—the black-earth country, they call it; the soil is very rich. Detvan was on the edge of the Alföld," the girl said, that bright look again illuminating her face as she mentioned her home.

"And what did you and the learned Mother What's-her-name do when you went to the Alföld, as I take it you did?"

"Oh, we were so fortunate! The lady we had worked for in Pest somehow arranged for Mother Scholastica to take a position as housekeeper and cook to a *wonderful* man, Father Antal, who had gone to be a village priest down there."

"Why was he wonderful?" Townsend asked—he was rather allergic to priests.

"Because he was holy, and learned, and wise, and also very brave," Hetta replied with her usual clarity. "He managed to say Mass almost daily, in spite of the Commissars; the peasants hid bottles of their wine for the Mass in the thatch. He went quite often to see Cardinal Mindszenty in his prison—"

"Goodness, was he allowed to do that?" the American interjected.

"Of course not—not allowed; he went disguised as a peasant, bringing in wood for the fires, or some such thing. It was a fearful risk."

"Did you hear how the Cardinal was?"

"Not much—it was better not to speak of such things. I gained the impression that he was not really ill, but not well; the confinement and the distress about his people were *eating* him," she said—"and the loneliness too, of course. It did him so much good when Father Antal went to see him; they were friends, they had studied at the same seminary—and it was a chance for him to hear a little truth, for a change. Lies, lies, lies, every day and all day long; these are suffocation. I think without the Father's visits he might have died. This is partly why I would do anything for Father Antal. I loved cooking for him."

"But were you the cook? I thought you said the nun was?"

"So she was supposed to be, but she was a terrible cook! First, she had no idea how, and further, she was always leaving the saucepans in order to recite the Office!" Hetta said, with an honest girlish giggle. "So, one cannot cook! No, I did most of it."

"And can you cook? How did you learn?"

"As a child at Detvan I was often in the kitchen with Margit, our old cook, who had been with us for ever; I used to watch her, and afterwards remembered, and did as she had done. Father Antal liked the food I made."

"Sounds as if the priest had been just as fortunate as you and the scholastic mother," Townsend said. He poured himself out another drink, gave Hetta a second sherry, and returned to his chair. He was impressed by what she told him, although all the stress on saying Mass and so on passed him by completely, indeed rather alienated him. But he could not help realising that here was a first-hand behind-the-curtain story, from a person who had the power to make it vivid; he began to see all sorts of possibilities. He asked more questions—about the deportations, how much luggage people might take, and so forth; and also about how the village commissars were organised. Her replies were satisfyingly detailed and lucid, especially about the commissars. "Everywhere are there not sometimes young men who are failures, and therefore dissatisfied?—and such turn often into *mauvais sujets,* small criminals; without conscience, and angry with a world in which they have no success. But give them the chance of *power* over other people, and they are delighted; they take this to be the success the disagreeable world has denied them, out of malice! Such were the commissars; sometimes from the villages themselves, or from some small town near by. Where we were, one was actually the village idiot—a lumping youth, with one eye squinting, his mouth hanging open always, his nose dirty! It was he who had the idea of sending the old Countess to stand in the fields to frighten the birds."

For a moment or two Townsend was fairly silenced by the horror of this. At length, pulling himself together, he said with an effort at lightness—

"I see that your nuns gave you a course in psychology, among other things!"

"Please?"

"Oh Hetta, you must learn not to say 'Please'! Say 'I beg your pardon?' or 'Would you repeat that?'—anything but 'please'!"

"Very well. Thank you for telling me. In German one says *bitte?* when one does not understand, but in English this is wrong?" she asked.

"Yes. It's—well somehow it's tiresome," he said, feeling ashamed. "I'm sorry."

"Do not be. This helps me—I have so much to learn. Will you tell me again what I should say when I have not understood?"

"Well, I think 'would you repeat that' is about the best," Townsend said, quite abashed by her humility.

"Thank you."

"Shall you feel up to meeting the Press tomorrow?" he asked presently.

"Oh yes—I have told Mama I would."

"Fine. I'll tell Perce—our Press Attaché, you met him this morning—that I think it ought to be as full-dress as he can make it. It will be a big thing."

"Can you tell me *why* one must speak to journalists?" the girl asked. "You and my mother both think so, but I do not really see why."

"But—" he paused, staggered by such ignorance. Then he began to expound the importance of publicity, the propaganda value of her story, so unique and fresh. Warming to his theme—"I'm certain Radio Free Europe would love a recording of a talk by you," he said—"You could do it in Hungarian, if you'd rather. And some articles, too—they'd be syndicated all over the States."

"Pl—I mean what does 'syndicated' mean?"

"Printed in about seventy papers. It's such a story!—the Press will eat it up."

She considered all this for a little while in silence; her first look of surprise changed then to one of mild and lightly charitable disdain.

"You mean, tell newspaper men, or write for newspapers, what I have told you?"

"Yes—exactly that."

"No," Hetta said—and the single syllable again had a ring. "I told you because you have been kind, and saw that I was tired and hungry. But I will not make this 'story,' as you call it, for journalists and the radio. What business is it of theirs?"

"I've just told you"—and again he tried to hammer home the importance of publicity and propaganda. But Hetta would have none of it.

"I feel all this to be quite false. If such things must be done, they should be done by people who know a great deal, and have importance. I am quite unimportant, and know nothing but what I have seen."

"That's the point—you *have* seen; you can tell the world." But Hetta would not give way; he was surprised both by her toughness, and at her reasons.

"If the world is to be told, it must be told by those who can speak with authority. The recollections of an ignorant girl are mere gossips."

The phrase made him laugh, but when he tried to press her further she quietly shut him up, saying—"If I could help my country in any proper way, I would; but this—please forgive me—is to my mind foolish, and almost indecent."

"Then you won't see them?"

"Of course I will see them—have I not said so?—because my mother wishes it. And I will describe my journey, and speak of small things. But I will not do what you suggest, and make 'a story.'"

"You're making a great mistake," the American observed, gloomily.

"Possibly. But I shall make it," Hetta said.

Chapter Three

IF the meeting with the Press next morning was not exactly a failure it was mainly owing to the Countess, who herself did a good deal of the talking, and *compèred* her daughter as far as she could, leading her on to describe the expedition to buy those dismal clothes, and so on—it was perhaps just as well really, she reflected, that Hetta hadn't felt up to going to M. Alfred the previous evening, for her shock-headed-Peter aspect fitted in very well with her ill-fitting ugly dress. Hetta, caught between her desire not to vex her mother, and her distaste for the whole idea as Townsend Waller had revealed it to her, did her best within her self-imposed limits, confining herself as far as possible to dates and generalities. "Looks to me as if she'd been brain-washed before she came out, so she'd give nothing away," one correspondent muttered to a colleague, going down in the lift.

"Maybe she's just born dumb, though she doesn't altogether look it," the colleague responded. "Anyway those *clothes* are a story in themselves!" They both laughed.

Townsend lunched that day with Atherley in the latter's small house up in the Lapa quarter of Lisbon, not far from the British Embassy. Richard Atherley disliked flats, and had been delighted to get hold of the little house: it was thoroughly Portuguese, with *azulejos* (coloured tiles) running in a bright cold 3-foot dado round the walls of the narrow hall and the small rooms, and rather sketchy plumbing; the furniture was distinctly sketchy too, except for a big sofa and some comfortable armchairs which the young Englishman, who was by no means poor, had brought out from home. But the house was perched on the lip of what was practically a ravine—although its broad bed was floored with small one-storey houses, their back-yards full of rabbits and washing, set in cramped little gardens equally full of onions, fig-trees, and vines trained over trellises, under which the owners cleaned their shoes, ironed their clothes, and ate their meals—and commanded a spectacular view across that end of Lisbon, white-walled and pink-roofed, to the great stretch of the Tagus and the green hills of the Outra Banda, the southern shore. It was very up-and-down, really like a small house in Chelsea except for the tiles and the view—and the food; unless the hostess cooks it, very few houses in Chelsea enjoy food like that which Atherley's elderly Portuguese servant habitually produced.

"Well, how did the arrival go?" Atherley asked at once, over drinks in the little upstairs drawing-room—and Townsend described the scene, and Hetta's instant and spontaneous refusal to talk. "But I went to see her yesterday evening—I knew Dorothée would be at the Belgians'."

"You never! What did you get out of her? Anything?"

Townsend's account of what he had got out of Hetta lasted through most of the meal—towards the end he recounted her unaccountable attitude towards propaganda and publicity. "Does that make sense to you?" he asked.

"What happened this morning? Did she meet them, or not?"

"Oh yes, she met them all right; but Perce says you'd have thought it was Dorothée who'd been in Hungary all this time!—she did most of the talking. I think they *just* got by. But can you understand why the girl won't tell a story like that?"

"Yes, I think I can," said Richard thoughtfully. "But she sounds interesting. I must meet her."

"Oh, you'll meet her all right! I'm sure Dorothée still means to cash in on her—though hoping for the best, poor woman, I expect after this morning!" said Townsend, with a rueful grin.

But in fact it was well over a week before Hetta Páloczy next appeared in public, and Atherley had the chance of meeting her. The interval was filled with endless visits to M. Lilas, the French-trained tailor, to Mme Azevedo, who produced blouses fine as cobwebs covered with what the French call *travail*, most delicate openwork and embroidery; to "Hélène" in the Chiado, one of the best shoe-shops in the world, for elegant confections in lizard and alligator-skin, and to Le Petit Paris, also in the Chiado, for simple becoming frocks. The Chiado (whose real name is the Rua Garrett) must be the steepest shopping street in the world; one pants going up, and is apt to slip going down on the tiny polished cobbles of the pavement—the shops are minute, yet produce superb craftsmanship. It is all very Portuguese; they are the most unobtrusive of races, preferring performance to advertisement. All this amused Hetta; and as she was dutifully anxious to please her mother she tried also to be interested in her new clothes—she ended, quite naturally and girlishly, in enjoying her pretty outfits.

She eventually made her début at a cocktail party at the hotel, for which her mother had sent out the invitations on the same day that Hetta met the journalists. In theory it was a purely social affair; in fact the Countess had invited Mr. Nixon, some of the better-known correspondents, and a pretty clever girl representing Radio Free Europe, hoping that on a less formal occasion they might contrive to "draw" her daughter. She therefore responded favourably when Mr. Atherley rang up in the morning to ask if she would perhaps allow him to bring a young Englishwoman who had just arrived in Lisbon to "cover" the royal wedding for an English newspaper.

"Of course I shall be delighted to see her, Mr. Atherley. What is her name?"

"Miss Julia Probyn, Countess. That's very good of you."

"Where is she staying? I might get a card to her."

"Oh please don't bother—I'll bring her. She's staying with some Portuguese friends." Atherley astutely refrained from mentioning that these friends were the Ericeiras; he knew that they were among the members of the *sociedade* of Portugal whose acquaintance Countess Páloczy had long sought in vain. Julia Probyn had spent some months teaching English to the Duke of Ericeira's only child, Luzia, and had become intimate with the family, and slightly acquainted with Atherley himself.

Hetta was about as inexperienced in social matters as a European young woman of twenty-two could possibly be, but perhaps just because of this she had the sharpened perceptions of a child or a clever dog. As she stood beside her mother, in a pretty and highly becoming cherry-red frock which exactly matched her new lipstick, and accentuated her clear pallor and the darkness both of her eyes and her now beautifully-arranged hair, she registered with considerable acuity which people her parent considered important, and to which she, Hetta, was supposed presently to talk. The young lady from Radio Free Europe began asking questions at once; Hetta was wise enough to leave her mother to indicate to the girl that she should do this later on—"When the receiving is over, my daughter will enjoy talking to you."

There were some other very concrete indications which Hetta did not miss. A short, brisk, cheerful Portuguese lady, greeted by the Countess as Mme de Fonte Negra, said as she shook hands, rather late—"Well, my dear friend, so this is the daughter! You must send her to lunch with me one day; I should like to talk to her." She glanced round the rooms. "I see the Regent is not here."

"No. They go out *so* little, as you know"—but Hetta recognised from long ago a sign of annoyance in the slight fluttering of her mother's eyelids. Later another guest said—"I've not seen the Archduke; are they here?"

"Oh poor dears, she is so lame, and it is such a long way for them to come, with no car," the Countess replied, again with that rapid fluttering —and Hetta at once seized on the situation. Oh, poor Mama! If the Arch-duke would have come, her mother's car would undoubtedly have been sent for him, however far away he lived. There was a lot of talk about the impending royal wedding, too, both while she stood beside her mother, and later when, as directed, she moved about among the guests: who was going and who was not was clearly the burning question at the moment, and she overheard enough of the jockeying for position, the intrigues for invitations suggested or boasted of, to cause her a rather painful astonishment. So much effort, so much emotion merely about being at any wedding struck her as unworthy, unreal. But she kept her ideas to herself. All through the innumerable introductions and the ster-eotyped questions she was actively recording in her mind—this was now to be her world, and however little she might like it, she must get to know it. In one way Hetta was rather well equipped for this particular task, since she had already had to come to terms with a world quite strange to her when she emerged from her convent school into a Com-munist Hungary, and she quickly marked down a few people as likeable and trustworthy among so many whom she found distasteful.

In particular she was delighted by a little old crook-backed Hungarian, an *émigré* journalist, who spoke to her in perfect idiomatic English. In-stead of the stock questions he surprised her by saying at once—"Are they bothering you to talk, and write? If so, don't do it—tell them all to go to Hell!"

"I have, more or less," Hetta replied laughing. She had just been firm with the pretty girl from Radio Free Europe and with Mr. Carrow, whose name in American journalism, Perce Nixon had told her, stood "right at the top."

"Well, go on. They will tell you it's for Hungary, or for freedom and democracy—but in fact as to fifty per cent at least, it's either to line their own pockets or boost their own egos, or to gratify a vulgar curiosity which has no moral or political importance whatever. Of the readers or listeners on whose behalf they are pestering you, how many would lift a hand, give a penny, or even cast a vote for Hungary or for freedom? Perhaps one per cent!"

The old journalist spoke the last words loudly and emphatically; they were overheard by Mme de Fonte Negra, who laughed, tapped his arm, and protested—"Monsieur de Polnay, do I hear you traducing the public of the free world?"

"No, Madame," he replied quickly, kissing the hand that tapped him —"for really it is hardly susceptible of being traduced! I am telling this young lady, who as yet knows nothing of our western monstrousness, the truth—which you really know as well as I."

"I hope we are a little better in Portugal—but, *enfin*, I am afraid I must agree with you on the whole." She turned her strongly-marked elderly aristocratic face to Hetta.

"I should like it very much if you would lunch with me one day. I promise you that no one but I will ask you questions, if you come! Your mother and I know each other well."

Hetta had taken to this frank lady, and accepted with pleasure.

"Very well—next Sunday, at 1:30. Your mother usually has people to luncheon on Sundays, so she can easily spare the car to bring you in to me."

As Mme de Fonte Negra moved away Richard came up.

"Good afternoon, Monsieur de Polnay. I hope I see you well?"

"My dear Richard, you know perfectly that nobody ever sees me *well*. As Maurice Baring once said—'I'm always worse, and *never* better!' However, thank you for the little phrase."

Atherley laughed.

"Moreover, your intention in greeting me is not in the least single-minded," the Hungarian went on. "You simply wish to be introduced to Countess Hetta Páloczy. Very well—Countess Hetta, allow me to introduce Mr. Richard Atherley, First Secretary at the British Embassy, who in spite of this lamentable exhibition of double-talk is really my very good friend."

Hetta, laughing, held out her hand. Richard Atherley was very good-looking in a rather neutral English way: that is to say that although he was very tall he had hazel, not blue eyes, and mouse-coloured hair, and his skin, though clear and healthy, was by no means pink. But his face was intelligent and expressive, something one noticed long before the excellent modelling of the features and the brilliance of the hazel eyes; he looked gay and amusing and pleasant. He was all three. He bowed over Hetta's hand and kissed it, surprising her.

"*Tiens!* We are going all Hungarian, are we?" said M. de Polnay. "Well, *je m'absente*—which in American means 'I'll leave you to it.' " He, too, kissed Hetta's hand, and hobbled away.

"What a very nice man this is," Hetta said, looking after him. When coaching her daughter for her first appearance in society Countess Páloczy's main injunction had been "Talk!"—she was now endeavouring to carry it out.

"Yes, he's an absolute darling, and as clever as paint, too."

To his immense surprise Hetta said—

"Would you repeat that?"

"Repeat what?"

"This that you said about his being clever."

"I said he was as clever as paint, didn't I?"

"Yes. Would you tell me what this means?"

"Oh, just that he's very clever—it's an expression one uses. But why did you want it repeated?"

"Mr. Waller told me I should say 'Would you repeat that?' when I have not understood, instead of saying 'Please?' It seems that 'Please' has a disagreeable sound in English."

Atherley gave his big laugh.

"Oh, Townsend! What a man! You go on saying 'Please?' as much as you like. Do you know, I believe I went to your house in Hungary once?" he went on.

"Did you really? When? Mr. Waller said you knew Hungary."

"It was in 1939—I was staying with the Talmassys at Bula, and they took me over to lunch at Detvan."

"1939—oh, then I was only six, so I could not have seen you! Did you like it?"

"Yes, I thought it a most charming place—dignified and yet so homely, with that great courtyard, and the farm buildings. And full of sun."

"Was it not? Oh, you have completely *seen* it!—this is evident."

"I liked the new chapel your father had just built, too. Of course it wasn't as perfect as the little old rococo one, but like that it was a part of the house, as well as being big enough for all the peasants to come to Mass in on Sundays, instead of trailing over to Bula."

"Oh, yes; that meant so much to them. Did you see the telegram?" the girl asked eagerly.

"You mean the one from Cardinal Pacelli that hangs up in the porch, framed, giving the building his blessing? Yes, of course I did—your father showed me that at once. It seems they were friends."

"Indeed yes—he was often at Detvan; they were close friends. And now one is the Holy Father, and the other is dead," Hetta said, on an elegiac fall of voice which struck Atherley with curious force.

"I'd forgotten—of course Pacelli is Pope now," he said, conscious of a certain lameness in his words after hers. What a strange being she was!— that smart hair-do and pretty frock, and the eyes and voice of a priestess at some Delphic shrine. Feeling his own inadequacy in a way most unusual with him, Mr. Atherley decided to call up his reserves.

"There's someone I want you to meet," he said. "May I bring her over? I think you might like her."

"But please do." Hetta was prepared to like any friend of the man who had been to Detvan and noticed how that long low house with its wide courtyard used to be full of sun—it was one of her own most vivid memories. She was still thinking how clever it was of him to have noticed the sun-filled quality of her home when Mr. Atherley returned with Julia Probyn, and introduced them.

Young women have mental antennae longer than lobsters', and as delicately fine as those of butterflies. Hetta's and Julia's antennae reached out and did whatever the lobster-butterfly equivalent of clicking is—in human terms, they took to one another immediately. There was a moment's check when Julia mentioned that she was a journalist, but Hetta's sudden expression of dismay was so obvious that it made the others laugh.

"Don't worry—Miss Probyn won't bother you. She's only concerned with the royalties," Atherley said.

"Oh, this wedding." Hetta's distaste for the whole subject of the wedding was so audible in her voice that Julia laughed again; as Hetta listened to that long slow gurgle a happy reassured expression came into her face.

"You, too, think it funny that people should care so much, whether they go or not?" she asked.

"Oh no—perfectly normal. There's surely more social snobbery in the

Century of the Common Man than ever before in the world's history," Julia said. "I *have* to go—it's my bread-and-butter."

The party was thinning, and Atherley murmured to Julia that they ought to leave. He turned to Hetta.

"Will you lunch with me on Thursday? So that we can talk about Detvan?"

"With Mama?"

"Of course if you say so—but Miss Probyn will tell you that in the free world young ladies do lunch with young men without their parents."

"So? This too I do not know."

"Ask the Monsignor—he's your mother's spiritual adviser, so if he approves, she can't object," said Atherley smiling. "Anyhow Miss Probyn will be there."

"If Mama has no other plans for me, I shall be happy to come. Thank you," Hetta said, with the composed decision that somehow had so much distinction.

"She *is* out of the top drawer, isn't she?" Julia remarked to Atherley as they drove back to Lisbon.

"Who, the young Countess? Yes. It's so curious, really, that little aristocratic air of hers, when she's been a convent school-girl for nearly two-thirds of her life, and cook to a rustic priest in Hungary for the rest."

"Oh, was she?"

"Yes." He repeated what Townsend Waller had passed on to him of Hetta's experiences.

"Mmm," said Julia, reflectively. "*She* can't be the frightfully important Hunk who was going to be got out to tell the world about conditions there, can she?"

"What important Hunk?"

"Oh well, I heard ages ago that one was to be got out, if it could be fixed."

"Who from?"

"Just a friend, who does those sort of things," said Julia airily, while the slight blush which always enraged her appeared. "But this girl would hardly be high-powered enough, would she?"

"She seems fairly high-powered, but I gather the one thing she *won't* do is tell anyone anything," said Atherley, "so I shouldn't say telling the world was really her line. Anyhow she came out quite openly, as the result of a piece of perfectly honest blackmail—didn't you read about Countess Páloczy's Press Conference?"

"Oh, that—yes, of course I did, but I thought that was some poor little tot."

"Really, Julia, you are too vague to live! Well, now you've met the little tot."

"Yes. She's certainly small, but so is an atom bomb, I believe."

"Is that your impression of her?"

"Oh well, I think all this convent life and cooking for country priests may simply have been smothering some sort of dynamite. Or developing it—did your American chum establish whether life was safe and easy for her in the People's Democracy, or risky and dangerous?"

"Not for her, I don't think. The priest she cooked for took risks, he said."

"Oh," said Julia. After a pause—"Well I hope I *am* coming to lunch on Thursday, or whichever day it proves to be. I'd like to have a go at her myself."

"Of course you're coming."

Two days later Mr. Atherley was sitting in his room in the Chancery, which looked out, not onto the Rua S. Domingos à Lapa, where the trams rattle up and down over the steep cobbles, but onto the green tree-filled space of garden behind, memorising phrases in that famous Portuguese lesson-book, a "must" for students of the language, *A Família Magalhães*. (These seem to have been a family rather like the Dales, and presumably descendants of the gentleman who gave his name to the Straits of Magellan.) Atherley's studies were interrupted by the rather brusque entrance of a small man who bore the title of assistant Military Attaché.

"Atherley, I've got one of our chaps downstairs—Torrens, from Morocco. I wonder if you'd see him?"

"Good morning, Melplash. Why does the man from Morocco want to see *me*?" Atherley asked rather repressively, putting a finger in the Magalhães family to keep his place.

"He seems to think he may want backing-up at a higher level than mine," Mr. Melplash replied, grinning cheerfully—"so he wants to put you in the picture. D'you mind?"

"What's it all about?" Atherley asked.

"Some top-secret, top-priority Central European who's been got out, and's coming here," Melplash said, in his usual hurried gabble.

"Not a Hungarian, by any chance?"

"Yes, I rather think it is—but he'll tell you all about it. May I bring him up?"

"Very well," said Atherley resignedly, putting the Magalhães family away in a drawer. H'm. That pretty Julia Probyn, whom he had met a good deal when she was with the Ericeiras, and had liked enough to take her along to Countess Páloczy's party two days ago—was she rather well-informed, or what?

Melplash reappeared with a tall red-haired man. Having introduced him he said—"Well, I'll leave you to it," and scuttled away.

"Now, what can I do for you?—or what do you hope I can do?" Atherley asked, pushing a gay Alentejo box of cigarettes across the table to his visitor.

"Thanks. We might not want you to do anything—but then again we might," said Major Torrens, grinning rather more subtly than his introducer had done. "May I hold forth?"

"Please." As he said the word Atherley was reminded of Hetta, and smiled a little.

"We have just got someone rather important out of Hungary—" Torrens began.

"How?" Atherley interjected.

"He came out as part of the Hungarian film unit which arrived a few days ago for the Film Festival at Cannes; they're showing two films this year—both rather good, I hear. And as you know, some of the stars and so on usually go too, for prestige purposes."

"Is this individual a film-star?"

Torrens laughed.

"Good God no! But he came out disguised as a technical director; one of the real stars is pro-West, and arranged with our man in Hungary to bring him along."

"Where is he now? In Cannes?"

"No. Our people have got him out. Not too easy—the opposition were watching them all the time like lynxes; but the star organised *five* different parties on the same day; to La Turbie, Vence, Grasse, and what-have-you; that rather foxed the sleuths, and our man got down to the Vieux Port and on board a little yacht, and sailed away to Port Vendres."

"Where is that?"

"The last port in France before the Spanish frontier—a tiny place. He's in Spain now, on his way here."

"May I know why he's coming here? To live?"

"No, he's going on to the States; primarily I suppose to boost the morale of the Hungarians there—you know there are something like 100,000 of them in and around Pittsburgh alone—and of course to give up-to-date information to the Free Hungary Committee, or whatever it's called. But I think the 'Voice of America' people have their eye on him too, for broadcasts."

"Then why is he coming here? Just to take a plane? If so, I hardly see where the Embassy comes in, if his papers are in order—and I'm sure your people have seen to it that they are," Richard said, in rather chilling tones.

"Oh yes, his papers are all right—a German technician with a specialised knowledge of printing processes and types! I'm told he speaks faultless German."

"Does he know anything about printing processes?"

"Seemingly he does, a great deal; but he isn't coming here for typography," Torrens said, looking a little amused. "He has to make an important contact, which may take some time. If all goes well there will be no need to bother anyone—but if we run into any trouble it might be necessary for the Embassy to step in."

"The Ambassador would hate that," Richard said, continuing to display the regular diplomatist's reasoned and wholesome distaste for any involvement in under-cover activities. "Have you any reason to expect trouble?"

For the first time his visitor hesitated. "Well?" Atherley pressed him.

"I'm not sure, really. There was no difficulty whatever at Cerbère—that's the Spanish frontier post near Port Vendres; but on the way to Barcelona, by car of course, there was what *might* have been an incident, at a little pub where they stopped to eat. Another car drew up, several men came in, apparently tipsy, ordered wine, and contrived to start a general fracas, in the course of which our men got the impression that there was an attempt to slug the Hungarian. We had three people with him, and two of them were middle-weight boxers, so they slugged the sluggers, and got clear. But of course he would have been missed in Cannes well before that, and presumably spotters spotted him as he crossed the frontier, and followed him."

Richard frowned.

"Probably—that's common form, of course. Anything since?"

"Not so far—but I only heard that this morning. We're holding him over in Barcelona for forty-eight hours before he flies to Madrid. We have a fairly thug-proof hide-out for him there."

"And from Madrid he comes here?"

"Yes, and stays a bit to meet his contact before flying on to America."

"I see." Atherley brooded. "You have an equally thug-proof hide-out for him here, I hope?"

"I think so. Melplash has it in hand."

Atherley restrained a groan—he had never been inspired with much confidence by Mr. Melplash. But he let it pass.

"Do you by any chance know a Miss Julia Probyn?" he now asked.

Torrens stared a little, surprised at the question.

"Yes, I do." He gave a sudden confidential grin. "She stood me up once, completely, out in Morocco."

"Oh, really? How amusing. When was that?"

"Year before last."

"And you haven't seen her since?"

Torrens looked still more surprised.

"Yes—I met her here in January, on my way home to report. But why?"

"No reason on earth," Atherley lied easily, pleased with the information he had picked up. "Except that I wondered if you would come to lunch on Thursday to meet her."

Torrens was caught off guard.

"Is she still here? I thought she went back to England in March."

Then they *are* in touch, Atherley thought to himself, but not in very close touch.

"She did, but she came back five days ago, to cover the wedding for some paper. So I hope you are free on Thursday. Little Countess Hetta Páloczy will be there too."

"Oh, really? The one who's just got out? Yes—thank you, I should like to come very much."

"Good—that will be very pleasant. Just the four of us, I thought—it will be easier for Countess Hetta. She seems a little inclined to find the West the *Wild* West," Atherley said. "Not really so surprising, in a way." He gave Torrens a card with the address of his house, and scribbled the hour on it. "Goodbye for the moment," he said, rising to terminate the interview.

When his visitor had gone Atherley sat for a little while, reflecting on what he had heard. Torrens himself impressed him favourably: he was in quite a different class to so many of these S.I.S. types—like poor little Melplash, for instance. He rang up the Military Attaché—the Embassy had a private exchange, unconnected with the Lisbon telephone system except for outside calls—and asked a few questions. The M.A. did not know very much, but the little he did was satisfactory: a sound man, thoroughly reliable, and with a high reputation. "He was in the Scots Guards to begin with," he said, with a certain finality.

"That won't make H.E. like it any better if he drags us into some mix-up over a Central European," Atherley said rather sourly—and Colonel Campbell laughed down the telephone. "Let's hope he won't," he said.

Atherley continued to reflect. Quite clearly it must have been from Major Torrens that the lovely Julia had picked up her rumour about the important Hungarian, presumably when he passed through Lisbon in January. Both his own impression of the man, and the Military Attaché's account of his record led Atherley to decide that his visitor was not a person to talk recklessly about service matters; he would only do so to someone with whom he was involved in some way, usually emotionally. But not necessarily emotionally, of course, he thought; they might be working together. Press assignments sometimes covered other activities. H'm. Perhaps he had better try to find out from Miss Probyn a little more about her relations with the Major, past *and* present. When dealing with these Secret Service people—or indeed with almost anyone —it was impossible to know too much. He had actually reached out his hand to the telephone on his desk when the instrument gave its low discreet buzz—he lifted the receiver.

"Atherley," he said.

"Good morning, Richard." It was the Ambassador's voice.

"Oh, good morning, Sir. How is her Ladyship?"

"Splendid, thank you—and the baby is putting on weight like anything! She gets up today, and I think we ought to have a cocktail party next week; we seem to have been more or less *incomunicado* for some time. I thought of Friday—Helen should be thoroughly strong by then. But we should like you to be there. Are you free?"

"Of course, Sir," Atherley said dutifully, even while he felt in his breast-pocket for his engagement book, and thumbed it awkwardly with his left hand to find next Friday's page. Before he had found it—and his conscious mind told him that it was merely to gain time—he added— "Shall you be asking Countess Hetta Páloczy? You know she's arrived?"

"Oh yes, so she has. How interesting—I expect Helen would like to meet her. Must the mother come too? Yes, I suppose she must. Very well—I'll ask Miss Cuthbertson to send cards to them both. *What* is the girl called?"

"Countess Hetta"—he spelt it out.

"Yes. The surname is the trouble; but I expect Miss Cuthbertson knows how to spell it. I never can be certain whether Polish or Hungarian names are the worst! Well, we shall count on you on Friday."

"I shall look forward to it, Sir. And I'll see that Miss Cuthbertson gets the name right! Countess Hetta is an interesting girl—unusual," Richard added; and then wondered why he had said that.

"I imagine that she has led a rather unusual life, by our standards," said the Ambassador a little drily, and rang off.

After a moment or two Richard lifted his receiver again and asked the bi-lingual telephone operator—the Portuguese wife of one of the English-born Chancery messengers—to ring up the Duke of Ericeira's house and get Miss Probyn for him. He then replaced the receiver, opened the drawer in his desk, and resumed his study of the life of the domesticated but so informative Magalhães family. When that discreet buzz came again he once more took up the instrument as before, saying "Atherley."

"Really, Richard," Julia's voice said indignantly—"what a way to speak! Atherley indeed! Have you become a Duke, or something?"

"No, it's simply common form—it avoids confusion," Richard said. "Can you come round to my house for a drink this evening?"

"Party?"

"No, you and me. Yes—No?"

"Yes"—rather hesitantly. "Yes, I think probably. Could I call you back presently and let you know? What time?"

"By all means. Sevenish—or whatever suits you." As he put back the receiver he added aloud—"According to what time your dinner with Major Torrens is, dear Julia!" The Major, he decided, had been uncommonly quick off the mark after learning that Miss Probyn was in Lisbon; indeed, unless he had telephoned from the Embassy he could hardly have done it in the time—he had left Atherley's room under half-an-hour earlier. Curiosity prompted Richard to find out about this.

"Mrs. Tomlinson, did a Major Torrens put a call through from the Chancery this morning?" he asked the operator.

"Yes, Mr. Atherley, he did—about twenty minutes ago, from Mr. Melplash's room. Mr. Melplash spoke to me first."

"Quite all right, Mrs. Tomlinson. It was to the Duke of Ericeira's, wasn't it?"

"Yes, Mr. Atherley. To the same young lady that you spoke to just now." There was a certain smugness, Richard thought, about the operator's voice. "Thank you," he said.

Julia rang back later to say that she would be with Richard at 6:45— "I've a dinner engagement."

"Do you want fetching?" the young man asked.

"No no—I have my own car; got it yesterday."

"I'm glad the firm's so rich," he mocked.

Julia was looking very lovely when she came into his drawing-room that evening, in a short full-skirted sub-evening dress of very rich dark-green brocaded silk.

"Goodness, Julia, what a frock!"

"It's my wedding dress. Do you really like it?"

"It's *quite* beautiful," Richard said. "But I am afraid you have probably put it on more for Major Torrens than for me."

The detested blush dyed Julia's cheeks to the tone of a fully-ripened apricot set against a sunny wall.

"What do *you* know of Major Torrens, pray?" she asked rather tartly.

"He came to see me this morning, and I very kindly told him that you were here, which he didn't know. You owe this dinner to *me*, dear Julia."

She laughed. "Oh well."

"Poor liaison, I thought," Richard pursued. "You didn't know he was here either, till he rang you up at 11:15 A.M., or as near as no matter."

"Richard, how *do* you know all this?"

"Never mind that, for the moment. But as a reward for my valuable services, will you now tell me exactly how you stalled him in Morocco last year? Come on—I have a feeling that it's a good story."

It was rather a good story—how she had gone to Tangier to look for her missing cousin Colin Monro, and in the course of her search for him had stumbled on Major Torrens' current activity of shipping a new and rare radioactive mineral out of Morocco; how her enquiries, quite without her intention, had raised so much dust that the operation had to be closed down. However, they had got all they needed for tests by that time, Julia said airily, so it didn't matter—"and now Morocco is such a muck-up that nobody can do anything there anyhow. I was blown up by a bomb!" she added, rather proudly.

"Good Heavens! Not that affair at Marrakesh? Wasn't some Duke blown up too?" Richard asked, quite driven off his usual careful-casual line.

"Yes, Angus Ross-shire. But nothing like as bad as me—here's my scar." She lifted her lion-gold hair to display a narrow white line running down her forehead.

"Golly! And did you ever find your cousin?"

"Oh yes; he was working for Hugh—for Major Torrens," she corrected herself hastily—"running the stuff on his little smugglers' yacht."

"Is he still with Torrens?—though I expect I shall soon be calling him Hugh myself," Richard said.

"Oh, rather—though he isn't here just now."

No, dear girl—I expect he and his little yacht have been scooting from Cannes to Port Vendres with a Hungarian passenger on board, Richard thought to himself. He gave his beautiful guest another drink, and when they parted it was on terms of greater intimacy and liking than before—Julia even, finally, vouchsafed laughing that at one point Major Torrens had suggested employing her.

"Oh, you would do them a treat—I can't think why they hesitate for a moment," Richard said, standing at his door, while she climbed into her rather large hired car. The bright Lisbon evening was soft and full of stars; lights from houses shone, warm and yellow, along the built-up sides of the ravine. "See you Thursday," he called as the girl drove off.

Chapter Four

THAT was on a Tuesday. On Wednesday evening, just as he was locking the drawers in his desk prior to leaving the Chancery Richard's telephone buzzed. It was Major Torrens, who asked if he could come round to see him.

"How soon?" Richard asked without much enthusiasm—he was dining out.

"Immediately."

"How soon is that? Where are you?"

"Oh, where I am! But I can be with you in eight minutes."

"Very well," the Head of Chancery said resignedly; he unlocked one of his drawers and took out the *Familia Magalhães*, who kept him company till Torrens arrived.

"Any trouble?" Richard asked.

"A little. The opposition seem to be rather active in Spain."

"Really? They haven't copped your man?"

"No—but it was only by accident that they didn't. I told you about the little hold-up between Cerbère and Barcelona—owing to that he missed the plane he was to have taken to Madrid. But *that* plane had engine failure and made a forced landing right out in the country somewhere on the upper Ebro—and the moment it landed a number of murky-looking types, who certainly weren't all innocent peasants, swarmed round it and made a rather thorough inspection of the passengers."

"Um. Cause of engine-failure known?"

"Yes. Sugar in the petrol-tanks—the Iberia people are quite solid on that."

"Did Iberia report the murky types?"

"No. One of our people from Madrid was on board, and mentioned them—he'd gone to Barcelona to meet our party, but had to get back at once."

"And where is your man now?"

"On his way to Madrid by train, I hope."

Richard considered. "Have you any idea who 'they' are, in Spain?—the actual operators? Spaniards?"

"I fancy so; leave-overs from the Civil War. Funny how little people in England realise what a Communist-dominated affair that was! A lot of them fled to North Africa—Morocco was full of them when I was there; but I suppose they are sent back to Spain as required. They would be more suitable than anyone else for the job. I gather some East Germans are in it too—Spain is full of German business men just now, doing an export drive, and nothing is easier than for an East German to masquerade as a West German."

"Well, that's all most interesting," Atherley said, glancing furtively at his desk clock. "But where do we come in?"

Torrens laughed.

"You don't, yet. I really only wanted to warn you that if they are as busy here as they seem to be in Spain, we might have to call on you. But I hope not."

"So do I, I assure you!" Richard said with considerable fervour. "Well, I shall see you tomorrow."

The cards for the cocktail party at the British Embassy arrived the day before Hetta set out for Mr. Atherley's luncheon. Hetta was always up early—lying late, let alone breakfast in bed, formed no part of her pattern of living; she usually went to Mass at half-past seven in the big church just across the gardens, and then ran on down to the sandy *plage* for a quick swim before walking back, glowing and contented, to breakfast—the water was still very cold, but she liked that. On this particular morning a letter lay beside her plate—apart from the note which Townsend Waller had sent with his flowers, it was the first that she had received since she arrived in Portugal. "Who should write to me?" she muttered, as she tore open the stiff envelope.

The formal card, with the Lion and the Unicorn embossed in gold, impressed her a good deal—and why, she asked herself, should Lady Loseley, who appeared to live at the British Embassy, ask her, Hetta, to a cocktail party? Hetta knew by now what cocktail parties were, her mother had taken her to several since her clothes arrived; but she knew no one at the British Embassy except Mr. Atherley. When she had finished her coffee and rolls she went to her mother's bedroom—the Countess always breakfasted in bed. After the good-morning kiss Hetta held out the card.

"Mama, I am invited to a party at the English Embassy."

"So am I," said her mother; she looked very pleased, Hetta noticed.

"But is it not rather strange, since I don't know them?"

"Not very strange—people are interested to meet you. The Loseleys are charming," she went on, "and of course as we know Mr. Atherley, and he is on the staff there, it is quite reasonable that we should be asked." Hetta realised then that this was her mother's first invitation to the British Embassy, and that it was a source of satisfaction to her. How peculiar!

Hetta set off in the Countess's car for her luncheon with Richard Atherley with sensations which were rather mixed. She was pleased to be going to see again, and in his own house, the man who remembered Detvan and the sun there; on the other hand she was a little nervous about this, the first social engagement that she had attended alone, though that big beautiful English girl whom she liked so much would be there—evidently a great friend of Mr. Atherley's. Bowling smoothly up the Tagus estuary, her thoughts were occupied with this new world of hers. She had asked Mgr Subercaseaux, at confession, about going to lunch with young men, and had received full sanction; later he had been to see her at the hotel when her mother was out, and spent an hour with her. He was kind, genial even, and clearly anxious to help her and to smooth her path in this unfamiliar life; but she did not like his kind of help, and she did not like him. The fact was that Hetta Páloczy found herself rather up against the Western world as presented to her at Estoril in many of its aspects, of which the social ease, the urbane worldly wisdom of her mother's confessor was most definitely one. The richly-dressed congregation at Mass on Sundays, with shiny cars waiting outside, the interior richness of the churches themselves, with all their treasures displayed, not hidden away in the deep reed thatch of some peasant's house for security—the very safety of it all jarred on her, after the passionate devotion of the people at home, holding with such stubborn intensity to the practice of their religion in the face of persecution and danger. She remembered the skilful, wary sermons preached—only very rarely—by Father Antal, when he knew full well that there would be several "Spitzel" (Communist spies) posted among the congregation, waiting to lay information against him if anything he said could possibly be twisted into an anti-Communist utterance. Here, priests were safe, and could preach as they pleased—and then go on to eat of delicate dishes at luncheon, bow to rich ladies, and make graceful little jokes. "Pfui!" said Hetta (who spoke German as well as she did French, English, and Hungarian) to herself.

Of course she was unjust. The young often are, and with less reason than Hetta, who had grown up in an unusually hard school; born courageous and tough, she had become intolerant. But as the car pulled up outside Atherley's little white house she forgot her criticisms in a warm feeling of happy anticipation.

A pretty smiling maid in a frilly apron and white cotton gloves led her up the narrow staircase and ushered her into the long narrow drawing-room; Atherley turned from the window at the far end as she entered, came over and kissed her hand.

"Here you are—how nice. Your chauffeur found his way to my slum all right?"

"How do you do. Please, what is slum?" she asked.

"Slums are where poor people live; I am not so very poor, but I live in one because I like it. Come and see my neighbours"—and he led her to the window, below which the family life and daily activities of the inhabitants of the ravine were spread out like a diagram, or a child's toy farm on the floor. Hetta studied them all, thoughtfully.

"This looks nice," she said at length. "So we lived in the Alföld, cooking and washing out of doors when it was warm weather. But this is 'slum'?" She pronounced the word with full Hungarian plumminess.

"No, it isn't really a slum at all," Richard said, forced into accuracy by her literalness. "I was being affected. Slums are degraded places in big cities, like London or New York, where people have no gardens, and no chance to live with decency or dignity. If there are gardens there is never degradation, and therefore no slums. That is Dr. Salazar's idea too," he went on—"When he lays out a new working-class suburb he insists that each house shall have a *bout de terre*, a small garden-plot where the husband can grow onions and saladings to bring in to his wife, instead of wasting his evenings and his money in drinking. He says that sociologically this is a fundamental principle, and he's quite right."

Some of this was rather too difficult for Hetta's command of English—she seized on Dr. Salazar.

"He dictates this country, no?"

"NO, and no twenty times!" Richard exploded. "He guides it." He went on for some time about Dr. Salazar, for whom he had a well-founded admiration.

"You must forgive me—I am still learning," Hetta said. She turned away from the window to the room. "But where is Miss Probeen? She does not come?"

"Yes, she's coming all right; she's only late, as usual. Come and have a drink. Townsend tells me you like sherry better than cocktails."

"He remembers this? How *nice* he is," Hetta said warmly.

Atherley, having given her a glass of sherry, was busy with the cocktail-shaker. "Oh yes, Townsend is nice," he said, without much enthusiasm—why should young Hetta think Townsend so very nice? "Tell me," he said as he filled his own glass, "did the Monsignor say that you might go out alone to lunch with young men? Did you ask him?"

"Yes, I did—and he said yes, certainly. He explained many things," said Hetta; a certain lack of enthusiasm was evident in her tones.

"Don't you like him?" the young man asked, slightly surprised.

"No—I do not. He—"

The door was opened by the befrilled maid to usher in Julia and Major Torrens. There were greetings, one introduction, drinks—then they went down to the little dining-room on the ground floor.

It was a pleasant meal. The other three bestirred themselves to draw Hetta out, and in this congenial company they found little difficulty in doing so. The food, which as always in Atherley's house was delicious, caused her to volunteer her most spontaneous observations: she ate carefully, consideringly, Atherley noticed with approval, and occasionally commented on a dish.

"There is something—yes, it is *fenouil*—how do you say that in English? —in this sauce," she said at one point. "So good."

"We call *fenouil* fennel," said Atherley—"but how smart of you to spot it. I always tell Joaquina to put very little of any flavouring in things, so that people shall wonder why they taste good, but not know why."

"This is so *right*—and she does it beautifully. I should not have known if I were not a cook myself."

"You a cook!" Torrens exclaimed. "What do you mean?"

"I have been a cook for six years in Hungary," Hetta replied airily—"to a priest. A nun whom I was with was supposed to be his cook, but she was so bad, therefore I did it. I love cooking."

"Do you really?" the Major asked, fixing her with a startled eye.

"Oh yes—also I love food," the girl said frankly. "And is it not a form of blasphemy to abuse the gifts of God by bringing them badly cooked, and therefore *horrible,* to the table?"

"Amen to that," Richard said, while the others laughed.

There was only one rough patch, and it was Hetta's fault. Inevitably the subject of the royal wedding came up, and Julia mentioned in all innocence the extreme desire of a certain highly-placed official's wife to attend it—through the Ericeiras she was *au courant* with all the social and political gossip of Lisbon.

"Well, if Madame de X. wants to see Princess Maxine married, X. will have to stop his opposition to the new ferry scheme," Richard said, equally innocently. "He's been making a perfect nuisance of himself to the Government about that."

"Oh, he will—I understand that he went round to the Ministry this morning in a plain van, carrying a small ladder to climb down by," Julia said gaily, causing everyone to laugh. Except Hetta, who leant across the table, gazing at the young Englishwoman with what Torrens later described as a basilisk's eye.

"May I know?—this Monsieur de X. attached importance to opposing the ferry scheme, whatever this may be?"

"Certainly he did"—Richard, rather negligently, answered for Julia.

"And withdraws his opposition at his wife's wish, because she will see a princess married?"

"Just that. Men are often rather at the mercy of their wives."

"But for this man, this Minister, it was a matter of principle to oppose?"

"One imagines so, or he would hardly have made so much fuss for so long," Richard said frankly. "But why, Countess? Does it matter?" He was astonished at her persistence.

"To me such a thing is infamous," Hetta Páloczy said, once again with that ring in her voice. "To sacrifice a principle for a social occasion! Where I come from people *die* for a principle!"

Of course that led to an awkward little pause. It was broken by Julia Probyn, who said gently—"I expect we all lead frightfully low, unworthy lives by comparison with the people you have been accustomed to live among. I'm sorry. That's the way we are—we have been too safe, and had it too easy, for too long. You'll have to be patient with us— I hope you will be."

"Oh, *you* are nice—you are *true!* I knew this at once! Please forgive me—everything here is so strange!" She looked ready to burst into tears.

"Of course it's strange to you—and in fact we are probably a lot of miserable bastards, as Miss Probyn says," Richard said comfortingly. "Don't worry, Hetta—if I may call you that?"

"Hetti, please," she said, the tears now falling.

"Very well. Dear Hetti, go upstairs with Julia and powder your nose, and then come and have coffee in the garden."

The garden was really only a small flagged terrace at the back of the house, shaded by a vine trained over a trellis, with two or three narrow flowerbeds; its low walls were both faced and topped with glossy blue-and-yellow *azulejos*. There was an azulejo-topped table too, and some garden-chairs with cushions, but when the two girls came out Torrens and Atherley were sitting on the wall, enjoying the view.

"Oh, how pretty!" Hetta said with her little *grande dame* air, to Richard's relief entirely ignoring the scene she had created only a few minutes before. "But this is perfectly charming." She went to the wall and looked over. "Another garden—is this yours also?" she asked him.

"No, that belongs to one of my neighbours," he said. In fact the gardens of the little houses below came right up to the foot of the wall; the nearest was full of ancient and enormous medlar-trees with grey leathery leaves, vegetables growing among them; similar gardens, divided from one another by the frailest of fences draped in runner beans, spread right down to the houses at the bottom. Torrens turned to examine them, standing with a foot on the wall.

"Where does that track between the houses go to?" he asked.

"It leads out into a maze of little streets, down towards the river, and that level-crossing where the goods trains hoot so frightfully at 2 A.M. Lady Loseley is always grumbling to the Commandant of the City about it; she says the noise comes right in at the Embassy windows," Atherley said.

"Perfect get-away if you wanted one—drop off the wall and down through those shrubs and creepers," Torrens pursued.

"Ah, but I enjoy diplomatic immunity, so I don't have to think of those things, Torrens. Hetti, have some coffee?"

"Richard, I think I've persuaded Countess Hetta to come out and have supper at the Guincho on Tuesday," Julia said—"Will you come too? Hugh, of course, goes without saying."

"Julia, I don't go *anywhere* without saying. What is the Guincho?"

"A place along the coast beyond Cascais, all sand and rocks, with one or two little shacks of restaurants where one gets the most delicious sea-food."

"Thank you, I shall love to come," said Atherley. "I like the Guincho."

"Good. Perhaps you'll bring Hugh, and I will take the Countess."

"If Mama has nothing else arranged for me—but I can let you know, if you will give me your address."

"Oh, I'll keep you in touch with one another," said Richard rather hastily. "Don't bother, Julia." He made a face at her over Hetta's head, and Julia obediently put away her card-case—she had become accustomed to the use of visiting-cards during her stay in Portugal.

Richard drove Hetta back to Estoril. The moment they were in the car she apologised for her behaviour at lunch. "To be so angry, and to cry! I am very sorry; I was silly—as silly as a nun!"

"Are nuns silly?"

"Only when they come out into the world, and everything is strange. Not in convents."

Richard had been startled, and rather upset, by Hetta's outburst. He was considerably taken with her, little dark thing that she was, with her splendid eyes and her remarkable voice—and he found her freshness of outlook interesting. But Atherley liked a certain ease and smoothness in social intercourse, and he had remembered Julia's uncomfortable remark about Hetta's conventual life possibly "smothering dynamite."

"Oh well, I don't think you are silly, only a little inexperienced, and perhaps rather too fierce," he said, turning and smiling at her. "You will have to learn to take people as they come. Tell me," he went on, "why you don't like Subercaseaux? You were just going to when the others came."

"He is part of it all," Hetta said slowly, looking straight in front of her.

"Part of all what?"

"This life here. So much is false, I think—the importance of attending the marriage of a King's child, of being invited to an Embassy—or that politician who sacrifices his principles to gratify his wife's snobbism! I cannot help it—I have said I am sorry that I burst out at your table—but to me all this is incomprehensible, *despicable*. And for a priest to accept it all, take part in it!"

"Oh, that's your quarrel with the Monsignor, is it? Well yes, he does take part, I agree. But can't he perhaps do good by doing so?"

"Possibly. Back there, where I come from, compromise is not possible;

our priests live in hourly danger. If you knew the risks Father Antal runs!"

"Is he the priest you cooked for?" She nodded. "What special risks did he run?"

"Going to see the Cardinal—" and she told him more of what she had told Townsend, ending up—"But he at least does not compromise with evil."

"But Hetti, *are* royal weddings and Embassy parties evil? Don't you exaggerate?"

"Oh, there are those lovely ships!" the girl exclaimed, forgetting the argument as the car came in sight of thirty or more big schooners, lying at anchor out in the Tagus. "These are the ones which go to catch the salt fish, no?"

"Yes; all the way to Newfoundland"—and Richard told her about the annual voyage of the Portuguese cod-fishing fleet to the foggy waters of the New World, to catch, salt on board, and bring home *bacalhau,* the dried fish which is a main part of the staple food of the nation, in town and country alike; at the next place they came to he made a detour through side streets to show her the flat triangular bodies hanging up in a grocer's shop. They were as hard as boards, and Hetta fingered one doubtfully. "Is it not very nasty?" she asked.

"Yes, if it's badly cooked it's quite horrible, but properly prepared it can be delicious. Next time you come to lunch with me you shall have it; Joaquina does it wonderfully, especially with braised fried onions, buttered rice, and a very mild mustard sauce."

"You speak like a cook yourself!" said Hetta laughing, as they drove on.

"Yes, I'm interested in food. I completely agreed with what you said at lunch about the blasphemous nature of bad cooking—I liked you for that," Richard said, again turning to smile at her. "But do you know"— and he went on to tell her how every spring before the bacalhau fleet sailed the Cardinal-Patriarch of Lisbon said a special Mass for all the men of it, out on the quay-side if it was fine, in the great Jeronimos church at Belém if it was wet.

"Oh, how I should like to see this," Hetta said.

"Get the Monsignor to take you—he always goes, and he'll get you a good seat."

"This he would *certainly* do!" the girl said ironically.

"Hetti, I think you're taking Subercaseaux up all wrong," Richard said. "Don't make up your mind in too much of a hurry. I think he's a splendid person."

"You are fond of him?" She sounded incredulous.

"Yes, and I admire him. He adapts himself to his world, of course—which you will have to do, sooner or later—but he *does* do good in it, for that very reason." He spoke with unusual earnestness; Hetta was silent.

Between the small towns strung out along the Tagus there are still open spaces of waste land, for the most part dry and sandy, where occasionally small flocks of sheep or goats, with tinkling bells, crop such scanty herbage as they can find—it is one of the charms of the environs of Lisbon, this artless penetration of the life of the country into the life of the town. In spring these waste spaces are misted over with the flowers of a minute dwarf iris, drifts of blue against the background of yellowish soil. A few moments after Atherley's last remarks about the Monsignor, which still remained unanswered, the car drew abreast of one such open space—"Oh, *could* we stop?" Hetta asked.

He pulled in to the side at once, by no means unwilling to prolong this tête-à-tête. "Of course—what is it?" he asked.

"The little lilies—for days I have wanted to pick them, but Mama is always in too much hurry for us to stop." She began to get out of the car.

"They die in five minutes," he told her, thinking—How she runs away from a subject! But he did not believe that it was from cowardice—why was it?

The girl came back after a moment or so with her hands full of the lovely little things; in the car she sat looking at them in silent delight.

"They aren't lilies really, they're irises," he told her as they drove on.

"So? The iris is the rainbow, isn't it?"

"I believe so; but it's this kind of flower too."

In a few minutes the small blossoms did indeed begin to wilt and shrivel together, as Richard had foretold; it is a fact that this particular species cannot endure separation from the soil.

"Oh!—oh! they *do* fade," Hetta lamented. "But it is so few minutes."

"I told you so," Richard said, slowing down again; he looked at her as she sat beside him, ruefully contemplating the flowers in her hands, noticing for the first time how strong and shapely those hands were, but also—in spite of nail-varnish and other evidences of careful manicuring—that the skin on the inside of the fingers was still cracked and roughened from, no doubt, hard kitchen work. They were strange hands to be associated with that pretty dress, the elegant shoes and hat, the careful make-up—somehow they moved him rather surprisingly.

"They say that if flowers fade quickly on a person it means a warm heart," he said. "But these anyhow fade the moment they are picked, so they tell me nothing about your heart."

"Do you want to know about my heart?" she asked, with a readiness that rather startled him. "Why? It is a most ordinary one."

Why indeed?—if he did; and to his immense astonishment he found that he did in fact want to know if Hetta Páloczy's heart was or was not warm.

"I think perhaps I might want to," he said, starting the car again. "People's hearts are interesting, don't you think?"

"I have never thought whether they are warm or not—if it is important, surely one knows this," Hetta said casually. "Mr. Atherley, I believe we should hurry a little—Mama is taking me to tea with some people at Colares this afternoon. Tell me," she went on, with one of her abrupt switches of subject—"This Major Torrens and Miss Probeen: are they fiancés?"

"I don't know. They could be. They have known one another for some time, but for most of it he has been in Morocco and she here. What do you think?"

"I think there is some sort of relationship between them, but I am not sure if it is this one," said Hetta, as Richard swung the car round into the road alongside the public garden which led to the hotel. "Mr. Atherley, thank you so much—I have enjoyed my luncheon, and it was very good of you to bring me home."

"If I am allowed to call you Hetti, shouldn't you equalise it by calling me Richard?" he said, drawing up before the door of the hotel.

"Possibly. I will ask your friend Monsignor Subercaseaux about this!" she said in a sudden laughing flash. "Goodbye." She sprang out of the car and vanished into the hotel.

"Lumme! Is she a coquette as well as all the rest?" the young man asked himself as he drove off. "That would be odd, in a convent-bred cook!"

At the same moment Hetta, going up in the lift, was also asking herself a question. When Atherley brought Miss Probyn to her mother's party, in her innocence she had assumed automatically that they were engaged; having seen Julia and Major Torrens together, and having just heard Atherley's detached assessment of the situation, she saw clearly that this, at least, was not the case. But why was she glad?

Mme de Fonte Negra's luncheon on Sunday was a very different affair from Richard's little party. She rang up in the morning to stress the fact that Hetta must be there "at 1:20—very precisely, please."

"How curious!—who can be coming?" Countess Páloczy said, when Hetta mentioned this. "All right, I will tell Oliveira." Oliveira was the chauffeur. "She didn't say why?"

"No—just what I told you."

In fact the party included the Duke of Ericeira and his sister—both elderly and rather silent, though when they did speak to Hetta it was in excellent English; but also the Comte de Bretagne, the Pretender to the throne of Armorica, and his tall splendid wife. Her hostess warned Hetta of their advent the moment she arrived, and kindly informed her as to the drill. "They are of the blood royal, but as he does not occupy the throne you merely sketch a curtsey to each; and you address him as Monseigneur, not Sire."

Hetta was rather vexed, partly because she was to meet these royalties behind her mother's back, as it were—and was it not all rather what she called "false," this business of the degree of curtseying, and whether to say *Sire* or *Monseigneur?* While they waited she expressed this view in an undertone to Mgr Subercaseaux, the only person she knew among the company.

"But why?" he said, raising his rather bushy iron-grey eyebrows. "It is exactly like Bridge."

"Bridge?"

"Yes, Contract Bridge—possibly you have never played it. But in this card-game there are certain 'conventions,' as they are called—rules, if you like; and unless all the players observe them it spoils the game."

"So one's life is to be as a game of cards!" said Hetta, rather contemptuously.

"Precisely. In effect, human life, particularly in its social aspects, is very like a game of cards! But the point of my observation, my dear young lady, is that it is as unfair to one's fellow-humans as to one's fellow-card-players not to observe the rules, and so to cause confusion or embarrassment. Did your Director at the Sacré-Cœur never tell you that courtesy is a part of charity?"

"Of course he did," Hetta said, flaring up. "But—"

"There is no 'but' in this case," said Mgr Subercaseaux, still urbanely. "Courtesy, and therefore charity, are to be applied to all human contacts. Our Blessed Lord never stated that one should be rude to Kings—on the contrary, He was rather specific about rendering the proper dues to Caesar, you may remember. Ah, here they are," he said, getting up.

The Comte and Comtesse de Bretagne in fact entered with very little fuss or ceremony, except that all the women made tiny bobs to them; they seemed to know nearly everybody, took cocktails, and stood about chatting easily. Presently the Comte came over, glass in hand, to where Hetta and Subercaseaux still stood together.

"Now, Monsignor, I am going to rob you of this young lady's company for a little while," he said; "I want to talk to her. Countess, will you indulge me by sitting on this charming canapé? I hope it will bear us both"—as he sat down on a fragile gilt settee, patting the shining brocade beside him. "I am heavier than I look."

"You do not look at all heavy, Monseigneur," Hetta said, remembering her instructions—her companion, though fairly tall, was far from stout.

"No, but I have heavy bones. There, now we are comfortable, well arranged, n'est-ce pas? Now tell me—"

Hetta's prejudices about royal personages melted rapidly in the next few minutes. Her companion asked innumerable questions, but all extremely sensible ones, and apparently based on a degree of knowledge of conditions in Hungary that astonished her. Could the peasants make any sort of living on four-and-a-half hectares? How were the collective farms going?—were they at all popular, and was their population increasing or diminishing? What proportion, if any, of the people had a real enthusiasm for Communism? Who directed it in the villages?—and what class of person provided the Commissars—Russians, or Hungarians? How about religion? Could Mass be said freely?—and freely attended? What had become of the monks and nuns when they had to leave their Communities?—how did they manage? And what about the Cardinal?

Hetta was soon answering eagerly, warmed by the intelligent quality of these enquiries; as usual she was lucid and categorical, and her replies provoked further questions—at the lively frankness of some of her statements the Comte de Bretagne laughed out loud, causing heads to turn in the direction of the flimsy settee. Their hostess was finally obliged to come and separate them, very deferentially, in order that the company might go in to luncheon.

"But this is a wonderful girl!" the Pretender said to Mme de Fonte Negra as he sat down at the head of her table—royalty, entertained, always takes the head of the table, and the hostess sits at his right hand.

"She is so observant and so uninhibited. Imagine her cooking for a *curé de campagne!*"

"Monseigneur, you have betrayed me!" said Mme de Fonte Negra. "I promised that if she came to my house she would be asked no questions."

"Oh, that is too bad! Why did you not warn me? Here, I will question her no more, but I shall ask her to come to our house, and there she shall talk to my family. She is immensely interesting."

"Her mother will not like that."

"*Pourquoi pas?* Do I know the mother?"

"No, Monseigneur, you do not. She is that enormously rich Countess Páloczy who lives in the hotel at Estoril."

"Ah, yes." He looked vague for a moment, a rather studied vagueness —then he turned to his hostess, his eyes twinkling.

"And you snatched away the daughter, alone, so that we might meet her?"

"*Je croyais vous procurer un plaisir, Monseigneur.*"

"Oh, you have, you have!—a genuine pleasure. She is thoroughly intelligent, and yet so naïve; it is as if she had just been born, at the age of—what, twenty?"

"Twenty-two." (That was the sort of thing Mme de Fonte Negra always knew.) "But I did not wish to involve Monseigneur in any *embêtements.*"

"Oh, I shall not let myself be *embêté!*—but I should very much like my wife and my children to hear her talk. If she comes alone to you, will she not perhaps come alone to us?"

"Monseigneur, you are a more serious proposition than I!" Mme de Fonte Negra said, laughing her stout jolly laugh. "And there is this complication, that Madame la Mère is dying to come to the wedding."

"Ah, *ça!*" His lively face became vague again, all of a sudden. "Too many wish to come to the wedding, which is after all an affair of the family! There is hardly place for a mouse." He twinkled again. "Is this an indispensable condition? I did not get the impression that the young lady is likely to be tied to anyone's apron-strings."

"I also think she is not—but she may have her own *embêtements,* poor child, with her mother."

"Do *you* know her?—the mother, I mean?"

"Oh yes, quite well. She is a kind woman, really, and spends much in charity—through Monsignor Subercaseaux, therefore it is well dispensed. But she has a certain *folie de la grandeur;* she lives for social success."

"I shall talk to the Monsignor about it," said the Pretender with decision.

"Do. He is her confessor, and can make her do anything."

The Comte de Bretagne did talk to Mgr Subercaseaux after lunch, while Hetta, summoned to sit on a larger sofa beside his wife, talked with her; again the girl had a small success, caused laughter. When the Bretagnes left, the Comtesse said warmly—"I hope you will come and visit us. I shall write to you."

Mgr Subercaseaux asked Hetta to give him a lift back to Estoril in the car, which had been sent to fetch her.

"The Comte and Comtesse de Bretagne wish you to lunch with them next week," he said when they were twisting down through steep narrow streets towards the speed-way along the Tagus.

"They are nice—I should like to go," said Hetta. "But does Mama know them?—visit there?"

The Monsignor was a little taken aback by this question—he hemmed. "In fact, no," he said at length.

"Then I shall not go."

He was surprised by her decisiveness.

"I think your mother might like it if you did," he said.

"I should not. Some other people gave me invitations today, but they seem not to know Mama; at least they did not come to her party. I will not go to such, just because they are curious to hear what I have to say."

She is really quite astute, the priest thought. He did not quite know how to tackle this new attitude; while he was considering what to say Hetta spoke again.

"Mama wishes very much to attend this wedding, does she not?"

"Yes, that is the case."

"Very well. If they invite her, I will lunch with the Comte and Comtesse de Bretagne with the utmost pleasure—but if they do not, I will not go."

At that he burst out laughing. This waif from the wilds of Hungary, issuing her ultimatum to a prince of the blood!

"I thought you considered any desire to attend royal ceremonies—unimportant," he said. He had seen Richard Atherley since that little luncheon, and been told of Hetta's outburst. But she was ready for him.

"My *ideas* on this must be quite unimportant, since I am so ignorant.

But I do not wish to be entertained by people who do not know Mama." She paused. "I am sure Pappi would not have wished it," she said, her face suddenly quivering.

Mgr Subercaseaux leant over and patted her hand.

"My child, you are perfectly right," he said, in an unwonted burst of sincerity. "Leave it to me—your mother shall attend the wedding."

Chapter Five

JULIA PROBYN'S party at the Guincho took place on one of those soft warm spring evenings which can make April in Portugal a heavenly thing. The two girls drove through Cascais and on into open country, a broken shore of pale rocks and Atlantic rollers on their left, to the right the landscape swelling up towards the seaward end of the Serra da Cintra—ahead the blunt bulk of Cabo da Roca, the western-most cape on the mainland of Europe, stood up with its lighthouse. They parked the car and strolled down through sand to the restaurant, past outcrops of rock studded with small bright flowers, and big silver clumps of sea-holly growing in the creamy sand. The restaurant was certainly shack-like, as Julia had said; it was built of wood, and approached by a wooden outside staircase—but passing in from the balcony, set with a few small tables, one entered a pleasant room gay with bright cotton table-cloths, and on each table an array of bottles, and bunches of the yellow flowers of the sea-holly. It was all simple, homely, and rather quaint—Hetta was delighted.

"Oh, what a nice place! Our country csardas at home are like this." She fingered one of the check table-cloths almost lovingly. "I did not know that there were such places here."

"Oh yes, lots of them, in almost all countries," said Julia. "Look, the men haven't come yet, I can't think why they're so late—but you and I might start on our drinks. Inside or outside?"

"Oh, can we be outside? There, please."

Julia had learned from Richard Atherley that Hetta had an aversion to cocktails, and it was a fine, dry Portuguese champagne that she caused to be brought out to the small table on the balcony. "I think cocktails before sea-food are a mistake," she said—"and here one eats nothing else."

"Sea-food? What is this?"

"Oh, it's an American expression, but rather a good one—whatever comes out of the sea. Tonight we're having bisque of langouste—well that doesn't come out of the sea, it's a sort of fresh-water lobster—and then crab, cold, and sole, hot, and cheese and salad to finish off with. But the cooking is rather good in this funny little place; I shall be interested to know what you think of it, as a professional."

Hetta laughed.

"Do not make fun! Me a professional! And as we have no 'sea-food' in Hungary, I shall not be able to judge of it very well."

"I'm sure you *will*, Hetti. By the way, Townsend Waller is coming; he heard somehow that we were dining here, and he's dying to meet you again, so I asked him."

"I am glad. He is so *nice*." But Hetta's gaze was constantly straying seawards, where big breakers surged in to fall on a narrow stretch of sand between two points of rock. "Yulia, I wish so much to swim!" she exclaimed. "Can I not? This water is so much more *alive* than at Estoril —I would love to swim in it."

"Have you brought bathing-things?"

"No—but I can swim in my petticoat! I often swam in my nightdress in the Tisza."

"It's frightfully cold, and pretty rough," said Julia doubtfully.

"I swim strongly!" Hetta pronounced firmly; "and at Estoril I swim every day—for the first time, here, I swim in the sea. Oh, I do wish to! Where can I undress?"

Rather unwillingly, Julia arranged for Hetta to undress in the bedroom of the proprietor's wife; the girl emerged in a crêpe de chine slip under her pale tweed overcoat and ran gleefully down to the little sandy bay. But instead of plunging thence into the breaking waves she nipped up onto one of the rocky points, threw off her long coat, and entered the Atlantic in a clean dive just as Atherley, Townsend Waller, and Major Torrens arrived on the balcony.

"Good God, who on earth is that diving in?" Torrens exclaimed.

"Hetta Páloczy."

Atherley swung sharply round, and like the others stared towards the sea, where Hetta's black head promptly reappeared.

"What on earth did you let her do that for, Julia?" he said brusquely. "It's not a bit safe bathing here, in water as rough as this, except for very strong swimmers. Surely you know that?"

"She says she *is* a strong swimmer," said Julia coolly—with a second's wonder as to why Richard should be so cross. Anyhow, she was not going to excuse herself to him.

"And *how!*—just look at her!" Townsend exclaimed enthusiastically, watching that black head smoothly surmounting the great crests of the incoming waves. Indeed she seemed to be an eel, a fish, and the water her natural element—as she got further out the watchers noticed that she took to turning onto her back to slide down feet foremost into the trough behind a wave, swinging over as the next approached to cross it with her powerful breast-stroke.

"She seems thoroughly in control," said Torrens.

"Yes. Have a drink," said Julia turning to the table, and filling their glasses with the delicate wine.

"Just the same, I think we ought to yell to her to come back now," Townsend said after a few moments; "she may get into a current—she's going pretty far out."

"Well, yell," Julia said. "She may pay attention to you—she wouldn't to me."

Townsend cupped his hands round his mouth and bellowed "Hetta!"

The black head turned on the summit of a green crest.

"Come on in!" Townsend roared. "We're hungry!"

They could see her laughing face as she turned round and started to swim towards the shore. But it is much easier to swim out through big waves than to swim back with them; each one bears you forward, but after it has passed there is a strong suck-back in the trough until the next carries you on again. Atherley could see Hetta frowning as she encountered this phenomenon—glass in hand, they all stood at the rickety rail of the balcony, watching her progress with some anxiety. But she soon learned the trick of it, swimming vigorously with each overtaking wave, then relaxing till the next came along.

"God, she is a good swimmer!" Townsend said, watching appreciatively. "Half the people who get drowned in swimming do it coming back in water like this. She must have had a lot of practice."

"No, she says she never swam in the sea in her life till she came to Estoril," said Julia.

"Well, really, Julia, I must say—" Atherley was beginning angrily when Townsend exclaimed—"Oh, watch out!"

The one thing that Hetta was not prepared for, strong and resourceful as she was in the water, was the merciless force of a breaking wave.

The tumbling crest picks the swimmer up and flings him forward like a piece of wreckage, rolling him over and over till sand and water fill eyes, ears, and mouth; the only way to prevent this is to turn and dive backwards through each following wave till the water is so shallow that one can stand, and even then it is not easy to keep one's feet. But all this the girl from the heart of Central Europe could not know. Even as the American shouted the watchers on the balcony saw Hetta picked up, thrown onto the sand, and tumbled over and over, helplessly, in the creamy surf—when the water dragged back again she did not rise, but was sucked back with it.

"She's stunned!" Atherley exclaimed. He was down the wooden steps in a flash, and raced across the beach, flinging off his jacket as he went; by the time the next wave threw Hetta forward again he had waded in waist deep, to snatch her up and carry her to the land. On the sand he set her down, for she was wriggling in his arms like a captive fish.

"Ow!" the girl said, spitting out sand and sea-water, and rubbing at her eyes with her fingers. "This is horrible!"

"Are you all right?" the young man asked.

"Yes, except for this sand!" But she was in fact shaking slightly all over, with cold and shock. "I must wash my face," she said, starting back towards the sea.

"No, do that at the pub," he said, catching her by the arm. As they passed up the beach he picked up his jacket and threw it round her shoulders.

"Thank you—oh, now you are all wet!" Hetta said, glancing at his soaked trousers. "I am so sorry. I do not know what happened; I—I was taken by surprise. These waves are so strong, when they come to the shore."

"They are. There's a trick about getting back through them—I'll teach it you some day."

"Will you? That I should like. But could you fetch my coat? It is up on those rocks." She waited while he brought it and then, modestly muffled, went up with him to the little inn.

Julia's dinner was rather late that evening. Hetta had to be sponged down, her hair dried, and dressed—minus her petticoat; a pair of the proprietor's trousers had to be borrowed for Atherley while his own were hung up to dry in the kitchen. Torrens and Townsend Waller, left to themselves on the balcony while Julia ministered to Hetta, became hungry, and in Torrens' case rather impatient.

"She's a beautiful swimmer, our little Countess, but not very considerate," he said, glancing at his watch. "It's nearly a quarter to nine."

"We started late ourselves, anyway," said Townsend, still rather resentfully conscious of having waited in Atherley's room at the Chancery for nearly half an hour for Torrens to appear; he had asked Richard why he didn't call his friend up and tell him to come along, but Richard had been evasive, merely saying—"No; he'll be here presently." Anyhow he, Townsend, disliked any criticism of Hetta.

"Yes, I was late—I couldn't help it," the Englishman said readily. "Sorry. Do you feel like a whisky?—I do. I wonder if they have it here?"

But just as Townsend was explaining that rum or Pheysey gin were all that could be hoped for in the way of spirits at the Guincho first Atherley, and a moment later the two girls reappeared, followed by the proprietor's wife with a second bottle of the local version of champagne. They had another glass, Hetta was dosed with hot rum-and-water, and then Julia hustled them indoors to dine. "Goodness, I do hope the soles aren't ruined," she said.

Nothing was ruined. The bisque was divine, the crab cold anyhow; and the resourceful proprietor—who was also the chef—on finding that the gentlemen were very late and one of the ladies determined to swim had not started cooking his lovely soles till he saw how things were shaping—they, too, were perfect. They had the restaurant to themselves, always a pleasant thing, and two courses of food—Guincho food at that —restored Major Torrens' equanimity; while the excitement of her swim (possibly aided by the rum) had put Hetta Páloczy into higher spirits than any of the others had so far thought her capable of. She sat between Torrens and Townsend Waller, her black hair hanging in damp elf-locks round her curious vivid face above her pretty cherry-coloured dress; she had already made profuse apologies, on returning to the balcony, for "keeping everyone hungry," but now, in response to Townsend's questions as to where she had learned to swim like that, she recounted her father teaching her to dive in the lake at Detvan, and later her solitary bathes in the Tisza on long hot summer afternoons, when for an hour or so quiet reigned on the Alföld. But she made it all natural, simple, and rather funny, told in her curious but expressive English— Townsend, it was evident, had fallen completely under her spell.

It was Hetta who urged that they should have coffee on the balcony, and when they went out from the small, rather steamy room to see whether it would be too chilly there, it was at once clear that she was right. The air was still warm, great stars and a young slip of moon hung in the sky, the Atlantic made a gentle thunder on the shore below.

"Atherley, do you feel like a stroll?" Major Torrens asked. "If Miss Probyn will excuse us?" He directed a glance at Miss Probyn as he spoke which did not escape Hetta—she thought there was complicity in it.

"Oh, very well," Richard replied. It had already occurred to him that there was probably some reason for Torrens having been half an hour late at the Chancery, and whatever it was he would have to hear it sooner or later. "May we leave you, Julia?"

"Of course—but come back for a cuentra."

The two men climbed down the rickety wooden stair. "Don't let's attempt to stroll in this hellish sand," Richard said.

"Don't let's stroll at all—we can sit on that lump of rock over there," Torrens replied, walking towards one of the flower-set out-crops. As they approached it a figure sprang up out of a dark crevice at the foot and raced away towards the road—when it passed through the broad bands of light cast on the sand from the restaurant windows they saw that it was a youth, wearing one of the loud tartan shirts affected by Portuguese fishermen.

"Hullo! Are we being watched?" Torrens said.

"Not at the Guincho, I shouldn't imagine."

"I think I'll just go and check on the cars," said Torrens, and strode up towards the road—before he reached it a third car, parked facing towards Lisbon, started its engine and roared off into the night, its headlights twisting and swooping till it disappeared.

"That's curious," Richard said, contemplating his and Julia's cars, still standing by the roadside. "There was no one but ourselves in this place, and the others aren't open yet."

"Have the people here a car?" Torrens asked.

"I don't know, but we'll soon find out." They went back to the restaurant, where Richard walked into the kitchen and put a question in his rather moderate Portuguese. Yes, the proprietor had an *automóvel*, a small van for bringing out supplies; but it had been in Lisbon all the afternoon, and had not yet returned.

"Um," said Torrens, when this was reported to him. "That wasn't a van—it was a rather big open car. Ask if they know whose it was?"

The proprietor and his family knew nothing of any car having come; busy with preparing the dinner, and getting the Menina washed and dried, they had not even heard it drive up.

"Looks as though we *are* observed," Richard said—"or you, rather. Now, where shall we talk?"

"In one of the cars, I think." He drove Julia's large machine out into the middle of the road, well away from the scrubby growth of heath and cistus on both sides, and switched off; Richard got in too. "Well?" he said.

"Things are getting rather hot in Madrid—we must get our man out as soon as we can."

"How hot?"

"They've tumbled to at least two of our people; they're followed the whole time. Two flat tires in traffic-blocks, and so on—a stiletto stuck into them, by the look of the marks. We think our passenger must either have been followed from Barcelona, or waited for when he was met at the station. Anyhow, the whole show there is compromised."

"Awkward," Richard commented.

"It is, damned awkward. He's got to come on here *prontito*."

"How?"

"By plane. But he'll have to travel alone, and board the plane alone, the way things are."

"Well, I suppose he's capable of that."

"Of course he is!" Torrens said, rather impatiently. "But the point is that neither I nor anyone else here knows him by sight; and as you know, one of our friends' favourite tricks is to abstract the person who's expected, and plant one of their own agents on us instead—that's why we usually try to have anyone like this escorted and handed over by a man we do know."

"Well, I don't see how *I* can help you," Richard said, frowning in the darkness. It sounded as if this affair was going to be quite as troublesome as he had foreseen.

"Oh, can't you come off that line for a bit, Atherley? After all, we're in the same show really—we work for the same country. And I need your help."

"All right—but how do you imagine I can help you?"

"Estoril is stiff with Hungarian refugees, and I expect you know a lot of them, and how reliable they are," Torrens said. "It occurred to me that you might be able to get hold of someone who would be certain to recognise this type and would be willing to come to the airport and point him out—one of these Archdukes, or Counts, or someone."

"Is he the sort of person Archdukes would know by sight?" Richard asked.

"Oh, probably."

Atherley was silent for a moment.

"Look here, Torrens," he said at length—"hadn't I, at last, better be told who your mystery man is? I can't, even if I were willing to, do anything till I know that."

"Yes, of course. He's a Dr. Horvath; a considerable theologian, I'm told."

"Christian name? I'd better have the whole works."

"Antal."

Richard started a little.

"Where has he been in Hungary before he came out? In Budapest?"

"No, down in the country somewhere, doing duty as a parish priest."

"Is he a friend of Mindszenty's? Been in touch with him recently?"

"Yes," Torrens said, surprise in his voice. "That's rather the point, as a matter of fact. Why do you ask?"

Richard burst out laughing, his great resounding laugh.

"What's the joke?" Torrens asked, slightly annoyed by this mirth.

"Only that he's the man that Countess Hetta has been cooking for for the last six years!"

"You don't say so!"

"Yes, it must be the one. She only calls him 'Father Antal,' but she told Townsend that he was immensely learned, and she told us *both* that he constantly went in disguise to see the Cardinal. Anyhow I expect she knows his surname—if it's whatever you said, there you are."

"Ye-es," Torrens said, rather slowly. "Yes," he repeated more firmly—"and I imagine she'd be reliable."

"Look, Torrens! Who would be more so?" Richard expostulated.

"Sorry—you see you know her and I don't. Well, we'd better talk to her—or you had," he said, opening the car door. "I ought to let them have a signal in Madrid tonight—the sooner they get him off the better." He paused, standing in the road beside the car. "I'm sorry I was so late this evening, but all this was just coming in, and I had to wait to help decode it."

"I don't quite see how we're to talk to her tonight," Richard objected.

"Oh, Julia's as safe as houses—Miss Probyn, I mean."

"Yes, but there's Waller. Or is he in on this?"

"Good Lord no. The Americans want this man out, but they have left it to us to do it—we know Europe better, after all. But couldn't you and I drive the little Countess back, and let Julia take the Yank?"

"I expect so. Anyhow do let's go and have that cuentra—any contact with secret service activities always leaves me feeling distinctly weak," Richard said, starting down towards the restaurant; Torrens followed him laughing.

"You'd better suggest it; you know her best," he said.

"Oh yes—I'll be cover."

Richard did it quite well, as the other readily admitted to himself. Sipping a second cuentra he said, very casually—"Julia, I've got to get back rather early, and so has the Major. And I'm sure the sooner Hetti is between the sheets the better, after all that swimming. How would it be if we three went off and left you and Townsend to make a night of it? He likes to drink till 1 A.M., I know."

"Richard, may you be forgiven!" Mr. Waller protested, while Hetta looked from one to the other of the faces about her; the phrase "make a night of it" left her completely at a loss, but once again she surprised a fleeting glance between Julia and Major Torrens, and her sixth sense —the particular sixth sense which becomes so strongly developed in countries where speech is never free, and spies always at one's elbow— caused her, together with this sudden change of plan, to think to herself: those two are up to something! But why, in that case, was it *she* who was being taken away?

She learned very soon. After goodnights and thanks the three of them got into Atherley's car and drove off. To her surprise he did not switch on his headlights—"You forget the lights," she said to him.

"No I don't. I can see by this moon and the starshine—and there's nothing on the road at this time of night." He spoke over his shoulder to Torrens. "No need to advertise ourselves, don't you think?"

"Undoubtedly not."

After a mile or so Atherley slowed down, and began to drive at a snail's pace. "Here we are," he said, suddenly swinging the car into a small side track; this wound inland between high heathy banks, and after some seventy yards a bend concealed the car from the road behind them—Richard stopped and switched off. "There," he said—"I think that's all right. You'll have to con me out later, Torrens. Now, will you talk to the Countess, or shall I?"

"You might begin, I think."

"Very well. Hetti, what was your Father Antal's surname? Do you know?"

"I *do* know—but it was not mentioned as a rule."

"I thought not. But would you tell it to me and Major Torrens?"

She hesitated. "I should like to know why you ask," she said—and Torrens, at least, recognised the ingrained caution of dwellers beyond the Curtain. He decided to speak himself.

"Countess, we need to know it because we may want you to help us, and him. I am in the British Secret Service," he added.

"No! Oh how nice. Yulia too?"

This question caused Richard to laugh out loud.

"Not altogether, no," Torrens replied, ignoring the laugh. "But will you tell me?"

Still she hesitated—for so long that Torrens finally said, rather brusquely—"Is he not really Doctor Antal Horvath, the theologian?"

"Of course he is—since you know it. But why then do you ask?"

"Because we have to be certain—just as you do, back there. Good. Now please listen carefully—would you know him by sight, even if he wore a beard?"

"He does not wear a beard."

"No, I know he doesn't—but would you know him if he were wearing one as a disguise?"

"His *eyes* I should know anywhere—but why?"

"You'd better tell her what it's all about, Torrens," Richard interjected. "You're only muddling her."

He thought that Torrens didn't manage his explanation very well when he did embark on it.

"He's in Madrid just now," the Major began.

"Impossible!"

"Yes he is."

"But how can he come to Madrid?"

"He was got out by our people—he's going to America, to do propaganda work."

"Talking to journalists? This also I do not believe!" Hetta said with energy.

"Suppose I have a go, Torrens?" Richard said. "Listen, Hetti—there are thousands of Hungarians in the United States who are all longing to know how everything is at home, as well as a sort of committee which acts almost like a free government, to look after the interests of Hungarians everywhere. Those are the people the Father is going to see in the first place. He's got as far as Madrid, and quite soon he's coming on here to fly to the States."

"Here? He comes *here?* Oh!" Her voice had that ring again. "Shall I see him?"

"That's exactly what we want you to do—see him, and recognise him," Torrens said, from the back seat.

Hetta ignored him completely.

"Richard, please explain more," she said.

Richard—curiously pleased by her unexpected use of his name—proceeded to tell her both how the priest had been got out, and that it was essential that someone who knew him by sight should be at the airport to meet him.

"Oh, of course I will go. Only what time? For me the morning is the best, because Mama does nothing in the morning—and of course it is best that she does not know of all this, isn't it? In such cases, the fewer who know the better, I think."

"Perfectly right," Torrens said approvingly. "Don't speak of it to anyone."

"Then when?"

"We shall have to let you know that. I'll make a signal to Madrid tonight, and tell them to arrange for him to come on a morning plane—then I can ring you up."

"If you ring up you should be most careful. Ought we not to arrange a form of words for the message, so that others do not understand?"

"Good girl!" Torrens said. "Yes, I think all we need do is to tell you which day. One of us will drive you out to the airport."

"I'll do that," said Richard. "If you let me know the day and time, Torrens, I'll bring the Countess out to Portela."

"You can invite me for 'drinks' when you telephone," Hetta said, with a sudden small laugh.

When this was settled Atherley reversed out onto the main road, Torrens walking to guide him; he continued to drive without lights till they were just entering Cascais, when he switched them on to pass through the town. Presently he was startled by some small strangled sounds beside him—they sounded like sobs. "Hetti, what on earth is the matter?" Atherley asked.

"Nothing. I am simply silly again. But to see *him,* after all these people here!—you cannot know what this is."

"Yes, I'm very glad. But cheer up now," Richard said—moved, and therefore embarrassed, he patted her shoulder rather awkwardly with his left hand.

"Hullo, there seems to have been a smash," Torrens said. "Had we better stop and see if the people are all right?"

Richard, who had begun to drive rather fast once he was on the Tagus speedway, braked; a little way ahead a car was tilted up against a bank hideous with the puce-and-white-wash flowers of mesembryanthemum, a revolting plant beloved of Portuguese road-planners. A man and a woman stood by it.

"It is Yulia!" Hetta exclaimed, as they came to a halt.

"By God, so it is!" Torrens said, jumping out. "Julia, what on earth has happened? Are you all right?"

"Some bastards quite deliberately crowded us into the bank," Townsend Waller said. "Forced us in. Don't know if they meant to tip us over, but they meant to stop us, because they pulled up just in front."

"They caught our wing," said Julia. "But Townsend's quite right— they overhauled us after we got through Cascais, and crowded us in— they weren't drunk, it was done on purpose. They came back and gave us the once-over, and swore in Spanish and drove away."

Torrens and Atherley exchanged glances—the latter walked quickly back to his own car and switched off the headlights; then he returned to the group.

"Was it an open tourer?" Torrens was asking Julia.

"Yes, it was—with three men in it."

"Was one of them a fisher-lad in a check shirt?" Richard asked.

"Oh, let's leave all that, Atherley," Torrens said hastily. "Julia, I expect you got the number of the car?"

"Naturally," she said, in her slow tones. "But I can't read it to you, since Richard has plunged us all in darkness."

"No, don't bother—you can give it to me later. I think we'd better get home. Have you got your things out, Julia—bag and coat and so forth?"

"Oh no—I forgot my bag." She went and groped for it in the tilted car; then Torrens hustled them all into Richard's Bentley.

"I'll sit in front, if you'll forgive me," the Major said.

"Richard, can you cope with the wreckage?" Julia asked from the back seat as they drove off—again without headlights.

"Oh yes—I'll see that someone goes over tonight. Don't worry."

.69.

"I'm not. Do you realise that you're driving without lights?"

"Oh, so I am. Well I don't really need them here with these arc-lights," Richard said easily.

It was only about a mile-and-a-half farther on that they came on an open touring car drawn up, also without lights, at the side of the great road. "Slow down," Torrens muttered to Richard. "Julia, is that the car?" he asked, leaning back.

"Yes, that's it," said Julia surprised. "Goody! Shall we ram *them?*"

"No. Step on it, Atherley."

Richard pressed hard on the accelerator—the Bentley roared forward. "They'll never catch this car—that's only a Vanguard," he said.

In Monte Estoril he swung up to the left, and began to twiddle his way through the maze of small tree-shaded residential roads which link it to Estoril proper, switching on his sidelights as he did so.

"Where are you going?" Torrens asked in a low voice.

"I thought we'd drop the little Countess, and perhaps Townsend too," Richard answered in the same tone.

"A good idea."

Atherley knew the two Estorils well, and presently pulled up outside the Casino, which overlooks the public garden—scores of cars were parked there.

"Townsend, I wonder if you would take the Countess home; it's only a few steps," he said, getting out and holding open the rear door.

"Why of course—I shall be delighted."

"Will you not all come in and have drinks?" Hetta, who was learning western ways, said as she got out.

"Not tonight, Hetti, thank you so much. We had better get on." While Hetta was thanking Julia, Richard drew Townsend a little aside.

"Take her right up to the apartment, and see that Dorothée or the maid is there before you leave her," he muttered.

"But why," Townsend began—Richard interrupted him.

"I'll explain tomorrow. Do what I say now, there's a good fellow. Would you mind making your own way home? So sorry, but I don't want to hang about tonight. I should take the train if I were you."

"That's pretty slow—I can get a taxi."

"All the same I should take the train. And don't *talk* to anyone about this, whatever you do."

"All right. I shall look forward to the explanation!" said Townsend, with his usual good-nature. Richard turned back to Hetta.

"Good-night. Sleep well."

"Thank you." Then she reached up to whisper in his ear.

"No, he doesn't—you're quite right. And not a word to anyone else," Richard muttered.

"But naturally."

When the pair had walked off towards the Castelo-Imperial Richard turned the car and drove back on his tracks into Monte Estoril.

"Where now?" Julia asked.

"Home, but via São Pedro da Cintra, I thought."

The car was climbing a hill; it passed through a small square with a bus-stop sign, and in a few moments was out in open country.

"It's *miles* round," Julia protested.

"It won't take us long," Richard replied, opening the throttle and at last switching on his headlights; the great car roared through the night.

"Well now perhaps one of you will explain," Julia said, in slow resigned tones. "You seem to know quite a bit about these types who ditched us. What goes on?"

"We'd better tell her everything, Atherley," Torrens said. "She'll find out for herself if we don't!—and she's completely reliable. Anyhow it looks as if we may need to make use of her before we're through, if things here are as hot as this already."

"Very well—you go ahead and tell her. The priest is your export drive, not mine," said Richard coolly.

Torrens proceeded to tell Julia the whole business of Father Antal; then of the watcher they had surprised among the rocks at the Guincho, and the car that had driven off.

"*I see,*" she said slowly. "That's how you knew about the tartan shirt. I suppose they took Mr. Waller and me for you, Hugh."

"I imagine they were waiting for both cars—first ditch one and then the other," he replied rather sombrely. "Only Atherley was too quick for them—in every sense of the word. You're sure they swore in Spanish when they found you weren't what they were looking for?"

"Certain. *Carajo* and plenty more in the same strain. Quite like old times in Morocco, isn't it?"

"A good deal too like to please me."

"Well, what's the next move?"

He told her of the plan for Hetta Páloczy to meet the plane, so that someone might recognise, indubitably, the Hungarian.

"I don't much like little Hetti getting mixed up in this," Julia objected. "Can't you get someone else? Some of all these Hunks here are bound to know him by sight."

"We might use Dorothée!" Richard put in, with his loud short laugh.

"My dear Julia, she's mixed up in it already," Torrens said. "Their spotter at the Guincho will certainly have seen her—she was sitting right by the rail of that balcony in a blaze of light. And besides, doesn't it occur to you that they must know perfectly well that she's here, after the roaring publicity of her getting out? If I know anything of them they will also know—nobody better—that she's been living in his house in Hungary for the last six years. Your little Hetti is involved up to the neck, whatever we do or don't do."

"Then you ought to warn her, Torrens," Richard said abruptly. He was disturbed—all these implications had not occurred to him.

"Oh, she'll know. These behind-the-curtain people can make rings round us," Torrens said—and Richard, remembering Hetta's whisper to him about Townsend Waller, realised that the Secret Service man might be right. "No, she's the person to do the plane job—it can't make things any worse for her. But you might suggest that she wears a veil, Atherley. Pity she's so short; it makes her terribly recognisable."

"Not here," said Julia. "No Portuguese women are tall. Oh, here we are at São Pedro—sharp right, Richard."

They sat in silence for a little as Atherley drove down the familiar road towards the distant lights of Lisbon—all slightly uncomfortable. Torrens was reflecting that he would need to satisfy himself pretty thoroughly as to the hide-out arranged by Mr. Melplash; to be of any use it would have to be thug-proof indeed. Richard was worrying about Hetta. He recognised that what Torrens had said about her being already deeply involved was obviously true, but he didn't like it any the better for that—and what on earth would the Ambassador say if he himself got still more mixed up in this affair? Julia was also worrying about Hetta—and about her press car. "How will you get my chariot mended?" she asked presently.

"Oh, I'm glad you reminded me—we'll go to a garage on the way home and see about it. Where do you keep it?"

"At the Ericeiras—in the stables. They're vast."

"Yes, I've always understood that that establishment is like a small town in itself, for all it's in the middle of the city," Richard said.

"Atherley," Torrens put in, "might it be a good plan if you got that car number from Julia, and mentioned it to the police? They might haul them in, or lay them a stymie, anyhow."

"I can't have them hauled in simply for tonight's performance, Torrens—that would be quite impossible, and particularly bad from your point of view, I should have thought."

"I didn't mean that, naturally—that *must* be kept quiet. But couldn't they be had up for something else?"

"I'll see. I daresay Colonel Marques of the Special Police could fix it; he's very resourceful." He pulled up. "Give me that number," he said, and wrote it among the telephone numbers in his diary by the faint dash-board light—then he drove on through Bemfica, with its lights and tram-lines, and into the city itself, where he presently drew up outside a large garage. "Give me *your* car number," he said.

Julia gave it—XL61-91-91. Richard turned the figures into Portuguese aloud—"X.L. *seis um nove um nove um.*" He went in, and returned after a moment or two.

"They're sending the breakdown van at once. I gave no name, just told them to report to me at the Chancery. They do most of the Chancery work, so they'll fix it properly and ask no questions." He got in. "Now Julia, we'd better drop you next—" he stuck his wrist out towards the dashboard, and looked at his watch. "Good Lord, it's after midnight! Have you got a latch-key?"

"Heavens no—that's not at all in the tradition," Julia said, with her slow giggle. "But I shall get in all right. An old old night-watchman sits just inside the front door, in one of those leather chairs with a high hooded back with brass nails in it—do you know?—to let in late-comers."

"Good God!" Torrens said.

When they reached the Ericeira town mansion, with its barred windows in the vast baroque frontage giving on a high narrow street, Julia proved to be correct. She got out, lifted a huge bronze knocker on the great panelled double door, and gave two gentle taps; a sound of shuffling feet was heard inside, the door opened a crack, and the aged retainer appeared in the aperture.

"*Boa noite*, Manoel," Julia said cheerfully.

"*Boa noite, Minha Menina,*" the ancient responded, with a happy toothless grin.

Richard had got out to see her in.

"Julia, do let me look at the chair."

"Oh, all right. O Manoel, this Senhor wants to see your chair. He comes from the *Embaixada Inglesa. Pode ser?*"

"*Pode, pode,*" Manoel replied—Richard stepped into the immense shadowy hall, and admired the chair. "Marvellous—just the place to park Hugh's priest!" he said. "Good-night, Julia—thank you for the party. I'll ring you up about your wreckage."

"Now, where do you want to go?" he asked Major Torrens, getting in and shutting the car door.

"I'm not quite sure," the Major replied. "We're so late that I doubt if I can get hold of Melplash tonight anyhow. Would it be a nuisance just to drive past my place, and see if there are any signs of our friends? They seem so unexpectedly well-informed."

"No trouble whatever. Where is your place?"

"Off the Praça José Fontana—I'll show you the street."

The Praça José Fontana is a long narrowish square with a rather modest garden in it. Richard drove in from the northern side and swung round the end of the garden, keeping his eyes open; at the mouth of a side street an open touring car was parked—he flashed on his headlights for a second, and read the number.

"That's them," he said, accelerating. "You'd better come home with me for tonight, hadn't you? I should say that you won't be able to function very usefully until the police have done something about that car and its occupants."

"I'm afraid I agree. Yes, if it won't be a bore I should be glad of a bed. It's very good of you, Atherley."

"The Queen's government must go on!" Richard said, as he shot through the midnight streets. He eventually pulled up, not at his own little house, but outside the British Embassy. The Ambassador's residence in Lisbon is quite separate from the Chancery, and stands in an angle between two streets, one sloping and one level—Atherley left his car in the level one, the Rua Arriaga.

"I hope you don't mind walking a little way," he said, as he pocketed the key and slammed the door—"usually I leave her outside my house, but I don't really want any stilettos in my tires, and your friends are so attentive."

"Is this any safer?" Torrens asked, glancing round him—he did not at once realise where he was.

"Oh very much so—patrolled day and night, as you see," Richard said, acknowledging the salute of a neat Portuguese policeman with a cheerful *"Boa noite,"* and walking off up the steep street.

"Yes, I see now," Torrens said, as they passed the front door of the Embassy. "I've only been here once, to write my name, so I didn't recognise it." He laughed. "Very convenient, to have a guard for your car."

"I told you I enjoyed diplomatic immunity," said Atherley.

Chapter Six

"JULIA's car's done for," Richard Atherley told his guest the following morning as they sat down to breakfast on the small vine-shaded terrace. "The chassis's fractured. I've been on to Julia and told her she'll have to hire a new car—she didn't seem to mind. She said everything was covered."

"It's the other car I'm worrying about," Torrens said.

"Naturally. I've arranged to see Colonel Marques about that—someone is having us both in for drinks before lunch."

"Oh, is that how you do it here?"

"Obviously. This is really your people's pidgin, so if for any reason I intervene myself, it is always on a very social plane. Could you look in at the Chancery about 1:30? I might know something by then."

Major Torrens said he would look in. "You seem to have been working rather fast," he said.

"Oh, the Portuguese get up quite early, however lethargic they may be when they have got up. Colonel Marques as a matter of fact is always on call—he's immensely efficient."

"Good." But Major Torrens looked rather abstracted.

"Have you any idea where your man is to be parked when you get him here?" Richard asked.

"No—I left that to Melplash. I must see him about it this morning; the way things are it will have to be cast-iron, a hundred per cent safe."

"Oh, Melplash!" Richard permitted himself that expression at this rather crucial point.

"Precisely. 'Oh, Melplash!' is the word for it," the Major said, with a rather wry smile. "But we have an *homme de confiance* of our own here, so if necessary I can lay him on."

"You'll have to settle that of course before you have your theologian come. You'd better let me know about that, so that I can get the little Countess a veil."

"Get her a veil today—we may have to move pretty fast when the time comes," Torrens said. He got up. "Well, if you will excuse me, I think I will go off. Thank you immensely for the 'bed and breakfast,' Atherley."

"It has been, as they say, a pleasure," Richard replied. "See you presently."

They met again four hours later in Richard's room in the Chancery.

"What a nice place you work in," Torrens said, leaning back in a comfortable leather armchair and glancing appreciatively out of the high windows at the green expanse of garden and trees.

"Yes. Lisbon is one of the more elegantly sited posts. Did you ever see those awful war-time hutments in Washington?—really the most sordid Embassy accommodation ever known, I should think."

Torrens laughed a little—he was beginning to like Atherley.

"Well?" he asked.

"That car was stolen. I told the little Colonel that we were interested in it, and gave him the number—he rang up his people there and then, and in less than half an hour they rang back and informed him that it belonged to a Mr. da Silva, who had advised the city police of its loss soon after tea-time yesterday. The police will soon get it, of course."

"Anything else?"

"Well, I told him as much as I judged necessary—an English journalist's car crowded into the ditch and so on—but he pricked up his ears considerably when I mentioned that the worthies in it had spoken Spanish. He quite properly has his knife into Spanish thugs operating in Portugal—'les Espagnols à l'étranger seront certainement des communistes!'—and he wants a description of the men in the car."

"Julia will be able to give that—she's very observant."

"So I should imagine. I'll get it from her and pass it on, today. Have you organised something for your man?"

"Yes—but through my own chap. The other, the local plan, was quite childish."

"That doesn't surprise me at all! Anyhow, when does he arrive?"

"Tomorrow morning, 9:40, at Portela. We thought an early plane would be best, perhaps. Can you marshal your young lady at that hour?"

"As she always goes to Mass at 7:30 A.M. it should be quite easy,"

Richard said—and then regretted having spoken so energetically. But Torrens appeared to take no notice.

"You won't forget to get that veil for her, will you?" was all he said —words which warmed Richard towards him. "Oh by the way, what about the Yank?" he added.

"The Yank?"

"Yes—the one who was there last night."

"Oh, Townsend." (Richard, having lived in the States, never thought of Bostonians as Yanks.) "Yes—he rang up to report having delivered his charge into her mother's hands."

"Was he curious?"

"Yes, of course, but I stalled him for the moment—he'll be at the Embassy on Friday anyhow. I told him the whole affair was classified," Richard said, grinning a little, "but that I'd give him a sanitary version when I saw him."

"Did he understand that? I confess I don't."

"Oh yes, perfectly. It's the new American jargon: 'classified' information is highly secret, and a 'sanitary' version is what one tells the press. Townsend won't give any trouble; he's very sensible and discreet, as well as extraordinarily nice."

"Good. Well, I expect you want to eat," the Major was saying when the telephone buzzed.

"That was the Colonel. The city police have picked up the car in a side street, *without* the ignition key," Richard said, having spoken into the instrument. "They're towing it back to Mr. da Silva's; luckily for him he has a spare key. But I think I shall have to go off now, if you will forgive me; I must see these young ladies—and buy a veil!—and be here again by five at latest. Unluckily H.E. *isn't* playing golf this afternoon."

Atherley left Mrs. Tomlinson to make his two appointments, and asked her to tell him the results at his house. There he sat down to, first, meltingly tender young french beans, then cold veal with salad followed by a delicious local cheese—all washed down with good red wine from a *garrafão*, the big wicker-covered glass carboy, holding five litres, in which the wise in Portugal buy their wine for household use; it works out at about twopence-halfpenny the half pint. While he was taking coffee on the little terrace Mrs. Tomlinson rang up to say that Miss Probyn could see him at "the palace" at any time after 2:30, and that Countess Hetta Páloczy would be in at four.

Richard was rather interested to penetrate into the Duke of Ericeira's town mansion. Though he knew the elderly brother and sister slightly he had never crossed their threshold till the previous night, when he went in to look at old Manoel's hooded chair; they lived much in the country, and in Lisbon entertained very little, and then mostly their contemporaries—except when they opened the house to accommodate floods of Bourbons for royal weddings. How typical of Julia Probyn to have inserted herself as a familiar into these legendary precincts!—and how rightly the Portuguese referred to the place as a palace, he thought, as he followed an elderly manservant in rich but rather threadbare livery up the immense staircase and along several wide corridors, all lined with treasures of furniture, pictures, ivories and porcelain which fairly made his mouth water with the desire to stop and examine them. In a broad upstairs lobby almost the size of a billiard-room the man handed him over to a pleasant-faced middle-aged woman, wearing a black silk apron over a tweed skirt and a silk blouse.

"I'm Luzia's Nanny," said this individual, in a pleasant Leicestershire accent—"Will you come this way? Miss Probyn is in the schoolroom."

The schoolroom was large and sunny, and looked out onto a big garden; with its bareness, shabby comfortable armchairs and sofa, and bookshelves full of tattered classics it was exactly like an English schoolroom, except for a magnificent ivory crucifix over the fireplace—which had a completely Victorian brass-topped fender standing in front of it—and a lovely polychrome sculpture group of St. Anne and Our Lady as a child on top of the bookshelves; both these holy personages were dressed in the height of 18th-century fashion.

"Here's Mr. Atherley, Miss Probyn," Nanny said comfortably. "Now, Luzia, you'd better come with me and feed the bantams."

Julia was sitting at a large round walnut table in the middle of the room beside a tall coltish girl of sixteen or thereabouts, studying, Richard noticed, a map of Morocco in the *Times* Atlas—she got up, as did the young girl.

"Hullo, Richard," Julia said holding out her hand. "Luzia, this is Mr. Atherley. Nanny, unless the bantams are *starving*, Luzia can stay—she won't be in the way."

"Oh Nanny, do let me! I have never met a diplomatist before! *Please!*" the girl said, imploringly. Richard, surprised and amused by this very Anglo-Portuguese little scene, noticed that Luzia had remarkable grey eyes under her dark hair, and a face which would presently be beautiful

—from its unusual vividness of expression as well as from the fine structure of the bones.

"Oh very well, Miss Probyn, if you say so," said Nanny, compressing her lips in the expression of disapproving acquiescence which has been classical among English children's nurses for over a century.

"Thank you, Nanny," Richard said as she left the room.

"Don't let her be a nuisance, Mr. Atherley," Nanny replied, closing the door.

Julia had not been in the least surprised to get Mrs. Tomlinson's message, in fact she had been waiting rather impatiently for some word from Richard all the morning. "Well?" she now asked, sitting down again at the table, and pushing the atlas across to Luzia. "See if you can find Tindouf," she told the child.

"Have you organised another car? When do you get it?" the young man asked.

"Tomorrow."

"Good."

"Oh, Miss Probyn, did you have an accident? I *do* wish you would drive me out in your car!" Luzia said. Completely ignoring the map of Morocco, she kept her surprising grey eyes steadily fixed on Atherley.

"Luzia, if you interrupt you will have to go and feed the bantams with Nanny," Julia said with cool firmness.

"I am sorry—I will be silent." But she did not relax that steady inquiring stare—Richard had difficulty in refraining from laughing. He had seated himself on the big shabby sofa, and as he did so he could feel that the springs were broken—this, combined with Nanny's behaviour, took him straight back to his own nursery days. But what a strange set-up to find in Lisbon!

"Julia, I want you to write down a description, as full as you can make it, of the people in the other car," he now said. "Can you do it at once?"

"Yes of course." She took a block out of a curved drawer in the round table as she spoke, and felt in her bag for her fountain pen. "Who wants it?—besides you?"

"How unflattering you are!" Richard said—Luzia giggled audibly.

"Luzia! Not another sound out of you, or off you go," Julia said crushingly. "Sorry, Richard—I was only enquiring."

"I saw the Colonel we spoke of on the way home, this morning, and it's he who wants it. The other car was stolen—but it was waiting for

Hugh outside his diggings last night, so he came and slept in my house."

"Not really?"

"Yes. So do get down to it. May Luzia talk to me while you do your home-work?"

"Yes, but somewhere else. Luzia, take Mr. Atherley to see the *Blanc de Chine* on the top corridor—you know, the white vases and things in those Chippendale cupboards."

Nothing could have suited Richard better than this arrangement, nor could anything have been more satisfactory to Luzia than to have a live diplomat all to herself. "For how long?" she asked earnestly.

"Oh, about ten minutes."

The collection of *Blanc de Chine* porcelain was magnificent, though not more so than the immense glass-fronted Chippendale cabinets in which it was housed. Goodness what wealth!—and what taste!—the young man thought. But on their way to it he had caught a glimpse of an equally spectacular display of the armorial porcelain known as *Compagnie des Indes*, the Portuguese equivalent of "Chinese Lowestoft"; this was really more in Richard's line than antique Chinese stuff, which was beyond the reach even of his rather ample purse, and presently he asked to be taken to it.

"This is quite marvellous!" he exclaimed, gazing at the vast dishes, the exquisite plates, and the tureens great and small. "It's even better than what they have at the Janelas Verdes." ("The Green Windows" is the name habitually used for the Lisbon Art Gallery, once Pombal's palace.)

"But naturally," Luzia replied. "For the Museum they had to buy, here and there; but this was all made for my great-great—well I don't know how many greats!" the young girl said, laughing, "but he was some sort of grandfather, and he was Governor of the Indies, like Albuquerque. These are our arms"—she indicated the coat so decoratively applied to all the larger pieces.

"It's fantastic. What treasures you live among! Do you like them?" he asked, a little curious.

"Yes—quite. I like the chapel better. Have you seen the chapel?"

"No."

"Oh, it is down on the next floor—I don't suppose we have time. There is a wonderful Zurbarán, and some really good sculptures—a Pietà from Viseu which I think marvellous! We say the Rosary there every night after dinner."

"Do you indeed!" For some reason this casual statement of a daily fact increased his curiosity about Julia Probyn's pupil. "Why are your eyes grey?" he asked, suddenly rounding on her.

"Because one of my grandmothers—I think my father's mother—came from the Minho, up in the North; there were many Celtic people there, and also Visigoths—and both, it would appear, had grey eyes. I do not know from which race my grandmother had them."

"From the Celts, undoubtedly—yours are Irish eyes," he said carelessly, amused by this display of ethnographic knowledge in someone as young as the girl beside him. But she blushed so deeply at his words that he began to wonder if she were really so young, after all; he was rather relieved to hear Julia's matter-of-fact voice calling—"Luzia! Where on earth have you got to?"

"Mr. Atherley wanted to see the *Compagnie des Indes*; he likes it better than the *Blanc de Chine*," Luzia explained when Julia joined them. Back in the schoolroom he studied the paper which Miss Probyn handed to him.

"Yes, that will do perfectly. It's very detailed. Did the imperial look genuine, or gummed on?"

"My dear Richard, one really can't see if a beard is put on with gummastic at night, by headlights, when you've just been tipped out of your car!" Julia said indignantly—Luzia, all eyes, nevertheless giggled again.

"Well never mind—thank you very much, Julia. That flat back to his head and the rolls of fat above the collar should be useful pointers, whether his beard is permanent or transitory—no one but Charles Laughton gums rolls of fat onto his neck, and that only for a film."

Julia as well as Luzia giggled at this remark—Richard, rather upset, took Julia by the arm and drew her to one of the windows.

"I say, is she all right? Little pitchers have long ears. Why on earth didn't you let Nanny take her away?" he muttered.

"Oh, Luzia's as safe as houses—she's a wonderful child. And she was so longing to meet a diplomat! You've *quite* come up to her expectations," Julia said, with her slow gurgle of pleasure—"I can see that."

"Julia, I do wish you'd grow up! What Torrens sees in you I can't think," Richard said irritably, pocketing the paper. "Now, will you please get me out of this museum? Am I allowed to walk downstairs alone?"

"Goodness no!" Julia replied, ringing the bell. "I'll start you, and Elidio will meet us on the way up."

"Goodbye, Luzia," the young man said, shaking hands with the girl who was so soon to be beautiful—his vexation faded as those astonishing grey eyes, so eager, so candid, were once again fixed on his face.

"Oh, goodbye. This has been a pleasure. Will you not come again, and look at more of the china? We have a great deal of celadon," the child said.

"Yes, I will, if your aunt will let me," Richard replied.

"Nanny likes you, and that is what matters," said Luzia. "*Oh*—oh, but we go to the country on Saturday!" she exclaimed dolefully: her mouth on the "oh" was a rounded sculpture of woe. Where was that head of the Medusa that it reminded him of, Richard wondered—and why should a Portuguese schoolgirl have a face moulded on the splendours of classical antiquity? Oh well, the Romans had colonised Portugal, so she might easily possess Roman as well as Celtic blood, he thought, as Julia and Elidio between them took him downstairs and out of that labyrinthine house.

He dropped Julia's paper at Colonel Marques' office, and then drove quickly to the Chiado and bought a charming veil set with black velvet stars; it was no good to try and make Hetta look like a widow, and anyhow, he found himself thinking, this was his first present to her, and he wanted it to be a pretty and an expensive one. (It was certainly expensive.) Afterwards he dropped down to the Tagus, and raced out along the road to Estoril.

Experienced drivers like Richard Atherley are apt to find speeding rather conducive to reflection. The pace, the automatic reactions to the need to brake, or accelerate, or avoid other vehicles produce something faintly resembling the effect of fingering the beads of the rosary, also automatic—one thinks almost involuntarily. Richard, afraid of being late for his interview with Hetta Páloczy and therefore driving extremely fast, was soon thinking about her with an unexpected and almost unwanted clarity. He had not been wholly unaffected by having carried her in his arms the evening before, in that clinging garment; her shape, so revealed, was as sturdily slender as a sapling willow, and had a willow's resilience—in the night he had found himself, almost with dismay, recalling the very feel of her small supple muscular body twisting and wriggling in his grasp to free herself. All the subsequent events—the watcher in the rocks, Julia's car, and Torrens' pursuers had pushed these impressions to the back of his mind at the time; but in the small hours, when the mind is peculiarly defenceless, they had returned on him with troubling force. And the splendour of her swimming, and the vivid gaiety of her face and her talk at supper! She was rather marvellous. Atherley, outwardly so much the conventional Englishman, and in addition heavily veneered with the watchful coolness of diplomacy, in his secret heart adored recklessness and *panache*—and this little creature, this convent schoolgirl turned cook, obviously possessed both to a high degree. But then her inexperience, her intolerance, the gaucherie which her prejudices engendered—how troublesome these were!

Hetta was in the little morning-room, alone; she was wearing a simple sleeveless cotton frock closely patterned in flame-colour and white, and white sandals; she looked as fresh as sunrise, and very pretty indeed.

"How do you do? When does he come, do you know now?" she asked at once. This neutral coolness should have put Richard at his ease; in fact, since his heart turned over at the sight of her, it suddenly irritated him. "She can think of nothing but her wretched priest," he told himself angrily. But he proceeded to the business in hand.

"His plane gets in tomorrow morning at 9:40. I will call for you here at 8:30, and take you out to the airport. There are some railings there where a little crowd always collects—the public, who are not allowed onto the apron; you will stand among them and watch all the people who get off the Madrid plane, and when you recognise Father Antal you will point him out."

"But do I not speak with him?" There was something like desolation in her face, her voice.

"Not there, no; it would not be prudent. Every plane from Madrid will probably be watched when it arrives here."

"Oh, by the Spitzel, of course—yes, I understand. But I shall see him properly later?"

"Yes, you shall," Richard promised recklessly, moved in spite of his irritation by the urgency of her tone. Damn it, Torrens could surely contrive that much, when she was so ready to help?

And so intelligently ready, as her next question showed.

"And whom do I point him out to?" Hetta Páloczy asked. "To you?"

This quite flummoxed Atherley—somehow or other he and Torrens had entirely overlooked that particular point when laying their plans. To whom *was* Hetta to indicate which of the passengers was the priest? Not to himself, if it was in any way avoidable—he thought gloomily of the Ambassador's justifiable reprobation if a member of his staff were to be involved in an affair like this, and anyhow he would not be having anything to do with the subsequent proceedings. It would have to be

Torrens, or Melplash, or Julia—Torrens and Julia were of course both known by sight to "the opposition," after last night, but that couldn't be helped. He thought rapidly. One person would have to be in the long hall at the airport through which the passengers entered, and where the customs examination took place; a second must stand at the railings with Hetta to be given the identification, and nip round to contact who-ever was in the hall. It was perfectly possible.

"I'll tell you that tomorrow morning," he said. "We haven't decided yet. But someone will be with you, and when you have pointed out Father Antal, he will go round and meet him." He pulled the little parcel with the veil out of his pocket, and said as he gave it to her—"And you are to wear this."

She undid the pretty flowered paper, drew out the veil, and shook it open.

"Oh, how pretty! But why? I never wear veils—they are for older women, with bad complexions, are they not?"

Richard had to laugh. "Yes, as a rule. But tomorrow you must wear this. And put on some dark, inconspicuous clothes—something shabby, if you have such a thing!"

"Oh, I have my *terrible* Hungarian suit; this is as ugly and shabby as possible! But please tell me why?"

He explained to her what Major Torrens had first made clear to him the night before—that she herself might well be in some danger, since her previous association with Dr. Horvath must certainly be known, and therefore she must not be recognised at the airport, if possible. Hetta jumped up, ran to a mirror, and held the velvet-starred veil before her face.

"Oh, it *is* pretty! I think I look very nice! Do you know me?" she asked, wheeling round on him.

"I should know you anywhere, I think, you silly little creature!" Richard said, restraining a strong desire to get up and hug her. "But Hetti, this is serious—it isn't a game. You must be very careful for the next little while. Don't go out alone, except in the car."

"I do not."

"I thought you went swimming before breakfast."

"Oh, this—yes."

"Well you positively mustn't do that, for the present." He spoke ur-gently—how appallingly easy it would be for her to be pounced on down on the beach, at an hour when nobody in lethargic Estoril was about. "Promise me," he said.

"I must go to Mass!"

"No, you mustn't do that either, unless your mother's maid or some-one can go too." Then, as she looked mutinous, he was inspired to say—"Not till the Father is safe out of the country, anyhow."

The mutiny died in her face. "Oh, if it is for *him*. Very well—I prom-ise. But *you* promise that I shall speak with him before he goes away?"

"Yes, I have promised you that. You shall."

They fell silent—a silence which to Richard became uncomfortable because of his own emotions. Hetta broke it with one of her character-istic switches to a fresh subject.

"I believe that Yulia really works with Major Torrens. Doesn't she? You remember I told you when you drove me back from your luncheon that I think they are involved together in some way—now I think it is in espionage, not as fiancés. What do you think?"

"I don't think about them at all," the young man said, getting up. He had got to catch Torrens and organise the arrangements for the morning, as well as clearing up his work in the Chancery, and he had no desire whatever to discuss Miss Probyn's relations with the Major with Hetti —his own relations with her threatened to become of overmastering interest.

"Goodbye, my dear," he said, taking her hand and kissing it. "Remem-ber what I've said, and be ready tomorrow morning at 8:30. Down in the hall."

The airport of Portela lies some distance outside Lisbon, farther up the Tagus; the drive to it is partly through suburbs, partly through open country now becoming increasingly studded with Dr. Salazar's new housing estates—these are rather straggling, since each house must have its *bout de terre*. Richard took Hetti there in a taxi, rather to her sur-prise; he thought it wiser not to take his own car with its red-and-white C.D. number-plate on this expedition. He had seen Torrens the evening before and they had settled that Mr. Melplash, who was small and suit-ably inconspicuous, should stand with Hetta at the railings, and then go round and tell the Major, who would be in the entrance-hall, which of the passengers was his man.

"What did you tell your mother?" Richard asked Hetta on the way out.

"Nothing. She will think that I went to a later Mass, or spent long in the sea—she is not interested in what I do before midday."

Torrens was there before them; Mr. Melplash was there too, and was introduced to Hetta; they went off to stand at the rails, where, early as it was, a small crowd had already gathered. Who these people are who have leisure to stand interminably watching the arrival and departure of aeroplanes is one of the standing mysteries of Lisbon life.

"I'll wait in my taxi," Richard said to Torrens—"I've told her to come back to me there."

"Yes, whisk her away. I hope to goodness Melplash doesn't perpetrate some clottery!" Richard recognised one of Miss Probyn's favourite phrases, and grinned. "I don't see anyone with rolls of fat at the back of his head, do you? Perhaps they haven't got anyone here for this plane."

Hetta Páloczy stood at the railings in the bright morning sunshine with Mr. Melplash. Beyond the white surface of the airfield olive trees stood out, shapely, silvered by the morning breeze, against a background of reddish soil shot over with the delicate green of growing corn; in a homely yet rich way the landscape had a certain beauty. But her mind was in a turmoil of excitement and anxiety. Mr. Melplash, eager to be helpful and thoroughly enjoying the situation, promptly pointed out to her the little motor affair, with its trailer for luggage, waiting out on the tarmac; there, he explained, the plane would come down. To Hetta it seemed appallingly far away; if Father Antal was really wearing a beard could she possibly recognise him at that distance? "Where do they go then?" she asked anxiously.

"In at that door, just to our right, where you see the police standing."

The police were reassuringly close at hand. There, surely, she would know his face and his eyes—though how hard it was to visualise that beloved stocky figure in anything but a dusty black soutane rather green with age, and either with his thinly-covered silver head bare or with an equally ancient and dusty biretta perched, rather askew, on it.

A faint hum sounded and grew in the blue bowl of the sky, above the red earth, the rising crops, the sculptured silver of the olives—grew till it filled the bowl, the air, and hummed in the ears of the watchers. "There she is," said Mr. Melplash, tilting his head, as a silver shape crossed overhead.

"But it's going away!" Hetta said astonished.

"No, only going out to turn over the Tagus—look, now she's coming in to land." And in a moment or two more the great machine touched down, gently, with one or two easy bounces, taxied along the run-way, and came to rest by the luggage-trailer.

Hetta leaned forward, straining her eyes to see through the stars on her veil, as the door in the aeroplane's silver side opened and the mobile steps were run up to it. A figure in uniform appeared, then withdrew again into the machine; some officials stood by the steps. Now, at last, the passengers began to descend. Three men with brief-cases, all too tall to be the priest; four ladies in mourning, heavily veiled; a man and a woman, apparently together, for she turned on the steps and spoke to him; three girls whose neat suits, clever shoes, and beautifully-dressed hair betokened Americans, followed by a tall man, also by the shape of his hat an American; two nuns. Then, one after the other, half a dozen men—all of medium height, all carrying the distended brief-cases which will hold pyjamas as well as papers, all wearing the light-weight slate-coloured rain-cloth overcoats which are practically a uniform among continental men travelling by air, brown trilby hats and sun-glasses! Hetta's heart sank as she watched them crossing the apron towards her, in the bright sun; the stars on Richard's veil were maddening, she pushed it up, impatiently, and studied the faces, panting a little. None wore a beard, she noticed with thankfulness, but how could she ever make this Mr. Melplash know which one she meant, when all were so alike, even if she managed in spite of their goggles to recognise Father Antal herself?

That, however, she *must* do, and as these stereotyped specimens of *Homo sapiens europaeus* came nearer, their eyes concealed by the tinted glasses, she was inspired to study the backs of their heads under the trilby hats. Yes—all but one had hair, and darkish hair at that; as the colourless stubble on the sixth head approached the group of police, she recognised—she could not fail to—the blunt ugly nose, the stubborn chin, the wide, wise mouth that she knew so well. She pinched Mr. Melplash's arm.

"That is he—the one whose hair is without colour."

"The bald-pate, d'you mean?"

"What is bald-pate?" Hetta asked, angrily—was this man's stupidity, or her lack of English, to spoil everything at the last moment?

"Well, he is nearly bald, isn't he? Is that the chap?"

"Yes! I said so. All the others have dark hair. Now *go!*" Hetta said, managing to speak in an undertone in spite of her fury with this silly little man.

"All right, all right," Melplash said, rather miffily. "There's no rush—they'll be ages in the hall." What a tartar this Hungarian secret agent was, he thought, for all she looked rather pretty—what you could see of her through that veil. (Major Torrens had thus promoted Hetta into the ranks of counter-espionage; he preferred not to reveal her identity to his local colleague.)

The little secret agent, left to herself, stood for a moment longer at the rails. She was trembling a little from reaction; a few tears fell behind her veil. He was *there*, in that building within fifty yards of her!—and yet she must not approach him or speak to him. It was almost more than she could bear; she clenched her hands round the rails, as if to clamp herself in position, to control the ferociously strong impulse to follow the detestable Melplash round into the building. But the crowd was thinning on either side of her, as it does after a plane has arrived; noticing this she sniffed, blew her nose, dabbed at her eyes, drew her veil down again, and walked back, very deliberately, to where the taxi waited on the parking-place.

"Well?" Richard asked as she got in. "All right?"

"Yes—but what a *stupid* person this Melplash is!"

The taxi-man started his engine.

"Oh, can't we wait just one minute? We might see him again!"

Richard himself would have liked to wait, but he remembered Torrens' injunction to whisk his young companion away at once, and he was going to be appallingly late at the Chancery as it was.

"No, Hetti—better not. Now, tell me what happened."

She told him about the six short men in sun-glasses and rain-coats, her terror lest she should fail to recognise the priest, and her final solution of the problem. "And then this *creature* used a word I cannot know! What is 'bald-pate,' if you please?" she asked indignantly.

"Poor Melplash—he isn't exactly a ball of fire," Richard said laughing. "You've done splendidly, Hetti. Those five or six ghastly little men in overcoats are always on every plane from Madrid. Anyhow," he added easily, "now everything is all right."

But in this he was unduly optimistic.

Chapter Seven

THE British Embassy in Lisbon is in various ways an inconvenient place for entertaining, not least because the main entrance is in a rather narrow and extremely steep street; moreover, the house is built on the slope of the hill, so that to reach the principal rooms all visitors must climb a quite considerable flight of stairs, broad and dignified as these are. However, once on the main floor, dignity takes over entirely. A splendid portrait of Marshal Beresford looks down on the guests even as they pant up the stairs to the wide hall; the long drawing-room is noble, with splendid views from its six windows; a glazed-in passage leads round a half-square to the great ball-room with its vast gilt mirrors, used for large receptions, and out into a small flagged court from which a flight of stone steps, overhung by the delicate sharply-cut foliage of a big pepper-tree, mounts up into the garden—immensely large for a town house—with its expanse of lawns, shady trees, and brilliant flower-beds. It is, in spite of its inconveniences, one of the most beautiful embassies in the world.

The drawing-room, fine as it is, is too long and narrow to receive in with any comfort—people fail to find their way out by the doors at the farther end, and get jammed in a solid block. Lady Loseley, who was as practical as she was short, neat, and pretty, therefore always awaited her guests in a smaller room, also with two doors, opening off the glass passage; this had a marble floor and marble tables, like mortuary slabs, against the walls—one of her predecessors had christened it "the morgue"; but it is too square for anyone to get jammed in it, and only a few steps from the long buffet in the great ball-room. Here the following afternoon Countess Páloczy, with Hetta in tow and deep satisfaction filling her heart, was for the first time received by the Ambassadress; Richard—looking very peculiar, Hetta thought, in morning coat and striped trousers, a uniform with which she was unfamiliar—stood at Lady Loseley's elbow and introduced them.

"So this is the young lady who is such a good cook!" Lady Loseley said smiling, as she shook hands with the girl; Hetta liked her immediately for this sensible frankness but the Countess's eyelids began to flutter—what a reputation for her daughter. "Henry, I don't think you know Countess Páloczy—and this is her girl who has been in Hungary for so long," Lady Loseley went on; the Ambassador turned away from a conversation with the Papal Nuncio to greet the two ladies. He was not tall, with gay blue eyes in a deceptively cheerful and open face; he had also a trick of picking at one thumb with the nail of the other, and did so as he said to Hetta—"I wish you would do me a *real* favour."

"What is that?" Hetta asked bluntly, entirely forgetting to say Your Excellency, as she had been told to do.

"Teach my idiot of a chef how to make *Hasen-pastete*. We used to have it for breakfast at the Budays—I never ate anything so good. Can you?"

"Yes—but hares will not be in season till September," said Hetta seriously.

"No more they will—though I doubt if that cretin in the kitchen would know a thing like that! All right—you'll come and make one in September." He turned back to the Nuncio.

"Countess, the buffet is round the corner, on your right," Atherley said. "This house is such a jig-saw! Ah, M. le Duc, *quel plaisir!*"

Hetta and her mother perforce moved on as the Duke of Ericeira and his old sister approached their hostess.

Hetta was rather upset by seeing Richard in this formal role—she felt that he was cold, distant; not at all the person she knew. And she had wanted to talk to him, and ask him if he had any more news of Father Antal, and when she was to see him. She followed her mother out of the morgue in a slightly gloomy frame of mind.

It was a fine warm afternoon, and all the glass doors had been thrown open onto the courtyard, making it almost an extension of the house; most of the many guests were congregated there, and the Countess and Hetta drifted out with the rest—a footman in livery brought up a tray of cocktails.

"*Je préfère le Xérès*," Hetta told the man, as her mother took a glass. "*Immédiatement, Mademoiselle.*"

"*Really*, Hetti—" the Countess was beginning, when Mgr Subercaseaux came up and kissed her hand.

"Good afternoon, Countess. What a lovely day! So you still prefer sherry, Hetta?"

"Yes—I do not like cocktails."

"Wise child. Countess, isn't this a charming house? Have you seen the *azulejos* with the coats of arms of the former Ministers and Ambassadors? Oh, but you must—the whole diplomatic history of the English in Lisbon is here; it is unique! Permit me to act as cicerone."

This particular feature of the Embassy in Lisbon is indeed unique, and rather decorative. Since the Moors, seven or eight centuries ago, taught them the art, the making of coloured pictorial tiles has become a Portuguese speciality; and some diplomatic genius initiated the idea of having the arms, crest, and name of each Minister—later of each Ambassador—emblazoned and set in the walls round the courtyard and up the steps leading to the garden. These the Monsignor now proceeded to point out to Countess Páloczy and her daughter. But the Countess was only slightly interested; living notabilities meant more to her than dead ones, and her attention strayed to the people about her. Not so Hetta.

"Oh, look—this Legate was here under *three* Kings!" she exclaimed, as she read the Latin inscription on one plaque.

M. de la Tour, the French Ambassador, who was talking to the Monsignor and the Countess, overheard her.

"*Tiens!*" he said, going up and poking his pince-nez over her shoulder towards the decorative panel—"So he was. Do all young ladies in Communist countries learn so much Latin?"

Poor Hetta had quite forgotten who this busy friendly little man was.

"Communists, Monsieur," she said coldly, "know nothing and learn nothing." She looked round, seeking an escape, and was delighted to be greeted by the old Ericeiras—she remembered them from Mme de Fonte Negra's party, and elderly as they were she liked them. She thus escaped for the time being her mother's vexation that she should have addressed an ambassador as "Monsieur"; the Countess, however, apologised on her behalf to His Excellency—"She has had *no* advantages, poor child."

"Countess, if I were as well pleased with everyone's daughter as I am with yours I should be a happier man and a far happier priest," Subercaseaux said emphatically; he bent a peculiarly benign glance on Hetta, who was working her way round the plaques with the Duke of Ericeira, pouring out Latin and lively comments. The Countess was startled by the priest's tone, and rather upset—she was not wholly pleased, either, to see her gauche daughter on such easy terms with someone whom she herself had never managed to meet. The priest gave her a fine, ironical smile as he moved away; he passed through the crowd, smiling and Dear-lady-ing right and left—Hetta, her tour of the diplomatic *azulejos* with the old Duke completed, observed him with distaste. Then she was fastened on by Townsend Waller.

"Oh hul*lo!* How nice to find you here. Isn't this a fascinating house?"

"I like this outside part," Hetta said, temperately.

"I saw you reading Latin aloud to the old Duque. What a lot you know —thanks to Mother Scholastica! Have you been round the garden?"

"No."

"Oh, come on. Wait—I'll get you another sherry."

Glasses in hand, they went up the steps under the pepper-tree, and out onto the broad lawns between their gay borders. Hetta was delighted. "Such a *huge* garden, in the heart of a city!"

"Have *you* any idea what was really going on the other night?" Townsend presently asked her, as they strolled about.

"No. I only heard what you heard," the girl lied blandly. "Do you not think these Spaniards were drunk, and came back to see if they had killed you and Yulia?"

"No, I don't," the American said bluntly. "I think it was something else, though I still don't know what. Who is Major Torrens, anyhow, and why is he here? Have you any idea?" They were approaching the top of the steps again, and could look down on the throng in the little courtyard. "Oh, there's Atherley," the Bostonian said. "Do you mind if I leave you, Hetta? I want to catch him."

"But of course. In any case I must find Mama—I expect we should go soon." She did not, however, at once leave her coign of vantage, but stood by the low parapet which overlooked the courtyard and watched what was going on below. She saw that Lady Loseley, the receiving over, had come out to talk to her friends and get a breath of fresh air; the Ambassador had done likewise, and so had Richard, released from his official duties; her mother was in a little group which included Mme de Fonte Negra. Hetta watched Townsend Waller forging his way through the crowd in Atherley's direction, but before he reached him Monsignor Subercaseaux was suddenly at Richard's side, and speaking in his ear; the young man made laughing excuses to the people he was with and began to move towards the steps, the priest beside him. They encountered

Townsend—the summary friendly decision with which Richard dismissed him was diagrammatically clear; Hetta laughed softly to herself at the American's disconcerted face. But how tiresome this was—she, too, would have liked to speak to Richard. Vexed, she watched them climb the stone steps, pass her, and move away across the garden. What *could* Richard and the ultra-social Monsignor want to talk about in private?

In fact they talked at first about her. As they strolled across the lawn Subercaseaux surprised Richard by saying, "What a delightful child Hetta Páloczy is."

The young man could only agree.

"I am glad that you see something of her—you do, do you not?—for I think she feels herself rather at a loss here; all her surroundings are strange to her, and I fancy there is a good deal that she finds uncongenial."

"That isn't altogether surprising, is it?" Richard said—he never beat about the bush with Subercaseaux, and certainly didn't intend to in this connection, if he was twenty times Dorothée's confessor.

The priest laughed gently.

"No—indeed it is almost inevitable. Her 'formation' "—he used that untranslatable French expression for the exterior forces which mould a person—"has been so unusual, and so different."

Richard was really quite glad to discuss Hetta's *formation* with the Monsignor, since it was one of his main preoccupations at the moment.

"Quite so. But though she is right about many things, she has some rather unreasonable prejudices," he said slowly.

"She has. I personally feel her prejudice against me not *wholly* reasonable," Subercaseaux said, with the ecclesiastical equivalent of a grin. Goodness, how sharp the old boy was, Richard thought, even while he laughed. "But it is quite understandable, in view of her background. And about certain things she is, as you say, entirely right. Did she tell you that the Bretagnes wished her to go to luncheon with them, and that she refused?"

"No. Why wouldn't she go? They're such very nice people, and I should have thought poor Dorothée would have loved it."

"She made it a condition—the invitation was transmitted through me —that her mother should be invited to the wedding, which is of course the poor lady's heart's desire."

The young man stood still for a moment—then he burst out laughing. "Oh, well done, Hetti! How splendid! And what happened?"

"It has been arranged," Mgr Subercaseaux said, smiling a satisfied smile. "The Pretender is so anxious to secure little Hetta's acquaintance for his children that he has agreed. The poor Countess will get that so coveted card this evening."

"Well, I hope, Monsignor, that you will make sure that Dorothée knows to whom she owes it!" Richard said. "Hetti never says a word, but I don't think she has too easy a time with her mother—or with herself, poor child," he added, with something like a sigh.

"You are right. But she suffers more from the difficulty 'herself' gives her than from any external cause," the priest said, bending his iron-grey eyebrows thoughtfully on the young man. "The defects of her qualities— that is her trouble. In fact she has few defects; but even her qualities at the moment are like a coat put on the wrong way out, and the lining is not becoming! We must help her to put this garment on the right way out."

Richard regarded him steadily.

"Who are 'we,' Monsignor?" he asked.

"You and I, at present. I endeavour to do what a priest can; you, I hope and believe, are doing what a young man can do for a young woman —which is something rather different! But equally important."

Richard was not really ready for anything so direct as this. He hesitated for a moment.

"Monsignor, what are you driving at?" he asked at length.

"At a whole host of things!" Nothing could disconcert Mgr Subercaseaux, and he spoke easily. "But she has special qualities which it is good for her to *use*, and which, here, have so far lain fallow. I think you did well to employ her at Portela yesterday morning."

"I beg your pardon?" Richard said, looking at the priest with a face completely devoid of expression.

"I said that I thought you did well to employ her at Portela yesterday morning—if I am to dot the *i*'s and cross the *t*'s, to identify Father Antal Horvath."

Atherley's face remained stony.

"May I ask how you know this?"

"Major Torrens told me when he brought me in yesterday afternoon to have my first meeting with his—protégé, shall we say?"

Richard stared at the ecclesiastic for a moment longer—then his huge laughter resounded all over the Embassy garden.

"Good Lord, Monsignor! You don't mean to say that *you* are the famous contact?"

"In fact I am," Subercaseaux replied, with a modest smirk. "My dear Richard, can it be that you underestimate me as much as the little Countess does? My vanity is wounded!—so useful for me really, of course."

"But why *you*?—and here? Do forgive me, but I'm all at sea."

"The Vatican. Naturally it is essential that they should hear, as directly as possible, all that this eminent, saintly, and heroic man has to tell of conditions in Hungary, and about the Cardinal—but there were too many practical difficulties about getting Dr. Horvath to Rome himself, so it was arranged that he should come here and see me, and that I should act as intermediary. When he is safely out of the country I can go and report—I was in Rome, you may remember, a few weeks ago."

"Getting briefed?"

"Exactly."

"I'm surprised," Richard said reflectively, "that Torrens should have taken you to see him the very day the Father arrived—I should have expected him to wait till he saw if everything was quiet."

"That was his intention, but he had to summon me to resolve a little difficulty."

"What? May I know?"

"Something the Major found it very hard to understand," Subercaseaux said with a small smile. "The Father wanted to say his Mass this morning; Torrens had forbidden him to leave his room, so I had to intervene."

"Goodness! Oh well, I suppose it's all right for him," Richard said, trying to be charitable. "But with all that's at stake, and the risks other people are taking! What did you arrange?"

"I took him very early to a little church in the Alfama where I often say Mass on week-days; I take an interest in one of those parishes, and by Countess Páloczy's bounty am able to relieve much want, much suffering."

Richard knew the Alfama, that very ancient and very poor quarter of Lisbon huddled below the Citadel; built on rock, the houses there were not destroyed in the great earthquake of 1755, and thus it escaped Pombal's town planning; its streets remain crooked, very steep, and almost too narrow for wheeled traffic—no car can pass another in most of them. It surprised him to learn that the Monsignor should have any connection with such a part.

"Does Dorothée go in for charity? You don't say so!" he said.

"My dear Richard, you should avoid hasty judgements. She does."

"How extraordinary! Well never mind—was it all right?"

"No," Monsignor Subercaseaux said, frowning. "It was not all right. I served his Mass, he served mine, in that dark shabby little building, so touching and so aged; we went just before six o'clock, and the street outside was empty then. But when we came out—it was not yet seven —a lorry was drawn up across the bottom of the *ruelle,* and a group of men stood round it; they were strangers, not people from the parish, in hats and smart rain-coats. This seemed to me rather peculiar, and I decided to go the other way; but even as we turned up-hill a taxi stopped at the top of the street, blocking the way there also, and more of these men, who certainly did not belong in the Alfama, got out of it and stood about."

"How *very* nasty. What did you do?"

"We went back into the church, which has an exit through the sacristy into the priest's house; we got out that way into a different street, and I took Father Horvath back to his lodgings."

"Safely, I presume?"

"Yes. But not unobserved, I am afraid—in fact they must be known, and an agent has been on the watch as early as 6 A.M., who traced us to São Braz and sent those men to entrap him as he came out."

"How did *you* get away?"

"Oh, your Major Torrens is very clever! He has hidden the Father in rooms above a small curio-shop, built right against the slope of one of the hills, and like São Braz it has a back entrance, not far from one of those extraordinary lifts. When I wished to leave I went down into the shop and examined some old prints under the window for half-an-hour, and was able to observe two men constantly appearing and reappearing on the pavement opposite. So I went out by the back way, got into the lift, shot up a couple of hundred feet, and took a taxi back to Estoril."

Richard, though he seldom used them himself, was familiar with that highly peculiar feature of Lisbon, the huge lifts which so conveniently take pedestrians from one level of the tip-tilted city to another. The ingenuity of the priest, and his self-satisfied expression as he recounted it made him laugh a little, but in fact he recognised well enough that this was no laughing matter. He didn't, being a diplomatist, at once say so; what he said was—

"I don't know why you call him 'my' Major Torrens."

"No—you are quite right; it was a slip of the tongue. In fact you are *his* Mr. Atherley."

"I'm nothing of the sort!" the young man protested.

"Oh yes you are—if only because the little Countess is involved in this. But my friend, something else must be arranged; the present situation is impossible. It is hopelessly compromised."

"I'm thinking about that, of course," Atherley said, ignoring the remark about Hetta. "He must be moved at once. It isn't really safe for you to try to see him in those rooms any more."

"Have you any ideas?"

"How you do go on dragging me into it, Monsignor!" Richard said, very good-naturedly. "Yes, I have had one, a quite wild one."

"Well?"

"To park him with the old Ericeiras. Private chapel in the house for saying Mass, and all."

"Do you know this idea came to me also just now, as I watched the little Countess airing her Latin to the old Duke while they studied those plaques together."

"Oh, was she?" Richard was pleased, and his pleasure did not escape the priest.

"Very much so. I thought him quite enslaved—as that young lady enslaves, and will continue to enslave, so many. Could it be arranged through her?"

"I shouldn't think so—he may have been enslaved today, but she barely knows them, and it's asking quite a lot, isn't it? Anyhow they go to the country tomorrow," Richard added, remembering Luzia's Medusa face when she had announced this.

"But better still! To this wonderful house up near São Pedro do Sul? Nothing could be more suitable for the purpose. Do you know them well enough to propose it?"

"NO, Monsignor, I don't!—and I wouldn't if I did," Richard said with vigour. "Why don't you ask them yourself?—you know everyone."

"The Ericeiras only very slightly. And to tell you the truth, Dona Maria Francisca is rather too holy for my taste!" Subercaseaux said, with a sudden boyish gleam of mischief.

Richard laughed.

"Well, in any case this is Major Torrens' pidgin, so let him arrange it —I won't."

"But how can he? He is a stranger here."

"I know that; but his friend Miss Probyn—how far she works with him I don't know, nor if they are fiancés—but in any case she is a close friend of his, and she's practically part of the Ericeira family; she was governess or something to Luzia, that lovely girl of the Duque's, for most of last year—she's staying there now."

"*Tiens!*" Mgr Subercaseaux said. "Ah, then through her no doubt all can be arranged. I think you will be seeing Major Torrens—will you suggest it to him?"

"I hope to goodness I *don't* see the Major!" Richard exploded; "and if I do I'd rather leave it alone. Once for all, Monsignor, I am a regular member of a law-abiding diplomatic mission, not one of your cloak-and-dagger men, and I do beg you to remember it."

Subercaseaux made no reply whatever to this except to smile his fine, rather subtly secretive smile as they strolled back towards the steps.

Their prolonged colloquy had not been entirely unobserved. When Hetta went down into the crowded courtyard she had found her mother by no means in a hurry to leave; she hung about, rather at a loose end, and was pleased to be accosted by M. de Polnay, the old Hungarian journalist whom she had met, and liked, at the Countess's cocktail party. "I hope no one is making you *do* anything?" was his greeting—Hetta laughed and said No.

M. de Polnay always knew everything, and had his private sources of amusement. "Come and let me show you something else," he said, after Hetta had expressed her pleasure in the *azulejo* coats of arms—he led her, hobbling up the steps, to the garden, and across to a small stone seat set in an embrasure in the parapet overlooking the Rua Arriaga, where a little tablet stated that King Edward VII had sat there on Palm Sunday, 1903.

"Such a pity they have not put up another one to say that Edward VIII sat here on Bank Holiday, 1936," he chuckled. But as they walked back towards the steps his sharp eye noticed Atherley and the Monsignor patrolling the lawn at the farther end of the garden. He stood still to watch them.

"I wonder what plot Richard Atherley and this old serpent Subercaseaux are hatching," he observed. "They are together for a long time. Do *you* know?" he asked, wheeling round on her.

"No—I have wondered myself," Hetta said, laughing.

"But is he not in your pocket?"

"No; in my mother's if in anyone's—which I doubt," the girl said. M. de Polnay pinched her arm gaily.

"I see you are learning—you are very ready. Well done—*mes félicitations!* But you know quite well which of them I meant."

"Of their plots, in any case, I am quite ignorant," Hetta said lightly—she thought, rather uncomfortably, that there had been a certain intention behind the journalist's question.

Her drive back to Estoril was uncomfortable too. The Countess was tired, and fatigue with her was apt to take the form of irritability, as it does with so many of us. She had not managed to meet the Ericeiras—something Hetti could so easily have brought off, if she had any tact and social sense at all!—and altogether she was thoroughly disgruntled, and took it out on her child. She was still scolding Hetta for her gaucherie with the French Ambassador when they reached the hotel; in the lift she was perforce silent, but as they went into the apartment she completed a long tirade by saying—"If you *will* perpetrate these gaffes in society, you will never make the most of your opportunities." She was thinking of Hetta's meeting the Pretender and his wife at Mme de Fonte Negra's, a thing which had rankled in her mind ever since.

Letters in the Countess's flat were always placed on a fine old chest in the lobby off which the main rooms opened—Countess Páloczy went at once to examine her mail. There was a note which she passed to Hetta and several, including a stiff white envelope, for herself—she carried them through into the salon and began to open them. After a moment or two she broke into joyful exclamations. "Oh, how wonderful! At last!" Hetta was reading her own note for the second time, and made no reply; but Dorothy Páloczy was one of those people who have to get a response to their own feelings of the moment, whatever they may be, and no matter from whom—forgetting her vexation with her daughter she got up, a little heavily, and went over to her holding out a large card.

"Look! Here is my invitation to the wedding!" she said. "How splendid of Monsignor Subercaseaux—I'm sure he arranged it, though he said he couldn't."

"How nice, Mama. I am very glad," Hetta said pleasantly—of her own part in the affair it never occurred to her to utter a word, but a tiny rather wry smile, which she could not help, played about her wide decided mouth.

"And what is *your* letter?" her mother asked, now all benignity.

"The Comtesse de Bretagne asks me to lunch on Sunday. But we are going to those American friends of yours at the Avix, are we not?"

"Oh, what nonsense! Of course you must go. A royal invitation is like a royal command; one cannot refuse. Let me see it." Hetta handed her the note in silence. "Very pleasant—delightfully expressed. The sudden visit of the Archduke of course fully accounts for the shortness of the invitation, but it is courteous of her to apologise for it. Write at once and accept—I will send Oliveira with the note this evening."

"Oliveira has been out all day," Hetta observed. "Can we not post it?"

"Certainly not—it must go tonight."

"Then what about the Salzbergers?"

"Oh, they don't matter in the least! I will ring up and explain to them. Write your note, Hetti," the Countess said, pushing the bell.

Richard Atherley, too, was slightly tired after the party. He did not dislike the social side of his duties, which came easily to him, but he took them seriously and did them well; and to spend two-and-a-half hours remembering faces and names, and thinking of something polite, and if possible not wholly meaningless to say to several hundred people is in fact quite tiring. When the last guest had gone and he had had a whisky-and-soda with the Loseleys—the Ambassador always liked such little relaxed post-mortems on these occasions—he had still to go back to the Chancery to sign letters and take a look at his tray. He walked round there—uphill, downhill, uphill again; the Lapa quarter is very *accidenté* —thinking longingly of the supper Joaquina would have ready for him, and of his armchair, his novel—a new Waugh, thank God—his slippers, and his small bright log fire. But when he pushed open the high heavy baroque doors of the Chancery and walked across the hall Tomlinson, the messenger, started up from behind the sort of counter at which he received messengers from other Chanceries, and similar lesser orders of creation.

"There's a gentleman to see you in the waiting-room, Sir."

"God Almighty! I really can't, at this time of night," Richard broke out.

"Gentleman's been there nearly two hours, Sir. I told him you was at the party and it was no good phoning, and that you'd be in a hurry when you did come in—but he said he'd wait."

"Who is it, Tomlinson?"

"That tall gentleman with red hair; Mr. Melplash's contact, Sir, isn't he?"

Richard groaned—and then with difficulty restrained laughter. Trust Chancery messengers to know everything!—especially if their wives, as they so often are, were Embassy telephone operators. He wasted a moment on a crazy speculation as to what Tomlinson would say if he were there and then to ask him—"Where shall we put Father Antal, this Hungarian?" Tomlinson, he felt sure, would not be taken by surprise; probably he would have some extremely sensible suggestion.

"All right, Tomlinson. I'll just go and clear up, and ring down when I'm ready."

"Very good, Sir. I hope the party went well, Sir?"

"Splendidly, thank you, Tomlinson." He went upstairs.

There was, mercifully, very little to do—Richard did it, then rang his bell; a moment or two later Tomlinson ushered in Major Torrens.

"I'm sorry to bother you so late," that gentleman said as he sat down, "but matters have become a little crucial."

Richard pushed the Alentejo cigarette-box across the table.

"I know—I've heard it all," he said rather brusquely. "And I want my supper! Of course Father A. can't stay where he is; he's got to be put somewhere else—*really* safe, this time. You'd better get Julia to take him to the Ericeiras' country place, hadn't you?"

The Major gaped at him in such complete astonishment that again Richard nearly laughed. "How on earth do you know about this?" he asked.

"The Monsignor has just been pouring it all out to me at the party." Torrens looked vexed.

"Why should he tell *you?*"

"Why indeed? Why you *all* go on pestering me about what is no concern of mine I can't think! But since you have waited nearly two hours to tell me yourself, I suppose Subercaseaux felt the same about it," Richard replied, unanswerably.

"What did the old boy want to go out and say Mass for?" Torrens said with irritation. "He was safe enough indoors."

"Oh rubbish, Torrens. If the opposition hadn't known something about your famous *homme de confiance's* hide-out already, they would never have spotted Father Antal creeping round to the Alfama at 6 A.M. Anyhow, it seems to me that the answer is quite clear—send him to the Ericeiras."

"But they're in Lisbon—Julia's staying there."

"I know she is—but they go to São Pedro do Sul tomorrow."

"Where's that?"

"Miles away, up towards the North. They have a vast baroque mansion there—complete with private chapel, so there need be no running *out* to say Mass," Richard said, grinning.

The Major reflected.

"Would they have him? And the Monsignor too? He'll have to go as well, as I daresay you've realised, since you seem to know so much!"

"There's plenty of *room* for him in that house, anyhow! But why don't you see Julia? She's the person to organise all this—the Ericeiras eat out of her hand. Rather a godsend for you, I should have thought." He got up, glancing at his wrist-watch. "I'm so sorry, Torrens, but I really must go."

The Major remained seated.

"Atherley, do let your supper wait for another ten minutes," he said, imperturbably. "This is quite important."

"I realise that, but fortunately for you you have the answer—Julia. Why don't you go to her and settle it at once?"

"But how is he to *get* there? That's a point, even if these people agree to take him in, about which you sound so uncommonly certain."

"I only know Julia—I thought you knew her even better than I do," Richard said smoothly; he observed with rather malicious pleasure a certain reddening of the Major's face. "As to how he gets there, I'm sure they will have a domestic chaplain, like all Portuguese of that class; borrow a clerical outfit from the Monsignor, and let him go up in the car, or the ox-wagon, or whatever chaplains travel in in this country! The real chaplain can follow on by train—if the thugs catch him they'll soon let him go when they find they've got nothing on their hands but a dumb antiquated priest, who can't speak a word of anything but Latin and Portuguese."

Major Torrens emitted a rather reluctant laugh.

"How detailed and knowledgeable you are! Why should you be surprised that we all apply to you?"

"Well, apply to Julia now—I'm going home," Richard said. "Come on; clear out—I want to lock my door." He spoke with a friendly firmness that made Torrens laugh again. "And *don't*, repeat don't, go ringing me up tonight to tell me in guarded language how you've got on, because I'm going to bed," he added, as they walked in single file along the absurdly narrow corridor and down the wide stairs to the hall. Tomlinson, behind his counter, heard them laughing, and reflected that Mr. Atherley would always have his joke.

Chapter Eight

WHEN in Lisbon the Ericeiras usually dined at eight-forty-five—if they were alone both Nanny and the chaplain dined with them; he did so at all times, to say grace. On that Friday evening Elidio, the elderly man-servant, after a muttered colloquy at the dining-room door with someone unseen sidled up to Nanny and whispered something. Luzia, whose ears were still sharp enough to hear the squeak of a bat on the wing, caught the words "Um Senhor Inglês" and "Menina Juli": she said at once, and out loud—"Who is it, Elidio? I wonder if it could be Atherley."

"*Mr.* Atherley, if you please, Luzia," Nanny said repressively. Asking permission from Dona Maria Francisca she got up and left the room; Julia went on eating her dinner in silence, with her usual relish. After a few moments Nanny returned and resumed her seat and her meal, also without saying anything.

"*Nanny!*" Luzia said after a moment, fuming—"who *is* it?"

"All in good time, Luzia. Go on with your dinner." She turned to Dona Maria Francisca with the announcement that she now had a full clutch of twelve bantams' eggs ready to set; could she have one of the grey hens to hatch them, if there was a broody?—the cook's wife had promised to look after them. (This in fluent Portuguese.)

"Better take the eggs up to Gralheira with you, Nanny; then you can look after them yourself," the Duke said, also in Portuguese. "You are a witch with those absurd little birds."

At last the meal in the great room came to an end; Dom Pedro, the chaplain, said grace a second time, they crossed themselves, and the little party filed out. The Duke asked for coffee to be served to him in his study, as he had work to do, but his sister said, as she always did—"Do you take coffee with us, Miss Probyn?"

Julia was speaking aside with Nanny.

"May I come presently, Dona Maria Francisca? It appears that there is someone who wishes to see me."

"Very well. Luzia, you can come with me," the older lady said, slightly compressing her lips; much as she liked and respected Miss Probyn she could not wholly approve of people who paid calls during dinner—or indeed called at all so late in the evening.

Julia Probyn, while exercising to the full the rather remarkable degree of freedom accorded by custom to a "Miss" in Spain and Portugal, had equally respected the privacy of her employers when she was Luzia's governess; indeed, until Richard Atherley had come to see her two days before no friend of hers had ever crossed the Ericeiras' threshold, apart from Richard's midnight peep at old Manoel's hooded chair, and she was not best pleased to learn from Nanny that Major Torrens was waiting to see her in the schoolroom.

"What a time to come!" she said, as Dona Maria Francisca and the reluctant Luzia disappeared in the direction of the drawing-room. "How boring."

"He's a magnificent-looking man, isn't he?" Nanny observed, suspecting the veracity of Julia's last words. "If Luzia saw him I daresay she wouldn't keep on so about Mr. Atherley." Julia laughed as she went upstairs.

"My dear Hugh, what on earth is this in aid of?" she asked as she entered that bare English-looking schoolroom. "Dona Maria Francisca doesn't allow 'followers,' and nor do I."

The Major, justly provoked, replied by enveloping her in a vigorous and rather stifling embrace.

"Hugh!" Julia protested, when she could speak—"What on earth has come over you?"

"Only you, my dear, as usual—except that I'm not usually as weak as I am at this moment."

"Why are you weak?" Julia asked, sitting down in one of the shabby armchairs.

"Because I'm starving; because I've been waiting to see Atherley in that revolting Chancery for two mortal hours; and because I'm in a jam which I think only you can get me out of."

Julia got up slowly, opened a cupboard, and drew out a tin of Huntley and Palmers biscuits, which she handed to him.

"That's all I can do about the starvation," she said—"Now tell me about the jam."

"Oh, wonderful!" Torrens said, cramming Petits Beurres into his mouth.

"Well?" Julia asked, after a few moments.

"Do you suppose—I expect you'll think me quite crazy—but do you imagine that your employers could conceivably be persuaded to put Father Horvath up for a few days?"

"Are you talking about the Ericeiras?—because they're not my employers any more."

"Damn you, Julia, don't be so pernickety! Yes, I do mean your *ex*-employers, the Ericeiras, as you know quite well."

"And who is Father Horvath? Hetta's priest, I suppose. I thought she called him something else."

"What does it matter what she called him?" Torrens asked, with all the irritation of a hungry and worried man. "Yes. But do you think they would put him up?"

"They're going away to the country tomorrow."

"I know. That's rather the idea."

"What's gone wrong?" Julia enquired. "I thought you'd poked him away somewhere here in Lisbon, to have meetings with a contact."

"So we had, but that's all compromised—don't ask me how! I thought it was cast-iron, but it isn't. They can't meet safely in Lisbon any more."

"So has the contact got to come to Gralheira too?"

"Well that would be the ideal thing, of course; but I daresay he could put up somewhere close by."

"There's nothing 'close by' at Gralheira; it's miles from everywhere. Look, Hugh," the girl said, frowning a little as she thought it out—"this is quite a large order, isn't it? Suppose you tell me a bit more. For one thing, who is the contact?—and why has Father What-not got to meet him?"

Torrens told her a great deal more, including the episode outside São Braz in the Alfama that very morning. When Julia heard that Monsignor Subercaseaux was the "contact" she hooted with irreverent laughter— "Him! Goodness, Hetti simply *hates* him." But she registered with satisfaction the fact that the Monsignor was representing the Vatican—"Of course that could mean a lot. You're *sure* about that?"

"Quite sure."

Julia continued to reflect.

"I think I'd better talk to Nanny first," she said. "Ring the bell, Hugh —by the fire-place." Torrens got up, and gazed about for an electric button, in vain. "No, pull that trace thing," Julia said, laughing a little— the Major obediently tugged on a broad strap of cut velvet which depended on the right of the grate.

"Whose idea is this?" she asked, as he came back and sat down in the other armchair.

"Atherley's really. But it seems that young Hetta rather mopped up the Duque at the Embassy this afternoon, according to him."

"Well, that may help. But the Vatican is the trump card." A footman entered. "O Francisco, I desire to speak with Miss Brown," Julia said. The use of the vocative is still current in Portugal, one of the many pretty archaisms in which the country abounds; it is really rather impolite *not* to say "O Manoel" or "O Francisco" when speaking to a servant.

Nanny, whose private apartments were on the same upper floor as the schoolroom, appeared almost at once.

"Nanny, you saw Major Torrens while we were at dinner—Hugh, you'd better meet Nanny properly; and until she gives you leave she's Miss Brown to you!" Nanny smirked; Torrens got up and shook hands. "Now listen, Nanny," Julia pursued—"The Major is in the English Secret Service." Nanny looked wise. "And he's in a difficulty, and he wants us to help him."

"Well, if it's in any manner possible, Miss Probyn, we ought to, of course," Nanny said, visibly if primly thrilled. "What is the trouble?"

Julia explained briefly what the trouble was: Nanny, a devout Catholic—there are quite a lot of them in Leicestershire—was even more thrilled when she learned that what was at stake was nothing less than to promote a meeting between an important foreign divine and an emissary of the Vatican. "This Father Thingumy-jig has seen Cardinal Mindszenty quite lately," Julia added at the end.

"Not really? Well, I must say I should like to meet him. And it would be an honour to have a person like that in the house. I think I'd better speak to His Grace about it first," Nanny said—"he won't get upset." Julia grinned—Dona Maria Francisca did get upset by anything unusual. "I'd better go at once; it's nearly time for the Rosary," Nanny went on. "When would the priest want to come, Miss Probyn?" She got up as she spoke.

"Well, that's rather the thing, Nanny. He ought to come *with* us to-morrow, with you in the second car—pretending to be Dom Pedro, you see. Everyone knows that we travel with a chaplain, so it would be a complete disguise."

Nanny gave a discreet giggle.

"And how is Dom Pedro to get up? Oh well, he can take his chance on the railway like another, can't he?—if he takes the slow train and gets off at Aveiro they can send the Land-Rover for him, and one of these other two priests can say Mass for us on Sunday morning, if he should be delayed. Is the gentleman from the Vatican to drive up with us too?"

Julia looked enquiringly at Torrens. The Napoleonic thoroughness of Nanny's strategy had taken her unawares.

"If the Monsignor could drive up with you and Father Horvath in the second car, Miss Brown, it would simplify matters very much," Torrens said at once.

"Nanny to you, Major."

"Oh, thank you. Well, when you have spoken to the Duke, and if he agrees, let me know what time you start, and I will have them both here."

"We start at ten-thirty. But I had better see His Grace at once—you wait here." She bustled out.

"That's a remarkable woman," Torrens said, taking another biscuit. He glanced at his watch—it was already after ten.

"Poor Hugh! When will you eat?" Julia said. "I wish I could give you a bite, but that isn't so easy."

"Oh, I'll eat when the job's done. I'm quite accustomed to Spanish hours, from Morocco," Torrens said cheerfully. "I wish I could get onto the Monsignor, though, to make sure of his being in—if they really would take him up with them it would be a great simplification. Those thugs outside the church this morning will have registered his appearance in detail—probably taken his photograph. Anyhow no one could miss his eyebrows!"

"Elidio can get onto him for you," Julia said, getting up and tugging at the huge velvet bell-pull. "There's an extension outside the chapel. I practically forced the Duke to put that in when I came to teach Luzia; I really couldn't go right down to the bottom of the house and scream in the pantry whenever I wanted to talk to my friends!"

Torrens laughed. "What an extraordinary set-up the whole ménage is! I wonder if there's anything like it left anywhere else in the world."

"Richard's description of Hungary sounded much the same, but I suppose that's all finished now," Julia was saying, when Francisco appeared. "What's the Monsignor's number?" she asked—she dashed it down on a half-sheet torn from one of Luzia's exercise books.

"O Francisco, take this number to Elidio. The Senhor Inglês desires to speak with the Senhor there—*um senhor eclesiástico.*"

"*Muito bem, Minha Menina.*"

"Have you got a car?" Julia asked. "I suppose you'll have to flash out to Estoril to settle this—you'll hardly want to do it on the telephone."

"No, I can't do that. I haven't a car; I'm using taxis at the moment—less conspicuous."

"A taxi to Estoril will take aeons. I'll run you out when it's all fixed—if Nanny manages to fix it."

"Why did you leave it to her?" Hugh Torrens asked, rather curiously. "I thought they were so devoted to you."

"Devoted is a strong word," Julia said slowly. "They are quite fond of me, I think, but Nanny has been here twenty years; she came for the little boy who died—such a tragedy—and stayed on to take over Luzia. Then the Duchess died too—poor Duque, he has had it hard!—and of course ever since Nanny has been an irreplaceable fixture. Dona Maria Francisca's a good old thing, but she's a bit of a *beata*," the girl went on, using the admirable Spanish expression for an ultra-religious woman; "with all her limitations, Nanny has been the salvation of that child."

"Yes, I can imagine that. She's a remarkable woman," Torrens said again—as he spoke the door opened, and the remarkable woman reappeared.

"Everything's going to be quite all right," Nanny said comfortably. "But His Grace would just like to have a word with the Major himself."

"All right for *both*, Nanny?" Torrens enquired.

"Yes, Sir. Miss Probyn, you might as well come along too, and do the introducing; Dom Pedro's been in the chapel this last ten minutes, and Dona Maria Francisca will fret if I don't go."

"Half a second, Nanny, while I get a coat," Julia said. "I must take the Major out to Estoril to fix up with the Monsignor." She hurried away and was back in an instant, a loose tango suède jacket slung over her shoulders.

"Bless you for this, Nanny," Torrens said, as they proceeded along the endless corridors towards the big staircase.

"We should be thankful to Almighty God if He gives us the chance to do a work of mercy, shouldn't we?" Nanny responded briskly. "And someone from the *Vatican!*"

Down in the shadowy hall, so vast that it was only faintly lit by the superb 18th-century chandelier which hung in the middle, Elidio stood waiting to inform Julia that he had got *"o número"* for the Senhor Comandante—Julia told Torrens to go with the man and take the call in the pantry, and sat down to wait on a high-backed chair of Dutch marquetry upholstered in magnificent but rather threadbare brocade; a dozen of these stood round the walls, and even one would have added lustre to most museums. When Torrens returned Elidio led them into the Duke's study.

This apartment, which opened off the hall, was not only very large, but stuffed quite full of original Chippendale furniture: enormous glass-fronted bookcases along the walls, with cabriolet-legged chairs standing between them; "occasional" tables, delicate and graceful; also two magnificent twin tall-boys, and a drop-front writing-desk from behind which the Duke rose to receive Torrens and Julia as they entered. Major Torrens was furniture-minded in the English way, that is to say he knew and admired English period furniture, and was blind to any other—but he fairly gaped at the contents of that room. Being new to Portugal he of course could not know that when the English wine-shippers in Oporto built, in the year 1785, the Factory House there, in which to dine and entertain their friends, they caused Mr. Chippendale to fabricate their two colossal dinner-tables, and the lovely chairs which still stand round them, each bearing the hidden "C.," the master's hall-mark. Presumably the Ericeira of that day had profited by the presence of these marvellous foreign craftsmen to furnish his own study; anyhow there it was, a room to stagger anyone.

There was nothing staggering about the Duke of Ericeira, except that he looked so very like a Scotsman. He was rather tall, with the same grey eyes as Luzia, iron-grey hair, and a deeply-lined rugged face which somehow also looked grey; he wore grey suits in Lisbon and greyish tweeds in the country—all made in London, and all with that indefinable appearance of being comfortably old from the moment they are first put on which is the special knack of London tailors. He greeted Torrens in perfect English, drew forward a chair for Julia, and then turned at once to the business in hand.

"I am delighted, naturally, to receive these divines," he said, speaking slowly, with a certain formal precision which was also rather Scottish. "I am familiar with some of Dr. Horvath's writings—in translation, of course. A very great man. Tell me, do you wish to bring them here tonight?"

Torrens was as much taken aback by the Duke's promptitude as Julia had been by Nanny's.

"Well, upon my word, I hadn't thought of that, Sir," he said.

"Might it not be better? It is dark now, which always creates difficulties for watchers; and it will be unexpected. Then they can both leave with us in the morning quite naturally; Dr. Horvath can travel in the car with my sister and myself—and my daughter, of course—and Monsignor Subercaseaux can follow in the second car with my secretary and Miss Brown, taking Dom Pedro's place."

"Dear Duke, don't tell me that Nanny remembered the Monsignor's name?" Julia put in irrepressibly.

The Duke smiled.

"No, Miss Probyn. But she did tell me that the second party was acting as the Vatican's representative in this affair, and that could only be Monsignor Subercaseaux." He turned to Torrens. "Well?"

"Yes, Sir. I will bring them both here tonight. That is much the best plan, if it won't be putting you about too much to have guests arriving so late."

"My household is never put about by anything that is my wish," the Duke said, pressing a bell on his desk. "For one thing they are paid to do whatever is required of them, and for another, there still obtains here in Portugal that happy sense of *unity* in a household between employer and employed. Do you know the Portuguese word for the domestic staff of a house?"

"No, I'm afraid I don't."

"It is '*a família,*' the family."

At this point a representative of the family appeared in the person of Elidio.

"O Elidio," the Duke said, "cause two rooms to be prepared for two guests; let *borachas* (hot-water bottles) be placed in the beds, for the gentlemen are old, and the night is chilly. You will wait upon them yourself, and will enquire if they desire any refreshment—tell the chef to have hot consommé and biscuits ready."

"*Muito bem,* His Excellency. And at what hour does His Excellency expect His Excellency's guests?"

The Duke glanced at the Empire clock on the chimney-place—it was twenty minutes to eleven.

"About midnight, or perhaps a little later."

"*Muito bem, Sua Excelência.*"

"And when the Senhora Condessa has finished the Rosary, tell her that I will come up and speak with her, and also with Dom Pedro—let him not go to bed," the Duke said firmly. Bowing, with another *Muito bem,* Elidio withdrew.

"Well, I think I'd better get going," Torrens said; he too had noticed the time.

"Duke, could Major Torrens have some of the consommé and biscuits when he brings his people along? He's had no dinner yet."

"Of course—how distressing." He pressed the bell again. "You must forgive my lack of hospitality," he said gravely to the Major—"I had no idea of this. Will you take something now?"

"Thank you very much, Sir, but I would rather get them safely here first."

"Very right. Do you come up to Gralheira with your charges? That would, of course, be a pleasure."

"I think not, Sir, thank you so much—there may be things for me to see to here."

"I understand—though I am sorry. Will consommé and an omelette, and some cold turkey, be sufficient when you return?—a poor meal, I am afraid."

"Ample, Sir. Don't bother with the omelette." He rose—"I really think we had better start."

"By all means. Does Miss Probyn go with you?" the Duke asked, suddenly noticing Julia's jacket, as she also got up.

"She is very kindly driving me; her car is faster than a taxi."

"Ah yes—she drives well. I will say goodnight, for I trust you and my other guests will excuse me if I should not be here to receive you when you return."

"Duke, there is one thing we ought perhaps to settle," Julia put in. "What names are they to go by?—their own, or should we make some up? I'm not thinking so much of the staff—it's things like the postman, and all the swarms of people who come and go at Gralheira."

The Duke, who had risen, sat down again behind his Chippendale escritoire.

"Elidio, tell the chef to be ready to serve an omelette and some cold *peru* and a salad, as well as the consommé, when the Senhor Comandante returns with the other guests," he said, when the man re-appeared.

As the servant left the room he turned to Torrens. "I think that is a good point of Miss Probyn's, as regards Dr. Horvath; the Monsignor must, of course, come under his own name—my chaplain, my secretary, my steward, in fact everyone knows him by sight. What do you say?"

"Yes, Miss Probyn is right—I ought to have thought of it myself. It would certainly be wiser for Father Antal not to use his own name."

The Duke doodled on his blotting-paper. "One can never think of names when one wants them," he said, drawing his eyebrows together.

"Why not Père Antoine for Father Antal?" Julia suggested. "A French name, as he's a foreigner."

"You are very ready, Miss Probyn! Will that do, Major Torrens?"

"No, Sir, not Antoine—too like Antal."

"Then what?"

"Oh, Père François—they'll call him Dom Francisco anyhow," Julia said abruptly; she was anxious to get off. Torrens agreed to this, and the Duke jotted down the name methodically in a little note-book— "I will tell Elidio and the steward," he said.

As this was settled Torrens gave a fleeting grin, which to Julia's surprise was repeated in the Duke's grey lined face. She registered suddenly that her late employer was enjoying the whole business considerably, and decided to waste two more minutes on increasing his pleasure.

"Duke, you realise that Countess Hetta Páloczy was cook to *Père François*"—she stressed the words, smiling—"in Hungary for six years?"

"Impossible! This young lady who knows so much Latin, a cook?"

"Indeed *yes*. I'll tell you about that when we get to Gralheira, and aren't in a hurry."

"Ought she to come up too?" the Duke asked—nothing, Julia felt, was beyond him that night.

"Not for the moment."

"But *you* come, of course?"

"Yes, rather—only I shall have to get back for the wedding."

"Oh, this wedding!" the Duke said. "That is not for another week, anyhow."

A groom swung back the great doors of the cobbled courtyard of the Ericeira stables to let Julia's car drive out.

"O Fausto, be here to let me in again—in an hour, or perhaps in two hours—but I must not be caused to wait," the girl said urgently. "I shall hoot three times, when I return." As she turned out into the street the gates clanged to behind them.

"Which first?" Julia asked.

"Oh, Estoril. They probably won't be watching Subercaseaux at this time of night—though you never know. How often have you had this new car out since you got it, by the way?"

"Once. It only came yesterday morning, and I took Nanny and Luzia to the Zoo in the afternoon."

"See anyone hanging about?"

"No—though I confess I wasn't looking."

"Well I *was* looking when we came out just now, and I swear that street was bone empty," Torrens said, as Julia twisted down towards the river. "There isn't cover for a cat along those huge house-fronts. We ought to be all right." There was a nervousness in his voice and manner that Julia had never met before—he's tired and hungry, she thought, as they raced along beside the Tagus. The young moon was fuller now than it had been three nights ago, and its light etched the Torre de Belém, the Manueline tower built on the spot whence the great Basque Vasco da Gama set sail to discover the Indies, in black and silver as they shot past it—a black-and-silver tower outlined against the broad black-and-silver river. Julia observed this with pleasure, but she was thinking of the task in hand in all its aspects. It was wonderful how the old Duque had played up, and there came into her mind Atherley's remark—was it really only three nights ago?—when she had taken him to see the night-watchman's chair: "Just the place to park Hugh's priest." Well, now Hugh's priest was going to be parked there—and at the thought she gave her slow giggle.

"What is it?" Torrens asked—she told him, and he laughed shortly.

"Yes, we're almighty lucky—having you there, and the old man being so splendid about it all. What a charmer he is—and so superbly off-hand about having people arrive in the middle of the night. I must say I'm looking forward to that omelette and consommé!"

"There's one thing," Julia said; the omelette had reminded her of it. "Do we pick up Father Antal on our way back or drop the Monsignor first and then go and fetch him?"

"I was thinking about that. It's between not putting all your eggs in one basket, and making as few calls as possible at the Duke's. On balance, I think the second is more important; anyhow I'll risk it. You know that big lift that goes up from near the Rossio—do you know your way to the top of it?"

"Yes."

"Well you can wait there, and I'll go down, collect Hetta's late employer, and bring him up in it."

"That's all right except for one thing, Hugh," Julia said.

"What?" He sounded impatient; she realised that the slightest check or hindrance played on his nerves tonight.

"It's easily got round," she said tranquilly. "That stub of street that leads down to the lift is a blind alley, and a car could block it; all I'm thinking is that it might be better for me to wait in the square near the other end, where I can't be blocked. It's barely a hundred yards from the lift."

"Yes. Yes, you're right. But don't just *sit* in the square, drive round a bit."

"I will. Don't worry, Hugh—I won't bog it." She reached out a hand to his.

"Bless you, I know you won't."

Mgr Subercaseaux lived in a small house with a garden in one of the shady streets between Estoril and Monte Estoril—the road was empty under the lamps as they turned into it; a light shone in one of the lower windows of the house. Torrens sprang out almost before the car stopped, and went up the little path to the door—at that moment the light in the window was quenched, and ten minutes later the two men appeared with a typewriter and a couple of suit-cases; the latter Torrens pitched into the boot, while the priest, clutching his machine, got into the back of the car.

"See anything?" Torrens asked as he got in beside Julia.

"Not a thing," the girl replied as she shot off down the road.

Cruising back along the Tagus speedway towards Lisbon, a small thought came into Julia's mind and nagged and fretted there. It was more a picture than a thought, really—a picture of a long line of goods trucks clanking slowly over that level crossing leading from the docks (whence the engine-whistles so troubled Lady Loseley at night) and of cars held up and standing stationary on either side of it, for as much as five minutes on end. She had a curious, insistent feeling that it would be better *not* to be immobilised for five minutes on the road tonight.

"Hugh, I'm going to turn up at Ajuda, onto the by-pass that goes out past the Stadium, and get into Lisbon from the top," she said.

"Why?" Again he sounded irritated.

"There's a level crossing if we don't, and at this time of night we might be held up by a train," she said, swinging sharply left as she spoke; the car climbed a hill, past the great Palace of Ajuda, past one of Dr. Salazar's new garden suburbs, and emerged onto the by-pass; this led into the city near the great aqueduct, whose gothic arches were as sharply defined in black and silver as the Tower of Belém had been. Torrens quite lost his bearings; he was surprised when Julia suddenly pulled up and said—"There. The lift's at the end of that short street."

He got out, glanced round sharply, looked at his watch.

"All right. Give me nine minutes. If I'm not back then go on cruising about, but close by. Keep moving." He was gone.

Julia too looked at her watch; it was ten minutes past twelve. As she drove away, Mgr Subercaseaux, for the first time, spoke from the back seat.

"Had you any particular reason for wishing to avoid the level crossing tonight?"

"Not what you could call a reason—except that there often *are* trains there as late as this. I just had a hunch that I'd rather not wait there, like a sitting duck, tonight." She was driving at considerable speed through the lamplit, almost empty streets; they came out by the Estrela Gardens, went up past the parsonage of St. George's, the English church, where among cypresses and judas-trees the novelist Fielding lies buried, and fetched a compass round; on the return journey they crossed the end of a long street filled on either side with the lofty frontages of baroque mansions—Julia slowed down as she passed it, and peered up its empty length.

"Nothing there," Subercaseaux said.

"No car, anyhow," Julia replied, accelerating again—it was the street in which the Ericeira palace stood.

"Is this your profession? You seem very good at it," the priest said, clutching the back of the front seat as the car swung sharply round a corner.

"Oh Lord no—I'm a journalist. I'm just helping Major Torrens out. I was governess for some time to the Duke's child, Luzia, so I know them."

"Do you come with us to the country, then?"

"For a few days—I've got to come back to cover this wedding."

"Ah. Do you know Countess Hetta Páloczy?"

"Indeed yes. She's a splendid girl."

"Splendid is the right word," Subercaseaux was beginning, when the car swung round another corner. "Don't talk now—do you mind?" the girl said, as they passed across the end of a square. She turned down one side of it, driving slowly now, and almost halted at the end of a short street. There was not a soul in it. Julia held her wrist-watch out towards the dash-board light. "Nine and a half," she muttered—"Drive round the block!" Rather slowly, now, she made the circuit of the square, and for a second time slowed down at the street. At that moment two figures appeared at the farther end, one carrying a small case. "Here they are—good-oh," she said.

Torrens and a small man got into the car, Torrens in front—Julia had kept the engine running, and even as the door slammed she shot off up the square.

"That's right—drive like hell," Torrens muttered. He was panting like a man who has been running. "I heard a car pull up outside the shop in a hurry, brakes squealing, as we left by the back way; and two men came racing up the passage to the lift just as it got moving. They yelled like mad, but I showed the man a huge note, and he kept on, thank God. I heard them swear—in Spanish, of course—before they ran back down the passage, and then I saw a car flash past along the bottom. They're after us all right."

"They've got to go all round by the Chiado," Julia said—she was driving very fast indeed, taking her turns with careful skill; nevertheless the two priests in the back were constantly ricochetting off one another. "We ought to be all right," she said, in her slow, tranquillising tones.

"Yes, but they were after us, damn them! They must have been keeping a round-the-clock watch on the Monsignor's house. I can't think how they missed us—six minutes sooner, and we were done."

"The level crossing, I expect," Julia said.

"Oh, *that's* why you came round by the by-pass! You thrice-blessed girl!" Hugh Torrens said, slapping his hand down hard on her knee, shining silken close beside his in the faint light from the dashboard.

Julia made no response. She was fully engaged in slinging her rather large car safely round a last corner—they passed now along a street which Torrens recognised. She pulled up on the left, hooted three times, leapt out and ran across to the great double gates of the Duke of Ericeira's stables; even as she reached them there came the dull clanking sound of heavy bolts being withdrawn, and one of the massive portals began to swing open. Julia nipped back and got into the car; she had placed it skilfully, and as the second big leaf of the high doors swung back the machine shot into the huge cobbled stable-yard. She switched off lights and engine instantly and ran over to the great gates, adjuring Fausto as she went—"Come—close everything. But softly, softly; do not make a clamour with your bolts." Noiselessly they eased the immense irons home into place; Fausto fastened a gigantic padlock, pocketed the key, and began a cheerful remark to Julia—"The Menina sees that I did not keep her waiting."

"*Não falar,*" Julia hissed at him—"*Por favor,* silence, Fausto. You did very well," she whispered to him then; "but silence for a few moments." She tiptoed back across the cobbles towards the others, who had got out of the car and were standing by it; Torrens had removed the suit-cases from the boot, which he closed, like the car doors, without a sound. Then they all stood in that open court, so strangely large in the middle of a city, listening. Julia stole a glance at Father Antal, but the moon was almost down, and a solitary electric bulb burning over the servants' entrance at the back of the house only cast a faint light immediately below it; all she saw was the silhouette of a small man in an overcoat, clutching an out-size brief-case. There was complete silence in the street outside, at that hour. They stood so for two minutes, three, four.

"We've diddled them," Julia murmured. "Let's go in."

"No, wait; isn't that a car?" Torrens said—listening again, Julia too heard, faint and some distance away, a car's engine. The note altered, then grew louder—"Changing down at the corner," Julia whispered. The sound approached very gradually—a car was evidently being driven extremely slowly along the street. But it did not stop, and presently the noise of the engine died away altogether.

"They must have spotted you at the Zoo and followed you home, or put two and two together somehow," Torrens said—"and so they were just taking a look at this place."

"Well they've drawn a blank," Julia said. "Now let's come in and you get something to eat; it's five-and-twenty to one!"

Torrens never forgot that meal in the Ericeira palace in the small hours. Fausto was horrified at the bare idea of guests coming in at the back door, and wished to send them all out into the street again to make a proper entrance, but Julia over-ruled him in rapid friendly Portuguese; as a compromise she sent him in to fetch old Manoel, the night-watchman, to escort them through into the front part of the house.

While he was gone she greeted the Monsignor and Father Antal in French—"I have treated you very brusquely so far, I am afraid, but chauffeurs are not really expected to talk!"

"Chauffeurs as good as you, Miss Probyn, do better than talk—your driving is a poem in itself," Subercaseaux replied at once; the Hungarian bowed, but said nothing. Then Manoel came shuffling out and led them in, through stone-flagged passages with *azulejos* on the walls: they caught glimpses of vaulted recesses piled high with wine barrels, with billets of chopped wood, with *mata,* the fragrant heathy prickly undershrub always used in Lisbon for kindling fires, with masses of the deep green lopped-off boughs of *Pinus pinaster,* throughout Portugal the fuel habitually used for baking bread. They passed the open door of the vast kitchen, where a chef in a high white cap stood before an enormous range; oval *azulejo* plaques of hams, fish, and game—hares, partridges, wild duck, quail—stared down, astonishingly life-like, from its walls. At last through a final door they emerged into the hall, where Elidio, bowing, awaited them—he almost gasped with horror at the sight of Major Torrens carrying the Monsignor's suitcases, and fairly snatched them from his hands; an underling bore them away, while Elidio grumbled at Manoel in Portuguese for having let such a thing occur.

Then they were seated in the vast dining-room at one end of the long table. Elidio held out a chair for Julia, and a footman brought cups of hot consommé, and a big rack of Melba toast. The chef had obviously decided that he might as well be hung for a sheep as a lamb, so there were omelettes all round, followed by an enormous *whole* cold turkey, which Elidio displayed to Julia before taking it to carve at the sideboard —also Chippendale, Torrens noticed, and at least fourteen feet in length. Only Julia and the Major partook of the turkey, since it was Friday; but there was salad, and red wine and white wine; both light, flowery, delicious. No one spoke much at first; in the soft light from the three big silver candelabras on the shining table Julia studied the face of the Hungarian. It was square-set, with the usual Central European prominence of lips and cheek-bones, but what she noticed was how rugged it was—the brow channelled with thought, round the mouth lines begotten of determination or courage, over all a strong expression of calm and benevolence. He really did look to be a splendid person; worthy even of Hetta's unbounded admiration, the girl thought. And at that moment Father Antal raised his deep-set eyes to hers, smiled at her, and said in French—

"This is very good. *Merci*, Mademoiselle."

"Does Hetta make omelettes as well as the chef does?" Julia asked, smiling.

"Oh, you know my little Hetta? Yes, she makes wonderful omelettes —though not often at one o'clock in the morning! How is she getting on, here?"

"Beginning to swim," Julia said—the priest smiled.

"I must see her before I leave," he said—he turned to Torrens. "This can be arranged?"

"Well, really, I don't know—" he was beginning, when Julia intervened.

"Oh yes, Father, easily. The Duke, your host, is a great admirer of hers—in fact he has already suggested that she should join us at Gralheira."

"Is our host a Duke? Which?" Father Antal asked calmly—and Julia was struck suddenly by his complete tranquillity and incuriosity on being whisked off in the middle of the night without having the faintest idea, obviously, of where he was going, or to whom.

"The Duke of Ericeira," she said.

"Ah yes. A great supporter of Catholic Action." Father Antal, it seemed, could place Dukes all right—Catholic ones anyhow.

But Torrens, having been set worrying again, apparently could not stop.

"Julia, we ought to tell the Duke about this," he said in a lowered tone, leaning towards her.

"About what?"

"All this business tonight, and that car coming past the house. It means that there's a certain element of risk about his having them."

"Well it's too late now," Julia said flatly. "They're here—and if you think the Duke will change his mind because of a vague risk, or *any* risk, you're greatly mistaken. Stop fussing, Hugh, and eat your turkey. Do you want coffee?"

"My God, no!"

"Oh, very well." She put the same question to the two priests, but they did not want coffee either—"No coffee," she told Elidio. The manservant, looking disappointed that he might not serve coffee at one-thirty A.M., when most of the household was leaving at ten that same morning, muttered a question in Julia's ear.

"Hugh, Elidio wants to know if you're sleeping here too, or if you want a taxi fetched?"

"Good God!" Major Torrens exploded—"What a place! A taxi, please." And in a taxi he presently drove away, while Julia and the two priests, the latter escorted by Elidio, climbed the shadowy staircase and betook themselves to bed.

Chapter Nine

THE main road from São Pedro do Sul, like all Portuguese main roads nowadays, is broad, and faultlessly surfaced with tarmac. Where it passes through a cutting the banks are planted with the horrible mesembryan-themum; elsewhere it is often bordered with neat little hedges, just high enough to obscure the view—every few kilometres a trim house stands back from it, built to accommodate the road-menders. But after several miles a small side-road turns up a valley to the north-east, through pine-woods which could make one imagine oneself in Scotland—especially when the mists from the Serra behind hang low over them—were it not for the fact that the banks, sandy like the road itself, are here draped with the dark foliage and brilliant blue flowers of *Lithospermum,* which English enthusiasts grow laboriously in their rock-gardens. In spring, if you were to leave the road and wander through the woods towards one of the many streams coming down off the Serra, the chances are that you would come on clumps of *Narcissus cyclamineus,* the exquisite little wild daffodil whose pale petals turn back and upwards like those of a cyclamen.

Presently, however, the pinewoods cease and cultivation begins: fields of arable, well-tended olive-orchards, terraced vineyards on south-facing slopes; the whole, as the road climbs, with an ever-increasing aspect of the tidiness that wealth and good husbandry bring: the motorist in Eng-land entering the Dukeries gets much the same impression. At last, on the right, one encounters a high demesne wall of grey stone with the formal, grey-green, plumed shapes of great cypresses rising behind it, and finally an enormous house, more formal even than the cypresses—rich with pedi-ments over the windows, with sculptured swags, with all the splendour and glory of a baroque mansion of the best period in northern Portugal.

A tall wrought-iron gate, between stone pillars bearing armorial shields, opens from the countrified little road onto a driveway which, skirting a court-yard surrounded by less ornamental buildings, leads up to the big front door, approached by a flight of wide shallow stone steps; beyond, open to the south and the sun, extends the great knot-garden of geometrical patterns of dwarf clipped box hedges with gravel walks between.

Strangely enough, this is the Portuguese idea of the sort of garden appropriate to a great house. It involves almost as much work as lawns and herbaceous borders, and is not nearly so pretty, but it is the local conception, and is practically inevitable as an adjunct to houses of a certain period and status. In fact the knot-garden at Gralheira had an added attraction: the house stood so high that its low parapet commanded a remarkable view over the rolling country of Beira Alta—small fertile fields, pink-and-white villages, patches of pinewood—stretching away farther and farther, fainter and fainter, to the dusty pallor of the sand-dunes along the coast near Aveiro, and the dim, barely visible blue line of the Atlantic.

Up this small road, to this house, there passed in the course of that Saturday a considerable number of cars, from the station-wagon with the chef and a selection of servants to the two Daimlers with the Duke, Dona Maria Francisca, Luzia and Father Antal in one and Nanny, the secretary, and Mgr Subercaseaux in the other, Elidio sitting beside the chauffeur. Very much later Julia also drove up it; later still, long after dark, the unhappy Dom Pedro, chilly and cross, bounced along it in the Land-Rover.

Julia had asked to see the Duke early that morning; she knew that he always took his coffee and rolls well before nine o'clock. In his study she reported to him the events of the night before—as she expected, they left him quite unmoved. "*Raison de plus* for taking them away," he said calmly; while she was still in the room he rang up the police of the quarter and arranged for a couple of men to be on duty in the street that morning, to check on any cars parked there. This done, he turned to her.

"Had you not better drive up with us?"

"Duke, if you don't mind I'd rather follow you later in my own car—I've got several things to see to this morning. I've packed, and I can leave this house while the police are still about; if I find I'm being followed I shall garage my car and come on some other way."

The Duke smiled.

"How shall you ascertain whether you are being followed or not?"

"Oh, pull up beside the point policeman in Alcobaça or Leiria or somewhere and fiddle with my engine," Julia said airily. "I shall soon see if another car stops and hangs about."

"You are very resourceful!" the Duke said. "Very well—I am sure you are perfectly able to take care of yourself, but do *take* care."

"Indeed I will—I don't want to cause you any extra bother. It is so frightfully good of you to take all this on anyhow."

"On the contrary, it is at once a privilege and a pleasure," said the Duke in his measured tones, and Julia knew that he meant what he said.

Her main reason for wishing to be independent and drive up to Gralheira alone was that she wanted to see Torrens and find out how he was, and whether he had slept—she had never seen him in such a nervous state as the night before, and she was worried on his account. Moreover, on her way downstairs to see the Duke a servant had intercepted her to take a telephone call on the extension outside the chapel—this was from Atherley, who asked if she wouldn't come round to the Chancery and tell him "how everything was going," before she went away to bury herself "in your ducal province." Julia, remembering Father Antal's expressed wish to see Hetta, and thinking that Atherley could probably arrange this, promised to look in at the Rua São Domingos à Lapa before she left. Richard told her that the Major had intimated that he might be coming along too. "Oh well, I suppose there's some ghastly waiting-room full of *Punches* and *The Illustrated London News* where he and I can talk quietly, isn't there?" she said.

"You can go into the garden, Maud—much nicer," the young man responded.

"Cheek!—all right. Soon after eleven."

Soon after eleven Julia pulled the inner wheels of her new car well up onto the pavement under the barred windows of the Chancery, out of the way of the trams—this being the recognised method in that inconveniently narrow street, where so many cars are of necessity parked for much of the day—and went in and asked for Mr. Atherley.

"Hugh hasn't come?" she asked, up in Richard's room.

"No, but I expect he'll be here soon. Patience is a virtue!" Richard said with a mocking grin. "Meanwhile, tell me what's happened. Did the Duque play? Is Father Antal going to Gralheira?"

"They've gone."

"What, the Monsignor too? Splendid. No wonder Torrens is late, if he's been tearing out to Estoril to collect the contact! I say, what is it?" the young man asked, suddenly struck by something in Julia's expression.

"We fetched them both last night," Julia said. "It was the Duke's idea, and like all his ideas, it was a good one."

"Did he put them up here in Lisbon as well?"

"Yes—three-course supper at 1 A.M.!" Julia said, with a wry fleeting smile. "But it was all rather disconcerting."

"Why, what happened?"

She told him, in her slow casual voice and with her usual tendency to understatement; even so Richard Atherley frowned.

"Nasty," he said. "But how can they have tied the Monsignor in with the Duke's house?"

"They may have been watching him, and I suppose they bribed the car-hire people and got the number of my new car, *and* my address," Julia said sourly.

"Give me the name of the car-hire people, will you? Campbell must see the Colonel about this," Richard said, drawing a block towards him. "Are you driving up alone?"

"Yes."

"Look here, Julia, I think you'd better take my car. That can outpace anything on the road. Can you drive a Bentley?"

"Drive any make!" Julia replied—"but don't bother, Richard. It's *frightfully* kind of you, but I should be terrified of someone else's car, especially a Bentley."

"No, you'd better. I shall feel easier. What's your hireling?"

"Oh, an old Packard."

"Well give me your key—here's mine." He tossed it onto the table.

Julia was considerably touched by this gesture of Atherley's. Indeed it is not nothing for a man to hand over his car—especially if that car is a Bentley—to a woman with whom he is not in love. She picked up Richard's key slowly, and gave him her own.

"By the way," she said, "Father Antal wants to see Hetta. Can you organise that?"

"Yes—in fact, I must. I promised her she should see him before he goes, and she's certainly going to. How long is he staying?"

"I've no idea. Personally, I feel that the sooner he's out of Portugal the healthier it will be for all of us," Julia said, with some feeling. "Look,

Richard, why don't you bring her up to Gralheira tonight for the week-end? Then it would be over with. Are you free?"

"I am, as a matter of fact—the de Freitases have got measles, and have had to cancel. But what about the Duke, and Dona Maria Francisca?"

"Oh, the Duke has invited Hetta already! That's to say, when we were arranging it all last night I told him that Hetta had been the Father's cook, and he asked at once if she was to come along?—but Hugh stood him off. There'll be no trouble about that, if she's free."

"But how can we catch them?" Richard objected. He was at once strongly tempted by the prospect of a country week-end with Hetta, and hesitant at the idea of inviting himself to people like the Ericeiras.

"They always lunch at the 'Lis' in Leiria on the way up, to give the staff a bit of a start—too easy!" Julia replied. "Ring Hetti up—go on. It would be such fun."

Still rather doubtfully, Richard asked Mrs. Tomlinson to get him Countess Hetta Páloczy. While they waited for the call Julia walked over to the window and looked out.

"Nice garden for Maud," she observed. Turning round—"I can't *think* what's happened to Hugh," she said. "When did he say he was coming?"

"About eleven—the same as you."

"It's after half-past now," she said, with a glance at her watch. "Did he sound all right?"

Richard's telephone buzzed.

Hetta Páloczy soon killed the week-end idea.

"Oh Richard, I am so sorry, but it is impossible that I should go away tomorrow," her clear voice told him. "I must go out to luncheon."

"Must you really? I was going to take you to see your late employer."

"Please?"

"The person you used to cook for."

"Oh!" A pause—then "Oh!" again, followed by silence.

"Hullo?" Richard said.

"I am thinking!" Hetta said curtly. "Please wait a little." After another pause—"No, even to see him, I do not think that I can alter this," her voice pronounced rather sadly.

"Who on earth is this luncheon tomorrow with?" the young man asked, slightly annoyed.

"With the de Bretagnes. You see—I am so *sorry*, Richard—I said that I would not go to them unless they asked Mama to the wedding, and now they have. So I think that I must go to déjeuner with them. What a pity!—for otherwise I am quite disengaged. Please do not mention this," she added.

"God Almighty!" Richard ejaculated—then his voice changed.

"Hetti, you're a darling and a wonder! God bless you—I'm sure He will, for this."

"I can see—him—some other time, can I not?" the voice on the telephone asked, now very small. "You did promise it."

"Yes, and I'll damn well perform my promise. Don't worry, Hetti darling—I'll see to it. You really can trust me."

"Oh, I do." She rang off quickly.

"What in the world was all that?" Julia asked, full of curiosity, as Richard put down the receiver. "Who *is* she lunching with tomorrow?"

"The Bretagnes." Richard's battle with his conscience was brief, and soon lost.

"Don't pass this on," he pursued, "but the little thing absolutely refused to go to their house unless they invited Dorothée to the wedding."

"And have they?"

"*Yes*; so now Hetti is paying Mama's debts, when she would give her right hand, this minute, to see that priest. You've no idea what it means to her."

Julia was struck by the fact that Richard apparently had such a very good idea of what it meant; that affair must be coming along faster than she had realised. But she only said—

"All arranged by old pussy-cat Monsignor, I suppose?"

Richard gave a rather unwilling laugh. "Well yes," he was beginning when Tomlinson tapped on the door and ushered in Major Torrens.

The Major was far from presenting his usual neat and slightly military appearance. His clothes were crumpled and his shoes dusty; he was unshaven, and there were dark circles under his eyes.

"Gracious, Hugh, you *are* a sight!" Julia said. "What's the matter?"

"Been spending the night on the tiles, Torrens?" Richard enquired.

"No—in the British Hospital."

"Good Heavens! You aren't hurt, are you?" Julia asked, now rather anxiously.

"Not in the least—but it seemed a good place to pass the little that was left of the night in. There was rather excessive thug activity outside my rooms when I got there, and no answer to the unutterable Melplash's bell, so I thought the hospital would be a good quiet place, and went there."

"I'm surprised they let you in, at that hour," Julia said.

"Night-sister is a charmer, and she remembered me: I often went in to see Campbell in January, when he had tonsilitis."

"Torrens, exactly *what* thug activity was going on outside your pub?" Richard asked.

"Oh, the usual half-dozen men, in the usual grey rain-coats, standing about in the street. I'm beginning to think that some, at least, of the ones who bothered the little Countess so at Portela on Thursday when she was trying to spot our man may have flown in with him from Madrid."

"You didn't see a club beard, or rolls of fat on any neck?" Julia enquired.

"Can't be sure. When I saw them I made my taxi-man step on it, and we shot through them—the fact was I rather wanted to get to bed, somewhere or other. May I have a cigarette, Atherley? I ran out several hours ago."

"Oh, I'm so sorry." He held out the Alentejo box. "Fill your case." He thought for a moment. "Julia, don't you think the Major had better go up to Gralheira with you, as things are?"

"Yes."

"I think I'd better stay here," said Torrens. "I ought to see Colonel Marques myself, and try to get those people cleared up."

"Campbell can do that," Richard said. "Julia's going to take my car, so it should all be quite smooth."

"I can't go like this," the Major protested—"and I've no clothes, or kit."

"*You* could fetch those in your car before we start, couldn't you, Richard?" Julia suggested.

"Yes of course." He glanced at his watch, dialled an interior Embassy number, and spoke. "Oh Campbell, could you ring up the Colonel's Office, *now*, and ask him to have a couple of men outside No. 35 Rua Dr. Antonio Pereira in ten minutes' time? I've got to make a call there, and I don't want any knives in my tires! What? Yes there was a little trouble there last night—I'll tell you later. No, he's all right; going to the country for a quiet week-end, which I may say I think he needs. I'll see you before lunch; can't stop now." He turned to Torrens. "Give me your key."

Torrens next objected that he couldn't go to the Duke's without at least letting him know in advance—"and they're on the road now. It's impossible."

"No it isn't." Julia explained again about the "Lis." "And the Duke did ask you."

"Yes, I'll do that when you've gone. Come on, your key, Torrens. In fact I am an excellent packer," Richard continued, "and you can shave at the Bau in Alcobaça when you stop for lunch."

The drive from Lisbon to São Pedro do Sul is long but attractive. Up the Tagus valley, rather industrialised; past the lovely red-and-white town of Alenquer, looking as Moorish as its name, piled up above the shallow river bordered with long brick-built factories of a Georgian and quite astonishing elegance; through Alcobaça, where the great church is gold flecked with grey; past the even greater abbatial church of Batalha, Portugal's Battle Abbey, grey lightly washed with gold—on and on through the charming *smallness* of Estremadura: little hills, little fields, patches of pine-wood, patches of vineyard or of blue field cabbage, all jumbled up together and studded with snug white-washed villages and elegant small towns—nothing large, nothing grandiose (except the bronze-coated slow-moving oxen, drawing carts laden with dung or country produce at a majestic snail's pace) but all serene, all delightful to a degree.

Through all this, in Atherley's Bentley, Julia drove Major Torrens on that Saturday. They lunched—and the Major shaved—at the Hotel Bau in Alcobaça, as Richard had suggested, but Julia firmly refused to allow her companion to so much as glance into the church—"Do it on the way back," she said. "I don't want to get in after dark." There was a trim little policeman on the wide sunfilled square, who saluted Julia, or rather the Corps Diplomatique number-plate, when she drew up beside him, and instantly undertook to watch over her car while she was taking *almoço* in the hotel, and to send in and report to her if any other car stopped close by and appeared to be taking an interest in hers.

"What nice people they are," Torrens said as he sat down to lunch, having been led by a beaming chambermaid with a jug of hot water to a clean bathroom in which to shave.

"Wait till you get to Gralheira, and you'll begin to see *how* nice," Julia responded.

The food at the Bau is simple and thoroughly Portuguese, but very good; the same applies to the wine. Restored by this, by driving through lovely country, and with a return of self-respect after he had shaved, Torrens began to recover his normal equable spirits, which were increased by the little policeman's report to Julia that no other car had approached the Bentley—"nor even cast an eye upon it." They drove on again, through Leiria and the long stretch of pine-forest beyond it; at Coimbra, a university city as old as Oxford and more spectacular, they crossed the Mondego, the river south of which one cannot, according to the Portuguese, drink *vinho verde*, the astringent, stimulating, prickling wine of the Minho, so rightly delighted in by the inhabitants, so wrongly alleged to be deadly to the foreigner. (Intoxicating it is; indigestible it is not.) At Mealhada they branched right towards Viseu, still through this rich, gentle, happy countryside; in Santa Comba Dão Julia slowed down to point out to her companion the little house where Dr. Salazar was born and where he still spends his rare holidays—a simple low building with a tiled roof, sitting modestly beside the road like the other houses in the village. But once again she would not allow sight-seeing. It was getting late; the light grew rich as the gold of evening deepened it, the air blowing in at the car windows was chill with the approach of night-fall—and it was in the glare of the Bentley's headlights that Torrens at last saw those tall cypresses overhanging the grey demesne wall, the great gateway, and the baroque façade above the front door of Gralheira.

The first stay in a Portuguese country-house usually produces a cer-tain impact on English visitors. There is the unwonted size and splen-dour of the rooms and their furnishings, to say nothing of the wealth of objects of art strewn about; the even more unwonted numbers of servants; the colossal quantity of wonderful if unusual food and, by way of con-trast, a quite astonishing absence of those modern conveniences which most of us have come to take for granted, even in our cramped flats. At Gralheira all these things—the splendour, the service, the food and the lack of modernity were present to a high degree, and did not fail of their impact on Hugh Torrens, though to Julia they had become second na-ture. Atherley had caught the Ericeira party in Leiria with the message from Julia, and the Major was expected; the Duke emerged from his study to greet him in the hall, already in a dinner-jacket. "I am so glad that you were able to come after all," he said. "Dinner will be in twenty-five minutes; Antonio will show you to your room."

Escorted by Antonio, a countrified-looking man in spite of his livery, Torrens mounted long stairs—on a landing he caught a glimpse of Julia gossiping with Nanny and being hugged by a tall beautiful girl. What first struck him about his room when he entered it was that no attempt had been made to unpack his luggage, though this had preceded him upstairs—nor did the worthy Antonio make any move to do so; he bowed and retired. This surprised the Major, who was familiar with one or two ducal households in England: there, if there *was* a footman at all, he unpacked. The second thing to surprise him was the washing arrangements. He looked round for a fitted basin; there was only a huge marble-topped washstand of Victorian aspect, with an equally Victorian ewer and basin adorned with immense crimson carnations. As he opened his suit-cases and began to fling his effects onto the bed, which had a high pointed wooden headpiece ornamented with faded paint and gilding, an even more countrified youth in a pantry-jacket appeared bearing a white enamelled can of hot water, which he set on the washstand and carefully draped in a colossal bath-towel before he, too, bowed and retired. Torrens, hurriedly but methodically placing his brushes on the high chest of drawers which served for a dressing-table, and emptying the contents of his sponge-bag onto the black marble of the washstand, swore at the immense spaces he had to traverse between each piece of furniture, even while he noticed with envious admiration the superb Arroiolos carpet across which he walked, and with amusement the carnations repeated on the lids of the soap-dish and the long receptacle for a tooth-brush. "Perfect, down to the last detail," he muttered, as he peered under the bed and observed that the china object there also bore red carnations.

There was a tap on the door; at his "Come in!" Nanny entered.

"Good evening, Major. I'm glad you've come. Now you haven't much time, His Grace is always so punctual, but I don't suppose Antonio thought of it, so will you excuse me if *I* show you the geography?"

"Oh yes, Nanny, do—thank you," Torrens said, shaking her hand.

"This way—and don't lose yourself! This is such a house-and-a-half," Nanny said, bustling ahead of him down three long corridors and round as many corners, while Torrens tried frantically to memorise his route. "There—that's the gentlemen's bathroom," she said at last, throwing open the door of an apartment the size of the back drawing-room in the average London house, which contained a bath with a sort of sentry-box at one end of it; the whole was encased in mahogany, and stood out in the middle of the room like a cenotaph; there was also a fitted basin and what should have been a hot towel rail—involuntarily Torrens went and laid his hand on it; it was cold.

"The water isn't always *very* hot in here," Nanny said, observing this gesture. "Dona Maria Francisca always has a hip-bath."

"Could I have one too? I love hip-baths."

"Certainly—I'll tell Antonio. In the morning? And you'd like morning tea, I expect."

"Yes please."

Nanny, leaving the bathroom, indicated a door across the passage. "And that's the other," she said. "Now I'll leave you. Don't lose your way going back!"

"The other," the lavatory, was also Victorian to a degree which highly amused Torrens; it took him back to his earliest childhood, and visits to his grandparents. The pan, set in a mahogany seat five feet wide, was covered all over with blue flowers, as was the little china bowl, let down in the wood, into which a brass handle shaped like a stirrup returned after being pulled up. "Marvellous," he said to himself, as he made his complicated way back to his room.

He just managed to get dressed in time for dinner. Julia was waiting for him at the stairhead, and led him down and into the drawing-room, where the rest of the party were already assembled; the Duke introduced him to Dona Maria Francisca and Luzia, who was in animated conversation with Father Antal—he was offered a very small glass of white port, and downed it hastily; then they all proceeded into the dining-room, which was large, and as gloomy as dining-rooms so often contrive to be, whether in England or in Portugal.

"Monsignor, as my chaplain has not yet arrived, will you say grace for us?" the Duke asked—Subercaseaux obliged with a brief grace in Latin, everyone crossed themselves, and they sat down.

Torrens found himself seated on his hostess's left, with the Hungarian on his other side and Subercaseaux opposite; Julia and Luzia sat on either side of the Duke, with Nanny beside Luzia, and that end of the table was soon gay with the lively chatter of the two girls and the amused benevolent comments of the grey-faced man between them. At Torrens' end there was considerably less animation. Dona Maria Francisca de Lencastre-Pereira was a small, pinched-looking woman in the fifties, who did her still-dark hair in the fashion of thirty years before, and wore clothes—invariably black—to match; she was sincere, kind, and truly good, but her only interests, apart from running her brother's household and rather vaguely supervising the life of her young niece, were religion and the welfare of young girls, for whom she organised schools and rescue-homes, according to their degree of innocence or the reverse. Torrens essayed one or two remarks to her, but with little success; the good lady concentrated her attention almost entirely on the Vatican emissary, who was much more in her line. A holy Venus, *toute entière à sa proie attachée*, the Major thought to himself with a sour little grin, and turned his attention to Father Antal.

He found the Hungarian good company: interested in everything he had seen on his drive up from Lisbon, and full of questions about the local methods of agriculture and so on which Torrens, himself new to Portugal, could not answer—Luzia, from across the table, stepped into the breach.

"They put those clappers or whistles onto the sails of the windmills so that they can hear at once if the wind changes, Père François," she said. Torrens was momentarily startled by the name; it took him a few seconds to remember that they had settled on it in the Duke's study in Lisbon only the night before. "You see most of the millers have a piece of land to till," the girl pursued, "and in this manner they can work at it without turning round to look all the time, because you can hear that noise more than half a kilometre away."

"And what does the miller do if the wind does change?" the priest asked, smiling across the table.

"Oh, of course he goes and adjusts the sails, so that they shall catch the air to the best advantage. There is such a nice old miller close by here—they call him 'The Blacksmith,' though he is a miller, because once when the real smith was ill he shoed a horse."

Père François beamed at her. "I should like to meet him," he said.

"Oh, you shall—I will take you to visit him tomorrow," Luzia said. It was clear to Torrens that the refugee priest and the very young girl with the remarkable grey eyes were delighted with one another—but at her last remark the Duke intervened.

"No, Luzia."

"Why not, Papa?"

"Because I say so. We will speak of it later." He turned and addressed a remark to Julia. And afterwards, when the party had adjourned to the drawing-room and drunk some rather weak coffee, he asked the two priests and Luzia to accompany him into his study—"You will excuse us for two minutes, *ma chère*, will you not?" he said to his sister.

"Provided you let them come back in time for the Rosary. I want the Monsignor to see the chapel."

The Duke of Ericeira's study at Gralheira was something completely unexpected and in startling contrast to the baroque splendour of the rest of the house. Apart from the inevitable crucifix over the mantel-piece —in this case a fine piece of Flemish work—it was as severely up-to-date as the business-room of a progressive Scottish landlord. Filing-cabinets and book-shelves full of works on agriculture, wine-production, and archaeology lined the walls; on the very large desk which occupied the middle of the room there were no less than eight telephones. A few leather armchairs stood about, to which the Duke waved his daughter and the two priests; he himself sat down in a workman-like chair in front of the telephones.

"I am naturally very reluctant to impose any sort of restrictions on guests in my house," he said; "and it is in your own interest that I am impelled to do so now. You have come here, in effect, to seek sanctuary; and within the walls of my estate you will, I trust, find it. But I must request you both, formally, not to go outside those walls without my knowledge or sanction. And there are two places within those walls which you must not visit—the kitchen, and the courtyard." He turned to Luzia, with an indulgent smile. "So if you wish Père François to meet 'The Blacksmith' you must bring him here. But in fact the fewer people outside who know that foreign priests are staying here, and see these priests, the better. Do you understand? It is not necessary for you to know the reason."

"Very well, Papa. I understand," Luzia said—something in her tone made Father Antal look at her rather keenly, but he said nothing.

Subercaseaux however was greatly intrigued by one of these prohibitions.

"My dear Duke, it is not my custom to visit the *kitchen* in houses where I stay, but I am intensely curious to know why I may not visit yours."

"Luzia, you can go now," the Duke said.

"Oh pouff, Papa! Really I know what this is all about; it is so that the man with an odd beard and the rolls of fat on his neck, who seeks Père François, shall not find him—and of course if he were clever he might come to eat in the kitchen one night, with all the others, and ask questions of the servants."

The Duke frowned; he looked greatly disconcerted.

"How do you know this? Can Miss Probyn have been indiscreet?"

"Not she—of course not. It was Atherley."

"Do you mean *Mister* Atherley, of the British Embassy? How did you meet him?"

"He came to see Miss Probyn about the accident to her car, and I heard what he said; she had to write down a description of the men who ran into her, and when he read it he was funny about the man with the fat neck, and Charles Laughton."

"What had Charles Laughton to do with it?" her father asked, in understandable bewilderment.

"*Nothing*, Papa!—I repeat, Monsieur Atherley was being funny. Then at dinner last night this red-haired Commandant comes asking for Julia, and sees you, and she takes her car and goes off with him. And soon after half-past twelve the car came back—I was awake, and as you know Tia Maria Francisca *will* make me sleep in this nasty little room which overlooks the stable-yard," Luzia said, clearly voicing a long-standing grievance—"so when I heard it I looked out and saw them all: Messieurs les prêtres and Julia and the Commandant, and Fausto, all standing like statues, *frozen*, listening to the sound of a car in the street; the luggage on the ground, no one moving or coming into the house till the other car had gone. And today these gentlemen drive up here with us, and *you* tell them that they have found sanctuary. So I have drawn certain conclusions. In any case, Tia Maria Francisca told me herself that the Monsignor is an emissary of the Vatican—she is quite *exaltée* about it!" the girl ended, a surprising gleam of irony lighting up her young face.

Father Antal laughed out loud.

"Monsieur le Duc, I think you would be well advised to take your daughter into your confidence! Any attempt at concealment from her will obviously be time wasted."

Rather reluctantly, the Duke laughed too.

"I am afraid I agree. In due course I will tell this inexcusably acute child of mine the little that she has not heard, or guessed."

But the Monsignor returned to his enquiry about the kitchen being out of bounds—he was not easily deflected from any point which had aroused his curiosity.

"Duke, do pray tell me who all these people are who invade your kitchen at night, and *why* they should come there?"

"They come to eat," the Duke said briefly. "It has always been the custom in this country that poor people, wayfarers, should be able to stop at houses like this and be given a meal at night, somewhere to sleep, and breakfast before they go on their way in the morning." His long, rather gnarled fingers tapped reflectively on the broad polished expanse of his desk.

"Here in Portugal," he pursued, "we have not as yet established very thorough 'social services' in the modern sense; we still hold to something which I myself regard as valuable, because it is more direct, more intimate—the personal responsibility of those who have wealth to supply some, at least, of the needs of those who have not. That is why my house is open to the traveller; and in fact Luzia is right—someone who was acquainted with this custom could easily enter the kitchen with the rest, and a silly maid-servant might answer his questions."

"But in the *kitchen!*" Subercaseaux was still inquisitive. "Is there room for them? How many come?"

"Tonight there are fifteen," the Duke said, smiling. "Elidio always tells me the numbers, but this evening before dinner I went out, as I often do, to see them and bid them welcome. And there is in fact plenty of room."

"At any price I must see this kitchen, which can accommodate fifteen guests while a dinner such as we have just enjoyed is being cooked!" Subercaseaux exclaimed.

"You shall see it tomorrow morning," the Duke said, rather pleased.

But the Monsignor's curiosity was not yet exhausted. His gaze moved to the telephones ranged on that enormous desk.

"My dear Duke, I have, as you will have observed, a prying disposition. May I ask, why *eight* telephones?"

Ericeira laughed.

"A measure of economy! It costs me less to install eight instruments than to pay the wages of someone to operate—almost certainly extremely inefficiently—a switch-board." He leaned forward, and tapped the machines one by one. "This is to the bailiff's office, and this to his house; that to the oil-mill, that to the stables; this one is to the farm, and this to the *lagare*, where the wine is made—of course it is only used during the vintage; this is to the garage, and finally, here is the one which connects me with the outside world."

"This same system used to operate in the big country houses in Hungary," Father Antal put in, "and for the same reason. Rustic people find these complicated mechanical contrivances difficult to manage."

There was a tap on the door, and Nanny's neat head, veiled in black lace, appeared round it.

"I'm sorry to interrupt, Your Grace, but Dona Maria Francisca wants to know if the Monsignor is ready to come to the chapel for the Rosary?"

"Oh yes," the Duke said rising, with a rather resigned expression.

"They will come immediately." He kissed Luzia—"Goodnight, my child" —and turned to the two priests. "I must ask you to excuse me—I have things to attend to. I wish you a very good night. Make my excuses to the Senhora Condessa, Nanny," he said urbanely. When they had all gone off to say the Rosary he settled down in an armchair and began to read *The Farmer and Stockbreeder*.

Chapter Ten

"You aren't by any chance poaching just a little on my preserves, are you?" the Military Attaché said to the First Secretary on the morning of that same Saturday, when after Julia and Major Torrens had driven off Richard Atherley went and asked Colonel Campbell to get Colonel Marques to come round to the Chancery.

"If I am it's most unwillingly, I assure you, my dear Campbell," Richard said heartily. "Your miserable clients are pestering the life out of me—even the Monsignor! However, thank you for organising police protection for me at No. 35."

"What on earth were you doing at Torrens' diggings?"

"Packing his clothes for his visit, under Miss Probyn's wing, to the Duke of Ericeira's country-seat."

"Oh, he's gone up there, has he? I think he might have told me."

"Between ourselves, I think he was a little distraught."

"Hardly too distraught to pack his own bags before he came away, I should have thought."

"He didn't know he was going, and anyhow he wasn't at home last night."

"Where was he, then?"

"In the British Hospital," Atherley said blandly, with enjoyment.

"Why? Is he ill?"

"No. He just thought it would be a good place to sleep in."

"Well, perhaps you'll explain all this," the Colonel said, leaning back and looking resigned.

Atherley explained at some length what had taken place the night before, and how he had dispatched Torrens and Miss Probyn in his own car, not twenty minutes ago.

"Good God, do you mean to say you're letting that girl use your Bentley?" Colonel Campbell asked—this fact seemed to impress him more than all the rest of his colleague's recital.

"Yes—in *your* interest, Campbell, I may say! But you realise, don't you, that her car is already compromised, though she's only had it two days; the car-hire firm she got it from must have sold the number, and her Lisbon address, to the opposition. That's what I want you to see Marques about."

"Well he'll be along in a few minutes. Yes, he ought to get after those car people. Where's Miss Probyn's car now?"

"Under your window. Here's the key"—he threw it on the table. "Over to you, Campbell—you can be your own game-keeper for a bit," Richard said, with an amicable grin. "By the way, what are you doing this afternoon?"

"Playing golf. Why?"

"I wondered if you would lend me your car? I want to take someone for a drive, and I don't particularly want to use Julia Probyn's, and be mobbed by Spanish Communists in rain-coats."

"Yes, of course take it—that's the least I can do, though as you know it isn't a Bentley! I can use one of the Chancery cars. Why, has the Countess turned up?"

Richard stared in incomprehension. His mind was on Hetta: she had said that she was free for the whole week-end, and he had conceived the idea of taking her out for a drive that afternoon; her self-abnegation over the luncheon with the Armorican Pretender on Sunday had moved him a good deal. "She hasn't left Estoril since she got out, so far as I know," he said, taken by surprise by Campbell's question.

"Oh, sorry—you're talking about little Countess Páloczy. I meant the Countess de Vermeil," Colonel Campbell said, looking slightly embarrassed.

Richard looked embarrassed too, and rather annoyed. Naturally he had not reached the age of thirty-five or thereabouts without having been "subjected to other influences" as the French so elegantly call it, and one of the foremost among these influences was a certain Countess de Vermeil; she had been very much in the ascendant during his time in Washington, and Colonel Campbell, there on some war-time mission or other, had met them both; when Atherley was at the Embassy in Paris before coming to Lisbon, he had in fact seemed quite dominated by her, and Colonel Campbell, then assistant Military Attaché there, had again registered the fact. She was a widow, older than Atherley; ultra-*mondaine*, skilful, witty, and well-dressed to a French degree of perfection which was like a sort of lacquer over her whole person—she was also tall, blonde, and sufficiently beautiful *just* to be visible herself through her wonderful clothes. (There are women who dress so well as to render their actual selves practically invisible, but Fanny Vermeil contrived to avoid that.) Lately Richard, absorbed by Hetta, had given very little thought to this enchantress, and the young man in his present mood felt his colleague's well-meant question peculiarly ill-timed.

"As far as I know, Madame de Vermeil is not expected here," he said coldly.

At that moment Tomlinson ushered in Colonel Marques. Both men, their minds fully occupied in giving the latest facts to the head of the Portuguese Security Service, forgot about any Countesses, young or less young. Colonel Marques was, as always, practical, brief, and shrewd: he noted down the address of the firm from which Julia had hired both her machines, and on learning that she had driven up to Gralheira in Richard's C.D. car nodded approval, and asked where the young lady's car was at that moment?

"Under this window," Richard said for the second time.

Colonel Marques asked who had the key. Campbell showed it to him.

"It would be convenient if I might borrow the key, and the car, for a day or two," Colonel Marques said—"If it is not required?"

"You can do anything you like with it, provided you take it away from under my window," Colonel Campbell replied. "We don't in the least want it standing about in the street!"

"Very well. Thank you. Leave it in my hands, Monsieur le Colonel."

"I'll leave you now," Richard said, rising, and went back to his room to ring up Hetta Páloczy.

After some thought as to what would please her most, he took her to Obidos, the little walled city lying between the main Lisbon-Alcobaça road and the sea, one of the most beautiful walled towns in Europe. In its smallness and completeness it compares with Gruyère, and like Gruyère a mediaeval castle dominates it from one end, but in some ways it is even more beautiful; the golden tone of its castle and walls is warmer and richer than the slate-grey of the Swiss town.

Hetta was delighted by it. They left Colonel Campbell's car outside the big fortified entrance, incongruously lined with blue-and-white *azulejos,* and inside climbed a flight of stone steps up onto the top of the western wall; a narrow path, originally a firing-parapet for bowmen, runs along the whole length of this to the massive block of the Castelo at the farther end. Neither the steps nor the firing-walk have any form of hand-rail, and people with a bad head for heights find them alarming, but to Richard's relief Hetta tripped up the steps and along the walk with complete unconcern—he had once had the disconcerting experience of taking a V.I.P. to Obidos, and finding that he could only negotiate the path along the wall on his hands and knees. The girl looked out through the loop-holes at the bright multi-coloured countryside, pink and green with plough-land and springing wheat; the dim blue of the Atlantic bounded the horizon, and nearer at hand was the brilliant blue of the great sand-enclosed lagoon, the Lagoa de Obidos, in which enterprising bathers can catch grey mullet in their hands. On the other side they looked down, very intimately, into the back gardens of the inhabitants, where shapely grey-green medlar-trees stand up among hen-houses, rabbit-hutches, and beds of vegetables. Hetta, inveterately practical, commented on the fact that these back-yards contained almost no lines of washing.

"No, they spread it out on those slabs of rock with the agaves on them, below the Castelo. Look." He took her elbow, and pointed to the open slope, gay with white and parti-coloured linen drying in the sun.

"Oh I see—how nice."

They were both very happy. In fact many people do experience an unexpected happiness in Obidos; it is a quality of the place. Moreover, this was Hetta's first expedition into the Portuguese countryside, and she was loving every moment. The Castelo has been turned into a *pousada,* a government-run hostelry, but when they descended from the battlements by another of those dizzy flights of steps just below it he did not take her there, but led her instead a few yards along one of the two streets, which are all that Obidos boasts, and into a tiny room barely ten feet square, with narrow benches along the walls and a broad wooden counter with wine-barrels below it. Richard knocked on this, and a bright-faced young woman with a flowered kerchief on her head came running in from the next room, and greeted him with cries of pleasure— these brought in a much older man, wearing the regular Portuguese country-townsman's rig of an open waistcoat, shirt-sleeves with floral stripes, and a black felt hat crammed down on his round head. He, too, showed the utmost satisfaction at the sight of Richard, and wrung him by the hand; he spoke to the young woman, who went out and reappeared after a moment with a big earthenware jug brimming with wine, which she poured into two thick tumblers and handed to the guests.

"This is their better wine," Richard said to Hetta—she sniffed, sipped, and then nodded her head.

"It is good," she pronounced. "This is such a nice place, Richard; it is like a Kis-Kocsma in Hungary."

"And what does Kis-Kocsma mean, pray?"

"A small wine-room. They are a little bigger, as a rule, but like this." She drank again. "Do you know, this is excellent."

"The Menina approves of your wine," Richard told the man—"And she knows of what she speaks; her father had his own vineyards."

"In what part of Portugal?"

"Not in Portugal at all—the Menina is Húngara."

This statement produced some rather surprisingly on-the-spot remarks.

"From Hungary, eh? Where they have put a Cardinal in prison? I thought the Húngaros were all Communists. Is the Menina a Communist?"

"No, she is a Condessa," Richard said laughing. "She has come to Portugal to escape from the Communists." But as he spoke he was seized with a sudden pang of the anxiety that had tormented him before on Hetta's behalf. "You don't go swimming alone in the mornings any more, do you?" he asked.

"Not since you told me I should not. Why?"

"I just wanted to be sure. Have some more wine."

"Yes please. But would he mind if we took it outside and sat in that square? It is so beautiful, this town—I cannot see it enough."

"There's nowhere to sit in the *largo*."

"Richard, do not be English, and diplomatic! We can sit on the steps."

On the steps they sat, their refilled glasses in their hands, looking up at the great bulk of the Castelo high above them.

"I'm glad you like Obidos; it's a place I love," Richard said. He felt warmed towards her, towards the whole world, as he sat drinking his wine, watching her face tilted up to gaze at the castle's golden crenellations profiled against the blue sky overhead. "Tell me why you like it?"

"Because it is happy, and simple. Much nicer than Estoril!" she said, with one of her sudden flashes of contempt. "I should like to live here—perhaps in one of those houses."

Below the *largo* stood a short row of houses considerably more elaborate than most of the town, with green shutters folded back from their windows, creepers on the walls, and in front of them neat little gardens with paved paths leading up to the doors; they had a sort of homely elegance.

"That one with the notice on it is to let," he said. "Would you like to live there with me, Hetti?"

He spoke on an impulse, born of his immediate happiness, his romantic love for Obidos, and his half-recognised love for the girl beside him. She turned her face towards him at his words, and studied him for some time before she spoke.

"Richard, I should like to live with you anywhere where you would be happy," she said at length. "But I am not sure that you would really be happy living in Obidos. Or indeed living with me," she added.

"Hetti, I really believe I should be happy with you anywhere," he said, taking her hand. This was really all he could do in the way of demonstration, since the square immediately in front of them had suddenly become filled with small boys, kicking a rather desiccated football about. The Portuguese have of late years developed an obsession for Association Football, which they call *futebol*; as professionals they play it extremely well, but the entire male population of the country, from the age of seven upwards, spends most of its spare time kicking some sort of ball about any available open space.

"I know you believe it," Hetta said, returning the pressure of his hand with the small firm clasp of her own. "But I am not sure, dear Richard, that—that your belief is true. I mean, I think that perhaps you do not know yourself. You would soon begin to think me too young for you, and in social ways of course I am—though in more real ways I think I am much older, because of how I have lived. Your reality has been easy, mine has been hard; and so a lot of the things you think important are to me quite unimportant. Looks, dress, *savoir-faire!*" the girl exclaimed, with a ring of contempt in her voice—"for you these are all-important; they fill your sky! But to me they are little, little, *little!* My mother has them all!" she ended, and sprang to her feet and walked away.

Richard, too, rose, and followed her slowly. He was rather disturbed —and startled by her perspicacity. She had sized him up with an accuracy which plenty of older women had *not* shown in regard to him, he thought ruefully. How clever she was! No, it was more than cleverness; she was wise. For a young man of his antecedents, living the life he did, Richard Atherley was rather unusually honest; he accepted Hetta's evaluation of himself as true, and did not resent it. But could one live beside such acuity? The remark about her mother—she would never have said that if she had not realised his own contempt for poor Dorothée, careful as he thought he had been to conceal it.

Hetta meanwhile was sauntering slowly along the lower of the two streets, her dark head sleek in the sun, that orange-patterned cotton frock of hers, that he liked so much, turning a deeper shade as she passed from sun to shadow—she walked beautifully, even in her silly white sandals and on that rough paving: she had that particular quality. He came up with her just as she had reached the spot where a church stood below the road; he laid a hand on her bare arm and said "Hetti!"—he could not find words for anything he wanted to say; he did not know, he was all at sea. She turned at once, with her wide gentle smile, and said with the blandest unconcern—"Should we not go into this church? I believe there are remarkable paintings in it, by a woman."

It again struck Richard, rather forcibly, that many women of the world could hardly have bettered her self-possession, immediately after receiving what practically amounted to a proposal; it was so completely incongruous with her clear-sighted statement that he would feel her "too young" for him that he burst out laughing, with his great laughter that resounded up and down the little street. But her knowledge took him by surprise too.

"What do *you* know about Josefa of Obidos?" he asked.

"Oh, she had a school of painting here—such an extraordinary thing for a woman, in the 17th century! And she was an etcher as well, and a silversmith, and modelled in terra-cotta. Do let us go in—I should like to see her paintings."

"How on earth do you know all this?"

"The Monsignor lent me that book about Portugal. I have read it twice, but, of course, I cannot easily go about to see all these buildings and pictures because the car is needed for other things."

Richard's heart smote him. He doted on Hetta, for his own pleasure he saw her whenever he could; but until today it had never occurred to him to do that quite elementary thing, show her Portugal—nor indeed that she would want, and want rather intelligently, to see its artistic riches.

"Look," he said, as they stood outside the door of the church, "if you can keep your week-ends fairly free I'll drive you out on Saturdays and Sundays, and show you anything that's within reach."

"That would be lovely," the girl said.

The parish church of Sta Maria in Obidos is in fact too dark for the visitor to see much of the versatile Josefa's pictures, particularly since these are skyed right up under the painted ceiling, above the decorative *azulejos* which adorn the walls. Hetta was disappointed. "Since we cannot see them, her pictures tell us nothing of her," she said. "How sad." Out in the sun again, she swung round on Richard.

"Our glasses! Did we not leave them in the square? We must take them back, those nice people will want them—poor people cannot afford to lose two glasses."

"Hetti, do you know that you are very kind and very good?" he exclaimed.

"*Niet!* It is only that you know nothing about poverty, and I know a great deal," the girl replied. "You are simply ignorant, not bad; I *know*, but I am not therefore good. Really, Richard, you are very ingenuous for a diplomat!"

"How censorious you are!" But he laughed and took her elbow as they went back to the *largo* below the castle. Their tumblers had gone; some of the youthful *futebol*-players, seeing them abandoned on the steps, had taken them back to the "small wine-room," as they at once explained to Richard when he began to peer about.

"What are you doing for dinner tonight?" the young man asked, as they drove back towards Lisbon.

It appeared that Hetta was doing nothing for dinner; her mother was dining out.

"Then come and dine with me," Richard said. He was in a divided mood. On the one hand he acknowledged the truth of her diagnosis of his own attitude towards her; on the other, the mere fact that she was shrewd enough to make it, and her subsequent lively uppishness about diplomats drew him to her more strongly than ever—and he had a sudden desire to push the thing further, if only to find out more about his own feelings, and hers.

She made no answer to his invitation.

"Well? Yes—no?" he asked.

"No," the girl said, turning to him—"It is No, please, Richard."

"Why on earth not?"

"Because we are not ready—I am not, you are not. You want me to come tonight so that you may make a little love to me, and see if that is nice. Oh, of course it would be nice!" she exclaimed—"lovely, delicious, *fun!* But you and I are not people to live just by fun; you have perhaps been a little spoilt, but you need *truth* in your love, and you do not know yet where the truth is, I think. I told you that on those steps. We have done enough for today about what is between you and me. Let us leave it—take me home."

Again her honesty and clear-sightedness took him by surprise; he felt something like reverence for her just then, mixed with admiration for the cool fearlessness with which she had spoken of love between them. Oh yes, she was right about him: he *had* wanted to try it out on the physical plane, leaving everything else in a warm happy fuzz; and Hetta, uncompromising as ever, wouldn't have that.

"Whatever *has* been done about us today, it's you that have done it," he said, putting his hand over hers.

"Because I am so old!" she said lightly.

As they approached Estoril—"Richard, will you let me know when I am to see Father Antal quite *soon?*" she asked. "I would excuse myself from almost any engagement, except just this one with the Bretagnes, for that. Where is this place in the country to which he has gone? Is it far away?"

"Yes—the better part of a day's drive. He's at Gralheira, the Duke of Ericeira's house near São Pedro do Sul, right up in the North." Richard had no scruples about telling Hetta this; she was in the whole affair up to her neck. "It would mean staying a night," he went on, "but I don't suppose your mother would object to your going to the Ericeiras. What about next week-end? I have something on, but I would cut it for that—for *you*, Hetti."

Hetta ignored his final words.

"So long?" she said dismally. "Could we not go sooner? You see, he may be going on to America. Do *you* know when?"

"No, I don't. But I'll find out. Don't worry, Hetti—I've promised, and I will keep my promise. Goodbye, my dear one. You will come and dine with me sometime, won't you?"

"Yes—at the *right* time!" she said, as they drew up at the hotel. "Thank you, dear Richard, for the lovely expedition. I have been so happy."

Hetta enjoyed her luncheon at the Bretagnes the following day. It was a homely, family affair. Innumerable Bretagne children, of all ages down to a seven-year-old, sat round the long table gazing at her, and occasionally firing off questions in her direction; the only guests beside herself were the young Archduke, a lively fair-haired youth whose questions about Hungary poured out like machine-gun fire, and a big, tall, lusciously beautiful woman who had, it seemed, only arrived by plane that morning, and having telephoned was bidden to this very unsocial meal—her name Hetta, too often absent-minded, failed to catch, though she realised clearly enough that this was a last-minute addition to the party. In this pleasant atmosphere the girl expanded, answered the Archduke briskly, and laughed heartily at the innocent question of one very youthful princeling—"Did you give the priest you cooked for soup? I *hate* soup!"

"You would not hate my soups; they are delicious," she told the child.

"Then I wish you would come and speak with our cook. He gives us *bouillon de légumes*, which is altogether horrible," the little boy pronounced.

"Countess, it looks as though I shall have to employ you to nourish my family!" the Pretender said laughing—"or are you tired of cooking?"

"I shall never be tired of cooking, Monseigneur—I love it."

"What a lucky man your husband will be! Well children, until she marries, shall we engage Countess Hetta to make your soups?"

"Yes!" the younger ones chorused.

"Monseigneur, I am not sure that I shall be able to enter your employment at once," Hetta said with a mock-grave face. "The English Ambassador has already engaged me to go and teach his chef how to make *Hasen-pastete*."

"*Jésus Gott!* Can you really make *Hasen-pastete?* I haven't eaten it for years!" the Archduke exclaimed. "Would you make one for me?"

"If Your Highness can bring himself to shoot three hares and two partridges out of season, I can make one for you at any time," she replied.

This was rather Hetta's hour, though a small hour. The talk soon turned back from food to Hungary, but presently the girl registered the fact that the beautiful golden-haired lady—a Frenchwoman, it seemed—looked on and listened with a detachment which seemed to contain an element of contempt; whether for Hungary and its affairs, or for a person who cooked, she could not be sure.

Towards the end of the meal the Pretender asked Hetta, who sat on his left, if she had seen much of Portugal?

"Very little so far, Monseigneur—but yesterday someone from the English Embassy took me to Obidos."

"Oh, this exquisite place! I am sure you liked it."

"I loved it. In fact I almost decided to live there!"

"You might do much worse." He turned to the Frenchwoman, who sat on his right. "Obidos is a most perfect little gem of a mediaeval city; you should visit it," he said, courteously drawing her into the conversation. Then he turned back to Hetta. "And did your English escort wish to settle there too?" he enquired teasingly.

"He played with the idea, but I did not think it would suit him!" Hetta replied—her small success had made her a little reckless.

"And may we know who this English diplomat is, who would like to live in Obidos?" the Pretender asked.

"It was Monsieur Atherley," Hetta said, still reckless. "But the life of a *petite ville de campagne* would not really do for him."

"No, I agree; he is a charming person, but *plutôt mondain.*" He looked rather keenly at Hetta, as if he found something amusing—but the girl was much more sharply aware that the big Frenchwoman had somehow stiffened at the mention of Atherley's name, and was staring at her in cold surprise. "Do you know Monsieur Atherley, Madame de Vermeil?" the Comte de Bretagne asked, once again courteously bringing his other guest into the conversation.

"*Very* well—and for many years," the lady said, with emphasis. "Certainly I imagine that *petites villes de campagne* and love in a cottage are not at all what would suit him—Mademoiselle is quite right."

"Yes—the *Countess* Hetta Páloczy has excellent judgement," the Pretender replied, in an urbane but rather unusually direct royal reproof.

The Comtesse de Bretagne, slightly preoccupied with making her younger family eat tidily, had missed this interchange, and when the three guests were about to leave she asked Hetta if she could drop the Archduke in Monte Estoril, and the Comtesse de Vermeil at the Castelo-Imperial—"where you are staying yourself." Hetta, making her semi-curtsey, of course agreed, and Oliveira bore them all away in the Rolls. The Archduke continued his flow of enquiries about Hungary till the very moment when he was set down before the small villa where he was staying—Archdukes, in the modern world, never put up in places like the Castelo-Imperial, they can't afford to; they leave them to the occupation of ship-owners and international financiers from the Middle East. He kissed the hands of both ladies, but it was to Hetta that he said—"Do please let us meet again. There is so much to talk about! Do you come to the wedding?"

"No, but my mother does," Hetta said, wishing that he were not getting out—she had no desire for a tête-à-tête with this big beautiful woman who professed to know Richard so well. *How* well, she wondered, as the car purred smoothly on again—every part of her went onto the defensive.

"You know Monsieur Atherley for long?" Mme de Vermeil asked at once, in an almost caressing tone.

"But naturally not, Madame la Comtesse, since I have been in Hungary until a few weeks ago," Hetta said casually. "He is quite a recent acquaintance—*du reste,* like everyone else in Western Europe, as far as I am concerned."

"Ah." The Frenchwoman appeared to reflect. "You must pardon my ignorance of your movements—but at luncheon I thought that you seemed to profess to a certain knowledge of Monsieur Atherley's character; this misled me."

"Some characters one can assess more rapidly than others, do you not think?" Hetta responded, trying to keep cool—she wished fervently that Oliveira would drive faster, and bring this conversation to an end.

"Possibly. Though not perhaps that of the person in question, who is, believe me, a rather more complicated character than he may appear." She spoke with an appearance of kindly indulgence. "Rapid assessments can be, also, mistaken ones," Mme de Vermeil added, with a fine air of detachment.

Hetta inclined her head politely in response to this observation, but said nothing.

"Has it occurred to you that *Richard*"—the Countess stressed the name —"is rather *volage,* as well as being very mature?"

"Indeed yes," Hetta said curtly. "That is why, as you doubtless heard me tell the Comte de Bretagne at luncheon, I said only yesterday to Monsieur Atherley that it would not suit him to live in Obidos." To her great relief she saw that the car had at last reached the public garden; in a few seconds this encounter would be over. But Mme de Vermeil had not finished with her.

"Did he propose to live in Obidos alone?" she asked.

"Madame la Comtesse, since you know him so well, why do you not ask Monsieur Atherley *himself* with whom he wished to live there!" the girl flashed, driven beyond all endurance by this final impertinence, as the car drew up before the hotel. She sprang out, not waiting for the swarming pages to open the door. "You will excuse me—my mother awaits me. I am happy to have been of service to you," Hetta Páloczy said, with an impeccable last word, and ran in through the revolving glass doors.

Up in the flat her mother, mercifully, was by no means waiting for her; after lunching with the Salzbergers at the Avis—where she had greatly enjoyed making elaborate apologies for Hetta's absence because the Pretender had summoned her to lunch with him—Dorothée had betaken herself to bed with two aspirins and *Time* magazine. So Hetta was free to run to her room, fling off her coat and hat, and then walk about, raging. What an insupportable woman!—and what unendurable insolence! *"Stupid,* too!" the girl muttered furiously—"As if I had not told him myself all, and more than all, than she told me!" But what lay behind all this? Could Richard really care for a person like that? Oh yes—alas, he could; Mme de Vermeil possessed, to an extreme degree, all the things which she, Hetta, had so ruthlessly belittled to him only yesterday in the *largo* at Obidos: looks, dress, *savoir-faire*. No, not complete *savoir-faire;* the Frenchwoman's good manners had failed her twice—at luncheon, when the Pretender, however elegantly, had corrected her, and again in the car, no doubt provoked by her, Hetta's, attitude. This must mean something—Hetta studied what it meant, and reached a not inaccurate conclusion. "Whether he loves *her* or not, she is in love with him, and means to keep him for herself!" the little cook from the presbytery in the Alföld said to herself, sizing up the beautiful Parisienne; having decided this, she burst into angry tears.

Hetta's distress was easy enough to understand. In this strange and difficult world into which she had so suddenly been plunged Atherley had been to her, from their first meeting, a link with home: a person who had been to Detvan and known and liked Pappi, the one adored and stable figure throughout her childhood, till he was swept away on the inrushing Communist flood, and she was left alone with the good nuns. In fact that loneliness had been extreme to the eager, positive, impulsive child, accustomed to the most expansive intimacy with so many people at home; the deliberate, carefully inculcated detachment and impartiality of the convent, easily endurable for three terms a year, had become a terrible thing to bear when there was *no* let-up, no times-off to be loved and spoiled and petted at Detvan.

Atherley, therefore, had come trailing clouds of all sorts of glory to her first cocktail party, when he had at once spoken of the Alföld; and he had been *kind* to her, patient with her when she made a fool of herself at his luncheon, interested in her even, she told herself with frank humility, before he began to be a little in love with her. And as she had said of Julia Probyn, she felt that *he* was nice, *he* was true; she trusted him and felt at home with him. The bare idea of being loved by, even possibly marrying such a person had made a sort of opening, however distant and uncertain, in a future which otherwise seemed to her dark and blank indeed—to lose him would be a desolating loss.

She soon dried her eyes—Hetta very seldom cried, and was ashamed of herself when she did; tears had not been approved of in the convent —but she continued to walk to and fro across her bedroom, thinking. This antagonist of hers, she recognised, was a powerful and dangerous one—in spite of being so old! (Mme de Vermeil was in fact thirty-eight, but to twenty-two thirty-eight is practically antique.) Hetta had begun to realise the sheer *power* of perfect clothes and social skill, even while she despised them; and certainly this full-blown rose of a Frenchwoman —the contemptuous phrase came of itself into her mind—had them to the last, the supreme degree. A smaller person might have entertained the foolish notion of trying to acquire a rivalling degree of elegance herself; this has often been done by young girls in her situation, with conspicuous ill-success. But Hetta Páloczy was too intelligent and too uncompromising to waste time on such ideas. She had no intention of remaining passive while her hopes and her future were drowned in a flood of perfect make-up and marvellous clothes, but she needed help, advice, reinforcement—and for these she absolutely *must* see Father Antal. She decided, rather reluctantly, to ring up Richard and ask him to help her to get to—what was the place called?—Gral something—as soon as possible. There was really no one else to whom she could turn—Yulia and her red-headed Major were already up there, and Hetta with the ingrained caution born of long years of living under Communism hesitated to suggest such a trip to anyone else.

If she had rung up there and then things would probably have turned out differently, for Atherley at that moment was sitting with his feet up in front of his little log fire, reading Evelyn Waugh and intermittently thinking, with a good deal of affection and a slightly worried admiration, about Hetta herself. But just as she was about to ask for his number Esperanza came in to say that the Senhora Condessa was going to take *chá*, and wished the Menina to join her. So Hetta went and drank tea in her mother's room, and good-temperedly underwent a detailed cross-examination about her luncheon at the Pretender's, and who had been there and what had passed. Dorothée was at once slightly annoyed and rather comforted that it had been, the Archduke apart, such a very family party.

"And this Frenchwoman who came at the last moment—what was her name?"

Hetta couldn't tell her name, she had never caught it. "She was a Countess, a great huge woman, very blonde and very well-dressed—I brought her back; she is staying here."

"Oh, then it must be Fanny de Vermeil. How nice that you have met her, and were able to give her a lift—I suppose her car is coming by road. Has she come for the wedding? I expect so; she and the Comtesse de Bretagne were at school together." Now that she was sure of a place at the wedding herself, Dorothy Páloczy could talk quite cheerfully about others who were to attend it.

Hetta could not say whether Mme de Vermeil had come for the wedding or not.

"Oh, you may be sure she has. She goes to everything! Didn't you find her charming? And her clothes are so wonderful."

Hetta, readily agreeing to the wonderfulness of Mme de Vermeil's clothes, managed with relief to avoid any reply about her degree of charm. But this conversation, which went on and on, increased her sense of desperation, and the urgency of her desire to see Father Antal at once. Jésus Maria!—if she was to be cooped up in this dreadful hotel (how *could* Pappi have borne it?) with that ageing French siren as well as her mother, what would become of her? The animosity of one, the contempt of both—it was impossible! And where was charity, in such a strait? When her mother at last went to take a bath the poor child, instead of ringing up Richard, flung a scarf over her head and ran across the garden through the sweet-smelling dusk to the church, where she knelt and prayed for pardon for her angers, for help, and for the man she loved.

She came back more leisurely, calmed and soothed; changed her dress so as to be ready for dinner, and then, at last, rang up Atherley. But by then the fortunate moment had passed—Mme de Vermeil had for the last half-hour been sitting in Richard's little drawing-room, and they were in the middle of a rather awkward conversation, largely concerning Hetta herself.

"Atherley," Richard said into the telephone. "Oh, it's you"—when she spoke. "Could you ring up a bit later on, or tomorrow? I'm busy just now." In his embarrassment he spoke more coldly than he intended, and his tone chilled Hetta—it also roused her temper.

"No, I would rather speak now—I will not keep you a moment."

"Oh, very well," he said resignedly. "What is it?"

The resigned tone angered the girl more than ever, even while it filled her with a vague terror.

"It is that I need to see Father Antal at once," she said, almost as coldly as he. "Tomorrow, perhaps?—or on Tuesday? It is necessary that I should see him quickly."

Richard had already heard enough from Mme de Vermeil to guess why Hetta felt it necessary to see Father Antal so urgently. He had, of course, been given a skilfully distorted account of what had passed at luncheon. "In your own interest, my dear Richard," the lady had said languidly, "I think you should try to prevent her from boasting that you suggested living with her in some country town." But though he had said "Oh don't be a fool, Fanny; I'm certain she never did any such thing. How disagreeable you can be when you try!" he was left wondering uncomfortably exactly what Hetta *had* said—she was so guileless, so unworldly, liable to be so indiscreet.

"I'm not sure that that will be possible," he said now, speaking carefully. "But let me telephone to you later tonight, will you?"

Hetta, at her end of the telephone, was making her own guesses; she might be unworldly, but it had occurred to her before she rang up that the French lady would lose no time in seeking Richard out and getting him into her toils again—no doubt she had done so.

"No," the girl said abruptly. "I need to know at once. *Will* you take me to see him? You made a promise, you may remember."

Richard in his turn was dismayed by the icy edge on her voice, but he was angered too—no man likes to be reminded of a promise that it is not at the moment convenient to fulfil.

"I did—and I will keep it. But I am not a free agent, as you know; I have my work to do. I will ring you up later tonight."

"No, do not trouble to telephone," Hetta said, trying to control her voice, which sobs now threatened to invade—was this the Richard who had told her yesterday that she was "very kind and very good," and that he could be happy with her anywhere? "I will make other arrangements—please do not concern yourself," she said, and rang off. After a moment she lifted the receiver again and told the hotel exchange to get her Mr. Townsend Waller, of the American Embassy. Also, she added, apart from the American Senhor, she would take no more calls that night.

Chapter Eleven

"Now, Monsignor Subercaseaux," the Duke of Ericeira said, coming in on Monday morning to the sitting-room overlooking the knot-garden which had been placed at the disposal of the two priests—"would you care to come and visit the kitchen, which interests you so much? Or do I disturb you? You both appear very studious!"

The two ecclesiastics did look rather studious. At the Duke's entrance Father Antal closed an atlas, while the Monsignor put an elastic band round a small leather notebook in which he had been making microscopic scribbles, and tucked it away in his soutane.

"On the contrary, my dear Duke, I shall be delighted," he said.

"May I come too?" Father Antal asked.

"Dom Francisco, I hoped you would." The Duke, not alone among the occupants of Gralheira, had begun to make comparisons between the blunt simplicity of the Hungarian and the florid politenesses of the Monsignor.

The kitchen at Gralheira was really something to see. It was roughly the size of two billiard-rooms placed end to end; the part nearest the entrance from the house was used for all cooking operations, the farther end for eating; another door led from this into the courtyard. Two great chimney-hoods descended over a pair of Briffault ranges, their bright-steel surfaces polished till they shone like silver, from a ceiling as lofty as the roof of a mediaeval tithe barn; a low brick-built shelf, with ovens set in it and open cooking-spaces on the top ran for several yards round the wall—an old crone knelt on the floor before one of these last, fanning the charcoal under a copper casserole to a glow with a palm-leaf fan. Down the opposite side of the great room several yellow marble sinks, with brass taps above them, projected from the wall; in these kitchen-maids were rinsing out crockery and copper pans, and washing vegetables. But the most remarkable sight of all was the tables. There were two, each fully twenty feet long; their solid tops were made of the same yellow marble as the sinks, and rested on carved marble trestles. The farther one was already being set for the mid-day meal by two more kerchiefed girls, who plumped down gay country-made earthenware plates, thick soup-bowls, and heavy tumblers for wine in some forty places; a cheerful array of bottles, and huge wicker platters of *broa*, the maize bread beloved of the Portuguese country-people, were already in position down the centre.

On the other table, nearer the two ranges, various culinary operations were in progress. (If you have a kitchen table seven feet wide and twenty feet long quite a number of different jobs can be done on it at the same time.) The chef himself stood, immaculate in his white coat and high pleated hat, rolling out delicate pastry; next him a youth was pounding *bacalhau* in a mortar; farther on two more boys were chopping parsley and slicing onions respectively, and another old woman was beating eggs in a bowl.

"Yes, you could practically feed an army here," Subercaseaux said. "Wonderful!"

"Where is the bread baked?" Father Antal asked.

"I will show you." The Duke led them out through the door at the farther end into the courtyard and to the bakery, fragrant with the resinous scent of the pine-boughs which stoked the ovens; here he sent a man, white with flour, back to the kitchen to fetch a key—"You might care to see the store-house."

This was on the same generous scale as the kitchen. Cheeses in scores were ranged on shelves round the walls; below stood vast wooden bins of dried peas and beans, and barrels of pork pickled in brine and garlic; from the raftered ceiling hung endless rings of sausages, hams in dozens, and white loops of lard. The Portuguese, so cleverly, do not preserve lard (which they call *banha*) awkwardly in a sheep's or pig's stomach, forming a clumsy oval lump, as the English do—or did; instead they pour it into the animal's large intestine, and tie the ends, so that Portuguese lard can be cut off in convenient lengths as required.

This magnificent demonstration of country self-sufficiency surprised Subercaseaux, who commented and exclaimed. To Father Antal it was nostalgically familiar—"So it used to be in Hungary," he said. "Ah, the good life! I am glad there is somewhere in the world where it is still led —*still* led."

The Monsignor wanted to see where the wayfarers slept, and the Duke led the way up an outside stone staircase to a great loft, fragrant from the mass of hay which filled the farther end; immediately inside, blankets lay tidily folded on a score of neat mattresses of hay, with coloured cotton pillows.

"*Tiens!* Whoever sleeps here is well lodged," Subercaseaux exclaimed, while the Duke was telling Father Antal that women travellers, who were rather rare, slept in a dormitory adjoining the house, supervised by one of the old kitchen-women—"This Maria do Carmo, who was fanning the charcoal. She is not only very sage, but also a *tigress,*" he said.

At luncheon the previous day Subercaseaux had praised the delicious odourless oil on the salad, contrasting it with the rank smell which defaces almost all salads in Portugal—now, as they descended into the courtyard, the Duke asked him if he would care to see the oil-mill? "It is not working now, of course; that occurs only in late autumn, when the fruit ripens. It is a short walk, and the day is pleasant."

The day was very pleasant indeed. The three men walked through the high delicate sunshine of spring in northern Portugal, which seems to throw a clear, an almost classical light, like the lambency of Latin prose, over a landscape in itself Virgilian—vines, white flocks of sheep and lambs grazing, olive orchards shimmering silver in the breeze, great oxen with coats like polished bronze turning up the rich red-brown earth. Behind, blue and immense, the great range of the Serra shouldered up into the sky. The oil-mill was one of a group of yellow-washed farm buildings, a large airy shed lighted by high windows; in the centre, now clean and at rest, stood the granite wheel which pounded the olives to pulp in a cemented basin, and at one side were ranged the metal butts in which the oil stood, mixed with water, to purify it. The Duke became enthusiastic as he expounded how one made *good* olive oil.

"First, the olives must be *fresh.* My rule is, two hours from tree to mill! Second, the oil must be drawn off in *cold* water; if hot water is used you get a slightly greater yield, but the smell of the pulp is transferred to the oil; with cold water this does not happen. But on most estates in Portugal there persists the lamentable habit of carting in the olives and leaving them in a heap for a week or more; naturally corruption sets in, creating a most unpleasant smell, and on top of that *hot* water is used in the butts, thus ensuring that the maximum of this foetid odour accompanies the oil to the table."

Both the priests had to laugh at the vigour with which their host expressed his view. They walked back to the house another way, which brought them by a flight of stone steps up into the knot-garden, where they came on Miss Probyn and Major Torrens, deep in conversation, on the most remarkable seat Father Antal had ever seen. A circular bench, curved in like a shell below with a high ornate back; the seat, the panelled back and curved support were all covered in blue, pink and white tiling, with lively 18th-century representations of hunting-scenes. One of these beautiful seats adorned each of the four corners of the knot-garden.

The two young people rose at their approach; Father Antal, with his usual lively curiosity, peered at the *azulejos*.

"Really, this is quite beautiful, though so strange," he said. He studied every detail. "Duke, here a bear pursues the hunter up a tree. Is this based on fact?"

Ericeira laughed.

"Yes. My great-great-grandfather was chased up a tree by a bear in the Serra, but when he gave the order for these *azulejo* seats he did not contemplate being immortalised in that situation! However, it had become a local legend, and the artist could not resist it." He turned to Torrens and Julia. "You come in with us? Luncheon will be in twenty minutes."

Of course they all went in together. Punctuality was one of the Duke of Ericeira's little manias; he could really only enjoy a meal if all those who were to eat it were safely marshalled in one of the great salons at least eight minutes before Elidio came in to announce that the Senhora Condessa was served.

Adept and skilful in worldly affairs, where his life's work lay, Subercaseaux naturally cultivated the art of making himself agreeable in his current surroundings, whatever they were; but at luncheon he rather overdid it. Seated as usual beside his hostess, he talked mostly to her; and Nanny's subsequent expression, "smarminess," described his conversation with painful accuracy. He praised the food, the oil-mill, Dona Maria Francisca's charities; there was a good deal of talk about royalties in connection with the impending wedding; there were remarks to and about Luzia—"this young lady who will have such immense opportunities." It was not sufficiently well done; Julia closed her immense eyes,

Luzia became openly restive, and upstairs in the school-room later, she burst out.

"Truly, the Monsignor is too detestable! 'This young lady'!"

Nanny reproved her. "But really, Miss Probyn, if one didn't know, I must say you would think Dom Francisco was the person from the Vatican, wouldn't you?"

Downstairs, in the sitting-room overlooking the knot-garden, the two priests prepared to resume their interrupted task. But Subercaseaux had not finished the excellent cigar provided by the Duke, and walked up and down—Father Antal, seated before the atlas, asked him a question prompted by the conversation at lunch.

"You said that Countess Páloczy was to attend the wedding—is that the mother, or the daughter?"

"Oh, the mother—though the Pretender would greatly have preferred that it should be the daughter!" And he told the Hungarian how Hetta had refused to lunch with the de Bretagnes unless her parent received the invitation she craved.

"This *good* child!" Father Antal exclaimed. "For really the Countess cannot be at all *comfortable* as a mother."

"Oh no, she isn't. She's a most difficult subject, poor creature," Subercaseaux said frankly. "Poor little Hetta could not have entered a more trying milieu for her introduction to the West."

"How is she getting on?" the other asked, turning an earnest gaze on his companion.

"In some ways quite well." The Monsignor continued to patrol the room, drawing appreciatively at his cigar. "There is a young man in the British Embassy, an admirable fellow, who has had the good taste to fall in love with her, and this is helping her in her adjustments." He gave his abrupt barking laugh—then he frowned. "But now I am afraid even this may go wrong."

"Why?" Father Antal asked—his eyes never left the other's face.

"Oh, the old story. The mistress of long standing is about to re-appear —of course for the wedding."

"Does the young man not appreciate Countess Hetta sufficiently to preserve him from the mistress?" Father Antal asked, severity in his tone.

"Oh my dear Dr. Horvath, *yes*, of course he does, or he would not have fallen in love with the child—who has, one must admit, the defects of her qualities to a degree which is rather marked in diplomatic society! *Voyons*," the Monsignor said, throwing the end of his cigar into the fire and spreading out his hands—"this young girl has done a wonderful thing—do not think that I fail to recognise it. With her world as she knew it in ruins she has managed to construct for herself a moral fabric of her own, and one of great integrity. But apart from her contact with you, the materials to her hand were very limited: a convent school, and the life of a servant! Now she is plunged into an international society—royalty, diplomacy, urbanity *in excelsis!* Naturally her formula is inadequate; she makes mistakes. But her admirer is born into this world, and he finds her mistakes embarrassing—whereas the old flame makes none! Surely you can comprehend the position?"

Father Antal continued to follow the Monsignor with an intense, unrelenting gaze.

"Of what sort is the mistress?" he asked.

"Well-born, and exceedingly clever. She has never allowed her reputation to become tarnished, for she is skilful, and her high social standing protects her. A stupider woman, or one less highly placed, would have little reputation left! Young Atherley is by no means her only lover—or was."

"And she is in Portugal now?"

"Is, or comes immediately." This was the sort of thing Subercaseaux always knew.

Father Antal got up, a little heavily, and also began to walk to and fro. "I am troubled," he said at length. "I am greatly troubled," he went on after a pause. "My little Hetti!" He rounded on his companion. "I must see her," he said—"quickly. Can she not come here?"

"For that we must consult Major Torrens—he is responsible for the security side. And Countess Hetta, you see, is already compromised."

"Compromised?—by whom? By the young Englishman?" Father Antal asked, with sudden anger.

Subercaseaux laughed gently.

"No no—by *you,* dear Dr. Horvath! Please!" he said, holding up a hand as if to ward off the Hungarian's furious glare—"I speak the language of counter-espionage now! In that sense only, Hetta Páloczy is what the Secret Service calls 'compromised,' since of course the fact that she worked in your house in Hungary is well known to the Communists."

"So." Father Antal expelled a deep breath, and stopped glaring. "Well, let us now speak with Torrens."

There ensued a whole series of consultations. Torrens, walking in the grounds with Julia, once again found his conversation with her interrupted by an active footman despatched in search of him by Elidio. When he came in, looking rather sulky, he said that if Countess Hetta was to come to Gralheira Miss Probyn would have to arrange it with the family. Julia was sent for, and walked, cool and beautiful, into the study; on hearing what was at issue she said, as usual, that she would talk to Nanny. "It'll be all right," she said comfortably to Father Antal. Julia then talked to Nanny, who talked to Dona Maria Francisca: in the end the Duke himself, looking more Scotch than ever in his grey country tweeds, appeared in the priests' sitting-room. He addressed himself to Torrens.

"I gather that there is some question of an addition to our party here."

"Yes, Sir. Father Antal wants to see Countess Hetta Páloczy," Torrens said glumly.

"Oh, but by all means let her come! I should like my daughter to know her. Telephone at once, and see if she cannot be persuaded to pay us a visit."

"There is just one catch about it, Duke, which you may not have realised," Torrens said, more glumly than ever.

"Which is?"

"Simply the fact that the Countess was employed in Father Antal's household in Hungary—which is, of course, well known to the agents of the other side. So she is certainly under observation—in fact you may call her something of a security risk."

The Duke smiled largely.

"What fascinating phrases the modern world coins!" he said genially. "A security risk!—it sounds quite American. Well, let us take this 'security risk'"—his tone made a mockery of the words—"and ask the little Countess to visit us. Who shall telephone?"

"I'd better," Julia said—"she knows me best."

"Will you come and do it from my study, Miss Probyn?"

Torrens again intervened.

"Excuse me, Duke, but before we ring Countess Hetta up we should arrange how she is to get here."

"Will she not come by car?"

Subercaseaux put in his oar.

"It is not certain, my dear Duke, that her mother will be able to spare her car for a whole day, at such short notice."

"And in any case she oughtn't to travel alone—we have asked her not to go out unaccompanied," said Torrens.

"Here, in Portugal?" the Duke said, looking bewildered.

"Duke dear, in a Portugal at this moment *full* of Communist thugs," Julia said, turning her immense eyes on him disarmingly. "No—I think I'*d* better drive down and bring her up; I've got Atherley's C.D. car, and she can either wear a veil, or crouch down in the back. Better the veil, I think—crouching makes one so stiff, and she won't be able to see the lovely darling country! Isn't that best?" she asked Torrens.

"Yes, I think it is. The diplomatic number-plate is a great safe-guard," the Secret Service man said, rather grudgingly.

"Very well—that's settled. So shall we go and telephone?" Julia said to her host.

But when they repaired to the study and the eight telephones, and eventually got through to the Castelo-Imperial at Estoril, it was only to be told that the Countess Hetta Páloczy had left.

"Left? When does she return?" Julia asked. The clerk said he would enquire.

"Where *can* they have gone? I should have thought wild horses wouldn't have dragged Mama Páloczy away just now," Julia speculated aloud, the receiver half at her ear. "The wedding's on Saturday. Unless she's flown to Paris to get a new frock."

The Duke laughed—in his private and rather silent fashion he derived a good deal of pleasure from Miss Probyn's uninhibited speech.

"Possibly that is the explanation," he was beginning, when Julia said "*Sing?*" sharply into the telephone. (Improbable as it may seem, this syllable in Portuguese, spelt *sim*, means "Yes.") "Sing, sing," Julia pursued, and went on saying "Sing" at intervals for some moments—"*Muito obrigada*" she said finally, and rang off.

"That's rather odd," she said. "Hetta left at ten o'clock this morning, with a suitcase, in a *diplomático* car, with a Senhor; she told the porter, who of course asked her, that she might not return for two or three days. The receptionist rang up her mother's apartment and the maid said that *they* had no idea where she had gone, nor who the diplomatic Senhor was! I don't think it can be Atherley, because I've got his car here."

"Does she know any other diplomats?" the Duke asked.

"Yes. That nice Townsend Waller, in the American Embassy. He's really her slave," Julia said, looking calmly amused.

"Then should we not ring up the American Chancery and ask, discreetly, if they know where this gentleman has gone? Or not?" The Duke looked a little bothered—running off in cars with *diplomáticos* rather upset his previous impression of Hetta as a desirable acquaintance for his daughter.

"Not," said Julia. "I think we ought to talk to Major Torrens before we do any more telephoning."

"Very well—let us speak with him."

The Major, who had been waiting with the two priests, flatly vetoed ringing up the American Embassy.

"They aren't in on this at all," he said, "except for my opposite number. They might start asking all sorts of questions." He looked put out, and gnawed at his small red moustache; the loss of one of the characters in this ill-assorted cast worried him. "I'll ring up Atherley; I can talk to him so that no one else understands, and he's pretty sure to know all about young Hetta's movements—they seem pretty thick. May we do that at once, Sir?"

Richard Atherley was sitting at his desk in the Chancery, staring out over the green garden, trying to make up his mind whether to have another shot at ringing up Hetta, when his telephone buzzed. Three times the evening before he had been infuriated by the smugness of the hotel operator's voice saying "The Countess Hetta Páloczy is not available tonight." What a remorseless little savage she was! He snatched off the receiver, hoping that she might have relented.

"A call for you from São Pedro do Sul, Mr. Atherley," Mrs. Tomlinson said. And then came Hugh's voice on the line.

"That you?"

"Of course." Richard's voice was cold with disappointment. "What is it?"

"I should be grateful if you could make some enquiries for me, unless you happen to know the answer yourself. Listen carefully, will you?—and don't use any names. Can you hear me?"

"Perfectly. What's the question?"

"You remember that you took a lady for a drive one day last week," Torrens' voice went on, with maddening deliberation.

"Well, what of it?" How the devil did Torrens know about Obidos, Richard thought, stiffening.

"In a taxi," Torrens pursued, ignoring the interruption—"and wearing a veil. Do you know who I mean?"

Richard relaxed a little.

"Yes, of course. Well?"

"We want to establish her whereabouts today, but we think it simpler for you to do that. Will you?—and call me back? You know where I am; you can look up the number."

Richard was embarrassed by this application in a way the Major could not of course have foreseen.

"I presume she's at home—I mean, where she lives," he said rather coldly.

"Ah, we don't want presumptions, we want facts," Torrens rejoined, dispassionately. "Your presumption is a little out of date. She left the place where she lives this morning, in a C.D. car, driven by a man, taking a suit-case with her, and said she might not be back for two or three days."

"Good God!" Richard could not control the exclamation.

"Quite so," Torrens said calmly. "You can probably make as good a guess as we can as to the identity of the owner of that car—since it obviously isn't you! You remember we all dined together not so long ago, outside Lisbon. We thought you might ring up his place of business and learn anything that is known of his movements, and then report back."

Every word Torrens said increased the fear, jealousy, anger and remorse that had begun to seethe in Richard, joined with a lively and positive hatred of Mme de Vermeil.

"The editorial 'we' including Julia, I suppose?" he asked waspishly.

"Of course. But don't use names." Torrens was quite untroubled. "How soon do you think you'll be able to ring back?"

"Damn it, why should I make your enquiries for you?" the young man exploded. "Haven't you got your own machinery?"

"Yes. Certainly I will do it through them, if you prefer it so. Can you have this call transferred to the little man we both despise?—I'll put him onto it at once. I have got to find out, you see."

Richard had been trained to think fast; clouded as his mind was by conflicting emotions, he instantly saw that anything was better than to have the ineffable Melplash prying into Hetta's movements.

"No, I'll do it," he said. "I shall get more out of them than your ghastly employee. I'll ring you up when I've got something—I can't say when." He rang off.

Sitting back in his chair he reflected, miserably, on his last conversation with Hetta. "I will make other arrangements; please do not concern yourself." Yes, of course she would have turned to Townsend, her faithful and uncomplicated slave, to get her up to Gralheira. But what a thing to do, to drive off with a man in a car, from the very door of the hotel. She really was too innocent to live!

The person he decided to ring up was the Counsellor at the American Embassy, a kind shrewd man with a passion for music.

"Townsend?" said this individual. "Oh yes, he called me last night to ask if he could take two or three days' leave. No, I didn't ask any questions—I thought maybe he just wanted to bury his grandmother! People do, you know, now and then. Why? Does it matter?"

"Not very much. Could you give me the number of his car?"

"Listen, Richard, do you mean you want to have him *traced?*"

"Arthur, I just want to know where he *is*—there's nothing to panic about. Someone's with him," Atherley said, unwillingly.

"Well so I supposed! All right—I'll get that number. But don't do anything embarrassing, will you? What in hell is all this about?"

"I'll tell you that some other time. Just let me have that number, there's a good fellow."

While he waited for the call from the American Chancery Richard relieved his feelings by ringing up Mme de Vermeil.

"*C'est toi? Bonjour,*" the lady said blithely.

"Good morning," the young man said. "I find I shall not be able to dine with you tomorrow night. I must ask you to excuse me." He spoke with an icy politeness which was not lost on the Frenchwoman.

"*Quel dommage!* Your Ambassador makes difficulties, or *la petite?*"

"It is out of my power to come," Atherley repeated stiffly, ignoring both questions.

"*Tiens!* So some other night? Which?" Mme de Vermeil still sounded blithe.

"I cannot say. Possibly never." He rang off before she could reply.

When the American Counsellor came through again he first gave Atherley the car number. "I happened to meet Perce while I was checking," he went on—"he's sort of a buddy of Townsend's, so I just asked casually if he knew what he was up to."

"And did he know?"

"Nothing very definite. Townsend told him, all in a hurry, that he had to take someone who was in trouble up to the North, and might not be back for two or three days. So then I had a word with our telephone operator."

"Well?" Richard asked.

"She says Townsend booked two rooms, on *different* floors, at one of

. 164 .

the hotels at that spa place near São Pedro do Sul, the Bela Vista. It's the best hotel anywhere up there except that British place at Canas da Senhorim, so I imagine the trouble is in or near São Pedro do Sul."

"Oh bless you, Arthur! Thank you very much," Richard said.

"That tell you anything?" the American asked curiously.

"Only what I wanted to know. Goodbye."

When Mrs. Tomlinson got the Gralheira number the Duke of Ericeira himself answered. Richard recognised his voice, and instead of pronouncing the name "Atherley," as usual, said—"Oh, how do you do, Duke. Could I speak to your red-haired visitor?"

He heard Ericeira chuckle before he replied.

"Certainly. He is here"—and then Torrens said "Richard?"

"Himself. *O Richard, o mon roi!* Here's the dope. Spending two or three nights at the Belle Vue at the spa near St. Peter of the Sun. Can you translate that? If not you'd better get Julia."

"Julia's here. Perhaps you had better tell her—I'm not so hot on all these names. Hold on."

Julia was much hotter.

"Oh yes, I know," she said, when Atherley repeated his Anglo-French version of the address. "Splendid—how clever you are! With the person we thought?"

"Precisely. His car number is"—he gave it. "His employers charitably assume that he is busy burying his grandmother," Richard said, rather sourly trying to conceal his own malaise under the borrowed crack.

Julia gurgled; then she said—

"Oh nonsense! You know perfectly well she adores you. I expect she just wanted to see the little man we all love, only she more than any. But why didn't she ask *you* to bring her up this way?"

"Damn you, Julia!—have you got second sight?"

"Oh yes—Highland blood! I see—and for some protocol reason you couldn't make it, so she turned to the boy-friend from Massachusetts! Well never mind—we'll get her all right now. 'Bye."

Julia was over-optimistic. After a consideration of time and mileage in the Duke's study—slightly hampered by the fact that none of them knew what make of car Mr. Townsend Waller drove—they decided that at the best Hetta and her escort were not likely to reach the Bela Vista before half-past four. It was now three-thirty.

"So we telephone then?" the Duke said. As in Lisbon that Friday night, Julia realised that he was rather enjoying the whole business.

"Oh, do we?" she asked, with a doubtful glance at Torrens. "I should have thought drive over and see them."

"Certainly," Torrens said. "There has been a most unfortunate amount of telephoning already."

"But surely this can have done no harm? You have all been so clever—it has been an entertainment to listen to you!"

"Unfortunately the people we are up against are quite clever too," the Major said wryly. "No, we had certainly better drive over."

"And bring her here?—I see. And the American also? There is plenty of room, of course."

"No, dear Duke. Boundless as your hospitality is, I think poor Mr. Waller had better stay at the Bela Vista tonight and scoot back alone to Lisbon tomorrow. Miserable for him of course, but we don't want an *unceasing* stream of C.D. cars up your by-road—don't you think, Hugh?"

"I *do* think. So good of you," he said to his host, "but Miss Probyn is right; it is much safer that Waller's car shouldn't come here."

Ericeira, in spite of the novelty to him of these goings-on was quite quick-witted.

"I understand," he said. "Then had you not better drive to São Pedro do Sul in one of my cars? They are a familiar sight there."

"That would be admirable, Sir. Thank you." Torrens glanced at his watch. "How long does it take to get in?"

"Twenty-six minutes to the town; to go on to the watering-place, another four-and-a-half." Times were one of the things about which the Duke was quite unfailing. He lifted the receiver of one of the eight telephones and ordered a car to come round to the house at once. "You will do it comfortably," he said. "Who goes?"

"I think we'll both go," said Julia. "Better for Hetta if I'm there. I'll just get a coat." She went out.

The post at Gralheira only arrived in the afternoon—on her way through the hall Julia took a look at the long walnut table on which letters were always laid out. The post was in, and there was a letter for her from her old and beloved friend, Mrs. Hathaway, forwarded from Lisbon on the very day she left; she read it hurriedly on her way to her room.

It announced Mrs. Hathaway's arrival in Lisbon that very day. "This will only give you very short notice of my advent," the good lady wrote, "but it was a last-minute decision. Since you left England I have been somewhat tied to the bed-side of an old friend who was lingering with cancer; but in the end he died very suddenly—it has been rather a shock, and I feel like the change. I have managed to get a plane passage on Monday; if you aren't at the airport—and *don't* bother; I know how many claims there are on your time—I shall go straight to the Hotel Lucrezia in Lisbon, which your Treasury friend Geoffrey Consett says is a very nice moderate hotel, near the main shopping street. I do apologise for this short notice, and you must not let me be a bother. But it will be blessed to see you." There was a P.S. "I have bought a Portuguese phrase-book, with instructions for pronunciation. How very odd that O should be pronounced OO, and OU O! And S as SH! Why have an alphabet?"

Julia laughed, and then frowned, over this missive. Damn! Of course it would have to happen that her precious Mrs. Hathaway must needs arrive in Lisbon in her absence, and while she was so tied up with Hugh's affairs that she couldn't race back to look after her old friend. However, once they had got Hetta safely tucked in at Gralheira she might get away tomorrow; anyhow she would ring Mrs. H. up tonight. She slung the orange suède jacket, which so delightfully matched her tawny-blonde hair and apricot complexion, over her shoulders and left her room.

In the corridor she encountered Luzia.

"Oh Miss Probyn, you are going out! I saw the car coming up to the door—I thought so. *Can't* I come too? I am so dull; and I *hate* cutting out aprons for Tia Maria Francisca's wretched lost girls to sew, which is what she will make me do if I am at home. I have hardly seen you today —you have been all the time with Torrens, or the priests! *Do* say Yes," the girl implored, twining an arm cajolingly through that of her ex-governess.

Julia, laughing and releasing her arm, decided instantly that she would say Yes. To drive into São Pedro do Sul, not only in the Duke's car but accompanied by the Duke's daughter was an excellent bit of cover for their errand.

"All right, you can come," she said. "Go and get a coat—but hurry."

Chapter Twelve

TORRENS, who had only come that way when it was practically dark, was especially pleased to see the countryside. Passing through the pinewoods clothing the slopes of the Serra they crossed ravine after ravine, each of which was spanned by small curved terraces on which spring crops were growing—they looked like whole strings of bright-green horse-shoes, suspended on silver threads of water between the dark pines.

"They don't waste an inch, do they, these people?" he said.

São Pedro do Sul is a pleasant unpretentious little town, lying, as its name implies, on a southern slope facing the sun. As the car drove into the curious raised square immediately below the Igreja Matriz, the Parish Church, Torrens' eye was caught by two things: the spectacular front of the Reriz Palace, with its huge impending cornice and innumerable balconies of wrought-ironwork, and the exquisite little façade of the Misericordia Church, whose baroque window-frames of dark granite are set, not as usual in pale plaster, but in aqueous blue-and-white *azulejos* which cover the whole surface of the building.

"Julia, do for goodness sake let us stop for five minutes and look at all this!" he exclaimed. "We're well on time, and some of these things are fantastically lovely."

"Oh very well"—Julia tapped on the glass and told the chauffeur to pull up.

Torrens sprang out at once, and strode off across the square towards the Misericordia, followed much more leisurely by Julia; Luzia got out too, but with her adolescent acuity decided to leave her companions to themselves—they get few enough chances in our house, she thought. She pottered contentedly about the little square in the warm sunshine, taking note of the various cars parked round its edges. Her eye was caught suddenly by the red-and-white number-plate with "C.D." and six figures, which in Portugal makes diplomatic cars unmistakable—she walked over to it. The car was American; it was empty.

"*Tiens!*" Luzia said to herself. Diplomatic cars were not a very common sight in São Pedro do Sul, especially out of season. She looked about her. As always in Portugal one or two beggars were sitting sunning themselves outside the parish church and she went up to them, feeling in her purse for small coins as she did so—at her approach they held out dirty hands and began their customary gabble.

"There, O Santinha! There, O Santinho!" the girl said, dropping money into the outstretched palms of a very old woman and a crippled man. In northern Portugal it is the delightful custom to honour poverty by addressing beggars as "Little Saint"; moreover, the giver thanks the beggar for affording him the opportunity of an alms-deed. Automatically Luzia did so now—"*Muitissimo obrigada*" (most greatly obliged) she said; then she briskly addressed the cripple, who looked the more intelligent of the two.

"What quality of persons came in this *carro diplomático?*" she asked. "Did you see them?"

"*Sim, sim, Minha Menina,*" the old man said. "There was a Senhor, who appeared to be an Americano, and a Menina—very dark, she was."

"And where have they gone?"

"The Menina went into the Igreja—she gave me *silver!*" the beggar quavered excitedly.

"And the Senhor?"

"He went to drink wine in that small shop across the *praça.* While he was within another big *carro* drove up, with four Senhores; they looked at the *carro diplomático,* and as the Menina has done one of them asked us where the *pessoas* in it were. So I told him; but he gave me no money!" the old man said angrily.

"And then?" Luzia asked.

"Then they drove the car close up to the entrance of the Igreja Matriz, and three went in, while one waited at the driving-wheel; and presently they came out with the Menina."

"Well?" Luzia pressed him.

"They put her into the car, and drove away all together."

"Without the Americano?"

"*Sim*—without him. Curious, was it not?" the cripple said detachedly. Julia had not bothered to mention to Luzia the reason for their drive to São Pedro do Sul—for one thing she was confident that the girl would have heard of Hetta's impending arrival from Nanny anyhow, and she had a firm trust in her pupil's tact and discretion. Her confidence was well-founded: Nanny had of course told Luzia that "we" were expecting a young lady—"Hungarian; a Countess it seems, and a great friend of Dom Francisco's. She's driving up from Lisbon today." It had not taken Luzia long to connect this fascinating fact with their expedition that afternoon, and when she saw the car with a diplomatic number-plate it took her exactly one second to leap to the conclusion that it had probably brought the Hungarian young lady to their remote district—hence her questions to the beggar. But she had heard, and guessed, enough of what was going on to be thoroughly disturbed by what the cripple said.

"How did the four Senhores look?" she asked, as casually as she could.

"Foreign—the one who talked with me spoke Portuguese very badly!" the old man said.

Luzia reflected quickly, then tried a further question.

"Had one of them a beard, and rolls of fat at the back of his neck?"

"*Sim, sim!* They wore grey," the beggar added.

The grey conveyed nothing to Luzia, though her mind recorded the fact, but the beard and the fat neck frightened her very much.

"And did the Menina go willingly with these Senhores?" she asked.

"*Não, não!* She struggled, and the bearded one put his hand over her mouth before they thrust her into the car. Was this not also curious?"

To Luzia it was not so much curious as horrifying. She gave the creature another coin, to stimulate his wits, and asked what the *carro* of the four foreign Senhores was like?

Black, large, shining, and closed, she was told.

"And by which road did it leave?"

São Pedro do Sul is the junction for four main roads: north to the valley of the Douro, south-east to Viseu and Guarda, but also to Coimbra and Lisbon; due west to Aveiro and the Atlantic; north-west—a poorish road—to Vale de Cambra and Oporto. But about this the cripple was less clear. The car had driven away very fast; and precisely at that moment a rich, a charitable lady had come up to him, and in speaking with her he had failed to notice which road the big black car took.

"Did you see its *número?*" Luzia asked, without much hope.

"Ah no, Minha Menina—I cannot read numbers."

"Is the Americano still in the wine-shop?"

"*Não, não*—when the big car has left he comes out, he goes into the

.170.

church, no Menina!—he comes out again, he runs here and there looking for her; I think he is gone to the *Policia*."

Luzia wasted no more time on the beggar except to thank him politely —she ran like a deer to the Misericordia Church, outside which Julia and Major Torrens now stood, admiring the delicious little narrow balcony—such a curious feature for a church front—immediately above the copper-green door. The girl caught Julia by the arm.

"They've got her! They've taken her away," she said.

"Who's got whom?" the Major asked. Julia was quicker.

"D'you mean Hetta Páloczy? How do you know?"

"It must be her. Come this way," she said, propelling Julia a few steps towards the square. "Do you see that diplomatic car? A dark girl came in that, with an American man; she went into the Matriz Church, he went to drink. And then"—she repeated the beggar's story of the men in grey pushing Hetta into the car. "One put his hand over her *mouth*," she said, staring at Julia, her eyes immense with horror. "It can only be her."

"How did you learn all this?" Torrens asked.

"From a beggar by the church. Beggars watch everything—what else have they to do? But do not waste time on him; I have sucked him as dry as a lemon! What must we do?" the young girl asked urgently.

"Ring up the Colonel, don't you think?" Julia said to Torrens. "They're pretty certain to make for Spain, and he can have the frontier watched—closed, if need be, can't he?"

"I suppose so." He looked worried. "Did your observant beggar get the number of the car?" he asked Luzia.

"No. He can't read. But it was a big black saloon. Oh, and I didn't tell you—one of the men had a beard, and rolls of fat at the back of his neck. Surely this is the person who smashed your car?" Luzia said to Julia, causing Torrens to gape at her—Julia nodded briefly.

"Well, that sounds like it," the Major said, rather slowly, to Julia. "But of course we're not certain it is the little Countess at all—Luzia doesn't know her by sight. Or do you?" he asked the girl.

"No—but who else would be forced, struggling, into a car? To me, it all fits. Do telephone!" she urged Julia.

"We'd better do that from the *Policia*," Julia said. "Where is it, Luzia?"

As Luzia led them towards the police-station a frantic figure came hurrying from that direction, staring about him as he ran; his hat and the cut of his overcoat blazoned him as American, in that European setting.

"Oh, there's Townsend," Julia said calmly. "Let's ask him about this. Oy! Townsend," she yelled—the Bostonian heard her, and raced towards them across the open space.

"Have you seen Countess Hetta?" he panted as he came up. "Julia, it's good to see you! D'you know where she is? She went into a church to pray, and I went to have a drink, and now I can't find her!"

"Relax, Townsend. We're looking after this," Julia said kindly. "Come along with us."

"But where *is* she?" the American asked.

"We think she's been abducted," Torrens said brutally. "By Communist agents. Why on earth did you let her out of your sight?"

"Oh shut up, Hugh," Julia said. "It's all our fault for keeping him in the dark."

"Communist agents?" the Bostonian asked, aghast. "Were they at the bottom of that business of crashing your car after the Guincho, Miss Probyn?"

To the surprise of the others, Luzia answered. "One man, at least, was the same both times," she said. Townsend, for the first time, noticed her.

"This is Luzia Ericeira, Townsend," Julia said, using the customary Portuguese form of identification. "But come back to the *Policia*—we want to telephone about this at once."

As they walked on Townsend's distress was painful to see.

"Shouldn't we go after her?" he asked. "Communists do frightful things to girls!"

"We might, if we knew where they'd gone," Torrens replied. "But we don't know the number of the car." He took Julia by the elbow and muttered in her ear. "For God's sake detach him somehow! We don't want him fretting round while we're telephoning to the Colonel."

"There—that is the *Policia*," Luzia said. She turned to the American. "I think you are quite right—we should go after her. Will you come with me while they are telephoning? I want to arrange something."

Julia didn't know whether Luzia's extraordinarily sharp ears had overheard Torrens' aside to her, or whether the girl was simply using her customary astuteness and tact, but she was thankful to be relieved so painlessly of poor Townsend's presence.

They got through to Lisbon rather fast—Colonel Marques' name and telephone-number seemed to act as a talisman. The local police, deeply impressed and much excited, stood round while one of them sat at the telephone; meanwhile Julia and Torrens examined a large map of northern Portugal which hung on the wall—she showed him the various routes from São Pedro do Sul into Spain.

"It just depends whether they choose a fast road, with a big, efficiently-manned frontier post on it, or a slower route to some dud little place where they might get through more easily—I don't suppose Hetta has her passport with her," she said. "Look—Fuentes de Onoro is fairly small; it's"—she worked out the distances with a pink-tipped finger—"nearly 200 kilometres, via Viseu and Guarda; the road's good all the way, but it's frightfully curly. Then, going north, there's Barca d'Alva—that's only just over 140 kilometres, and it's a *tiny* place, but the road's appalling; they'd have to turn off the Guarda road at Celorico, and trickle through Pinhel and Figueira de Castelo Rodrigo. And I don't know whether the bridge has been re-built yet." She turned and questioned the policemen. "They're not sure," she told Torrens. "So I think we can count that out."

The Major nodded. "Yes, I see," he said, though he saw little but the map before his eyes; he was bewildered by the flow of difficult names, and amazed at Julia's apparently inexhaustible fund of information about Portuguese roads.

"Well that only leaves Vila Nova de Foscoa and Chaves. Vila Nova's a long way too, about 180, though it's a fair road almost all the way—and it's not a very big place. But the fastest of all would be—"

"Minha Menina, I have the connection!" the policeman at the telephone called out.

"*Muito bem*—I will speak." Leisurely, she went over and took the receiver. "No," she said in Portuguese—"I must speak with the Chief himself. A name Inglês—Probeen." And in a moment the Colonel was on the line, and she handed the instrument to Torrens.

Colonel Marques' admirable command of English was an enormous asset on an occasion like this; so was his quickness at the uptake. Torrens did his part quite well—"We suspect an abduction of a little foreign lady—do you know who I mean?" he began at once.

"The identifier? Certainly. What do you know? Speak openly, but fast—English is difficult for these others, if spoken quickly."

Torrens told him, speaking rapidly, the little they knew. "But we have failed to get the number of the car."

"Oh, I have that," the Colonel said cheerfully. "I sent some stooges"

—he pronounced the word with a certain relish—"out in a certain car over the week-end, and as I anticipated, it was followed! How long ago did this abduction take place?"

"Hold on." Torrens consulted Julia, his hand over the mouthpiece; they both looked at their watches—it was five o'clock.

"We've been here at least half an hour—no, more," Julia said—"but of course we've no idea how long Townsend was drinking and Hetta praying. Say about four."

Obediently, Major Torrens said, "About an hour ago," down the telephone. "We imagine, of course, that they are making for another country," he added.

"So I also imagine. From where do you speak? The house, or the town?"

"From the town."

"*Muito bem!* Excuse me if I ring off now—I want to close the frontier to this car. Wait! Where can I contact you later?"

Once more Torrens consulted Julia.

"Tell him to try the house—we may be there, or we may not, but we certainly shan't be *here.*"

"Well that's something—he'll stop all the exits now," Julia said, when Torrens had rung off.

"If he's in time. I wish we knew how fast that car is."

"I think he's bound to be in time—the shortest route, the one with the dubious bridge, is eighty-five miles, and that's an appalling road; they'd have to *crawl.*"

"Which was the one you were saying was the fastest, just when we got through to him?" Torrens was beginning, when Luzia and Townsend Waller walked in. All the police greeted the young girl with a combination of affection and deference which amused the Englishman.

"You have got him?" Luzia asked. Julia nodded. "But look, pipe down a moment, Luzia," she added. "Mr. Waller, you don't mind waiting a second or two, do you? I want to explain something to Hugh." She turned again to the map on the wall, and traced a line with one finger.

"Much the fastest is to blind straight north to Chaves, crossing the Douro at Regua—see?—and on through Vila Real; it's the main route north into Spain, and a good road all the way. But it's over a hundred miles, and a major frontier post, of course. Could they do it in the time?"

"Touch and go," Torrens said, looking at his watch—it now said 5:10. "No, they would hardly do it, even on an auto-strada, in under an hour-and-a-half—unless the black saloon is a super-charged Mercedes-Benz or something like that." He thought, frowning. "It all depends, really, on how quickly our friend gets the frontier alerted. Very fast, I imagine—he is so enormously efficient."

Luzia suddenly spoke up.

"If they were well-informed, and clever, they might not cross the frontier on the main road at all. In Chaves they could turn left to Montalegre, in the Terras de Barroso; and from Montalegre there are two little, small roads into Spain—so tiny, I doubt if the frontier posts have telephones at all. One goes to Baltar, and one to Lucenza; both in Spain."

"How do you know all this?" Torrens asked, staring at her doubtfully.

"Papa has a small house—do you call it a shooting-box?—near Montalegre, where he goes to shoot wild goats; so I know the roads there."

"Luzia, is there a telephone at the shooting-lodge?" Julia asked, while Torrens digested this information.

"Of course."

"And they're sensible people, discreet?—the keepers, I mean?"

"Martinez is wonderful—he is a *Gallego* Spaniard."

"Could he do something about having the car stopped? How far is the lodge from Montalegre?"

"Only eight kilometres. But let us start to telephone now; there is no car up there, and Maria-Rosa at the exchange at Montalegre is not very prompt!" She turned to one of the police and gave a number. "Expressly for the Senhor Duque, tell them," she added brusquely, "and *urgente!*" —grinning, the policeman did as he was told.

"How will your keeper stop the car?" Torrens asked, lighting a cigarette.

"Oh, leave all that to Martinez!" Luzia said cheerfully—pushing aside some dusty and faded files she had perched herself on the office table, and sat there swinging her long thin legs, the legs of a very young but thorough-bred colt. "He will stop it by some means or another, if he is told to."

"I think we ought to ring up the Duke and say we may be delayed," Julia said presently, also seating herself on the table beside Luzia.

"I've done that," Luzia said. "Mr. Waller and I went and did it from the Câmara, while you were telephoning to Lisbon."

The Câmara is the name used in Portugal for the municipal offices of any town. In São Pedro do Sul this rather uninspiring organisation is most splendidly housed, behind superb baroque façades, in what was formerly the Convent of the Frades; along corridors where once religious walked in stately meditation, little clerks now scurry to and fro on errands concerned with street lighting and sewerage disposal. It is something when these noble buildings, left vacant when the religious orders were driven out in the 19th century, are used as Câmaras or barracks, for then at least the fabric is preserved; all too many are simply abandoned to the ravages of the elements and the tender mercies of squatters, who crouch in one corner of some vast ground-floor room—probably with a magnificent painted ceiling, now rather damp-stained—along with their skinny fowls and their stinking goats. Julia grinned a little at her pupil's resourcefulness. But just as she was about to speak the telephone rang; Luzia leapt off the table, and gabbled into the instrument in Portuguese.

"That is arranged," the girl said, as she put down the receiver. "Now, do we go after her?"

Poor Mr. Waller, who had perforce remained a rather passive spectator since he and Luzia returned to the *Policia*, now spoke up.

"Of course we do. We have to! We can't just leave her in their hands!"

"Just a moment"—Julia spoke very calmly. "Luzia, who did you speak to at Gralheira?"

"Elidio—Papa was out."

"And what did you say?"

"That there was a contretemps, and we should not be back in time for dinner; we might be very late, and they were to keep food hot for us. I was *exceedingly* discreet!" the girl said.

"That all sounds in order," Townsend said to Julia. "Let's go. What are we waiting for?"

"Let's go and talk about it in the open, anyhow," Julia said. "I think these polite policemen must have had about enough of us." She spoke courteous farewells and thanks, which were received with a perfect ballet of smiles and bows and a chorus of *um muito grande prazer!* (a great pleasure). "I told you you'd see up here what nice people they were," Julia said to Torrens as they walked towards the square. "Well now, had we better go after her?"

"I think some of us must, anyhow. I wish to God we knew which road to try, though."

"I think Chaves is much the best bet. The others are all far slower," Julia began, when a piercing whistle just behind them made both her and the Major jump.

"Oh, I am sorry! But there it *is*," Luzia said; once more she put two fingers in her mouth and emitted that frightful sound, usually a shepherd's secret, and waved vigorously. The Gralheira Land-Rover, driving slowly into the square, swung round in their direction.

"Good gracious, what's this doing here?" Julia said astonished.

"I had it sent. For these bad, small roads in the Terras de Barroso it is *much* better than the Daimler, and on a good road it can do a hundred kilometres an hour easily," the girl said earnestly. "So I told Elidio to send it in."

Torrens burst out laughing.

"Splendid! Send back the other car, and we'll go in this. Waller, have you locked yours?"

Townsend had. But Julia began to feel some slight qualms about her pupil.

"Luzia, you'd better go home in the Daimler," she said.

As Luzia opened her Medusa mouth in a bitter protest, Torrens broke in.

"Damn it, Julia, you can't do that! The child has had the wits to produce the right machine for the job, and she may be very useful in dealing with all these types on the spot. For pity's sake let her come along."

Julia glanced at him in surprise. "Oh, very well," she said—Luzia, in her thankfulness for this mercy, swallowed the Major's use of the humiliating word "child." The Daimler was despatched to Gralheira, and the four of them piled into the Land-Rover and roared off towards the north. From habit Torrens glanced at his watch—it was a quarter to six.

From São Pedro do Sul to the frontier, a few kilometres beyond Chaves, is about 106 miles. The Land-Rover did it in two-and-a-quarter hours, battering its occupants almost to jelly in the process; for the road goes up hill and down dale, descending to cross the deep golden-schist valley of the Douro at Regua, and then climbing up onto and over the wild high-lying country of Trás-os-Montes, the most remote province of Portugal. Exactly at 8 P.M. they drew up in front of the wire barrier closing the road, climbed down, and went to interview the frontier officials. By common consent Julia did the talking. She showed the man at the barrier Torrens' "white card," an invaluable document issued by the Security Police only to senior members of diplomatic missions and to Portuguese Cabinet Ministers; Torrens had, of course, been furnished with one of these coveted objects, which enable their fortunate possessors to go practically anywhere, and—most useful of all—to park their cars in places where parking is normally forbidden. (In fact they do confer *carte blanche* on their owners.) The frontier guard recognised this portentous document when he examined it by the Land-Rover's headlights; he pushed the long slender barrier back a little way, beckoned the party through the gap, and led them to where his superiors were smoking cigarettes and drinking red wine in a small office.

Here Julia introduced the Senhor Comandante Inglês as a friend and colleague of Colonel Marques, and then began her questions about a large black car. Yes, such a car had driven up about 6 p.m., but it did not bear the number advised telephonically by the Colonel, so the occupants had not been held; however, the Colonel had closed the frontier tonight, so it was not allowed to pass—it turned round, and drove back towards Chaves. Was there a Menina in it? Ah, that they could not say; since it did not bear the specified number it was not examined—it came, and it went.

"Well that gets us exactly nowhere," Torrens said gloomily when Julia passed on this information.

"Shall I ask if the men wore grey overcoats?"

"Might as well."

Julia did so. Yes, in effect the Senhores had worn grey top-coats—"like most travellers who are not Ingleses," the customs officer said, with a side-long glance at Torrens' rather vivid tweed. Luzia laughed.

"That really tells us nothing either," Torrens said, as they walked back towards the barrier. "I wonder what our next move is?" Luzia, however, was speaking to the frontier guard in his own tongue; she rounded briskly on the Secret Service man.

"They consulted a map when they got back to the car!—he *saw* them. They might have seen these little roads on it. Oh, do let us go to Montalegre and see if Martinez (she pronounced it Marteensh) has done something!"

On to Montalegre they went. The young chauffeur in the Land-Rover was new, and Luzia sat with Torrens beside him on the front seat to show the way. As they drove through that wild upland country they met nothing but one rather broken-down old car, with weak and wavering headlights; Luzia, however, drew the Englishman's attention to one of the most peculiar features of the place—the stone walls dividing one field from another, almost as frequent as the walls which turn Connemara into a chess-board. But whereas the Irish walls are loosely made of shapeless lumps of the local lime-stone or marble, these Portuguese ones, also dry-stone built, are of a most elaborate, even elegant construction—between upright slabs of silvery granite nearly two feet across, slender and much smaller flakes of dusty-gold schist are piled slant-wise, producing a quite extraordinary effect of golden hammocks or curtains, slung between broad silver pillars. Seldom can peasants merely in search of utility have created anything so beautiful.

"Are they not strange, and pretty?" the girl said. "I wish you could see them by day; the colours are beautiful."

Montalegre is a very small town indeed, and so remote that the cheerful friendly people who live in the little houses of its narrow primitive streets often only see a stranger once in two months; so, as Luzia explained to Hugh Torrens, it was an easy place in which to make enquiries. As they drove in, the enormous mediaeval castle, looming high above the town clustered at its foot, was beginning to be illuminated by the rising moon—"Goodness! That is quite magical," Torrens exclaimed. Luzia ignored the remark; she had just told the young chauffeur to drive slowly, and was peering out through the wind-screen. "There is Francisco—stop!" she said. The Land-Rover pulled up before Montalegre's nearest approach to an inn; outside it stood a little group of people. Luzia bounced down out of the high seat and spoke with a handsome dark youth who leant across a bicycle—Torrens climbed down after her and saw, close in front of them, a large black saloon car drawn up. He walked quickly to it and looked inside; it was empty; moreover, he then observed that all its four tires were flat! He went back to where Luzia was talking to the young man with the bicycle, the inn-keeper, and the town policeman; an attentive audience hung on every word.

"They *did* come here!" Luzia said to him excitedly as he came up. "Did I not tell you they would? And they went into this house to drink wine, and ate an omelette, and bought some bread and cheese, and made enquiries about the roads to Lucenza and Baltar. *She* was with them! While they were within—they got here just before seven o'clock—Francisco put a knife in all their tires! Martinez has sprained his ankle, that is why he sent Francisco; if he had come himself he would not have let them go."

"Oh, they've gone, have they? Where to, and how?"

"Back to Chaves. There is a sort of taxi in the town, and when they found their tires flat, they took it; Senhor Antonio here"—she indicated the tubby figure of the inn-keeper—"got it for them."

"That must be that ghastly old rattle-trap we met on the road," said Julia, who with Mr. Waller had now joined the group. "How maddening!—I wish we'd ditched it! Then we should have got her by now." She turned to the inn-keeper. "*Que pena* that you ordered the *carro* for these people. They are Communistas!"

"*Minha Senhora*, I did not know! How could I know? And they offered poor Pedro such a magnificent price to drive them to Chaves—he with all those children, and for weeks now not a single person requiring his machine! I thought I did well." The little man was pitiably distressed—Luzia cheered him up.

"Do not fret, Senhor Antonio—as you truly say, you could not know. But tell me the *número* of Pedro's machine."

Twenty voices gave her the number of Montalegre's one hire-car—"In any event, everyone in Chaves knows it by sight," said an enormous man, the local butcher. "*Sim, sim,*" said Luzia, "naturally." She turned to the others. "We should follow them back to Chaves, should we not?"

The Montalegre policeman now spoke.

"My Countess, what shall be done about the strange *carro*? Does it remain?"

"Of course it remains—since its tires are flat, it cannot move," Luzia said laughing.

"An outrage was committed upon it," the policeman said rather anxiously, casting a baleful eye upon young Francisco, who still leaned, now visibly wilting, across his bicycle.

"This was done by the orders of the *Chefe* of the *Policia* in Lisbon," Luzia said majestically. "*I* transmitted them. But if you are in doubt, telephone to Lisbon yourself." The policeman subsided; Julia spoke up.

"Hadn't we better search the car?"

They did—but their hasty examination revealed nothing. "You'd better tell the bobby man to seal it up, and leave it where it is," Torrens said to Luzia. "The Colonel can send someone to search it properly." Luzia passed on these instructions to the policeman, who was clearly inflated by this idea—"Certainly the priest will have sealing-wax," he observed hopefully.

"Oh, how is Dom Gil's rheumatism? No better? Ah, *pena!*—please give him my love." She went on with local enquiries, as about the inn-keeper's wife's new baby, and replied to similar questions concerning the health of the Senhor Duque and the Senhora Condessa. All this drove poor Townsend Waller nearly distracted; he stood in a fever of anxiety.

"Look, Miss Luzia," he broke in at last in desperation—"Shouldn't we get going? You say they left here at 7:15; well it's nine now, so they have nearly two hours start."

"All right—yes."

It was just after 9:30 when they drove across the splendid Roman bridge of sixteen arches which in the 20th century still carries all traffic from the South into Chaves. They had arranged on the way that Julia and Torrens should be dropped at the *Policia* to ring up Colonel Marques, while Luzia and Townsend were to rout round the few garages and try to ascertain the number of the car which Hetta's captors had taken—assuming reasonably that no one would try to go very far in the Montalegre taxi.

When Torrens reported to the Colonel he gave the number of the car which they had found, and left, at Montalegre.

"But this is not the one!" the Colonel exclaimed.

"No. We found that out at the frontier; that was why they didn't hold it."

"These *fools* of mine!" Colonel Marques said angrily. "They must needs have a puncture just before Coimbra, and of course lost sight of the car! It will be in Coimbra that these others changed to a different one, no doubt." His voice ceased for a moment—"Hullo?" Torrens said.

"Do you know the number of the car they have taken in Chaves?" the Colonel asked then.

"We're trying to find out. I'll let you know if we get it."

"*Très bien*. In any case I will now ensure that *no* car passes the frontier anywhere for the next twenty-four hours—this is troublesome, but it cannot be helped. They may of course try to take the girl away by sea or by air; I will have the ports and air-fields watched."

There was no sign of Luzia and the American when Julia and Torrens emerged from the police-station, so they walked by moonlight to the hotel where they had all agreed to meet for dinner. Chaves is now a thriving spa; in past centuries, owing to its proximity to the frontier, it was a favourite meeting-place for diplomatic missions between Spain and Portugal, and even the scene of dynastic intermarriages—probably its hot springs, which are alleged to cure everything from rheumatism to syphilis, pay better. Anyhow it has two really rather good hotels with excellent food; Julia and Torrens sat down in the one recommended by Luzia and ordered dinner for four with a certain enthusiasm—it was now just on ten o'clock, and they had eaten nothing since lunch at 1:30. The waiter produced gin and French Vermouth; after a deep preliminary gulp the Major sank back in his chair, relaxed and thankful.

"Feeling better?" Julia asked.

"Yes, much. But this is a ghastly show—I've never touched anything so hopeless."

"Hugh, *why*? It seems to me that you've been getting no end of help —thanks to Luzia of course."

"Oh yes—she's a wonder-child! But where are we now? At a dead end, as far as I can see—and that poor little creature in the hands of those bastards at this moment."

Julia, woman-like, poured him out another drink.

"Sup that—I'm going to ring up Gralheira," she said, and went out. The Duke himself answered.

"From where do you speak, Miss Probyn?"

"From Chaves. *La petite Hongroise* has been abducted—that's why we came here. It was Luzia's idea, and it was a good one, but we just missed them."

The Duke sounded grave.

"This is a terrible thing! How could it happen?"

"Oh, her poor Yank boy-friend left her alone in a church, and they pinched her," Julia said, deliberately using these slangy expressions in case of line-tapping. "It was our fault; he didn't know. I'm sorry we shall be so late; do please apologise for me to Dona Maria Francisca. We're just going to dine now; I suppose we shall get back about one. Don't keep any food."

"You abandon the pursuit?"

"We've lost the trail—there's nothing more we can do tonight. And Luzia ought to get to bed. Oh, can we bring the American with us? I don't like leaving him alone, he's in a terrible state."

"Of course."

"You *are* kind."

"By the way, the British Embassy constantly telephones, asking for you—three times, so far."

"Oh, let them wait!—say I'm dead!" Who *could* have told Atherley what was going on, Julia speculated—it could only be he who was ringing up. She said Good-night and rang off.

When she returned to the hall where she had left Torrens she found Luzia and Townsend Waller; the latter was drinking gin too.

"Miss Probyn, could I have a *porto branco*? I *feel* like one!" the girl said.

"She'd much better have a brandy," Torrens interposed—Luzia's pearl-pale face was now white with fatigue.

"Yes—order one, will you?"

While Luzia sipped brandy-and-water, Townsend recounted their fruitless endeavours to trace the car to which Hetta had been transferred from the Montalegre taxi. "They were seen at at least three garages, but the people just weren't talking."

"Not even to *me!*" Luzia added, with a naïve indignation which amused Torrens. "They must have given *huge* bribes!"

"We'd better let the Colonel know about this—he can have the heat turned on them," the Major said rather reluctantly—he wanted his dinner. "Back to the police-station, I suppose."

"Oh nonsense! Let's do it from here; the whole town will be buzzing with it by now," said Julia, and put the call through for him.

Over their much-needed dinner they discussed what further moves they could make.

"My own bet is that they'll go back to Lisbon and think again," Torrens said. "It's clear that they have quite an organisation there."

"I agree," said Julia.

"I don't see how you can talk about it so calmly," Townsend burst out. "What will they do to her in the meantime?" He was in a pitiable state, only playing with the good food in front of him.

"As to that, for the present you can only pray," Luzia told him, rather severely. "That is why I took you into the Igreja Matriz; but I think you did not pray—you only looked at those lovely carved angels which stand on top of the organ, and the two golden deformities of dwarfs that hold it up!"

Julia and Torrens burst out laughing.

"Well, that organ *is* extraordinary," the Bostonian said defensively. "It's so beautiful, although it's so queer."

They did not linger over the meal; they climbed into the Land-Rover just before eleven, and set off on the two-and-a-half hours of pounding and shaking back to Gralheira. Luzia fell asleep, and toppled off onto the floor—Torrens picked her up and took her in his arms, arranging her long thorough-bred legs across Julia's knees.

"It's all right, sweetie—just you go to sleep," he said when she opened her eyes—"You've done a splendid job." Luzia closed her eyes again and relaxed like a baby, her head on his shoulder; Julia slid one arm out of her suède jacket and spread part of it over those long legs. Then she too closed her eyes, in silent endurance of the prolonged battering. But several times during the next two hours she opened them to glance at the Major, holding her pupil so tenderly in his arms, with an indefinable expression.

Chapter Thirteen

JULIA was surprised and touched, when they reached Gralheira a little after one, to find the Duke still up and waiting for them in his study, with a blazing wood fire and a tray with whisky. Nanny was hovering in the background; she pounced on the sleepy Luzia and bore her off to bed—over her shoulder she threw Julia an indignant "Well, Miss Probyn!" Julia apologised to their host—"I really am so very sorry. It seemed the only thing to do, to go on and try to get hold of her."

"Of course you could do nothing else. But now you must all drink something."

Julia was touched afresh by the degree of the Duke's concern for Hetta, when over their drinks they told him their adventures. "This *poor* young girl! What happens to her at this moment?"

"I daresay they won't dare to do anything very much—they just want to hold her to ransom, and worry us," she said as convincingly as she could, for Townsend's benefit. At that moment a telephone bell rang sharply.

"This is doubtless your friend at the Embassy!" the Duke said, selecting one of the eight machines, and lifting the receiver. "Yes," he said in English—and handed it to Julia with a smile.

It was Atherley—and Julia handled him rather roughly. "My good friend, do you realise that it's going on for *two*? You really can't ring people up at this time of night! And I gather you've been pestering this house the whole evening. What is it?"

"Have you got her back?" Julia hardly recognised his voice, it was so strained and toneless.

"No, we haven't, I'm sorry to say. But how did you know she was missing?"

"From Hugh's Colonel. After I'd spoken to Hugh this morning I thought I might as well let him know where she'd gone, by way of no harm; so when you told him what was going on this afternoon, he told me. But what happened? Weren't they stopped? He said he had their car number."

Guardedly, Julia told him why that car number had been of no use, and of their fruitless pursuit right up into the North-West.

"So you have absolutely no means of tracing her?"

"No—except that we've alerted you-know-who, so they can't leave the country by road. But otherwise, we're completely at a dead end." Between fatigue and distress Julia's own voice fell away on the last words. She was tired out, she was tormented about Hetta; but she was also irritated by Richard's ringing up at such an hour. She felt—more rightly than she knew—that it was really all his fault for not bringing his girl-friend up to Beira Alta himself. "Well, goodnight," she said.

"No, wait! This is too frightful! We *must* do something. I'll come up."

Julia managed not to utter the words that came into her head—What good do you think *that* will do? Too exhausted to protest, really at the end of her tether, she merely said resignedly—"Oh very well. Come early, come all, and vote for Eisenhower!" and banged down the receiver.

"Duke, I fear we may anticipate a visit some time tomorrow from the First Secretary at the British Embassy," she said, as she returned to the fire.

"This is your friend who telephones so persistently? Atherley? An agreeable young man," the Duke said, very courteously, in view of the hour at which the call had been made.

"Well I suppose I may call him a friend, but he's little Countess Páloczy's young man, and that's what all the telephoning has been about," said Julia thoughtlessly and indignantly. "Personally, I think he has probably perpetrated a *total* clottery of some sort! Silly ass!" She emptied her glass and added—

"Duke dear, I'm dead. I simply must go to bed. You've been an angel," —and left the study. In less than two minutes the others followed her, Elidio escorting Townsend Waller to his room.

Nothing is more tiring than distress and anxiety; and however she might preserve her outward composure, Julia Probyn was in fact deeply distressed and cruelly anxious about Hetta, and had been for the whole of the eight hours that she had spent bucketing about North Portugal in the Land-Rover. Never had she so much craved a solid twelve hours' sleep; but before settling into bed she took steps both for and against this. *For,* she swallowed some Seconal with a gulp of water from the Victorian tumbler, exquisitely engraved with vine-leaves, on her washstand—which like the Major's had a marble top; *against,* she set her little American folding alarm-clock on the bed-side table to ring its pretty but persistent chime for 7:30. "Good God! Only five hours!" she muttered with a glance at the tiny luminous face, as she snuggled down to sleep.

At Gralheira Father Antal had taken to saying Mass in the chapel at 8:30, just after Dom Pedro, the chaplain; the Monsignor said his rather later. Julia, roused by her little Travalarm, pealed her bell for Manoela, the housemaid who attended on her, demanded her morning tea *pronto,* drank it thankfully, and was dressed and waiting on the landing outside the chapel in time to catch the Hungarian priest before he went into the little sacristy, with its carved rococo vestment-cupboards, to vest himself for Mass.

"Dom Francisco, just one moment," she said, gesturing away one of the men-servants, who took it in turns, eagerly, to serve Mass for these eminent foreign divines.

"Oh, good morning, Miss Probyn. You are up early! Is there anything I can do for you?"

"Yes, Father, there is. I want you to pray like *mad* for Hetta Páloczy!"

He looked troubled.

"Why, please?"

"Come here." She led him a little way along the landing, out of earshot of the hovering footmen, and told him hurriedly of Hetta's disappearance and their fruitless pursuit. "So now we've completely lost track of her, and so have the Security Police; there's absolutely nothing we can do—God simply *must* take a hand," she said, with a direct earnestness which made the words far from irreverent.

"Thank you for telling me, my daughter. I will offer the Mass for her release. Pray yourself," he added as he went away.

"Oh, I will—for what *that's* worth," said Julia. She drew from her pocket a little black lace scarf, such as all women in Portugal carry in their handbags for use in church, twined it round her tawny-gold hair, and went and knelt down in the chapel. A moment later Dona Maria Francisca sidled in and knelt also, followed by Nanny and some of the maid-servants, among them the old kitchen crone, Maria do Carmo, whom the Duke had described as a tigress; several shabby-looking men with broken boots crept in too, escorted by Antonio, and knelt on the opposite side of the aisle—these Julia recognised, without surprise, to be some of the Duke's wayfaring guests who had passed the night in the hay-loft above the courtyard. At Gralheira not only food and lodgement, but Mass itself were available to the poorest traveller who desired it. How lovely that was, the girl thought, most unwonted tears suddenly filling her eyes. She glanced round at the pictures and small statues that made the chapel a treasure-house: the Grão Vasco Crucifixion over the main altar, and an enchanting Nativity by the same hand in the Lady-chapel on the right, the faces in both vividly alive; everywhere delicious polychrome sculptures of Our Lady and various saints, mostly dressed in the height of 18th-century fashion, but nevertheless possessing an unmistakable devotional tone that is all their own. The odd thought struck her: how idolatrous, how papistical, this beautiful rococo building and its rich ornaments would seem to thousands of people—to her low-church Aunt Ellen in Scotland for instance. But Aunt Ellen would not ever see those shabby poor men, with their cracked boots and their stubby chins, fingering their rosaries so devoutly just across the aisle from her. No, this was *real*, a reality that the normal Protestant world would never understand unless, like her, they could come and live with it.

The thought of Aunt Ellen reminded her of Mrs. Hathaway, always her poor aunt's mentor and stand-by in any emergency—she *must* ring her up the moment after breakfast.

A tiny silvery chime of bells, jangled by the footman-server kneeling at the altar steps, announced that Mass had begun; Father Antal in a wonderful faded chasuble of silvery rose brocade was saying the *Judica me*. Like everyone else Julia crossed herself, recalled her wandering thoughts, and began to pray. She was not a Catholic, she was just a very usual type of casual Anglican, who went to Church when she felt like it—because she was in Durham and the Cathedral was so beautiful or, elsewhere, because the singing would be good or the preacher interesting. She made her Communion at Christmas and Easter, because she always had; she lived a kind and generous life partly because she had a kind and generous nature, but even more because she was unconsciously drawing on an enormous bank-balance, so to speak, of inherited Christian traditions of living. But during her long sojourn with the Ericeiras she had got into the habit of attending Mass, and going up to the chapel after dinner to say the Rosary with Dona Maria Francisca, Nanny and Luzia—partly, again, out of a generous impulse not to separate herself from her pupil in anything; so this morning's proceedings were all perfectly familiar, and in her present distress on Hetta's account she found them deeply comforting.

When Father Antal went up to the altar to say the Introit there was a slight rustle and a tiny push beside Julia—Luzia had slipped into the pew. The Mass pursued its brief, majestic course—so stately, so impersonal, so overwhelming in its implications. After the dismissal Father Antal left the altar, and at the foot of the steps began the prayers "for the conversion of Russia"; Julia said them with unwonted fervour, realising as never before that under "Russia" were comprised all Communists, everywhere. As the priest left the chapel Luzia whispered to her—"It is frightful! I was too late to ask Dom Francisco to offer his Mass for Hetta. This idiotic Anna let me sleep. Now I suppose I must ask the Monsignor."

"Dom Francisco *did* offer it for her—I asked him to," Julia whispered back; she felt a curious gladness and relief as she told Luzia this. The girl's great grey eyes glowed under the black mantilla that shadowed her pale face.

"You did? Wonderful! How thankful I am!"

Emerging from the chapel with Luzia, out on the broad landing Julia heard a voice she knew coming up from the hall below—Richard's voice, talking his rather peculiar brand of Portuguese to someone; looking down over the carved walnut banisters she saw him in conversation with Elidio. Luzia saw him too, and shot down the three right-angled sections of the wide staircase like a rocket.

"Oh Atherley, she is lost! She is lost! We followed her, we tried to save her, but we failed!" She clung to his arm, her face more Medusa-like than ever, and more beautiful.

"Luzia! Luzia!" Dona Maria Francisca and Nanny, on the landing above, hissed vainly in reprobation, without producing the smallest effect; Julia was reminded irresistibly of geese by the roadside hissing at a high-powered car—laughing a little, she walked down the broad shallow stairs. Just as she reached the hall the Duke, disturbed by his daughter's high-pitched lamentations, came out from his study to see what was going on.

"Ah, Atherley, it is you. This is very pleasant—welcome to Gralheira! I hope you stay with us?" He turned to his daughter. "My child, must your greeting to a guest be to wail like an Irish peasant or a Chinese woman at a funeral? You make a most lamentable noise. I think you had better go and have your breakfast."

"Papa, I was only telling him"—Luzia began, when Townsend Waller walked in at the front door, and simultaneously Major Torrens appeared from the direction of the smoking-room. Meanwhile Father Antal, having divested himself, was proceeding calmly down the stairs in search of breakfast, which was normally served to him on a tray in the priests' study.

"Hullo, Atherley, you're very early!" Major Torrens said. "You must have been driving all night. Well don't accuse *me* any more of involving you in our affairs! You've bought it this time, coming up—" He broke off suddenly at the sight of Richard's stricken face; but not soon enough to forestall Luzia, who said brusquely—"Major! You are being tactless!" While the Duke stared in amazement at this unwonted behaviour on the part of his offspring, and Julia stifled unseasonable laughter—even as she tried to think of some remark to tide over the awkward little pause which followed Luzia's words—yet another figure appeared in the hall: the rather portly soutaned shape of Monsignor Subercaseaux.

"Good morning, good morning! My dear Duke, good morning to you!" He glanced about him. "Quite an assembly—*both* our young ladies! And Atherley! *Mon cher,* this is an unexpected pleasure! When did you arrive?" Then his eye lighted on the American. "Monsieur Waller, too! —how very pleasant." He shook hands. "My dear Duke, are you giving a breakfast-party, or what?"

The Duke of Ericeira was exceptionally well able to deal with such situations. "Come into my study a moment, Monsignor," he said. There he explained the events of the evening before. Subercaseaux, who like Father Antal and everyone else had only been told that Luzia and her companions had been "delayed," was horrified.

"This child in the hands of the Communists! But this is frightful. What is being done? Does Colonel Marques know?"

"Colonel Marques?"

"The Head of the Security Police. Oh yes, Major Torrens will certainly have told him. But this is an appalling thing! How could it happen?"

"Major Torrens will be able to tell you that," the Duke said. "But it seems that Monsieur Atherley is greatly attached to the young lady, and his feelings need to be spared. The American, too, is apparently devoted to her, and feels to blame. And now I think I must rejoin my guests."

"And I will go and say my Mass." Chastened in a way most unusual for him, Mgr Subercaseaux left the study and went slowly up the staircase towards the chapel.

His rather unfortunate little joke about a breakfast-party had inspired Julia to more drastic action than she usually took in the Ericeira household. Nanny and Dona Maria had stopped hissing like geese on the upper landing, and vanished; she sent Luzia up after them, then rang the bell and gave some orders to Elidio. When her host re-appeared she muttered to him in an aside—"Duke, I hope I haven't done wrong, but I told Elidio to order breakfast for all these people, to save time. Poor Atherley must be starving, he's been driving all night; and I'm sure Mr. Waller usually eats a steak in the morning! All right?"

The Duke laughed, with his usual appreciation of this lively sensible young woman.

"Perfectly right. What a comfort you always are, Miss Probyn! But I am not sure that there is beef-steak, properly hung, in the house," he added seriously.

"Oh, hang his steak!—I mean bother it!" Julia said briskly. "I said tomato omelettes all round, in the morning-room; then we shan't interfere with all Elidio's fusses over flowers and polishing in the dining-room."

To her great surprise the middle-aged man bent and kissed her hand.

"No congratulations will be sufficient for the man who becomes your husband!" he pronounced.

"Dear Duke, you really are a poppet!" said Julia, touched by this praise. (Several hours later the Duke, in his study, consulted an Anglo-French and an Anglo-Portuguese dictionary for the meaning of the word "poppet"; since both described it as some form of doll, he was left mystified.)

Richard Atherley was in torture over the whole business. Ever since Torrens had telephoned to him the morning before he had recognised that he was responsible for Hetta's having gone off with the American —he, and he alone; and the quite hideous outcome, though it could not have been foreseen, was his fault. On the long drive up, first through waning moonshine, then through the sweet-smelling Portuguese dark, the young man had spent those hours of solitude doing what Housman has perhaps described better than anyone else:

> I took my question to the shrine
>   that has not ceased from speaking,
> The heart within that tells the truth,
>   and tells it twice as plain.

—and his heart had told him, with loud and piercing distinctness, that whatever her mistakes and her gaucheries, for him henceforward it was Hetta, only and always; and that unless she was somehow restored to them he would have lost the person who meant more to him than anything else in the world. A frantic impulse of remorse had sent him off in the middle of the night in one of the Chancery cars, leaving a cryptic and abjectly apologetic note for the Ambassador with the night-watchman; by daylight, over breakfast at Gralheira, he realised plainly enough that he had made a fool of himself. What could he hope to achieve that would not be better done by Colonel Marques or Torrens?—or indeed, it seemed, by Luzia? These reflections left him with an extreme consciousness of his own folly and misery, and a great desire to unburden himself to someone. For this last purpose who could be more desirable than Mgr Subercaseaux?—and the instant they rose from the table he asked the priest if he could spare him a few minutes?

"But of course, my dear young friend. Shall we walk in the garden? —the sun shines."

French windows led from several of the groundfloor rooms into the knot-garden; stepping out, they walked there. For years afterwards any sense of shame or embarrassment would bring back to Atherley, quite unbidden, a picture of dark geometrical patterns on a pale ground, so deeply were the close-clipped shapes of the tiny box hedges burnt into his mind that morning during his talk with the priest.

"Monsignor, I want to tell you—I—in fact this is all my fault," the young man began, with none of his usual aplomb.

"You wish to explain to me why Countess Hetta made this journey with Monsieur Waller rather than with you?" Subercaseaux asked as Richard paused.

The young man stared.

"You know, then?"

"No, I deduce. Did she ask you to bring her here?"

"Yes, and really I wished nothing more than to do so; but she happened to suggest it at—at an awkward moment. I said I would telephone to her later, but when I tried she was not taking any calls."

"This was when?"

"Sunday evening."

"Had Madame de Vermeil arrived?"

Richard stared again—then, in spite of his distress, he gave one of his baying laughs.

"Monsignor, there is no end to you! Yes, she had; in fact they met at the Pretender's, at luncheon."

"Ah, that explains much. I expect this detestable Fanny—I am sorry, my dear Richard, but to be honest with you I do really regard this person as one of the most pernicious of creatures!—did or said something perfectly hideous to that poor child. And then she asked you to bring her up here, and you temporised? Is that it?"

"Yes, that was it." He kept his eyes on the box hedges. "She said she would make her own arrangements," he said wretchedly. "Well we know what those were, and what they have led to! I would give *anything* that it hadn't happened; I could kill myself!"

"More practical is to decide, finally and definitively, which of these two ladies you now propose to pursue," Subercaseaux said, with elegant severity.

"Hetta! I've broken with Fanny. She doesn't believe it yet, but it's true."

"She will find plenty of consolations, believe me," the priest said sardonically. "But if—when—" he sighed and looked distressed. "If and when you are able to renew your addresses to Countess Hetta," he went on, "I think you should realise that there must be no sentimental harking back, in fact no outside flirtations at all. This young girl is not the sort of person either to understand that kind of thing, or to tolerate it."

"I know she isn't," Richard said humbly. "And honestly, Monsignor, I didn't start it this time. I had no idea, even, that Madame de Vermeil was coming to Lisbon till she turned up at my house on Sunday evening. That was the damnable part of it."

"Damnable is indeed the word, especially for this poor child, in the event," the Monsignor said. He could guess at the details of the "awkward moment." "But can you explain one thing to me—how came the American to let her out of his sight?"

"That was my fault too," Richard said miserably. "He was with us the night Miss Probyn's car was crashed, and I promised to tell him what it was all about—or at least enough to make him careful; but what with one thing and another I never did. He isn't in the least to blame."

"I see—no."

A little silence fell, as they walked to and fro in the strong sunlight.

"If only there were something one could *do!*" Richard broke out.

"You could pray, of course, if you have that habit." Richard shook his head. The priest looked at him quizzically.

"Of course if you were a Catholic I could give you a swingeing penance," he said. "That would do you all the good in the world. But for a Protestant penitent, who doesn't even pray, I hardly know what to prescribe! I suggest that you go and do something to distract poor Mr. Waller—play billiards with him, or take him for a walk. Not in the least as a penance, he is too nice. And when you are alone—" he paused.

"Yes?"

"Reflect long and carefully on what your relations are to be with Countess Hetta, if by God's mercy she is restored to her friends, and to you. If you were to marry her, both her integrity and her naïveté would irritate you twenty times a week! Spend this time of suspense and distress in asking your heart whether you can school yourself to abide that with patience, and with *sweetness*; if you cannot, leave her alone."

He turned away and went into the house.

When the breakfast-party broke up Julia had gone first to find Dona Maria Francisca, and make her apologies both for returning so late, and for keeping Luzia out. Then, at last, the girl felt free to do what had been at the back of her mind all the morning, namely to ring up Mrs. Hathaway in Lisbon. They had so tormented the Duke with all their telephoning the previous day that she went straight to that inconvenient instrument by the pantry, and put through a call to the Hotel Lucrezia; she lit a cigarette and waited, perched on a case of wine. When the call came through she demanded Mrs. Hathaway, and presently heard that familiar voice.

"Darling Mrs. H., there you are at last! I only got your letter up here yesterday afternoon, just as I was going out; I meant to ring you up last night, but we didn't get back till one o'clock this morning. I am so sorry. How are you? Is the pub all right? I do wish I hadn't been away."

Mrs. Hathaway replied, cheerfully, that she was quite all right, and the hotel charming; also she had been astonished to see how *red* Portugal looked from the air—"like Devon—quite extraordinary!" Then as usual she brushed aside her own concerns to enquire into Julia's. "Dearest child, what *were* you doing, out till 1 A.M.? A ball? Was it fun?"

"No, it wasn't a ball, and it wasn't fun," Julia said sombrely. "I can't tell you properly now, but a quite darling girl has been carried off by perfectly *deadly* people, and we were chasing after her. You can probably guess for yourself who the deadliest people in the world are today! —well it's them, and we're all in agony till we get her back. I don't know when I can come down, Mrs. H. dear, with this going on."

"Was she carried off in a car?" Mrs. Hathaway asked sharply.

"Yes," Julia said a little surprised. "Why?" It wasn't like Mrs. Hathaway to ask futile questions.

"She isn't short and dark?—and her initials P.H. or H.P.?" Mrs. Hathaway pursued very briskly.

Julia was utterly amazed.

"Yes—yes to both. But how on earth do *you* know this?"

"I've got her here in my room in the hotel, at least I think it must be her. *Exquisite* H. and P. monograms on all her underclothes! The Doctor thinks she's been drugged, but he gave her an injection, and we've *poured* black coffee into her, and now she seems to be sleeping it off fairly naturally. There's a policeman outside my door, too, and another at the front door; they seem quite concerned about it."

"But why is she with you?" Julia asked weakly.

"Because when the car she was in rammed my taxi and we all got out, I saw her lying in the back, with a gag in her mouth, and I was worried. I *peeped*, you see," said Mrs. Hathaway, in a satisfied voice. "So I got them to let me have her carried up to my room in the hotel, and made that nice police official, who speaks such *good* English, get a doctor. I really couldn't let her be left to the police."

"Well!" said Julia—all other words failed her.

"Oh, here's the police officer again—I think I must ring off," Mrs. Hathaway said. "I'll ring you up later."

"No, *wait*, for goodness sake!" Julia protested. "I must—"

But Mrs. Hathaway, implacably, had rung off.

Julia sank down again on the wine-case. After a moment she got up. "Hugh must hear this," she murmured as she walked towards the hall; and then, "How *like* Mrs. H.!" She was all astray, between relief, astonishment, and uncertainty; but Colonel Marques could soon settle whether it *was* or was not Hetta Páloczy whom Mrs. Hathaway was, so improbably, nursing in her room in the Lucrezia.

"Anyhow if it *is* her, that's Father Antal's Mass," Julia said out loud, as she stepped into the hall.

Chapter Fourteen

MRS. HATHAWAY, descending from the sky at Portela airport on that Monday afternoon, soon registered that her young friend Julia Probyn, at whose instance she had decided to visit Portugal at all, was not there to meet her. Resigned and calm, she submitted quietly to the inquisitions of the Portuguese Customs, and presently, by air-line bus and taxi, found herself at the hotel recommended by Mr. Consett. There she lay down and rested in the double-bedded room which the management, untruthfully, said was all they had free; later she took a bath, and went down and had a very good dinner. Afterwards she caused the hall-porter to ring up the Ericeira Palace—which created a great impression—and learned that the Duke with all his party had left for Gralheira two days before. Still resigned, she decided to start looking at Lisbon by herself, and told the porter to order a taxi to be at the hotel at 9:15 next morning to take her to Belém to see the Tower, the Jeronimos Church, and the Museum of the Coaches; she also ordered *petit déjeuner* for half-past eight. Then she went to bed, and slept the sleep of the just and the sensible.

The taxi was a little late, and Mrs. Hathaway first bought a camellia from a man on the pavement with a tray of them for what seemed to her nothing, and then stood at the door of the hotel watching with interest the brisk morning bustle of traffic in the street: cars and taxis shooting by in the bright sunshine, women in black mantillas returning from Mass, and, what completely charmed her, the *varinhas*, the women fish-sellers, striding up barefoot from the river-side markets with shallow oval baskets of fish balanced on their heads, their shoes perched casually on top of the fish. The Lisbon City Fathers wage an unequal contest with the *varinhas* over this matter of shoes: they hold that barefooted women in the streets of a capital create an impression of poverty and backwardness, and insist on shoes; the fishwives, who have always walked barefoot and prefer it—and anyhow how much more economical!—conform to the point of having shoes with them; but they habitually carry these objects not on their feet but on the fish, a charming piece of individualism in our regimented modern world.

When the taxi finally arrived the hall-porter handed Mrs. Hathaway into it with the deference due to someone who telephoned to the Duke of Ericeira's, gave the requisite instructions to the driver, and slammed the door; Mrs. Hathaway drove off, full of the happy anticipation of the intelligent sightseer in a strange city on a fine morning.

She did not get very far. Less than a hundred yards from the door of the hotel a large grey car, shooting out of a side turning, collided with her taxi; both vehicles were slewed round sideways by the force of the impact and came to a halt, partly blocking the steep and crowded street. Three men in grey overcoats leapt out of the car, cursing and gesticulating at their driver—their fury surprised Mrs. Hathaway; her taxi-man got out too and examined the damage, shrugging his shoulders phlegmatically. Cars started to hoot angrily; a little crowd gathered round the accident, and a small, neatly-uniformed policeman came up and began to ask questions.

It was at this point that Mrs. Hathaway, realising that she would certainly not reach Belém in this particular taxi, got out of it. The calm demeanour of the little policeman impressed her, but she was struck afresh by the fury, almost desperation, of the three men when the policeman produced a note-book and began, obviously, to demand names and addresses, while two more of his colleagues appeared from nowhere. It was probably this curious display of emotion, combined with her natural curiosity, which caused the good lady to "peep" into the other car; there to her immense astonishment she saw, lying across the back seat, what she at first took to be the corpse of a young girl, white and motionless.

After that there was of course no holding Mrs. Hathaway. She opened the door to examine this corpse more closely; took a wrist and felt a very faint pulse—moreover, she then noticed, projecting from one corner of the pallid lips, a piece of material. Rather gingerly she pulled at it; the lax jaws allowed her to draw out a sizeable piece of some rough, coarse, rather dirty rag, sodden and disgusting. Mrs. Hathaway stared at it incredulously; then quietly put it in her handbag, from which at the same time she drew out her Portuguese phrase-book, and stood for a moment ruffling the pages, looking for words which would enable her to say—

"There is a young lady who has been gagged in this *automóvel*." Unfortunately phrase-books seldom contain information of that sort, and after a few seconds of fruitless search Mrs. Hathaway decided to rely on English and on herself, and went to tackle the policeman.

By now the crowd had concentrated round this worthy, his colleagues, and the three furious men in the grey overcoats; the group was joined by an elegant slender man in a green uniform at the very moment when Mrs. Hathaway, tall, grey-haired and imposing, lifted up her voice and said—"Does anyone here speak English?"

"I do, Madame," said the man in green. "Can I help you? Or you have information to offer?"

"Yes, a little information. But I think you should put those three men under control immediately—the ones in grey."

Police in all countries, but especially in the Latin ones, make a regular practice of stalling in any emergency; as she spoke Mrs. Hathaway saw incredulity appear on the face of the official in green.

"Oh very well; never mind. Just come here"—and taking the elegant man by his green elbow she propelled him firmly towards the grey car and opened the door. "Look there." While he stared in at the helpless form on the back seat Mrs. Hathaway opened her handbag and drew out the piece of rag. "Please look at this, too," she said—"I myself pulled it out of her mouth not two minutes ago."

The official in green picked the horrid object up in gloved fingers, and examined it.

"You say this was in her mouth?"

"Yes. I saw it and pulled it out. My taxi was run into by this car," Mrs. Hathaway stated in explanation, "and I thought the behaviour of the men in it so very odd that I looked and found this girl—gagged. To *me* it seems rather abnormal; but of course I am a stranger to Portugal."

The man threw her a shrewd glance.

"This is abnormal in Portugal also, Madame, believe me," he said.

"Well, what are you going to do? Oughtn't she to have attention? She's alive, I felt her pulse; but I think she's very ill. Can't I take her into my hotel and look after her while you make your enquiries? I think a doctor should see her."

Mrs. Hathaway saw the expression of official obstructiveness reappear in the man's face.

"Where is your hotel, Madame?" he asked.

"The Lucrezia—it's just up there."

"This young lady is known to you?"

"Not in the least! I've just found her. But she's ill, and needs help. Isn't that sufficient?"

"Your charity does you credit, Madame," the man in green said smoothly, still stalling. "But this is obviously a case for police enquiries and the utmost caution; and frankly, I have no idea who you are."

"Of course not," Mrs. Hathaway replied, as smoothly as he. She took her passport from her bag and handed it to him. "Naturally this tells you nothing but that I am an English visitor," she pursued, still smoothly. "If you want further credentials I suggest that you ring up Gralheira, the Duke of Ericeira's country-house; my friend Miss Probyn, who is staying there at present, can tell you all about me—I have come to Portugal at her invitation."

This told, Mrs. Hathaway saw the green-clad official prick up his ears at the mention of the Duke's name, though he said nothing except to ask how to spell PROBYN while he jotted down notes in a pocket-book.

"Thank you, Madame," he said politely. "This shall be done."

"Yes, but what about this poor girl? You can't just leave her lying in a car in the street while you telephone; it's monstrous! Do let us get her into bed, and call a doctor. I certainly shall not run away, and she *can't*."

Mrs. Hathaway's mixture of common sense and imperiousness might have prevailed anyhow; combined with the Ericeira connection they did —though slowly. The official summoned yet another policeman to watch over the grey car, and invited Mrs. Hathaway to wait in it, which she did; he asked for her room-number at the hotel, and went away. From the car window Mrs. Hathaway saw the three men in grey being led off in custody; then she waited. At last a stretcher was brought and the unconscious girl placed on it and carried to the Lucrezia, accompanied by the man in the green uniform and Mrs. Hathaway; she noticed that a policeman now stood at the entrance to the hotel, and when they reached her bedroom another was standing outside the door.

"Oh, excellent," Mrs. Hathaway said. "Will he stay?"

"Yes, he will stay," the official replied, with the hint of a smile.

Mrs. Hathaway had the unknown girl placed on her own bed. "I *know* this is aired," she said. "Can you arrange to have a doctor sent immediately?"

"I will. And will you, Madame, be on the look out for any marks or labels which might identify this young lady?—and if she speaks note down what she says?"

"Of course. The Doctor must speak *French*," Mrs. Hathaway added firmly. "I know no Portuguese."

"He shall," the official said, now smiling openly. "Au revoir, Madame; I shall return soon."

One of the Portuguese words Mrs. Hathaway had carefully memorised on the plane was *boracha*, which means hot-water bottle; she used it freely now, while she took off the girl's overcoat and suit and removed her shoes, stockings, and suspender-belt; and soon several *borachas*, carefully wrapped in towels, had been disposed all round the figure in the bed. It was during these operations that Mrs. Hathaway's attention was caught by the beauty of the monograms with H.P. on the delicate underclothes. She had only just finished when the doctor arrived, a tall man with an intelligent square face who spoke, not French, but extremely good English. He felt the pulse, lifted the eyelids, put a stethoscope to the heart, and turned to Mrs. Hathaway.

"Drugged!" he pronounced.

"What with?"

"I don't know." He drew back the bed-clothes again, examined the bare arms, and showed a tiny pink spot to Mrs. Hathaway. "An injection here, do you see?"

"Well, what do I do?"

"You order black coffee, very strong, and when it comes make her drink it. I will give an injection; I am guessing, but it is probably a barbiturate."

While the doctor prepared his injection Mrs. Hathaway rang the bell; when a servant appeared she said, "Doctor, will you order the coffee? They may not understand me." The doctor gabbled vigorously in Portuguese, and then asked Mrs. Hathaway to turn the helpless body onto its side—she did so, and he jabbed a needle into the buttock; then he turned the girl back onto the pillows and washed his instruments. As he was finishing the coffee appeared, brought by a waiter. Mrs. Hathaway tasted it.

"Yes, that's quite strong, but I shall want someone to hold her up while I get it down," she said. "Will you have a chambermaid sent, please?"

Like the police official, the doctor smiled.

"Madame, you are a hospital in yourself! Perhaps you have nursing training?"

"Certainly not—just common sense," said Mrs. Hathaway rather repressively, as she pushed the bell. When it was answered the doctor demanded the manager, and on his appearing, nervous and troubled by all these goings-on, the doctor asked him to send "a strong and discreet" chambermaid, to assist the Senhora Inglesa in carrying out his treatment. "Let her bring a small basin," he added. Then he bowed over Mrs. Hathaway's hand.

"I shall return in an hour or two, but continue with the coffee; give it over and over again," he said. "It is the best of all antidotes. If she is sick, so much the better—that will help to clear off the poison."

Only those who have actually undergone the experience of trying to restore a drugged person to life—fortunately they are few—can realise what Mrs. Hathaway now went through. To begin with it was all quite new to her—far more than the doctor she was "guessing"—and moreover she had to carry out this unwonted task labouring under the terrible sense of helplessness engendered by being in a country where one cannot speak the language, a thing quite extraordinarily defeating. When an elderly chambermaid with a severe and rather negroid face appeared, carrying a small enamel bowl, Mrs. Hathaway had to indicate to her by signs that they must lift the inert figure up to drink the coffee, which she had already cooled in the wash-basin; but an unconscious person is astonishingly heavy and clumsy to handle, and though when Mrs. Hathaway pushed the flaccid lips open and held the cup to them the girl gulped and swallowed automatically, a lot was spilt—the maid clucked in dismay at the dirtied sheets.

"Bring the bath-towel," Mrs. Hathaway said, but of course the woman didn't understand; she went and fetched it herself, but by the time she returned to the bed the flabby body had collapsed again. Patiently Mrs. Hathaway heaved it up once more and placed the maid's hands under the clammy armpits—"Hold her *so*," she said, with an emphasis which transcended language, while she spread the bath-towel in front of the girl and placed a soft shawl over her bare shoulders. Then she applied the cup again.

They kept on at it for what seemed like an eternity to Mrs. Hathaway. Before the first lot of coffee was exhausted she sent for another; half-way through the second brew the girl was sick—Mrs. Hathaway held out the basin almost in time, but not quite; the maid clucked again, but very intelligently hustled out and returned with fresh bath-towels, shortly followed by a waiter with yet more coffee. So they went on: the girl gulping down, being sick, gulping down again. At last the vomiting ceased, and it seemed to Mrs. Hathaway that the swallowing was performed more consciously; still guessing, she decided that they had done enough for the moment, and shook her head when the chambermaid held out the coffee-tray questioningly. The pulse seemed to her stronger; quite definitely the hands were getting warm, and that chilly perspiration had stopped. She put another blanket over the girl, and drawing an arm-chair up to the bed sat down in it; she suddenly felt extraordinarily tired.

But she had only been resting for five minutes when she was summoned by a page to the telephone. The Hotel Lucrezia has one of these on each landing, and edging out past the small policeman Mrs. Hatha-way took the call from Julia Probyn already recorded; in the middle of it the official in green re-appeared, and Mrs. Hathaway, ignoring Julia's protests, rang off.

"How is she?" he asked.

"Better, I think. Come in," Mrs. Hathaway said, once more by-passing the policeman, who raised his hand in salute to the officer.

"She has not spoken?" the man said, after glancing at the figure on the bed.

"No—and as she seems to be sleeping fairly naturally I think she should be left alone. But I rather *think*, from what I heard on the telephone just now, that she was abducted by Communists."

The official suddenly became very alert.

"May I know to whom you were telephoning?"

"I wasn't, at all. My friend Miss Probyn rang me up from Gralheira. But she said that they had been out half the night chasing after a girl who had been carried off by Communists; so I asked if she was short and dark, and whether her initials were H. and P.? And Miss Probyn said she was, and they were," Mrs. Hathaway said, not very lucidly.

"These are the initials, H.P.?"

"Yes, they're on all her underclothes."

"No papers in her pockets?"

"Oh really, Senhor, I didn't look," Mrs. Hathaway protested. "I have been trying to revive her! I'm not a detective! Do by all means search her clothes yourself."

The official slid a practised hand into the pockets of M. Lilas's trim little suit and the pretty matching overcoat, and drew out a rather grubby handkerchief, and a tiny copy of St. Thomas à Kempis; the hanky bore the monogram H.P., and on the fly-leaf of *The Imitation of Christ* was written—"P.H. from H.A., Easter, 1953."

"So!" the green-clad official said, thoughtfully. "H.A.—or A.H., perhaps. The other initials are reversed also." He put the little book in his pocket. "Please excuse me if I leave you now. I must make a report."

"*No*," Mrs. Hathaway said firmly. "I see you have learned something. Do *you* think that this is the girl Miss Probyn was hunting for last night? If so I think you ought to tell me what you found out?"

At this the green-clad official laughed out loud.

"Madame, you are *impayable!* In strict confidence I may tell you that we believe the three men we hold to be what you suspect."

"And my patient? What does H.A. or A.H. tell you? Something, I can see."

But here the man in green was firm.

"Madame, I am sorry that I can really tell you no more at present. But I am most grateful for what you have done. If the young lady becomes sufficiently conscious to speak, please ask her her name and anything she can tell you of what happened to her—especially as to whether she was questioned, and revealed any facts under pressure. This could be of the utmost importance, and the sooner we know it the better." He drew out a small card on which was printed—

"T. Soubrinho de Almeida." On this he scribbled a telephone number, and handed it to Mrs. Hathaway.

"If you will have this number rung up and mention my name, I or another officer who speaks English will come round immediately. But I cannot impress on you sufficiently that the very greatest discretion is essential. As you see, I am reposing great confidence in you," he ended, and bowed and went away.

Mrs. Hathaway returned to her chair by the bed. She asked the grim chambermaid her name—most unsuitably, it was Flora—and indicated by signs that she would ring four times if she wanted any more assistance; the woman departed, and Mrs. Hathaway sat reflecting on what she had just heard. The man in the green uniform certainly knew more than he was willing to say. Well quite soon she must ring Julia up again—she had promised to—and then she might learn more; but she would rest a little first. That struggle to get the coffee down had been quite exhausting; it was so *tiresome*, how fatigue got the better of one as one grew older. Thinking how tiresome old age and fatigue were, Mrs. Hathaway, in her armchair, fell into a doze.

When Julia Probyn got up off the wine-case outside the pantry at Gralheira her first intention had been to tell Major Torrens what she had heard, but in the hall she changed her mind and went along the corridor to the priests' study. To relieve Father Antal's anxiety was more important than anything else; if the girl in Mrs. Hathaway's room *was* Hetta she was safe anyhow, with the indomitable Mrs. H. in charge, and English-speaking police officers—damn the man, turning up just then!—popping in and out.

Father Antal was alone. The Monsignor was still giving Atherley the treatment out in the knot-garden; beyond the high windows their figures could be seen passing to and fro. The old Hungarian was sitting at the table, his head sunk in his hands; he raised it as Julia came in.

"Dom Francisco, I think it's *almost* certain that she's safe!" Julia said, going over to him.

He got up, slowly.

"Why 'almost,' my child?" he asked, rather heavily.

Julia told him all that Mrs. Hathaway had said, and asked, and how their conversation had been interrupted.

"Drugged, and cannot speak!—poor soul, whoever she is. And who is this lady who so charitably took her in?"

"The best person in the world! She's been all the mother I've had since my own mother died."

He considered. "Still, it is not sure," he said at length.

"Dear Dom Francisco" (Julia automatically used the agreed name) "don't you think it *is* pretty sure? Granted that there might easily be two, or even three short dark girls in Portugal who have H.P. embroidered on their underclothes, would any of them but Hetti be likely to be found drugged and gagged in a car? I don't see how it *can* be anyone but her."

He smiled at her conviction.

"You have made a good point. Yes, I believe I agree. Let us give thanks to God."

"Oh, I do!—or rather I will in a minute, when I've told Major Torrens. I just wanted to let you know, Father dear." She hurried away.

The smoking-room at Gralheira was an apartment seldom used except on the rare occasions when the Duke entertained a shooting-party, and Torrens had more or less appropriated it to his own use. As Julia went in at the door Atherley was in the act of entering by the French window; in obedience to the Monsignor's instructions he had come in search of Townsend Waller. Townsend was not there. "He went out," the Major told Richard.

"All right, I'll go and find him."

"No, wait, Richard—you'd better hear this too," Julia said.

"Don't say you have some news?" Torrens asked.

"Well, near-news, anyhow." She recounted what she had heard on the telephone. Richard said, "Oh, thank God!"—the Major, like Father Antal, asked who on earth Mrs. Hathaway was?

"Oh, a darling—and just the sort of person who *would* go and look in the other car when she'd been crashed in an accident!" Julia said.

"Well, whatever it's worth, I think the Colonel ought to hear it," Torrens said temperately.

"Let's find out first if the poor Duque is in his study." Julia rang the bell as she spoke. Elidio, who answered it, said that His Excellency was gone out to the vineyards to examine the vines.

"*Muito bem, Elidio—muito obrigada.* All right; he's out," she said.

"*Which* of these accursed machines gets the exchange?" Torrens asked gloomily, surveying the array of telephones on the Duke's desk with distaste.

"Well really, Hugh, by now you ought to remember that much!" Julia said laughing—her own conviction that Hetta was safe had put her into the highest spirits. "Second from the right."

It was getting on for noon when Major Torrens got through to Colonel Marques. He made a guarded beginning: "I think perhaps we have some news of the lost lady." The Colonel interrupted him.

"Oh, the little identifier! Yes, I know," he said breezily. "She is in the care of this admirable lady, who nevertheless did not think to look in her pockets! One of my men did so, however; he found a book with an inscription which I think makes the matter certain—but to leave nothing to chance I have sent a car to fetch the maid-servant from a certain place, to make the identification absolute."

Torrens asked about the men who were with "the identifier" when the so lucky accident took place. The Colonel was still breezy.

"Just the ones we wanted, and expected!—three. We are holding them; their papers are not quite in order!" Torrens could hear the pleasure in the Colonel's tones. "But one is missing; the principal, I am afraid. I must ask you not to relax *any* precautions; after all, the little person in question was only a means to an end, and the *end* is still with you. I will ring you up again when the identification is confirmed; in the meantime I must ask you to be very watchful." He rang off.

Torrens had just begun to retail all this to Atherley and Julia when the Duke walked in with Luzia. He was delighted at the news of Hetta Páloczy's almost certain safety, and fascinated by Julia's account of her rescue. "But this must be a most remarkable lady!"

"Oh, she is!" Julia responded. Torrens however was particularly concerned to impress on his hearers what Colonel Marques had said about the escape of "the principal," and the importance of relaxing no precautions; he did so at some length. Atherley saw Luzia listening to this intently, her grey eyes very wide.

"Yes yes, of course we will continue to observe all our rules," the Duke was saying a little impatiently when Dona Maria Francisca sidled in—her manner of entering a room always gave the impression that she felt it immodest to walk straight forwards. "Yes, *ma chère?*" her brother asked.

"I only came to enquire—I hear there has been telephoning—whether we are to expect the young Countess today?"

"No, not today, my dear sister. I will advise you of her advent in good time."

Dona Maria Francisca looked disapproving; she muttered something about the notice yesterday having been very short, and when the room was prepared, after all no one came.

"Yes, the American came," Luzia piped up. "And now also Atherley!" —looking with great satisfaction at Richard, who grinned back at her. Luzia was a source of endless pleasure to him.

When Dona Maria Francisca sidled out again she took the reluctant girl with her. Before the door closed they heard Luzia's voice from the hall—"Go in, go in; there is good news; she is safe!"—and Townsend Waller appeared.

"Is it really all right to come in, Duke?" he asked apologetically. "And it is true that the little Countess is safe?"

Torrens told him that it was almost certainly true, and how it had come about.

"But it's not a hundred per cent certain yet?" the American asked doubtfully.

"*Yes,* Townsend, it really *is* a hundred per cent," Julia assured him. "It's only a police fuss, sending for the maid. Don't worry."

The Duke was pursuing a train of thought of his own.

"As soon as the young lady is well enough to travel, should she not come here?"

Before anyone else could answer, Atherley said, "Yes, Sir; she ought to come as soon as possible." He was still acutely conscious of his own responsibility for Hetta's misadventure. "The whole reason for her making this expedition at all was to see Father A."—he checked himself.

Townsend stared at him in bewilderment.

"Father A.? Who's he? She never said a word about any Father; she just said she was upset about something, and to take her mind off it she wanted to see the North, and to call on some friends."

Julia intervened.

"She was only being discreet, Townsend," she said with kindness. "People get to be, you know, when they live under the Communists. But the friend she *most* wanted to visit up here was one of the two priests you saw at breakfast."

"Not Subercaseaux, for goodness sake!" the Bostonian exploded incredulously.

"No, the other one," Julia said. She turned to the Duke.

"When Hetta is better, since you are so kind, we can arrange for her to come up. Now we'll stop invading your study! Come on," she said to the three men. "Let's go and put Townsend properly in the picture—it's high time."

This briefing was conducted in the smoking-room. Julia took upon herself to expound to Mr. Waller how Father Antal had been got out of Hungary, and the necessity for his having ample opportunity to report to Rome through Mgr Subercaseaux—"he's the Vatican contact, you see. Then Father Antal will go on to the States and do things there, broadcasting and so on." The mere name of the Vatican was slightly repugnant to Townsend Waller, who belonged to the straitest sect of the Unitarian Pharisees of New England, but he took the point all right.

"I remember seeing a cable about some high-powered agent who was to be got out of here by plane; our Security people were to send someone over to meet him, but I didn't register exactly when."

"Well the priest we're calling Dom Francisco *is* the high-powered agent," Torrens said; "and the escort will fly over to meet him when I tell my opposite number in your outfit that we're ready—he'll cable for him, and your Security man will be here in thirty-six hours."

Waller reflected for a moment or two.

"What I don't quite see is why you British are handling this here, if he's coming to the States, and being flown across by our people," he said then, looking rather straight at Torrens.

"I think I can tell you why, Townsend," Richard put in before the

Major could answer. "This is a small, but a very explosive operation where Europe is concerned, and one that has had to be organised hand-in-hand with the Catholic net-work over here. And though your Catholic net-work is much wider than ours, it's looser mesh!" He smiled very pleasantly at his friend. "As one Protestant to another, I expect you'd agree that European Catholics during these last years have become admirably security-minded—they've had to; the English ones of course have been ever since the days of Good Queen Bess! And security was Word Number One, in this."

Townsend looked a little uncertain.

"But is *he* a Catholic?" he asked, glancing at Torrens.

"No," Richard said, laughing. "But he's been working in with them now for a long time, and they know him. It was just a case of how to get the job done in the safest way. Maclean or no Maclean," he added with a grin.

Townsend, who was far from a fool, and moreover had the admirable quality of great honesty, took the point.

"I see," he said. "Yes, that makes sense." Suddenly he too grinned, ruefully and disarmingly. "Well seeing I was stupid enough to lose Countess Hetta, I suppose I must let you say what you like about wide mesh! But you never told me what it was all about, Richard, as you promised to; if you had, I wouldn't have been so careless."

"I know. I've told you I'm sorry about that," Richard said.

A gong boomed, the preliminary summons to luncheon. "Goodness, where's the morning gone?" Julia exclaimed, and went upstairs to attend to her face.

It was shortly after lunch that Mrs. Hathaway, as promised, rang up again; Julia took the call outside the pantry—"Oh, the inconvenience!" she muttered bitterly. The girl was now conscious, Mrs. Hathaway said; the doctor had been again, and said that she was quite all right.

"And has the servant been?—is she really who we thought?" Julia asked.

"Oh yes, there's no doubt about that; she *is* your friend."

"Is she fit to travel?"

"Oh, do you want her? The little fat man thought perhaps you might." (By the little fat man Julia guessed that Colonel Marques was meant.) "Not today, but tomorrow I think she could."

"Is she going back to her mother, or staying with you?"

"She will stay with me tonight anyhow. The fat man seemed to think it better, and of course I like having her; now she's awake, she's charming. But she seems very troubled about something she's said, or done—I wish I could get her mind off it."

This is it, Julia thought; she *has* given something away, poor little wretch. Down the telephone—"I couldn't speak to her, could I?" she asked. "Is she still in bed?"

"Oh no, she's up and dressed. I'll see. But this isn't a very *convenient* place—it's out on the landing, and there's that man at the door, and people going up and downstairs all the time. Wait a minute."

Even more inconvenient than here, Julia thought, grinning to herself, as she sat down again on the wine-case, the receiver at the full stretch of the flex held to her ear. There was a long pause. At last—

"Here she is," said Mrs. Hathaway's voice. "I'm sorry to have been so long, but the bobby—I'm sure you understand me—didn't want her to leave the room, or use the telephone. I got the manager to overpersuade him, but it took some time. I've told her not to use any names. Now!" And then Julia heard Hetti's rather deep voice saying—"Is it you?"

"Yes, darling. How good to hear you! Are you all right again?"

"Yes yes, quite all right. But oh Yulia, I am so miserable! I have done a terrible thing. Only I cannot tell you about it on the telephone."

"No no—for goodness sake don't try!" Julia said hastily. "I shall be seeing you very soon; either I'll come down, or you will come up. Do you understand?"

"Yes, I do. Is *he* still with you?"

"Of course. Tell Mrs. H. she will be rung up later about plans."

"Please? Mrs. Who?"

"Oh, the lady you're with, silly! Ask *her* her name!" Julia said impatiently—to her relief she heard Hetta laugh.

"She is an *angel!*" the girl said fervently.

"I know she is. Goodbye. Do exactly what she tells you, and don't worry."

"Yulia, I *must* worry! And please be so careful, because of what I have done."

"All right. Now you do what you're told! Bless you. Goodbye."

After ringing off Julia went at once in pursuit of Major Torrens. She had some difficulty in finding him. Richard, still anxious to implement the Monsignor's recommendation to do something to distract Townsend Waller had offered to take the American round that remarkable house, and Torrens had gone with them. She ran the party to earth at last in one of the huge salons, full of Boulle and Empire furniture; as she went in the Major was commenting in some astonishment on the fact that though the room contained seventeen armchairs there were only two table lamps, both heavily veiled in grey crêpe-de-chine. "How on earth do they *read?*" he asked.

"Oh, the women don't much; anyhow no one ever sits in here," Julia told him. "Listen, Hugh—Hetta's all right again, quite fit to come up tomorrow, so we must settle how to get her here. Should I go down in Richard's car?—if I might?"—glancing at Atherley.

The two young men broke into eager enquiries, which Julia answered rather brusquely. "Yes, *per*fectly all right; I spoke to her. But for goodness sake be quiet for a minute and let me settle this with Hugh." She pursued the thing with Torrens. "She's given something away, I gather."

"What?"

"Of course I wouldn't let her tell me. I presume simply that Father Antal is here—she begged me to be very careful. And I imagine, too, that by now the pavement outside the Lucrezia is stiff with Commie agents, disguised as camellia-sellers!" Julia ended, with vigour.

Torrens laughed. "We'd better consult the Colonel," he said. "Where's the Duke? Out, please God."

The Duke was out.

"Spilt some beans, has she?" the Colonel said, displaying his usual pleasure in using English slang. "Well no wonder. Was she tortured?" Torrens couldn't say. "In any case, you and her friends are much more likely than I am to find out what she *has* said, and it would be useful to know—*precisely*, please, if she can remember. But people under torture are apt to forget what they have said; it is part of the psychological blotting-out of distress."

Those words, so casually uttered, caused Major Torrens to shiver a little. He knew that Communists do use such methods, and merely said—

"The thing is how to get the person in question up here. Miss P. thought of going down to fetch her, in the car in which she brought me up."

"Oh, do not let her go to this trouble! Why not allow this admirable Englishwoman who succours her—and to whom we owe the fact that the young person was discovered so soon—to bring her up? I can supply a car and chauffeur, which will be closely followed by another car with my own men. No one knows the old lady by sight, and *la petite* can wear a veil, as she did at Portela. Can Miss P. arrange this at your end? I gather she is the contact for the Englishwoman."

"Hold on," Torrens said, and spoke to Julia.

"Of course. Lovely! The Duque will adore Mrs. H.—and so will you. Say *Yes*."

Chapter Fifteen

MAJOR TORRENS thankfully left it to Julia to organise the reception of these extra guests. How on earth, without her, could all this have been managed? A perfect hide-out, too, with those high walls all round the place. In the circumstances he did not worry over-much about what the poor wretched little Countess might have given away.

Julia took no immediate steps. The Duke was out on the farm, and Nanny usually had a shut-eye in the afternoon. She observed with amusement that both Hetta's admirers showed every sign of remaining where they were—"Oh very well!" she muttered to herself, as she went in search of Father Antal.

She found the dear old man in the priests' study, just about to set out for a walk; he looked rather like Hilaire Belloc, arrayed in an extraordinary cloak with a shoulder-cape and a broad-brimmed hat, produced by the Monsignor as chaplain-disguise; he had a breviary in his hand.

"Oh, you are going out?"

"Yes—will you not come too? It is a most beautiful day," he said, smiling on her.

"Well, just a little way—I have some good news for you," she said, stepping through the open French window. The sun stood high and hot over the knot-garden, bringing out the aromatic woody scent of the tiny box-bushes; men with rakes were smoothing the walks between them. "Let's go into the park," Julia suggested.

They descended by the flight of steps near the corner seat with the *azulejo* picture of the hunter being treed by a bear; as they walked over short pastures, where sheep were grazing, Julia told Father Antal that the girl at the Lucrezia was undoubtedly Hetta, that she was nearly recovered, and was coming up to Gralheira tomorrow. His delight at this news moved her a good deal. "Tell me more about Hetti, Father," she said.

He told her, obviously happy to be asked, how Hetta had come to his country presbytery as the protégée of the poor incompetent old nun, and how promptly and energetically the girl of sixteen had taken over the running of the house, the cooking, and all the dealings with people who came for help or advice when he was out. "This poor Mother Scholastica could seldom get a message right!—but Hetta always had everything clear for me. In no time at all it was the old religieuse who was really *her* protégée; but she never failed in showing her all deference and respect. This dear child followed so completely the example of our Blessed Lord —she 'took on her the form of a servant.' And so happily, and with obedience."

"That's funny—I can't see Hetti very obedient," Julia said.

"In one thing she was *not*," the priest replied, smiling reminiscently. "I could not stop her, in summer, from going to swim in the Tisza—in her night-dress! She went in the afternoons, when in the great heat there was no one about in the fields, but it was unsuitable; however, in this she would not be controlled. She had the passion for water of a little fish!"

Julia had begun to tell him of Hetta's swimming at the Guincho when suddenly Father Antal stood still and held up his hand, enjoining silence. "What is this sound?" he asked.

Julia listened too. "Oh, that's from the windmill," she said, now hearing the "clock, clock, clock, clock" that filled the sunny air. "Look, there it is, just over the wall."

They had reached the eastern boundary wall of the demesne; a narrow iron gate, heavily padlocked, led through into the open country outside, where the four blunt-ended sails of a whitewashed windmill revolved rhythmically, clock-ing at each revolution. Father Antal went and stared through the iron bars.

"Is this the mill of the miller whom they call The Blacksmith?" he asked.

"Yes," Julia said. "How on earth do you know that?"

"Luzia told me." He continued to peer through the bars. "Is this he, this old man who digs?" he asked.

Julia also looked through the gate. A rather bent figure, using the outsize hoe which in Portugal takes the place of a spade, was diligently turning up the reddish-brown soil. Europe is divided into the races which dig *away* from themselves, as in France and England, and those who dig *towards* themselves, as in Portugal.

"Yes, that's him."

"It is true—he does not look round as he digs," Father Antal said. "Luzia was quite right."

"She's usually right, about country things especially," Julia replied.

The sound of their voices did cause the miller to look round, not at his mill, but towards the gate; seeing Julia he waved.

"*Boas tardes!* (Good afternoon) *Minha Menina,*" he called.

"*Como estai, O Ferreiro?*" Julia called back. *Ferreiro* is the Portuguese word for blacksmith; the old man, grinning at this greeting, shouldered his heavy tool and walked over to the small gate, quite ready to break his toil with a little gossip. He asked who the priest was?

One of the Duke's chaplains from the house, Julia told him promptly, but foreign—he spoke no Portuguese. The miller expressed regret. "I could have wished to speak with him; he has the countenance of a saint." Not being able to converse with the saint he asked after Luzia, and then broke into a paean of her praises. "Ah, there is one who has all the loving-kindness of *a mãe* and the intelligence of *o pai.* A noble child!"

Julia translated this for Father Antal as they turned homewards: loving as her mother, intelligent as her father; she knew it would please him.

"Yes, she is a noble child," he said. After a moment's silence he asked suddenly—"How well do you know my little Hetta? Have you seen much of her?"

His train of thought was obvious to Julia—for him Hetta was another noble child.

"I haven't seen as much of her as I should have liked," she said. "What I have seen I like very much." This sounded cold and inadequate, and she added quickly—"I think she's intelligent, and brave, and very honest; perhaps too honest for her own comfort, let alone that of the people about her."

He laughed. "You are very right! How often I have seen this in my own house. She would give me, as I told you, a perfectly clear message from some peasant; but when I asked what she had said in reply, nine times out of ten her answer would be—"I told him not to be a fool, and not to bother you!"

Julia could hear Hetta saying it.

"And this young Englishman?" Father Antal pursued—"What is he like? Is he serious, good? You must know him well—I notice that you call him Richard."

"That means nothing. Everyone calls everyone Richard or whatever their name is, if they don't call them 'darling,'" Julia said rather impatiently. "I don't know him particularly well, though I've known him for some time. He's intelligent too, as you can see, and rather unusually open-minded for a diplomat, but I've no idea whether he's 'serious' or not; in fact I'm not sure that I know what you mean by serious. 'Sérieux,' in the French sense?"

"Yes."

"Well no, I shouldn't have thought he was; rather *volage,* really. But I do think he's seriously in love with Hetta—I suspect for the first time in his life! Funny, isn't it? Because I imagine his other affairs have been with middle-aged married women who never put a foot wrong socially."

The priest stared at her.

"You know of Madame de Vermeil, then?" he asked in surprise.

"No—who's she? One of the middle-aged mistresses?"

Julia had merely been guessing, rather shrewdly, at the component parts of Atherley's love-life hitherto—she gurgled with pleasure when Father Antal burst out laughing at her last question.

"Miss Probyn, I think you must be a witch!" he said.

"The last person who thought I was a witch was a half-caste barkeeper in Tangier!" she exclaimed gaily. "But one needn't to be a witch to spot the normal line of a person like Atherley. All the same, I do think he's really nice, underneath all the diplomatic stuff; if he were to marry Hetta, though they'd have a rough passage at first, I think she might be the making of him."

"You answer my questions before I put them," the old man said, bending a benignant smile on her. "Witches I believe wait to be asked; so probably you are something better than a witch—wise! I speak openly to you. While this child lived in my house I came to love her dearly; now she has left my care and my world, and I know as little of her new world, and the people in it, as I know of the great geographical New World to which I soon go, and of the people in that—though I confess that I dread this experience! So I seek to learn all I can about her surroundings."

"Well of course her mother is a perfectly *pestilential* woman, in my opinion," Julia said flatly. "Anything to get Hetta away from old Dorothée."

"You mean, even take something of a risk in marrying this young man? Is he, in your opinion, *fundamentally* able to love her and value her?"

Julia reflected before answering.

"He *loves* her, anyhow," she said. "You'd only to watch his face this morning to see that. I fancy he did something frightfully stupid which made her come rushing up here with Townsend—the American; and he's been in agony over it. But as for being capable of valuing her—honestly, Father, one has to take some risks in any marriage; you can't expect safety on a plate! If she's in love with him—and I think she is—I should say they'd better marry as soon as possible, take a *long* honeymoon, and Richard get himself transferred to some other post in the meantime, out of the way of the old Countess."

He smiled at this blue-print for Hetta's future. "Thank you. I believe I agree with you," he said.

"Good." She paused for a moment and then added—"As Hetta's Father in God, couldn't you tip her off to be a little less uncompromising herself, and bottle up her prejudices? It really won't do in diplomacy for her to tell her husband's visitors not to be fools!"

"I had it in mind to do this," the priest said smiling. "So much I see."

On their way back to the house they encountered the Duke deep in conversation with his head shepherd and the bailiff about some new rams from England, who were nibbling away in a small hurdled enclosure in the pastures; he joined them.

"Duke, there's good news," Julia told him.

"Is she found?"

"Yes, found and safe. And with your consent she will be coming up here tomorrow."

"Of course I consent! To whom do I say so?"

"Well in fact as you were out, and as you *had* asked her already, I gave your consent myself," Julia said. The Duke laughed.

"Miss Probyn, I think you must never leave us again! You manage my affairs better than I do. I am delighted."

"Yes, but there's just one thing," Julia pursued. "She'll have to come with an escort."

He looked alarmed.

"Not the mother?"

"Oh Lord no—heaven forfend! With that English lady who found her. Would you mind? You see, no one in Portugal knows *her* by sight, so she's good cover."

"Indeed I do not mind! I should like to meet this spirited lady, and as a friend of yours she is doubly welcome. Have you given my consent to this also?" he asked slyly.

"Well yes, I have," Julia admitted.

"Excellent! I will tell my sister. Really, how interesting it makes one's existence to be involved in these matters! Usually here at Gralheira we lead a life which is tranquil almost to the point of being a little dull," he said to Father Antal. "But since you and the Monsignor came we have the house full of handsome young men, we have alarms and excursions, the telephone ringing at all hours—and now a rescued heroine and her duenna! So amusing."

"You are all goodness; and so is this young lady," Father Antal said, with a benevolent glance at Julia.

"There you are right!" But the Duke raised a question which had not occurred to Julia.

"Who pacifies the formidable Mama, whose daughter ran away from her yesterday morning with this so well-mannered young American? Has she been told?"

"Good gracious, I never thought of that. Well whatever happens, don't let *us* do the pacifying!" Julia exclaimed. "I'll talk to Major Torrens, but personally I think all that had much better be left to Colonel Marques; he's on the spot, and after all he can cancel her residence permit tomorrow, if he wants to. Then she'd miss the wedding!" Julia added cattily.

"Ah yes—the wedding! Dear me, I had quite forgotten it, with all these other affairs. We shall have to go down on Friday, I suppose," the Duke said ruefully, "And you also, Miss Probyn?"

"Yes, I must. I'd forgotten all about it too."

The Duke turned to Father Antal, with careful courtesy.

"You will remain here, of course. The absence of my sister and myself will make no difference, and in any case we shall only be away for forty-eight hours; we return on Sunday."

"You are more than kind," Father Antal said, measuredly. "In fact I think I have almost completed my work with Monsignor Subercaseaux; my movements are in the hands of Major Torrens after that."

"Let us both leave it all to Miss Probyn, then," the Duke said, again slyly.

At the house she promptly put the point about Dorothée to the Major. "We simply can't have her coming storming up here, when the Duque is being such an angel; but he's quite right—she's got to be sorted somehow," Julia said, using the West Highland expression for dealing with a person. "Ring the Colonel, don't you think?"

Torrens did think; and the Duke being now in possession of his own study, he gloomily telephoned from outside the pantry, while Julia as usual sat on the case of wine.

"Oh this mother!" Colonel Marques barked angrily. "*Well* may you be worried about her; for two centavos I would send her out of the country tomorrow! I went myself to see her, to relieve her anxiety: she is playing Bridge with Madame la Comtesse de Vermeil, she can see no one! When I send word that I desire to examine her *permis de séjour*, out she comes flying! But she made great difficulties about the daughter: threatened to go to the American Embassy, and Heaven knows what! Since I cannot and will not tell her where her daughter *is*, or where she goes, this is very troublesome."

"What *did* you say?" Torrens asked.

"That her Father Confessor—you know who I mean—would come to explain matters to her; meanwhile, that her daughter was in his care. After all she will be tomorrow, so what difference does it make?"

"Oh, none," Torrens said cheerfully. This Dunne-like treatment of time did not worry him in the least. "But have we got to send the old holiness down?"

"Yes, *mon cher*, I am afraid you must do this. Brief him first, of course; but that one needs little briefing!—merely *no* indication of where *la petite* is or will be, and of what has happened. He is the one person who can keep her quiet. How soon can you send him?"

Torrens, after consulting Julia, repeated her airy assurance of—"Oh, Richard can drive him down first thing tomorrow; they can be there by lunch-time, in that car."

"*Très bien.* Then I inform *Madame la mère* that she may expect her Director for luncheon tomorrow, and that he will explain everything."

When Marques had rung off Julia and Torrens went back to the smoking-room.

"I suppose it's all right letting him go," the Secret Service man said. "After all, they were watching his house on Friday night."

"Only to try and catch Father Antal," Julia said. "And he'll be in a C.D. car. Let's go and tell him, and the wretched Richard. How furious he'll be at being sent off, just when Hetta's coming!"

Neither the ecclesiastic nor the diplomat were in the least pleased at their assignment. The Monsignor took it best. "Yes, I understand," he said resignedly. "Of course maternal feelings must be placated, but how one wishes that in Americans they were not so pronounced! Very well —at what hour do we start tomorrow?"

"At eight sharp," Julia told him firmly.

"*Miséricorde!* That means saying Mass at seven!"

"I'll see that Antonio calls you in good time," Julia assured him, not without malice.

Richard was much more recalcitrant.

"But it's tomorrow that she comes up here!" he exclaimed unguardedly. "Why do I have to drive him down? Can't he go in one of the Duque's endless cars?"

"No. It's much wiser that he goes in a C.D. car," Torrens told him.

"Well, Townsend has his car sitting in the *praça* at São Pedro: can't he do it?"

"*No*, Richard," Julia said firmly. "We've had quite enough of Townsend driving people about!—and his car's nothing like as fast as yours. Anyhow, whose fault is all this Hetta thing?"

The young man stared at her.

"Why do you say that?"

"I'll give you three guesses!" she said. "No, Richard; you take him down."

Atherley capitulated.

"Oh, very well. Must I stay down there to bring him back, or just dump him?"

"Well oughtn't you to get back to your Chancery? Of course that's between you and your Ambassador," Julia said remorselessly. "I shouldn't think the Monsignor will want to come up here again before the wedding; that's on Saturday, and tomorrow is Wednesday. By the time he's flattened Dorothée there'll only be forty-eight hours before he has to put on his war-paint and assist at the Nuptial High Mass."

"Oh Lord, yes!" Richard groaned. "I'd forgotten that infernal wedding. Haven't you got to come down for it too?" he asked rather sourly of Julia.

"Of course. But I don't really mind!" she replied with a grin. "The

Duke and Dona Maria Francisca are going, of course; I shall take a lift off them, in one of their endless cars."

"Damn you, Julia!"

Torrens weighed in.

"You're going rather too fast, Julia. The Monsignor has got to come back here to finish off with Father A., and anyhow Marques has already told Countess Páloczy that he is looking after Hetta. That's in the future conditional tense, but we're bound to run into trouble if Subercaseaux stays in Estoril; he's sure to be seen, and she's sure to be told."

"Oh, ah, yes; I see your point," Julia said blandly. "Very well, let Richard bring him back tomorrow night. And the Monsignor can go down again on Friday with the Duque and me and all. Old Dorothée won't make any fuss *at* the wedding—she'll be much too excited! But I wish I could be a fly on the wall when he tackles her tomorrow."

"He'll win—you can bet on that," Richard said.

Monsignor Subercaseaux did win, although he was playing on a bad wicket and the Countess on a good one. When he walked into the apartment at half-past one he saw at once that she was all set to give him a rough passage; but the Monsignor was not at all inclined to submit to rough passages, and did not on this occasion.

"Well, Monsignor, I hope now you will have the goodness to explain to me what goes on about Hetta?" she began. "That quite *insufferable* Colonel Marques said you would."

"You dislike him?" the priest said, raising his bushy eyebrows. "I find him so intelligent, and invariably *courteous.*" He glanced towards the tray of drinks under the window; after being driven at nerve-wracking speed by Atherley for five and a half hours he felt like a glass of sherry. The Countess saw his glance, and interpreted it; already a little cowed, she moved towards the tray.

"A glass of Tio Pepe, Monsignor?"

"Thank you, my daughter." The last words put her back in her place as his spiritual child. He sipped, gently, and sniffed appreciatively at a bowl of roses.

"Well?" the Countess asked sharply. "Why did she rush off like that? And was it with Townsend Waller or with Atherley? I know she went with a man—right from the door here! She has *no* sense."

"Do you remember a conversation we had about her, just after she arrived?" the Monsignor asked tranquilly. "You complained then of her independence, and I made certain recommendations as to your own course of behaviour. I am beginning to wonder if you have carried them out."

"Now look here, Monsignor, you're trying to put me in the dock, and I don't like it," the angry woman said. "Are you really suggesting that this performance of hers is *my* fault?"

"I am not sure. Your treatment of her might have been a contributing factor, let us say."

"No, let's not say that, or anything like it! I've been doing everything in the *world* for that child, gauche and difficult as she is, since she came." In her anger the Countess's voice took on the rasping accents of the Middle West, and she reverted to her native idiom. "Quit stalling, Monsignor, and tell me where my daughter *is?*"

"She is in my care," he said, in tones of studied moderation. "She is well, and she will return to you presently; but I am not going to tell you her address, I am not going to send her back till I think fit, and I am, above all, not going to enter into explanations as to why she left, or with whom, at this stage. Later I may do so; but the present is not the moment."

The calm authority in his voice checked Dorothy Páloczy momentarily; then her resentment flamed up afresh.

"In fact you're taking my own child out of my hands? Is that it?"

"No. Your child left your hands of her own free will and without my knowledge; you may ask yourself why. But now, I repeat, she is in *my* care."

"It's—it's absolutely outrageous!" the Countess said fuming, walking up and down the pretty flower-filled room. It was, of course, and no one knew it better than Mgr Subercaseaux. But security demanded that the wretched woman should be kept in the dark—to say nothing of their obligations to the Duke, to Father Antal, and to Hetta herself. The Monsignor had no qualms at all about the line he was taking. He drank some more sherry, and sat relaxed in his chair, waiting for the storm to blow itself out.

"Well, when *is* Hetta coming back?"

"Oh, soon after the wedding, I think. You do not want her to come before that, do you? Will you not be very much involved in your own preparations, till then?" There was a hint of irony in his tone, and Dorothée, who was not altogether a fool, realised that he was thinking—quite rightly—of all she would be having done to her clothes, her feet, her hands, her hair, her face. She gave an angry laugh. "Oh very well—

you win! But when what you call 'the moment' for explanations comes I shall want a full one, remember!"

"I shall not forget." He pulled out a thin gold watch in a Cartier case from somewhere in his soutane, and glanced at it. "My dear Countess, I have to leave at three. Will you do me the honour of lunching with me downstairs?"

"No, I won't!" the Countess said flatly. "We're lunching here, in the apartment, where the chef will send us something fit to eat."

"You are very kind. Do you wish me to ring?"

Dorothy Páloczy had been slower than most American women married to Europeans about learning to let things be done *for* her; after twenty-five years she was still liable to do them herself, especially when her nerves were out of order. She moved now to the telephone and ordered luncheon to be served immediately; then she poured out another glass of sherry for her guest. Subercaseaux was relieved by this promptitude. He had undertaken to walk up and meet Atherley outside the Casino sharp at three, but he was exceedingly hungry, and did not at all want to cut his meal short.

Atherley lunched more briefly, and rather less well. After dropping the Monsignor he raced in to Lisbon and from the Chancery rang up the Ambassador's residence to ask how soon he could see him? Sir Henry was in, and luckily had no luncheon-party; he sent a message to say that his First Secretary could come at two-fifteen.

"Tomlinson, what can you get me to eat, *here*, in five minutes?" Richard asked, sitting at his desk, and groaning inwardly at the sight of three laden "In" trays.

"Well in five minutes, Mr. Atherley, that isn't so easy; there aren't any restaurants close round here. Must it really be *five* minutes?"

"Yes, Tomlinson, it must."

The messenger reflected, wrinkling his pale forehead.

"Well Mr. Atherley, I hardly like to suggest it, but Mrs. Tomlinson and I often bring along some of her meat pies if we're liable to be busy; I could bring you up some of those at once, if you would fancy them. They're fresh-baked; she did them last night."

"That's very good of you, Tomlinson—the meat pies by all means. But what will *you* do?"

"Oh, I can go out, Sir. We're not so rushed as we expected; the Messenger's plane was held up, so the bag isn't in. Would you like some wine, Sir? We can get that just round the corner, and it isn't too bad either—though not what you're accustomed to, of course."

No district in Lisbon is without its small wine-shops, however lacking it may be in the matter of restaurants, and the Lapa quarter is no exception; in less than five minutes a tray was placed on Atherley's desk with a china jug of wine, tomatoes, and a plate of Mrs. Tomlinson's meat pies. These were the most English food the young man had eaten since he came to Portugal—stodgy, wholesome, and the pastry in fact rather good; he was ravenous, and helped down by the tomatoes and the rough cheap wine they made quite an adequate meal. Richard grinned as he ate, amused by this side-light on the domestic arrangements of the messenger and the telephonist—imagine that little thing going home, after her day's work in the head-phones, to roll out pastry and bake meat pies!

Punctually at a quarter past two he was waiting in the Embassy drawing-room, where a coffee-tray stood before the fireplace at one end of the long room; in a moment Sir Henry and Lady Loseley came in by the door at the farther end—Lady Loseley, after a pleasant greeting, took a cup of coffee and said that she must go and see the baby, and tactfully went out.

"Well Richard, does this visit mean that you contemplate returning to us?" the Ambassador asked, turning a quizzical blue eye on his Head of Chancery.

"Not if you can spare me for another forty-eight hours, Sir. I came to beg you to do that"—he spoke with an earnestness so unusual that it rather impressed his chief. "And to apologise for rushing off the night before last."

"Oh! Have you really driven all the way down from Beira Alta just to say that?"

His shrewdness embarrassed Atherley.

"Well no, Sir. I brought Monsignor Subercaseaux down, and I'm afraid I must take him back. But I can be in the Chancery by nine tomorrow morning if you wish it," he said rather stiffly.

The Ambassador chuckled.

"Had to bring him down to tranquillise the troublesome Countess, eh? I'm not surprised; she's been making a terrible commotion. And where is that nice little daughter who cooks? Up at Gralheira? I don't wonder she ran away."

"She's on her way there," Richard said. "But she didn't go off just to escape from her mother; she had a more valid reason than that."

"Oh, ah." The Ambassador, his eyes always gay and shrewd, picked at his thumb-nail. "Am I to be told the more valid reason?"

"Well really, Sir, at this stage I think you had better know the whole thing," the young man said rather desperately. "I tried hard to avoid getting involved in this, but that infernal Secret Service man simply dragged me into it. You see—" and then he poured out the whole tale of Father Antal.

"Oh yes, I know about that," the Ambassador said airily, still picking at his thumb, his eyes still amused. "The Duke of Ericeira really is a *galant' uomo* to take on the whole boiling like that, though of course all these ecclesiasticos are just his sister's cup of tea! But why do you say the little lady is on her way to Gralheira? Didn't she go there on Monday with her *cavaliere servente?*"

"No Sir; she never got there." Seeing how much the Ambassador already knew—probably from Campbell, Richard reflected sourly—he decided to tell the rest of the story. "At São Pedro do Sul the wretched American went to have a drink while she went to say her prayers, and in his absence she was pinched by some Communist agents and carried off."

"Good God! What a frightful thing!" The Ambassador was startled by this development. "But how on earth was she recovered? I should have thought they'd have swept her straight off into Spain."

"They would have but for Luzia, that beautiful little girl of the Duke's —do you know her, Sir?"

"No, alas."

"Well, she prevented it. Everyone in São Pedro do Sul eats out of her hand, of course: she got an eye-witness account of the kidnapping, so Torrens rang up Colonel Marques and had the frontier closed."

"What a wonderful story!" the Ambassador interjected, his blue eyes gleaming. "Do go on. Did the remarkable Luzia go after them and catch them?"

"They went after them all right, and Luzia telephoned and caused some thug to give their car four flats before it crossed the frontier! But they got away in the local taxi."

"Ah, she probably rang up Martinez at the shooting-box," the Ambassador said reflectively. "Lovely country up there; and those wild goats give one some very sporting shots. But how was the little Hungarian recovered in the end? Where is she on her way to Gralheira *from?*"

"Here, Sir. When the agents found all exits blocked they hived back to Lisbon; by God's mercy their car was involved in a street crash yester-day morning, and Countess Hetta was found, and saved."

"It sounds as if there was another story there," the Ambassador said. "However, I won't delay you by going into that now, since you have got to get out to Estoril and drive the Monsignor back to Gralheira. I know that the Duke likes to dine punctually! Just tell me this—how much did the little Countess give away?"

Richard blinked slightly at this further instance of the all-knowingness of his gay, bland chief.

"Something, Sir, but we don't yet know what. I'm sure we shall find all that out this evening; she will tell Miss Probyn—she trusts her."

"I think I really must meet this Miss Probyn; she seems to be a sort of lynch-pin in this whole business," the Ambassador said. "Very well, Richard; take your extra forty-eight hours of leave—let boy meet girl! You know your way out. Goodbye."

And with this final shattering display of omniscience the Ambassador walked up the long room and went out by the farther door, leaving Atherley blinking after him.

Chapter Sixteen

Mrs. Hathaway and Hetta, with their police escort, reached Gralheira soon after five. Dona Maria Francisca was dispensing prizes for needlework at a local "Instituto Bom Pastor," i.e., a rescue-home; the Duke, with Townsend Waller and Torrens, was off at the far end of the estate inspecting his forestry plantations, but Julia and Luzia, the latter bursting with curiosity, were out on the steps to greet the new arrivals. Hetta looked pale, Julia thought; she consigned her to Luzia's care—"I'll see you later, Hetti." She turned to Mrs. Hathaway. "I thought you and I would have tea up in your room. Dona Maria Francisca was so sorry—" She led her guest upstairs.

"My dear child, what a wonderful house!" Mrs. Hathaway said, her eye travelling round as she went. "And what a beautiful room!" she exclaimed a moment later, taking in the carpet, the period furniture, the space and dignity, and the view from the two high windows.

"Yes. We'll have tea in here while Marta unpacks," Julia said, opening another door into a sitting-room. "This is yours too; you have a suite, all but the bath-room!" While Mrs. Hathaway took off her hat and coat Julia explained about the only two Gralheira bath-rooms. Mrs. Hathaway was as amused as Major Torrens had been by these Victorian dispositions. Lying on a brocaded chaise-longue in the boudoir, drinking tea, she gave a little sigh of pleasure.

"How nice this is! Really I am wonderfully lucky to be here, however it came about."

"Tell me every word," Julia said—and so Mrs. Hathaway did; to Julia she even admitted the agonising helplessness and distress of that first hour or two of her efforts to bring Hetta round. "But who is the little fat man who sent the car to bring us up here? He wouldn't let me pay a penny! Is he something to do with the police?"

"Yes, he's the head of the Security Police."

"Well now Julia my dear, I should like it so much if you were to tell me what all this is *about*," Mrs. Hathaway said. "You call this girl Hetti, but who is she?"

"She's Hetta Páloczy; a Hungarian." Julia told the whole story, ending up with Father Antal's escape.

"You'll meet him at dinner; he's the dearest old creature you can imagine."

"That is all quite fascinating," said Mrs. Hathaway. "But, Julia, I feel that you ought to go and see that poor child; she's on thorns about something, and I know it's you she wants to talk to."

"All right, I will. Just tell me how Edina is."

"Splendid, when I last heard. But do go to your Hetta. If I could just have a *boracha* I think I would lie down for a little. At what time do we dine?"

Julia laughed and kissed her old friend. *"Boracha!* You know the words already! Dinner is usually at eight-thirty; tonight it may be a little later because the Vatican contact has to get back from Lisbon. But Marta shall call you, and I will come and take you downstairs to meet them all. Oh, what fun this is!"

She found Hetta in Nanny's sitting-room, lingering over an ample English tea and actually laughing at some nonsense of Luzia's; at the sight of Julia, however, the gaiety left her face, and she sprang up, saying—"At last there you are! Now, please, I *must* speak to you." She turned to thank Nanny and Luzia for "so delicious a tea," and looked anxiously at Julia.

"Come along to my room. Countess Hetta is next to me, isn't she, Nanny?"

"Yes, Miss Probyn. It's rather *small*, really only the dressing-room, but I thought the Countess would put up with that for the sake of the communicating door."

"Perfect, Nanny," said Julia, who had in fact herself asked her hostess to put Hetta there. She glanced round as they passed through to see that Manoela had unpacked properly, and led Hetta on into her own room, which was big, and as much a sitting-room as a bedroom; Julia had organised this for herself during her spell as Luzia's governess. The two girls sat down on a comfortable English sofa under one of the windows. "Now, Hetti, tell me what the trouble is," Julia said.

Hetta's account was rather confused, to begin with.

"Yulia, first I must tell you that when Richard would not say that he could bring me here when I asked, though he had promised, I was angry. There was a reason for that, but it does not matter," Hetta said, on a falling note of the voice.

Aha and oho, Julia thought to herself—enter Mme de Whatnot!

"Well never mind; go on," she said.

"So then I asked Townsend instead, and he drove me up to this beautiful little town—but how beautiful *all* Portugal is! He wanted to drink wine; I did not, so I went into a church. That is always a nice way to spend time, and this is a beautiful church; I grew more happy. Then these horrible men come in, though how they can know I am there I cannot imagine!—they drag me out and put me in a car and drive away; a *long* way. At last we stop, and I see it is a frontier; I try to get out, and shout; but they pulled me back and held my mouth, and tied something over my eyes so that I should not see. Then the car is turned; I could feel it going backwards and forwards, so I knew that it had not crossed the frontier, and this was *something*."

"Indeed it was! And then?"

"We drove, not for so long now, and presently stop while one of the men asks questions; then they bring me into a *very* small inn, first taking the bandage off my eyes. In this place *they* ate, bread and butter, and an omelette, and drank wine, but to me they gave nothing; I must sit and watch them eat!" Hetta said indignantly. "And I was now very hungry, for Waller and I had taken lunch at one. But I would not ask for food!"

Julia sat listening, with a sort of pang at the strangeness of it, to Hetta's blindfold account of the journey that they had so painstakingly traced out only two days before—one story, but from two how different angles.

"And after that?" she prompted.

"They take me out again, but there is some trouble about the car; one takes me back into the inn, swearing! And presently we get into another most *terrible* old car, and again they tie my eyes; but even through the bandage, just once I could see the lights of another car that met us, and I tried to put my hand out of the window to wave—but they snatched my hand away, and struck me."

Julia was shaken by this, realising that it was the lights of the Land-Rover that had pierced the bandage over Hetta's eyes; that it was to her own friends that she had tried to beckon. But all she said was—"Well, after that?"

"We stop several times, and there is more talking with people; at last we get into another car, much better, with a chauffeur, and drive again."

"I wonder where to?" Julia speculated.

"To the frontier, I think. Is there a place with the word honour in it? I thought I heard 'Onoro' several times."

"Yes, there is. Fuentes de Onoro."

"*That* was it. And again the car is stopped; they cannot pass, but turn round and drive away. Then they got out a map, I heard the paper crackle, and one says, 'No no, Lissabon!' Now this is how *Germans* say Lisbon," Hetta said, opening her eyes at Julia—"so I begin to think that though they speak Spanish, one or two are perhaps really German. We drive a long time, very fast, and then stop; it seems the driver does not know the way. They swear and swear; it is dark, the road is empty —no people, no houses; the chauffeur speaks only Portuguese. One of them speaks that, a rather fattish man, with a short beard; I can see this when he gets out to look for which road they shall take, because after we leave this Onoro place, by bending down and rubbing my face against my knees I managed to push the bandage off my eyes."

"Why didn't you use your hands?" Julia interrupted, making a horrified guess at the reason.

"After I tried to wave to that car we met they tied my hands behind my back, so tight that it hurt; it was most disagreeable, because now I cannot lean back, and I am *so* tired."

Julia wondered whether to ask for more details about the fattish man with the beard, but decided that it was better to let Hetta get her story out in her own way.

"You must have been—*poor* Hetti! Do go on."

"So presently we drive again, the man with the beard always telling the chauffeur to go faster; but in their anger two speak now altogether in German, and one says—'*Eine verfluchte Geschichte!* It is nearly four, we shall not reach Lissabon before it is daylight!' And the bearded man says he will get out when we pass through a town called Santa something, and '*allein arbeiten*'—this means work by himself," Hetta explained.

"At Santarém, I expect," Julia said. In her mind she was tracing the route of the car after leaving Fuentes de Onoro: down through Beira

Baixa on the farther side of the Serra da Estrêla to hit the Tagus valley at Abrantes, and on to Santarém. "Well?" she asked.

"Then another man says, 'So had we not better stop and do the questioning of the little one now, that you may profit by what she knows?' Oh Yulia, when I heard that I was so much afraid!"

"Darling Hetti, I don't wonder! But do tell me everything. You'll feel better when you've got it all out, and we must know because of Father Antal." She was full of nervous distress herself, dreading what might be coming.

"Him! That is just the thing! But I must ask you to try to understand," Hetta said, speaking with a curious quietness. "I am very tired, and I am also very hungry; it is now four in the morning, and I had last eaten with Waller at one o'clock the day before. Also these men do not allow me to go to the lavatory in that small inn where they ate, nor to leave the car; so for *fourteen* hours I do not go, and I am quite *miserable!*"

"Hetta, I do understand. Frightful!"

"Then the car stops," Hetta said, speaking slowly now, "and in bad French they ask me, 'Would you like to get out, and go to the side of the road?'—grinning most vulgarly! They have switched on the light inside the car. 'Yes,' I answer. 'You shall,' they say, 'when you have answered one quite small question: where is now Dr. Antal Horvath?' At that I shut my mouth; I think No, better endure shame, stain my clothes, be disgusting, than do this! When I shake my head the one with the beard strikes me across the face with the palm of his hand, first one side, then the other—five, six times! This is a horrible thing," Hetta said flatly, "but I do not speak, except to say No. Then they untie my arms, and twist them so hard that it hurts very much, and the bearded man slaps my face again, but still I do not speak. Then he looks at his watch, and says, quite furiously—'We cannot lose any more time; it is dangerous. She *must* speak.' And they whisper together, and I am more afraid than ever! Another says, aloud—'Let us search her first; we have not done that yet.' And they begin to feel me all over, in my pockets and inside my clothes, also touching me in a very disgusting way. But one takes my handbag and looks in that, and suddenly he gives a shout—'I have it! Give yourselves no more trouble; here is what we want!' "

"What had he found?" Julia asked.

"This is what is awful of me! I had written a note to Father Antal, and put the name Gralheira on it. I thought I would make Townsend drive by the house, and that we could send it in by a servant, and then the Father could get someone, you perhaps, to telephone to me at this hotel where we were to stay. It was quite *id-yot*, I should have known better; in Hungary I should never have put a name and a place on paper. But that is what I did, and what they found. After I was taken from the church I ought of course to have eaten the letter," Hetta said matter-of-factly, "but I was confused at first, and by the time I thought of this, my hands were tied. So now they are all quite cheerful, and say 'Very well; now you can get out.' But one stands near and flicks the torch on me; it may be in order that I should not escape, but I think also to humiliate me! For where could I escape to, in the night, in Portugal? And I am so—Yulia, I cannot express it properly, but *weak* with relief—that I just go back afterwards to the car, like a silly person!" Hetta said, with an expression of profound distaste.

"I don't see what else you could have done, Hetti dear; if you *had* tried to run away they would simply have caught you," Julia said. "What happened after that?"

"They offered me wine and bread, but I would not take them!" Hetta said, with a lift of the head. "Accept anything from such animals?—no! Those two go on talking in German—so stupid, this, to think that I should not understand German, brought up in Hungary!—and I heard one say: 'We must be careful as we enter Lissabon; she must not make a *Geschrei*.' Then they push some piece of stuff into my mouth, so that I cannot speak; this dries the mouth quite up; my mouth is still sore. But he with the beard says, 'If we do not tie her hands again she may pull it out, and shout, and we cannot drive her through the streets with bound hands; it could be seen. Better to make her *ohnmächtig*.' And he turns on the inside light of the car again, and tells the chauffeur to stop, and takes out a little case and fills a syringe from an ampoule. I *see* all this, while the others hold me!" Hetta said, in a tone which brought that moment vividly before Julia. "Then he pulls off my coat and jacket, and pushes up my sleeve, and gives me the *piqûre*. I remember them putting on my jacket and coat, and the car starting, and after that *nothing*, till I wake in bed in Mrs. Hattaway's room."

It seemed to Julia that Hetta had very little to reproach herself with. (The idea of *eating* compromising letters she had only encountered up to now in books about the *maquis*.) Still, Torrens must be apprised of the fact that the bearded man knew, and had known for thirty-six hours, that Father Antal was at Gralheira. She kissed and consoled Hetta, told her to lie down till she was called to dress for dinner, and then went off to see if the Major had returned. Elidio informed her that he had, and was in His Excellency's study; Julia betook herself there, and poked her leonine-golden head round the door.

"Oh, but come in," the Duke said, rising.

"Please, no—I've just come to snatch away the Major, thank you so much." She gestured with her head at Torrens.

"Our new guests arrived safely, I hear," her host said.

"Yes. They adore Gralheira already! Do excuse us"—and she swept the obedient Torrens out of the room.

In the smoking-room she told him, without any details, what the Communists had found in Hetta's handbag, and how the "bearded man" had proposed to leave the car at Santarém.

"Yes, Marques said they'd only pinched three of them," Torrens said. "Well, we'd better let him know at once. That ghastly telephone in the passage, I suppose?"

Even heads of Security Police must, one imagines, sometimes eat; anyhow on this occasion Colonel Marques was not to be got on the telephone. They tried for Colonel Campbell, but he too was out.

"Well don't attempt to get Melplash," Julia said. "Stupid clot, he'd only make a muddle. Let's try the Colonel again after dinner. Nothing much can happen between now and then."

Dinner that night was rather late. The Bentley only crackled over the raked gravel to the front door at eight-thirty, and Gralheira was not a house where people were told not to bother to change for dinner; Atherley and the Monsignor hurried away to their rooms. Julia had warned the Duke that they would almost certainly be late, so he was not fussing acutely when the rest of the company assembled in the drawing-room, Julia shepherding Mrs. Hathaway and Hetta. The Duke greeted Hetta with warm kindness, his sister with her usual rather pinched courtesy; Townsend was duly presented to Mrs. Hathaway, and wrung Hetta's hand in almost speechless relief and apology. The girl spoke gently to him, but her eyes were straying round the enormous room; this actually contained as many as five lamps, but it was nevertheless out of a certain degree of shadow that Father Antal's voice came, saying—"My child?"

They all heard it; for a moment they all watched her as she flew to him and kissed his hand. Then in the blessed half-dark the pair spoke together in that impossible language, Hungarian, which no one else could understand. The Duke with his impeccable courtesy began a conversation with Mrs. Hathaway, Julia did the same with Dona Maria

Francisca. Presently Elidio appeared to announce that *Os Senhores* had returned, and that in *mais dez minutos* (ten minutes more) they would come down. The Duke nodded and looked at his watch; then he glanced round the room and observed that two of the company, who should have been there, were missing.

"My sister, where are Luzia and Miss Brown? They do not seem to be present."

They were not—and they were still not present when Atherley and the Monsignor came in, followed by Elidio, who whispered in his master's ear that the young Condessa and Meess Brown begged to be excused from dining; they would eat upstairs. The Duke frowned—this was unheard-of—and muttered a question to Elidio; he was answered by the ineffably evasive shrug of the old and privileged Portuguese servant. "My sister, we will not wait for Nanny and Luzia," Ericeira said authoritatively, and they all trooped into the great dining-room, where the Duke, as Julia had foreseen, was quickly beguiled by the cheerful astringent quality of Mrs. Hathaway's conversation. Hetta, of course, sat beside Father Antal, and neither had eyes or ears for anyone else; but Atherley, seated next to Julia, asked uncompromisingly—"Where on earth *are* Luzia and Nanny? I thought everyone simply had to show up for meals, here."

"I haven't a clue," Julia said airily, though in fact she was quite as curious as Atherley could be about the reason for their absence. Atherley was not a very lively companion that evening; his eyes strayed constantly across the table to where Hetta, her face pale, but alight with happiness, talked eagerly and incomprehensibly with the old priest. "Have you found out if she had a bad time?" he asked anxiously.

"Uncomfortable, but nothing serious," Julia told him. "They found a note in her bag addressed to Dom Francisco, *here*, before they resorted to extreme measures; and as that was all they wanted, they just drugged her and took her on to Lisbon."

Atherley was much relieved.

"Does Marques know they know he's here?" he asked.

"No. We couldn't get him before dinner; Hugh's going to ring him up afterwards. That will give him something to think about!" Julia said, with what Atherley thought misplaced levity.

But when Major Torrens did eventually ring up Colonel Marques he had something rather unexpected to tell the Chief of the Security Police. In the drawing-room after dinner Elidio, holding out a silver tray with small cups of weak coffee to Julia, murmured that Meess Brown desired to speak with Meess Probyn in the schoolroom. Julia drank the cheerless coffee hastily, made her excuses to her hostess, and hastened upstairs.

In the schoolroom she found Nanny and Luzia tucking into cold chicken and salad, on both their faces a remarkable expression of smug triumph, as of two cats who have each swallowed an out-size canary.

"Well Miss Probyn, I hope His Grace isn't too much upset, but really there seemed to be nothing else to do," Nanny began, in a busy sort of voice.

"Nanny, please!" Luzia interjected. "Do let *me* tell Miss Probyn. Did I find him or did you?"

"Tell away, tell away," Nanny replied cheerfully. "Blow your own trumpet!—I will say this time you have the right to."

"Oh do get down to it, Luzia!" Julia said impatiently. "Who have you found?"

"Him! This 'principal' of whom Torrens spoke, the one with the beard, who was not taken in Lisbon with the others," Luzia announced triumphantly.

"Where, for goodness sake?" Julia asked, half incredulous.

"In the kitchen. You see after I heard Torrens yesterday telling Papa in the study that he had escaped, and that we must continue to take all precautions, I went out last night to the kitchen to look at the travellers who were eating there, to see if any looked suspicious. None did; just poor Portuguese working-people. Tonight I went again, and there at the table, eating with the rest, sat a man with a beard, in poor clothes, but they do not fit him very well; and moreover, he had rolls of fat on the back of his neck!" said Luzia, her eyes like saucers.

"Gracious! Well?"

"So I went round the table greeting all the people, there were only six or seven tonight, and at last I came to him, and he spoke *very* bad Portuguese, just as the beggars said of the man at São Pedro do Sul. I said nothing then, but went to find Nanny."

"Well Miss, of course I went down at once," Nanny said, taking up the tale with evident pleasure. "Luzia was quite right not to say anything in front of the servants, but to come to me. And I find my gentleman talking to one of the kitchen-maids as she served his food, asking if there weren't foreign *eclesiásticos* staying in the house? The cheek of it!" said Nanny indignantly.

"Goodness! What on earth did you do?"

"Well, I felt sure you and the Major would wish to see this person, but the chef was just about to send dinner in, and I knew I couldn't get you then. So I spoke to the man myself, and said, if he wanted to see the foreign priests I could arrange it, if he would make it worth my while, and come with me."

"And did he?" Julia asked.

"Indeed he did; he got up at once and came along as meek as a lamb. I gave a sort of wink to the chef and old Maria do Carmo, so they made no trouble—for as you know, Miss, those people never come through into the house, except for Mass. And I just caught Elidio in the passage, and sent the message to His Grace. But then I had to think where to put him."

"Heavens, yes! Well, where *did* you put him?" Julia was beginning to gurgle with laughter; this performance on the part of Nanny and Luzia was too superb, if it really was "the principal" whom they had got.

"Out in the old night-nurseries, Miss Probyn. You see there are bars on the windows, so he can't get out. His Grace had them put in for the little Count, God rest his soul!" Nanny said, sadness for her long-dead baby boy for a moment eclipsing the satisfaction in her sensible time-worn face. "And those rooms are right at the far end of the East corridor, and give onto the garden, so he can scream his head off, and no one will hear!" the good woman pursued, triumph again returning to her expression.

"And he's there now?"

"Yes. I told him the priests were just about to sit down to dinner, and it would be an hour or more before he could see them; but that he *should* see one of them, if he made it worth my while. I repeated that, so as to lull his suspicions, as you might say," Nanny concluded, looking smugger than ever.

Julia laughed loudly. "Nanny, how marvellous! *Did* he make it worth your while?"

"Indeed he did, Miss Probyn. He gave me a conto." (A conto is a thousand escudos, worth about £12 : 10 : 0 in English money, but a small fortune in Portugal.) As she spoke Nanny drew a bundle of notes out of her bodice. "I shall give it to Dona Maria Francisca for her poor girls, of course. Then I told him that all this was very irregular, and I should get into terrible trouble if he was found, and I was going to lock the door so that none of the servants could get in and find him. He didn't seem to mind that; in fact he looked quite pleased, and settled down in my old armchair as cool as a cucumber! So I locked the door on him, and rang and ordered our supper—and there he is, and here's the key." She laid it on the table.

"Nanny, that is splendid. And Luzia, *how* well you did!"

"I expect you'll want to tell the Major," Nanny observed, falling to once more on her cold chicken.

"Yes, I must. Don't go near him again till I've seen you, Nanny." She got up.

"*Can't* I be with you when you tell Torrens?" Luzia implored, getting up too. "I *did* find him!"

"*Major* Torrens, Luzia. And you haven't finished your supper!"

"Bother my supper! Miss Probyn, *please!*"

"All right, come on," Julia said.

Down in the hall she summoned Elidio and told him to fetch the Senhor Comandante out to her. "But discreetly, you understand—so as not to attract attention."

Major Torrens did not really relish the long formal evenings in that huge, inadequately-lit room, and was relieved at the chance of escape.

"What goes on?" he asked Julia in the hall.

"Come into the smoking-room and hear."

When he had heard what Julia had to tell he considered for a little.

"You haven't seen him yourself?" he asked. She shook her head. "So we don't know for certain that it is the man we want."

"Oh Hugh, would any *other* man with a club beard and a German back to his neck show up here in the kitchen, and ask about foreign priests? We know that the 'principal' knows that Father Antal is here, and now we have this person arriving. If you won't ring Marques, *I* shall."

"I was going to ring Marques anyhow," the Major said calmly. "Of course I shall tell him what's happened. I suppose we can do it from the study this time? I hope to goodness he's in now."

Colonel Marques was in. Torrens told him first, very guardedly, what the Communists had found in Hetta's handbag, and went on to relate how someone "corresponding to the description of the fourth man" had been found in the house, making enquiries about "divines from other countries."

"Where is he now?" the Colonel asked.

"Under lock and key upstairs. He was promised an interview with one of the divines, and has paid a large bribe to secure it. Should we afford him any interview?"

"*Ah non, mon cher!* That would be too great a risk. I will come up at once; this is certainly worth investigation. You have not seen him yourself? Nor your lady colleague?"

Neither, Torrens told him; only a very youthful member of the family, and an old member of the staff, a foreigner.

"*Bon!* Now listen closely, *mon ami.* It would be highly desirable that this inquisitive individual should pass the time till I arrive in a deep and restful sleep; the old servant might perhaps offer him a glass of wine, or a cup of coffee. Can this be arranged? Have you what is necessary?"

"Of course I have the stuff. But not *coffee,* here; it wouldn't disguise the taste of barley-water!" the Major exclaimed hastily, causing Miss Probyn to laugh. "Hold on," he added, and turned to his ribald lady colleague, his hand over the receiver.

"Can Nanny administer a drug to the beard? I've got the dope."

"Yes, I'm sure she'd love to," Julia responded heartily.

"That can be done," Torrens said into the telephone.

"Excellent. And please arrange for us to be let in when we arrive: in about six hours from now. An awkward time, I am afraid."

Torrens glanced at his watch—it was just after ten.

"I'm sure that will be all right," he said, remembering his entry into the palace in Lisbon with the two priests in the small hours. "See you then." He rang off.

"So Nanny is to drug him. Oh, what fun for her!" Luzia exclaimed. "I *wish* I could do it!"

"Let's go up and see Nanny," Julia said, ignoring her. "You get your drug, Hugh, while I get something from Elidio to put it in. Vintage port, don't you think? Oddly enough the Duke has some, and that should mask the taste of your stuff as well as anything, though mind you it isn't really *good.* Port simply won't hold in this climate—the summers are too hot."

It is a curious fact that the Portuguese themselves have small taste for their country's supreme product, vintage port; they greatly prefer lighter wines. The Duke of Ericeira, however, with his wide circle of English friends, kept a small stock of some of the more noted vintages; only, as Miss Probyn had truly remarked, owing to the very hot summers and the lack of adequate cellerage they were seldom at their best.

"All right," Torrens said. "Only how am I to find Nanny? This house is like the maze at Hampton Court!"

"I go with you, and bring you to Nanny," Luzia said eagerly.

"Yes, you do that, Luzia," her ex-governess said. "Take Major Torrens up. I'll meet you there."

It gave the measure of Miss Probyn's standing in the Ericeira household that she had little difficulty in causing Elidio to decant a bottle of Graham's 1945 port; this, with a rather large glass, she took from the old servant.

"*Minha Menina,* let *me* bring this to wherever you desire it," the butler said earnestly. Julia shook her head.

"On this one occasion, Elidio, I will take it myself," she said smiling; an answering smile, coupled with an expression of ineffable intelligence, overspread the rather monkeyfied visage of the Portuguese. "*Muito bem, Minha Menina,*" he said, and let her depart. Elidio had not failed to draw his own conclusions from the arrival of two priests in Lisbon after 1 A.M. the previous Friday; nor from "Meess Brown's" escorting, tonight, a *pessoa* from the traveller's table in the kitchen into the house.

Torrens, Luzia, and Nanny were waiting in the latter's sitting-room when Julia arrived with her salver.

"Well, Nanny, has the Major told you what he wants?" she asked.

"Yes, Miss Probyn. Quite an unusual request!"

"Do you think he'll take a glass of port?"

"I'll see that he does. I shall stay and talk about the foreign priests to him while he drinks it, and ask for more money. Asking for money always sort of carries conviction," Nanny stated, making Torrens laugh.

"Let's taste that wine, Julia," he said.

"I did. It's quite strong. I'd say it would mask most flavours."

The Major took out the stopper of the decanter, and sniffed. "Wonderful! What is it?"

"Graham's '45. I asked for that because it's still fairly young. Are you going to put your dope into the whole decanter, or pour out a glass?"

"I am certainly *not* going to ruin a whole bottle of Graham's '45!" the Major said emphatically. "I see you've brought a fairly large glass— good." He filled it; then before the fascinated gaze of the others he drew a small ampoule from his pocket, sawed off the neck, and emptied the contents into the glass of port. He stirred the fluid, carefully, with his little finger, then sucked the finger.

"Perfect," he pronounced. "This particular thing has very little taste."

He replaced the glass on the silver tray. "There you are, Nanny; go and do your stuff. I'll come along behind you, just in case he smells a rat and tries something on." He picked up the poker from the grate and followed her as she took the tray and went out.

He reappeared in about five minutes. "It all seems to be going all right," he observed. "He's drinking it, and talking to her, quite jolly. This acts very gently and gradually, you know." He looked at the table. "Pity we haven't some port-glasses! We could use some of this decanter."

"*I* shall get them!" Luzia flew from the room before anyone could stop her.

"This really is the most extraordinary set-up," Torrens said when she had gone.

"Rather fun, don't you think?" Julia said contentedly, lighting a cigarette.

"Put that out, Julia, if you're going to drink port," Torrens said peremptorily. "It's desecration to smoke before stuff like this."

"Oh, very well." Always good-natured, Julia flung her cigarette into the fireplace—the Major looked on her with love.

"Darling, do you know that you really are an *absolute* darling?" he said, getting up as he spoke.

"Hugh dear, cut it out! Luzia will be back any minute, and you remember that we agreed to cut all this out till the Hetta-Antal business was finished, only the other day in the knot-garden, when the Duque and the holies interrupted us."

"It isn't easy to cut it out when you're so sweet," the Major was beginning, when Luzia flew in.

"There you are! Nanny *loves* port," the young girl said, banging four exquisite Marinha Grande port-glasses down on the table. Like port, the beautiful glass of Marinha Grande is a product which Portugal owes to English enterprise; as long ago as 1748 a factory was started there by John Beare, and carried on by the Stephens brothers, who prudently secured from the great Pombal the right to buy wood for their furnaces in the neighbouring forest of Leiria, the oldest man-controlled forest in the world; since the 13th century this has been felled, re-planted, and thinned under human direction. Julia was telling the Major about this when Nanny came in.

"Gone down?" Torrens asked.

"Yes, Major; he quite enjoyed it. I *hinted* about some more money, so he gave me another conto!—and he was half-asleep when I left."

"Splendid, Nanny!"

"Hugh, hadn't we better go and have a look at him presently, to see if he really is the man I saw on the road outside Cascais?" Julia asked.

"Give him another quarter of an hour," Torrens said, looking at his watch. "He'll have passed clean out by then. And meanwhile, I think we might drink Nanny's and Luzia's health."

After fifteen minutes pleasantly spent drinking admirable port they proceeded along the East corridor to the old night-nurseries, where Nanny unlocked the door. There, slackly sunk down in an old-fashioned nursery armchair, upholstered in faded cretonne patterned with turkey-cocks, lay Nanny's captive, snoring gently, his mouth half-open. Major Torrens went over to him and lifted an eye-lid; getting no response he briskly felt him all over, and from a pocket extracted a small revolver, which he pocketed himself. Then he turned to Julia.

"Is that your man?" he asked.

"The beard's all right. Let me see the back of his head."

The Major heaved the inert figure upwards and forwards, out of the comfortable cup-shaped back of the old chair.

"Yes, rolls of fat! I'm sure that's him."

The Major replaced the man in the chair and they all went out, Nanny locking the door.

"Nanny, I'd better have that key," Torrens said. "The head of the Security Police will be here about 4 A.M. to collect this person, and I don't want to dig you out of bed at that hour."

"Very well, Major. Does His Grace know? Elidio will have to wait up."

"No, I must see His Grace now." He looked at his watch. "We'd better get hold of him at once."

"Yes. And you're for bed, Miss!" Nanny said firmly to Luzia, and swept her off.

Chapter Seventeen

THE drawing-room party was just breaking up when Torrens and Julia got downstairs. The girl shepherded Hetta and Mrs. Hathaway to their rooms, while in the study Torrens, over a whisky, was about to inform his host of the events upstairs when Mgr Subercaseaux poked his head round the door. "Do I intrude?" he asked; the Monsignor liked a nightcap. Torrens frowned, involuntarily.

"Yes, I see that I do. Goodnight, my dear Duke."

"No, Monsignor—come in, come in!" his host said. Then he, too, noticed Torrens' face. "You did not wish to speak to me *privately?*" he asked, recalling that the Major had rather formally requested a few minutes with him.

"Well, as a matter of fact I did, Sir; but I don't suppose it much matters the Monsignor hearing what I have to say."

"Then shut the door and come and sit down, Monsignor. Say when."

Torrens told his tale. The Duke listened with half-incredulous delight. "Incredible!" he ejaculated. "And you mean that man is in the house now?"

"Yes Sir; in some disused rooms upstairs."

"Do let us see him!" Subercaseaux exclaimed. "A spy spotted by a *jeune fille* and drugged by a *bonne* is really something worth looking at!"

The Duke was also quite anxious to see his daughter's prize.

"I hope I can find the room," Torrens said rather doubtfully as they went upstairs; however, on the landing they encountered Miss Probyn, who had just said Goodnight to Mrs. Hathaway. "Ah good, Julia. You can conduct us to that creature. The Duke and the Monsignor want to see him."

In the old night-nursery the Duke did not at first so much as look at the man lying slackly in Nanny Brown's armchair by the fire-place; instead his glance strayed to a little cot in one corner, a tiny chair and a low table, miniatures for a child's use. Julia knew why. He was thinking back to the little son who had not lived to carry on his name and care for his estates. When at last he did examine the drugged figure— "He looks like a Baltic German," he observed. "How strange."

Julia and Torrens exchanged glances. But Torrens wanted above all to get the business in hand organised.

"Quite so, Sir," he said briskly. "Now, Colonel Marques and his men are coming to fetch him about 4 A.M. Can someone stay up to let them in? And do you agree to his staying here till then; locked in, of course?"

The Duke pondered—Julia saw him glance again at the cot in the corner, and guessed at his distaste.

"Yes, of course," he said then with a shrug, as if shaking off his private thoughts. "Elidio shall let these people in and bring them up by the back stairs, so that they will not be heard."

"Thank you, Sir. I shall wait up myself, of course."

"In that case you had better use my study. I will tell Elidio to keep the fire in. Now let us return to our drinks. Miss Probyn, will you not join us?"

In the study Mgr Subercaseaux suddenly put a question.

"Major Torrens, I think you said that this creature upstairs is probably the principal in the organisation?" Torrens nodded. "That being so," Subercaseaux proceeded, "and at least three of his associates being also laid by the heels, might not this be a good opportunity to get Dr. Horvath out of the country, before they have a chance to reorganise?"

"That was my idea. Have you done with him?"

"Substantially, yes; we could finish in a couple of hours. And since His Grace will be driving back to Lisbon on Friday for the wedding, it occurs to me that Dr. Horvath could travel down as he came up—if you agree, Duke?"

"Of course. Strange how one keeps on forgetting this wedding!" the Duke said. "It had quite passed from my mind again."

Subercaseaux turned to Torrens.

"You would, of course, have to make your transatlantic arrangements," he said. "How quickly could you do it?"

Torrens considered.

"Do you know, Sir," he said, "I think I had better go down with

Colonel Marques when he comes to collect the body—a *corpus vile* if ever there was one!"

"Leave at four in the morning?" The Duke looked horrified.

"Yes, Sir. Of course I must hear whether Marques agrees with the Monsignor's estimate of the situation; if he does, I think we should go ahead. Could Father Antal spend just the Friday night in your Lisbon house again? You have been so good already that I hesitate to ask it, but it would save a lot of complicated arrangements."

"I am vexed that you should hesitate to ask!" the Duke said warmly. "I think you must know what a privilege it has been to have so great a man as Dr. Horvath under my roof."

Major Torrens was rather crushed by this. He had never realised that Father Antal was in any sense a "great" man in his own right; he regarded him as a little priest—a bit of a theologian, apparently, and as nice as you like, of course—whose special knowledge of conditions in Hungary made the Americans covet him for broadcasting on the Voice of America. As for the Vatican, God knew *whom* they attached importance to, or why: though one had to admit that the Roman Catholic Church was one of the few things that really seemed to worry the Kremlin, so good luck to it! He was relieved when the Monsignor put another question.

"You think you can get the agent from America over by Saturday to take him back? That seems rather quick work."

"Oh, no. This is only Wednesday—well it will be Thursday in half an hour!" he said, glancing at the clock. "But if Marques is on time we should be in Lisbon by ten-thirty tomorrow morning, and I ought to get through to Washington in an hour at most."

"That is only seven-thirty there," the Monsignor observed.

"Yes, but that office works round the clock. I don't know how long they'll take to lay on the special plane, but even their smaller jets do the trip in nine or ten hours."

"You will telephone to Washington?" the Duke put in, much interested.

"Radio-telephone, Sir. With a scrambler, of course: that is how Roosevelt and Churchill used to have those long heart-to-hearts during the war."

"They will come to Portela?" Subercaseaux asked.

"I shouldn't think so—much more likely Montijo. But Marques will have to arrange all that. He can have the plane advised which airport to use when it stops at the Azores to re-fuel. Then they can take Father Antal off some time on Saturday."

Julia spoke.

"Is all this rush really necessary?" she said coolly to Torrens. "It's a little hard on Hetta, don't you think? She'll hardly have any time with Father A. at this rate; only tomorrow, and I gather the Monsignor proposes to mop up most of that. Considering what she's been through for the sake of seeing him, I think it's rather tough."

Torrens looked annoyed and hurt; the Monsignor gave his barking laugh.

"Dear Miss Probyn, you remind us of the human element, so rightly the woman's role! But in this case perhaps there are over-riding considerations."

The Duke did not laugh.

"Miss Probyn, could not Countess Hetta come down with us to Lisbon on Friday? Then she could spend a quiet evening with Dr. Horvath, and possibly Saturday morning also. It is easy to take a third car if we need it."

"Duke dear, you're an angel! Yes, that's perfect. But I don't think you'll need to take a third car; Mr. Atherley has to get back to Lisbon on Friday, so *he* could drive Hetta down."

Subercaseaux threw her an enquiring glance, but he said nothing.

"Of course all this is subject to Colonel Marques approving of the plan," Torrens said. "Duke, if you will excuse me I think I'll go and put my things together now, so that there will be no delay when he comes."

"Certainly, my dear Torrens. Ring when you are ready, and Elidio will have your luggage brought down." He rose as he spoke. "I am afraid that this is Goodbye," he said, "but I hope only for the present. We shall see you in Lisbon, of course. Your visit has been a great pleasure."

Once again Major Torrens was abashed by his host's words; he spoke almost haltingly as he tried to express his own thanks. "You've been unbelievably good to us, Sir." Then, hastily, he made his escape.

"I think I'll go up too, Duke," Julia said, observing that her host was still on his feet—that was the sort of thing the darling Duque managed so well, she reflected amusedly, as she watched the Monsignor reluctantly heaving himself up out of his comfortable armchair.

Miss Probyn once again set her little Travalarm, and appeared in the study a few minutes after 4 A.M., in a highly becoming black velvet house-coat.

"Good heavens, Julia!" the Major exclaimed, surprised and glowing. "What on earth are you doing down here?"

"I just thought I'd come and see the coffin carried out, and hear what the Colonel has to say."

"*Darling!*" But the embrace on which Torrens was just embarking was forestalled by a sound of car-wheels on the gravel outside the windows; he stood back, and listened.

"Coming in with his engine shut off—good man," Julia commented.

"He's early," Torrens said resentfully; a moment later Elidio ushered in the Colonel.

"Well, our man is still fast asleep, I hope?" Marques said, shaking hands. "An excellent piece of work, this."

"You'd better come up and see if it *is* your man, Colonel. He should be quiet enough still."

"Oh, I know it's our man," Marques said. "Our people traced him to São Pedro do Sul this evening, but there was an inexcusable delay about getting the report through. However, the counter-espionage in this house is so good that it didn't matter! If you will just give me the key of the room, Major, my men will carry him down."

"We'd better go up with them; no one in the house knows where he is," said Torrens.

"Oh yes, the Duke gave instructions to his butler." Indeed at that moment Elidio appeared at the door and asked the Colonel for *a chave*; Torrens, amused, handed over the key.

"There; now we need not disturb ourselves," the Colonel said, going across to the fire and holding out his hands to the blaze. "Do I see whisky? That would be very welcome—the night is quite chilly." And soon the Chief of the Security Police, glass in hand, was listening very contentedly while the Major outlined his plans.

"Admirable. Yes, by all means come down with me; I have two cars. And this is an excellent moment to get Horvath out; their organisation here is disrupted for the time being—there were note-books on the three we caught, so we were able to land several others as well."

"*Did* any of them come in on the plane with Father Antal?" Julia put in unexpectedly. Marques glanced at her with amusement.

"Yes; four. How much you know, Mademoiselle!"

Presently Elidio, perfectly impassive, appeared at the door and announced that *este homem*, the agents, and the luggage of the Senhor Comandante were all now in the cars.

"Oh, but look here—*momentinho*, Elidio—they must have some coffee or something before they start off again!" the girl exclaimed. She spoke to the servant; Elidio said smugly that the policemen had already partaken of coffee and bread.

"Are you sure *you* don't want coffee or something?" she asked Colonel Marques.

"*Au contraire*, whisky was much better. So, *en route*." He bowed over Julia's hand, Torrens gripped it hard; a moment later she heard the cars crunch over the gravel and hum away up the drive.

When Julia told the Duke in the morning that Torrens was gone, and that the Colonel had given his blessing to the plan for getting Father Antal out of Portugal at the weekend, her host drew a pad towards him and began one of his careful computations, jotting down names as he spoke.

"So you go, and I, and my sister—the wedding party; also both our divines; five." He drummed with his fingers on the desk. "I think if possible we must take Dom Pedro by car; he was miserable coming up. He dislikes riding in the Land-Rover, it seems."

"I don't wonder!" Julia exclaimed bluntly. The Duke laughed.

"But you say Monsieur Atherley is driving down, and could take the little Countess; could he not take Dom Pedro too?"

"No, Duke; not on any account!"

"Oh?" He raised an eyebrow at her. "You have some combination in your head?" he asked.

"Yes—'a consummation devoutly to be wished,' and you really *mustn't* spoil it. Let Townsend Waller drive Dom Pedro down; if he does mislay *him* it won't matter," said Julia coolly. "The Communists wouldn't hold that poor old creature for twelve hours! Townsend can't stay here for ever, either."

Ericeira burst out laughing.

"Miss Probyn, I sometimes envy your remorselessness! It simplifies many problems. Very well: Dom Pedro either with us or with the American, Atherley and the Countess." He made more notes, and looked up at her again.

"But your delightful friend, Mrs. Hathaway! We are forgetting her. Presumably she will wish to return to Lisbon also. How vexatious that we must leave just now! I should have liked her to pay us a much longer visit; she is interested in agriculture."

"Why shouldn't she stay here, then? We shall all three be back on Sunday evening—if I may come back?"

"Of course you come back! But you think Mrs. Hathaway would not mind this, being left for two days in the company of a child and a nurse?"

"Judging by a talk I overheard between her and Nanny this morning I think she'd love it. They were getting on like a house on fire."

"Very well; so it shall be. You are the best judge. I must say," the Duke said thoughtfully, "that it would give me great pleasure to show your friend something of the estate, and of my plantations. She appears to have a considerable knowledge of forestry."

Julia, who knew Mrs. Hathaway's knowledge of forestry to be confined to conducting acrimonious disputes on her Aunt Ellen's behalf with the Forestry Commission about "dedicating" some of the woods at Glentoran, was delighted, though not surprised, that her old friend should have spent the previous evening to such good purpose, and hastened off to open the plan to her.

In the hall, however, she was intercepted by Atherley.

"Julia, be a good friend! Can you somehow break through the sort of harem system that seems to operate in this house? I really do want to talk to Hetti, but the women apparently never appear downstairs except at meals, or in a covey."

Julia laughed. Richard's picturesque description of Portuguese country-house life was in fact extremely apt.

"I'll do what I can," she said. "But of course you realise that the really important thing is for her to get as much time as possible with Father Antal, since he's flying to America at the week-end."

"*Is* he? When was that settled?"

"With Colonel Marques, early this morning. Oh, of course you don't know—it's *such* a performance!" And she told him about Luzia's and Nanny's exploits. Atherley bayed with delight.

"That *glorious* girl! Really she is a wonder." But then he pressed his request about Hetta.

"Well have a little *patience*, Richard!" Miss Probyn said, her voice displaying a marked absence of that quality. "Anyhow on the Duque's car-and-passenger schedule for returning to Lisbon tomorrow you are billed to drive Hetti down, *alone*."

"You've arranged that? Oh bless you."

"Yes. He wanted to plant you with Dom Pedro as well, but I suppressed it. So even if you don't get much time with her today, you'll have all tomorrow."

"Do I have to take her back to Dorothée?" Richard asked apprehensively.

"Oh Lord no! To the Palace; she's staying there till after the wedding, anyhow."

Julia had made up her mind that it was important that Father Antal should have an opportunity to give Hetta his guidance in what lay ahead of her—life in the western world, probably a diplomatic marriage —before Atherley started on the poor child. But on her way to the priests' study she was caught by Hetta's other admirer.

"Oh Miss Probyn, *there* you are!" Townsend Waller said. "I was wondering—do you know where Countess Hetta is? I never had a chance to speak to her last night, and I really *would* like a talk with her."

"Townsend, I know you would, and I expect it can be fixed presently. But just now I'm trying to arrange for her to have a long, *quiet* talk with Father Antal; you see he's probably flying to the States on Saturday, so she and he won't have much time together; and honestly I think you young men can wait!"

"Leaving on *Saturday!*" the Bostonian exclaimed.

"Yes. I'll tell you the story later—it is quite a story! But Townsend, I must go now." She felt ready to shake both these greedy grasping creatures, thinking so much more of their own desires than of Hetta's real needs, and walked into the priests' study in a mood of strong impatience.

Subercaseaux had been sufficiently impressed by Miss Probyn's *démarche* in the study the previous evening to raise no objections when she stated that *now* would be a very good time for Father Antal and Hetta to have a little talk, alone. "If I don't arrange it no one else will," the girl said. "There are all these wretched suitors clamouring for her all over the house—she might be Penelope! Can't the Vatican take your infernal revisions as read, Monsignor?"

Both men laughed; Father Antal rose at once. "I am at your disposition."

"Splendid. Come along."

Julia had decided that the knot-garden or anywhere out of doors was too liable to interruption, and led the priest to one of the huge deserted salons; there she looked round for an ash-tray, another rarity in Portuguese country-houses, and ruthlessly grabbed a small celadon dish off the chimney-piece.

"There you are—now smoke away! I'll bring her down."

She looked in on her way to see if Mrs. Hathaway was all right; she found Nanny seated with that lady in the latter's boudoir, deep in conversation, and both mending stockings—Mrs. Hathaway's stockings. "Oh, the young Countess is in my sitting-room, helping Luzia with her puzzle," Nanny said. Julia found Hetta, and bore her off with "Father Antal wants to talk to you."

Will it work? she asked herself as they went downstairs; these arranged things sometimes didn't. But unless this *was* arranged they would get no chance. She pushed Hetta into the great room, and left them to it.

"This is nice," Hetta said happily, pulling a brocaded tabouret over to the rather severe upright Louis XV armchair in which Father Antal, regardless of his own comfort, had settled down, and seating herself at his feet. "How did Yulia get this tedious Monsignor to release you? For I am sure she *did*. It seems he never lets you out of his sight!"

"Who told you this?" the priest asked, non-committally.

"Luzia; there is nothing she doesn't know. I find her—but *quite* enchanting!"

"She is. Now tell me why you describe Mgr Subercaseaux as tedious?" He was still perfectly non-committal.

"Oh but really, Father, surely you can see this for yourself! Flattering this poor old *beata* Dona Maria Francisca last night, being agreeable to the Duke, to everyone; enjoying his wine and his cigar!" Hetta said contemptuously. "And he is always the same: with my mother, with the Comte de Bretagne, with anyone who is rich or great! I dislike it. He is so—so *utterly* different to you!"

Father Antal made no direct reply to this outburst.

"Do you know about your mother's charities in the Alfama?" he asked quietly.

"Charities of *Mama*'s?" She sounded incredulous. "No, I never heard of them. And where is the Alfama?"

"It is one of the districts of Lisbon where only quite poor people live, and money for the necessary charities is therefore hard to come by. But for the last few years the parish priest has received practically all he needs—from your mother."

"This is *very* odd! At home it was always Pappi who took an interest

in poor people, and charities. That parish priest must be a most per-
suasive person, if he has succeeded in interesting Mama!"

"She has never met him," Father Antal said. "It is the Monsignor,
whom you so despise, who has tapped this source of wealth to help the
poor. Also he goes and says early Mass there at least twice a week, to
give the parish priest a chance to rest and say his Mass later. As you
know, working people must hear Mass early, or not at all."

Hetta pondered.

"He drives in from Estoril to say Mass? At what time?"

"At seven."

"Then he must leave his house soon after six. Well, that is something
for him!" She pondered again. "Father, you mean some particular thing
by telling me all this—what is it? Do not leave me to guess; you know
that I am stupid at guessing!"

He patted her head gently.

"My child, I think you are in a certain confusion. Partly it is due to
ignorance and inexperience, partly to the natural intolerance of youth;
what is unfamiliar to you is necessarily wrong! This is a mistaken idea,
believe me. What I wish you to recognise, and accept, is that there are
other ways of serving God than those which obtained in the Alföld!
God's plan for the world, and His wisdom, are not limited by your personal experience; He uses other means, other men, and it is presumption
not to recognise the fact."

She was silent, troubled.

"I fancy this is, in you, a certain spiritual pride," he went on. "That,
as you know, is a sin. You have only seen certain aspects of Monsignor
Subercaseaux's activities, and in a certain milieu which, since it is unfamiliar, you take upon yourself to disapprove of—you, an ignorant girl
of twenty-two! Who are you to judge?"

Hetta was deeply disturbed. In all their years together her beloved
Father Antal had never spoken so severely to her before.

"But Father—he is so different to you," she repeated lamely.

"And am I the only model for God's servants? Must they all be cast
in the mould which Hetta Páloczy approves? The Monsignor is quite as
efficient as I am in achieving God's ends, and as uncompromising; and
those ends are always worth achieving, even if it should be done by
associating with the great or the rich."

Hetta burst into tears.

"Oh, it is all so difficult!" she exclaimed, between sobs. "To me, nearly everything here is a muddle! Compromise, compromise!—dress well, say always the right thing, whether it is true or not, and you are safe, you are accepted! But how can I live so? It is not my nature, and I have never learned it."

Father Antal let her cry for some time; then he put out a hand and raised her tear-stained face to look at him.

"This is what you must now learn," he said. "What made you a good little cook in a country presbytery, and a dutiful helper to Mother Scholastica will not suffice here. You must learn tolerance, and control, and moderation—but tolerance above all. Listen," he said, as she shook her head rebelliously, scattering tear-drops on his knees and her lap, "God has some particular work for each of us to do—yes, even for His little ignorant obstinate Hetta! But we must accept the place, and the conditions, which He chooses to set; if we do not accept them we are useless. And part of our acceptance must be a willingness, a *humble* willingness, to learn the appropriate technique. This for the present is your duty, since you have been set down by Almighty God in the free world, and in rather *mondain* surroundings. I shall be distressed," he ended rather sternly, "if you do not accept these terms."

This time Hetta did not cry. She shook back her hair and frowned, concentrating on his words; it was some moments before she spoke.

"I *have* tried to accept Mama," she said at last. "And truly I have tried to be docile: to go forever to the coiffeur, to put stuff on my face, to wear the right clothes. But—just lately—other things have come in, too; they make me wonder what I must do. Oh, I don't know whether I *can* live out here!"

"Are you thinking of M. Atherley?" Father Antal asked.

She stared at him. It was a strange expression that came over her strong face just then: surprise, hauteur, uncertainty—but, he would have sworn, also joy.

"But—why—I know that he is here; has he spoken?" the girl asked. Her words were confused, but there was no confusion in her manner; as always it was perfectly direct.

"Not to me. Has he to you? My child, I do not wish to force your confidence but before I leave I should like to know how this affair stands."

"Asked me to marry him—no," Hetta said thoughtfully. "I think he has become attached to me, in a rather unthinking way; he did once say to me that he thought he could be happy with me anywhere."

"And what did you say?"

"That he had not given the matter any thought; that I should drive him mad by—by my lack of control and tolerance and moderation!" the girl said explosively. "All the things you wish me to learn." She paused. "In any case, he is not a Catholic, and that is difficult," she ended in a different voice.

"Might he become one?"

"Well, at least he very much admires the Monsignor!" Hetta exclaimed. "We have arguments about him. Perhaps this is the road to Rome!"

Father Antal burst out laughing.

"This is a hopeful sign!—though it may only mean that Monsieur Atherley has more experience, and therefore more tolerance, than my late cook! One would expect this of a diplomat, of course."

Hetta laughed too, then became grave.

"Father"—she hesitated.

"Yes, my child?"

"Supposing he—Richard—did not wish to become a Catholic at once, should you approve of my getting married to him all the same?"

The priest took his time over replying. The question itself told him much. Clearly Hetta was anticipating a proposal; and his mind returned to what that so excellent young Englishwoman had said to him only yesterday about the importance of getting the child away from her mother. But there was the official Catholic view on this matter. At last, with deliberation, he spoke.

"My child, as you know the Church does not approve of mixed marriages. But Mother Church also takes particular circumstances into consideration; and in your case I should not oppose your marriage to this Englishman, provided that you love him, and are prepared to try to fit yourself to be his wife. Do you love him?" the old man asked bluntly.

"Oh yes—very, very much!" Hetta said in ringing tones. There was no bashful hiding of the face; she threw up her head as she announced her love for Richard Atherley. "Only I think we might have fights! But not so many if I practise these things you have told me of. And—" She stopped, her face clouding, as if the sun of her love had gone in.

"Yes?"

Hetta, too, delayed her reply, frowning in thought.

"Look, Father dear," she said at last, "I am young, and as you say without experience, unsophisticated"—there was a note of contempt on the word. "So it is hard for me to know if this, I mean to marry me, would be right for *him*. He *is* sophisticated, and the other day I met a person, a"—she faltered—"well, to me a most *disagreeable* person, who claimed to know him very well; and she made it plain that in her opinion I should make him miserable. This I have so much wanted to ask you about, for me it is important—in quite a different way to how it is important to her!" the girl said, with sudden anger. "She is an old woman who wants to keep a young lover; I am young, and I think of a husband, and having children, and a life together!"

He stroked her dark savage little head; he could not help smiling, though he was moved.

"Monsieur Atherley has broken with Madame de Vermeil. That affair is finished," he said.

"*You* know about this? How extraordinary!"

"No, personally I could not know. But Monsignor Subercaseaux, owing to this worldliness which you so contemn, knows all about the lady in question. And only two days ago young Atherley told him that the thing is over, and that he will never willingly meet this person again."

"So," Hetta Páloczy said thoughtfully. "So," she repeated slowly. She was considering this information. It must mean that the two priests had discussed her and her relation to Atherley; almost certainly it must mean as well that the Monsignor and Richard had also spoken of her relation to him. Now, no young girl whose heart is engaged before her hand really relishes the idea of her relations with the man of her choice being discussed by other people, but in Hetta's realistic Central European make-up there was no room for the quivering sensibility of the Nordic races over matters of romance. If they had all talked her and Richard over, well they had, and that was that; at least she had learned one really most precious fact—that this hitherto redoubtable enemy, the Frenchwoman, was no longer to be feared. She got up off the tabouret.

"Father, I do thank you. You have helped me so much: cleared my mind and my conscience. Now I see my way, if it should turn out so." Her deep voice hung suspended on the last words. "And now I am sure the Monsignor wants you!" She knelt on the Aubusson carpet. "Father, will you give me your blessing?"

His hands on her head, he did so, tears at last running down his face.

Chapter Eighteen

ON the Friday morning preceding the nuptials of the son of the Comte de Bretagne another procession of cars passed down the by-road from Gralheira to São Pedro do Sul. In the twenty-four hours before an event of this sort one might have expected a certain degree of fuss to prevail; in fact there was none. For such occasions Dona Maria Francisca invariably donned a slightly richer version of her usual out-of-date black, and unlike Countess Páloczy gave no thought whatever to her hair or her face, let alone her feet; as for Julia, she had left the green brocade dress, which had so *épaté* Atherley, in a cupboard in the Ericeira Palace in Lisbon, all ready to put on.

The Duke had apologised deeply to Mrs. Hathaway for his own absence, and for taking away Elidio.

"This poor Antonio! I hope that he will wait on you well; but on the telephone he is hopeless, and there may be many calls in Lisbon. In any event we shall be back on Sunday evening, and you have only to ask Nanny for anything you want."

"Oh, Nanny and Luzia and I are going to enjoy ourselves thoroughly," Mrs. Hathaway said. "It is so good of you to keep me. Please don't worry. Nanny is a host in herself."

Nanny, for her part, expressed similar sentiments to Julia.

"Well really, Miss Probyn, it's quite a privilege to meet someone like your friend. It's not often I come across anyone that I could have such an esteem for."

"Yes, Nanny, she's grand, isn't she?" Julia said.

"A great advantage for Luzia, too, the company of a person like that," Nanny observed rather patronisingly; Julia went away laughing, realising how little of Mrs. Hathaway's advantageous company Nanny was likely to allow her charge.

So down the sandy road between the pines the cars poured that morning: a station-wagon containing Elidio and other servants, then Atherley's Bentley with Hetta and a rather gloomy Townsend Waller, who with Dom Pedro was to be dropped in São Pedro to pick up his car. Poor Townsend had not achieved a talk with Hetta—for which, rightly, he blamed Julia. Some time after the Bentley came two of the Daimlers with the rest of the party.

Atherley had made his own dispositions about this drive. He, too, had not yet succeeded in talking to Hetta; therefore he asked Elidio the day before to provide *lanche* for two—*lanche* being the Portuguese word for any form of meal carried in a basket to be eaten out of doors. After dropping the chaplain and Mr. Waller in São Pedro do Sul he shot on to Aveiro, the so-called Venice of Portugal. Here the flat coast-line is broken up into a maze of lagoons, and a net-work of canals brings the brine of the Atlantic into shallow salt-pans, divided by low earthen banks; these are filled through small sluices and then left to be evaporated by the strong sun; the good resulting salt is scraped off the floor and the pans re-flooded. This process goes on all through the summer, and by early autumn conical mounds of snow-white salt cover this peculiar landscape, like ranges of miniature Alps. Richard had seen this once, and he wanted Hetta to see it too, but in his urban ignorance he had ignored the seasons; this was Spring, and hardly any salt had accumulated; there were no snowy mounds.

"Oh well never mind, we'll go and see the Convent of Jesus instead," he said. "That's there all the year round." And he drove Hetta to that amazing place, where the interior of the chapel gives the visitor the impression of standing inside a golden box, covered all over with the richest possible gilded carving. Hetta was more surprised than pleased by this— "Must one have so much gold about to worship God?" she asked, causing the young man to laugh. But she stood long before the portrait of Santa Joanna, the King's daughter who became a nun, with her plain melancholy face, her heavy jowl, and her exceedingly long nose.

"Yes, that one could really have been a Saint," she said. "About some one wonders, but not her. It must be a true portrait. Who was the artist?"

"Nuno Gonçalves, who painted the triptych with Prince Henry the Navigator in it. Have you seen that yet?"

"Oh, *that* painter! Yes; no wonder," Hetta said, turning back to stare at the sainted Princess again.

"Who took you to see the triptych?" Richard asked, slightly annoyed; he would have liked to do that himself.

"Waller. He is very *gebildet*; he comes from Boston, where it seems that all are extremely cultivated," Hetta said, again provoking Richard to laughter. The priest's cook was coming on if she had already registered the Boston passion for culture!

The Bentley's speed was so great, on the almost empty Portuguese roads, that in spite of their détour they overtook the stately convoy of the ducal Daimlers, proceeding at a majestic pace, several miles short of Leiria; Hetta waved gaily to Julia and Father Antal, in the second car.

"Now we are ahead!" she said.

"Yes, but we're not going to eat with them all at the Lis; you and I are going to have a picnic by ourselves," he pronounced; the arrogant happiness in his voice sent a vibration through the girl. A mile or so farther on he swung the car sharply to the right down a small road which led through pinewoods to the village of Pinheiros, already on the edge of green open country with a river running through it, all brilliant as enamel in the spring sunshine, and the great church of Milagres standing up across the valley, a lonely wonder of baroque. Richard carried the lunch-baskets up a path to the fringe of the pinewoods, where he spread a rug on the clean mixture of silvery sand and fragrant needles; there, the dusky shadow of the trees behind, the shining river with its crumbling bridge in front, they had their lunch.

Portuguese servants have rather exalted ideas about picnic food. The *lanche* provided by Elidio included a bottle of sherry and another of red wine, with their appropriate glasses, thermoses of soup and coffee, and a jar of cream; these were merely adjuncts to a boned stuffed chicken already cut up and slices of *paio*, loin of pork spiced, salted, and rolled into a sausage; there were also buttered French rolls, a dish of dressed salad, and a box of chocolate éclairs. Richard ground the bottles and flasks into the shining sand to keep them upright, and poured out the sherry.

"Well, darling Hetti, here's to your future happiness!" He raised his glass.

"Prost," she said, and drank to him.

"You don't drink to *my* happiness, I notice," he said.

"Prost means 'to your well-being.' Isn't that enough?" she countered.

Her readiness pleased him. And she looked so *right,* there on the sandy edge of the forest, in her unobtrusive suit, open-necked blouse, low-heeled shoes and heavy-weight nylons. That a woman should look right in the country is always very important to Englishmen; another thing to which they often attach considerable importance is legs. Richard Atherley now observed that Hetta's legs, stuck out carelessly in front of her on the sand, though strong and shapely were rather thick, as Central European legs are apt to be; they were not in the least like Julia Probyn's long lovely ones. And with a sort of pang of surprised emotion the young man realised that in this girl, at any rate, he could even love thick legs.

"No—my well-being, like patriotism, is not enough," was all he said. "I would like you to drink to my happiness, Hetta. Do you know the one thing necessary for it?"

Again that vibration shook her, but she spoke deliberately.

"Richard, I am not certain that I do, truthfully. If your happiness requires two women, and I am to be one, I am afraid that you will have to go without it."

"Meaning?"

"That if I were to marry, I cannot share my husband with anyone— least of all *you* with this Frenchwoman! If I am married my husband must be mine!" she exclaimed.

He put down his glass so quickly and carelessly that it fell over; the sherry seeped away into the white sand as he took her in his arms.

"Darling, you won't have to share me with *anyone!*" he said, between kisses. "That nonsense is all over." He paused. "I learned the other night, when I thought I'd lost you, what I really want—you, and to spend my life with you. But in fact I had that idea before; do you remember what I told you at Obidos? Anyhow, will you marry me? This is a formal proposal, and requires an unequivocal answer," he said, giving her another kiss and then holding her away from him so that he could watch her face.

To his infinite delight she gave a tiny laugh; then she put up her hand and stroked his cheek. It was a very small gesture, but combined with the laugh to him it seemed to demonstrate comprehension, humour, and great love.

"Yes, Richard, I will marry you," she said. "On these terms that you have just stated—I hope, unequivocally also!"

He shook her shoulders. "Oh, you are a proud piece! Yes, unequivocally! And now, my fiancée, please give *me* a kiss. This affair mustn't be altogether one-sided, you know."

The kiss Hetta gave him was so satisfactory that it demanded a rather protracted response; it was some time before they returned to the normal world and the business of drinking and eating.

"See, you have upset my glass as well as your own—what waste!" Hetta said. "How shall I live with a husband who is so careless? Hungarians are thrifty."

"Oh, go ahead with your thrift, my saucy darling! We shall need it; diplomacy is a ruinous career. I never knew an English Minister or Ambassador who didn't end up several thousand pounds down out of his private pocket."

"But you are not an Ambassador."

"No, sweetheart, but it is quite inevitable that I shall become one— unless the demands of your love extinguish me before my time!"

She gave him a little slap.

"Do not be id-*yot!* I am hungry. Do you allow your wife, or your wives, sometimes to eat?"

In such a mood Elidio's *lanche* went down very well: the soup was drunk, the French rolls munched; between them the two young people demolished the whole of the boned chicken, the salad, and the spiced pork, to the accompaniment of the Duke's good red wine. Seeing Richard take up a final slice of *paio* before he vulgarly wiped out the salad-dish with the last roll, Hetta asked rather anxiously, "Do you like *l'ail?* I think the English call it something else."

"Garlic. Yes, I do."

"That is well. I should find it almost impossible to cook *good* food without it, though one should not always recognise quite so clearly that it is there as one does in this curious *Schinken*." (*Paio* in fact reeks of garlic.)

"Sweet, you won't have to be *my* cook, as well as the old priest's," Richard said. "We shall have a cook, please God."

"I shall be much in the kitchen, nevertheless," Hetta averred firmly. "A good *maîtresse de maison* is constantly there, taking counsel with the cook, as my Grandmother did at Detvan. And so I shall do with our cook."

Those two very ordinary words, "our cook," were astonishingly sweet in her mouth to Richard's ears. His fears, the inevitable hesitations of a lively handsome young man finally and definitely confronted with matrimony, began to fall away as another picture opened on his imagination: of a home with a wife in it, who would "take counsel" with his cook about his food, and never allow dead or dying flowers, one of his particular phobias; of a hundred homely domestic intimacies—perhaps even children. Richard Atherley had never hitherto contemplated any picture of the sort; now he did, in a wondering silence, and found it strangely delightful. He was silent for so long that at last Hetta touched his hand. "I have said something stupid?" she asked.

"No, you've said something very nice indeed. Look"—he held her hand —"how do you feel about having children?"

"*Feel* about it? What should I feel? I hope we have many; one child is not a good thing." She paused and looked at him, uncertainty coming into her face. "Do *you* not want children? Richard, I cannot marry without."

"No, I do. Darling, this is all so new—don't be impatient with me." It was he who was anxious now. "We'll have lots of children! Well say four; they cost the earth to educate! Will four do you? But I do want *some*; I'd like to have a son, I must say."

Hetta laughed at him.

"And what shall you do if you only have a daughter, like the Duque? And my poor Pappi," she added, no longer laughing.

He caught her to him. "Try, try, try again!"

They arrived in Lisbon rather late, because Richard had insisted on giving her at least a glimpse of Batalha and Alcobaça; and then they felt that they must drive out to Obidos and have another glass of wine in the tiny room that Richard so idiotically called "The Ritz," and look again at the house in which he had first suggested living with her. During those hours of driving through the sun-drenched countryside, laughing and touching hands, there grew in them both, strongly, the extraordinary sense of *security* that becoming engaged brings, and the quite irrational self-satisfaction at having achieved this security, this feeling of being anchored. Richard told the man in the flowered shirt-sleeves who poured out their wine in the Ritz that they were going to be married, whereupon a surprising number of relations crammed into the minute space to laugh and drink their healths.

As they drove on again Hetta asked a question.

"So do we tell everyone, now, that we shall marry?"

Richard reflected, but only for a moment. Thinking of Fanny—

"Yes, immediately," he replied. If everyone in the Ericeira Palace knew of their engagement tonight it would ring all round the wedding reception tomorrow, and could not fail to reach Fanny's ears, and Fanny would always accept a *fait accompli* that was publicly proclaimed, however unpalatable; she was much too clever to make a fuss which might jeopardise her position in the eyes of the world. But even as he reached this reassuring conclusion another quite fresh idea struck him: how low and calculating such considerations were—his, and Fanny's—compared with Hetta's spontaneous and unself-seeking honesty. Even loving and desiring her, he had thought patronisingly of her lack of sophistication; now, startled, he saw that there was such a thing as moral sophistication, that fierce delicate rectitude in relationships, regardless of one's own position. And Hetti had it, and he and Mme de Vermeil had not. Oh, once she had mastered a little of the technique of tact and discretion she would be able to make rings round all the Fannys in the world!—as Maggie Verver had made rings round Charlotte Stant in *The Golden Bowl*, in the end of all.

Hetta was silent for some time.

"If we tell others, I should tell Mama," she said at length.

"Yes, you must of course. But may I give you a piece of advice?" She nodded.

"I shouldn't do it tonight. She's not worrying about you; you know I took the Monsignor down to see her, and he straightened all that out, and if you telephone to her this evening she'll only get in a fuss, just when she ought to be resting, to be at her best for the wedding tomorrow." Feeling slightly like Judas, he added, "You should know how much that means to her."

"This is true." She frowned a little, thinking. "But if she hears it from others at the wedding, she might be hurt."

"She's not likely to hear it from the Ericeiras," Richard said bluntly. "Why don't you leave it to the Monsignor? He's made himself responsible for you to her."

"Yes, Yulia told me. He has been kind, in this. All the same, that someone else should tell a mother that her daughter is engaged: this is not very nice, do you think?"

He reflected. "I suggest that you write a note to your mother tonight —after all, we've only got engaged today—and let the Monsignor give it to her tomorrow. Then she will hear it from you, and at once."

Again Hetta considered.

"Yes, I will do that. It is—*just* adequate."

Julia and the Monsignor were down in the hall when they reached the palace; Subercaseaux at once asked Richard if he was staying to dinner? "If not, perhaps you could take me out to Estoril. The telephone has ceased to function, so there is some difficulty about a taxi; and the chauffeurs appear to be at supper."

"I shall be delighted," said Atherley unwillingly. He turned to Julia. "Hetti and I are engaged to be married."

Julia gave Hetti a warm hug. Still with an arm round her—"I hope, Richard, that you realise exactly *how* lucky you are," she said.

"Truly, Julia, I believe I do."

"Well don't go forgetting it later on!" Miss Probyn said crisply.

The Monsignor also made appropriate congratulations. "I think this match will be welcome to your mother," he added to Hetta.

"My note!" Hetta exclaimed. "I must write to Mama, so that you can give it to her the *moment* you see her, Monsignor, please. Yulia, *where* can I write?"

While Julia took Hetta away to write her note Richard explained the advice that he had given the girl about telling her mother; Subercaseaux nodded approval.

"Yes, for the Countess to telephone tonight might create complications. For the moment the instrument is out of action, but that cannot last long." He looked shrewdly at Richard. "You will have many things to learn from this child," he added.

"Monsignor, I've realised that." He liked and trusted Subercaseaux enough to expound his sudden enlightenment about moral sophistication.

"Precisely—that is what I mean. She needs to acquire the lower forms of this necessary but uninspiring quality, sophistication; but you, my dear Richard, would do well to master the higher ones! Ah, there they are!" he said, as Julia and Hetta cascaded down the great staircase; he took Hetta's note, and they drove off.

Too many descriptions of royal weddings can be tedious. This particular marriage was both exclusive and brilliant; it was followed by a reception, in the course of which the British Ambassador found himself practically pushed into the rounded front portion of Mgr Subercaseaux. "Oh, how are you, Monsignor? Everything going well? Tell me, is that Miss Probyn here? If she is I should like to meet her."

The Monsignor threw a practised eye over the throng. Not far off he saw Miss Probyn, whose height made her conspicuous; he and Sir Henry slowly made their way towards her between the jammed, richly-dressed bodies. Julia, in the green brocade dress, with a close-fitting toque of cock's feathers which continued down one side of her white neck to curl over her left shoulder, was really a very splendid sight; the Ambassador's blue eyes rested on her with pleasure.

"At last," he said. "I've been wanting to meet you for some time."

"Oh. Why?" Julia asked, in her near-drawl.

"You seem to be a sort of key to all these doings in which my First Secretary has been involved. Tell me, is he going to marry the little Countess?"

"Yes, they got engaged yesterday. Do you think it's a good idea?"

"It's always a good idea to marry a woman who can cook," Sir Henry said. "Especially nowadays. He will be comfortable when he retires, which is more than I shall; my good wife can't boil an egg."

"Oh how sad!—poor you!" Sir Henry chuckled. Few people say "poor you" to Ambassadors.

"A marriage with a foreigner won't *help* his career, of course," this one said, "but I expect he will surmount that. He's very able, and she is such a charmer. *Good,* too; you know lots of diplomatic wives seem to lose practically all ethical sense—if they ever had any."

Julia laughed. But she was thinking more of the present than of Richard's retirement some thirty years hence.

"Look, dear Sir Henry," she said coaxingly, "can't you push him off now somewhere else, out of reach of Mama?"

Sir Henry threw her a glance of half-comic outrage.

"So you want to rob me of the best Head of Chancery I've ever had, in any post?"

"Certainly I do. What do Chanceries matter compared with love and marriage? And for two such unusually nice people, in this case. I think they come even before the convenience of Ambassadors."

He laughed, and picked at his thumb.

"Miss Probyn, you fully come up to my expectations! No wonder everything hangs on you." He considered. "In fact I know that the Office wants someone of about his seniority for Rome."

"Then do get them to send him there, for goodness sake! Rome would be perfect for Hetta—it's full of expatriate Hunks, isn't it? And, of course, the Holy Father as well."

The Ambassador laughed again.

"I promise you that I will try—against my own interests." He gave her a shrewd glance. "Wasn't that exceedingly nice American, Waller, one of her admirers too?"

"Oh yes, but that didn't work. Hetta likes him, he was kind to her when she came; but—well, these things happen in one way and not in another."

He mused.

"Yes; yes, of course." He went on picking at his thumb. "Thirty-five years ago, no, more, when I was a Second Secretary in Washington I often met Emily Waller; his mother, you know. She was a very forceful woman. And their toffee doesn't always set."

Julia laughed so loudly that heads turned in their direction.

"Ah, but that isn't confined to America," the Ambassador said. "My dear Miss Probyn, London is full of such men."

At this point the Duke of Ericeira appeared beside them.

"Duke, you are the other person I wanted to see," Sir Henry said. "Miss Probyn I have, at last, met." Julia took this rather broad hint, and drifted off. "You have been unspeakably good to our people over all this," he went on. "I do thank you."

"Your Excellency, I cannot tell you the pleasure it has been to have them all in my house. I have long been a student of Dr. Horvath's writings, but I never hoped for the privilege of meeting him, let alone to have him as my guest. And the good Torrens: an admirable person, especially when galvanised into life by our dear Miss Probyn; and Atherley and the nice American, to say nothing of the enchanting little Countess. I assure you, my friend, it is long since Gralheira was so full of life."

"You like the little Countess? Good. I hear she and Master Atherley are going to make a match of it."

"Yes, so Miss Probyn tells me. From the little I have seen of her I should count him fortunate, for she seems to have real *fonds de caractère*. Would you agree?"

"Well, yes and no," Sir Henry said. "I think the girl is a good girl, with plenty of individuality; but the Service still takes a curiously *static* view about our diplomats not marrying Englishwomen, you know, and this girl comes from a Curtain country. Her father had a great reputation, of course, as an anti-Communist, back in 1919. But the poor boy will be saddled with a rather dreadful mother-in-law."

The Duke agreed. "Look out, *mon cher!*" Sir Henry suddenly exclaimed—"We are going to be *coincés par la mère!* Can we get away?"

They couldn't; the crowd was now too thick. Only someone of Dorothy Páloczy's ruthless determination could have forced a way through it just then; she succeeded, and appeared beside the two men, a formidable apparition in all her war-paint—the clothes, the hair, the make-up. Mme de Vermeil was at her elbow. After greeting the Ambassador, "I don't know the Duke of Ericeira except by sight!" the Countess said gaily.

Sir Henry was both firm and adroit.

"My dear lady, I am in precisely the same situation in regard to Madame de Vermeil," he said promptly. "Do please present me." This introduction was followed up by a flow of questions from Sir Henry about people in Paris, during which the Duke, thankfully, contrived to edge away.

"Oh, he's gone!" the Ambassador exclaimed, after a final earnest enquiry concerning *"cette chère Violette."* "What a pity! Well, some other time. Now tell me—are you happy about your little daughter's engagement to my admirable Head of Chancery? I do hope so, because I am very fond of him. Moreover, he's extremely able; he has a great future before him."

"I'm very glad to hear that. Yes; I haven't seen a great deal of Richard, but I like what I have seen," Dorothée said. A certain sharpness came into her voice. "Did Monsignor Subercaseaux fix this up?"

Sir Henry looked shocked.

"Oh my dear lady, NO. What an idea! Richard has been head over ears about your daughter ever since they first met; and when she—well, disappeared—" the Ambassador said carefully, "he was quite distracted. My good young man, my right hand, you might say, deserts both his chief and his job, and rushes off in the middle of the night to look for his lost love! Personally I regard this as practically a *crime passionnel,*" the Ambassador observed, chuckling. While he spoke he had kept one shrewd blue eye on Mme de Vermeil; she took it as he had expected she would, unblenchingly, but he decided to rub the thing in thoroughly.

"This really *is* Love's Young Dream," he went on; "I can assure you of that. The Monsignor I know is delighted—as well he may be, since he is extremely fond of Richard too. All this young man's friends can only rejoice at his great good fortune."

Dorothée was rather swamped by these complimentary phrases. Thrown off her balance—"I still don't know where she is," she said. "Do *you* know, Sir Henry?"

"No notion! Mustn't we both leave all that to the Monsignor? I gather he's in charge. Au revoir, chère Comtesse; au revoir, Madame de Vermeil. I see the Cardinal Patriarch over there; I must have a word with him."

The crowd was beginning to thin a little; skilfully, the Ambassador, too, escaped.

At that very moment Hetta Páloczy was standing out on the apron of Montijo airport, seeing Father Antal off. Thanks to the kindly planning of Julia and the Duke she had had a long quiet evening with the old priest the night before, and another blessed two hours with him this morning. She had told him of her happiness, he had given her his final blessing as she knelt devoutly in front of him, pressing his hands strongly on her little black head. Afterwards, "But do not forget what I told you at Gralheira," Father Antal said. "Now you enter upon a life in which your husband will be among those who wield power and influence. See to it that you do not diminish his influence by any mistakes of yours, any roughness or clumsiness. Be humble; be gentle. Do you remember what Ruysbroeck said? 'Be kind, be kind, and you will be saints.' I think, my Hetti, that you are not always kind in your judgements, as for instance concerning the Monsignor! And you must be good to your mother, too. She is very much alone, now." With tears, Hetta had promised to obey these injunctions.

That was her real farewell, but all the same she could have hugged Major Torrens for saying, off-handedly, that she might as well come along to the airport. Now, in the blinding sunshine, she stood in a little group which included Colonel Marques, the Major, and the Military Attaché, forcing herself to talk politely to the agent from America, a quiet, soft-voiced Southerner; at any other time he might well have charmed her, but now all her eyes and half her ears were concentrated on the stocky little figure of the priest. Once more he was wearing his European disguise of the grey overcoat and sun-glasses; the silver stubble on his head was half-concealed under the incongruous Trilby hat. The mouth and that cropped hair were really all she could see—she looked and looked, trying to force into her mind a picture that might have to last her for the rest of her life.

"And you cooked for him?" the Southerner said. He had heard enough of Hetta's story to be interested in her.

"Yes. I like cooking. Oh, but where does he go now?" Hetta exclaimed, as Marques, Torrens and Father Antal moved away. The man from Louisiana glanced at her with compassionate understanding.

"You go after him; you don't have to worry about me." Hetta followed the others.

"She loves that old man, the poor child," the American muttered to himself, as he moved after her.

On military airports like Montijo there is none of the civilian vulgarity of loud-speakers braying commands, only a brief discreet summons to the official passengers by word of mouth. This had just been given: the American followed Hetta slowly towards the great silvery bird-like shape poised for flight on the tarmac. He saw his special cargo, the freight he had to deliver safely to his employers in America, pause and look round; saw the pretty girl with whom he had just been talking break into a run, seize the old man's hand and cover it with kisses; when she turned back towards him Captain Glenny averted his eyes from the pain in her face. But he took her hand, saying, "Countess, I'll look after him; please don't worry."

Hetta made no reply. She stood stock still, watching, while Father Antal and the American climbed into the plane; watched while it rose, circled, and hummed away in flight over the red earth and the silver olive-groves, till it disappeared, seawards, behind the Serra da Arrabida.

It was just about then that Richard Atherley and Townsend Waller were sitting down to cocktails on the terrace of that restaurant above the Tagus. Richard had asked Townsend to lunch; one way and another he had rather a bad conscience about his friend, and he particularly did not want the Bostonian to hear of his engagement from any outside source.

"We've not been here since the day before Hetta arrived," Townsend said, tilting the Martini round in his glass thoughtfully.

"No. It's warmer now," Richard said, idiotically; he felt nervous. He pulled himself together. "Townsend, Hetta and I are engaged. I proposed to her yesterday on the way home, and she has accepted me."

"I was really expecting that, I think," Townsend said, after a moment's pause. He drank half his cocktail at a gulp, and set down his glass. Then he lifted it again.

"I don't have to wish you good fortune, Richard, because you have it! But I do wish you every conceivable happiness; you and her"—and he drained the glass.

Richard was touched by this. But there was nothing more to be said, really, and all through their meal they rather carefully talked diplomatic shop. Presently cars returning from the wedding reception began to stream along the broad road immediately below the terrace, and they amused themselves by noting the occupants. The Duke and his sister in one of the Ericeira Daimlers were among the first, shortly followed by the Loseleys in the Embassy Humber: on this highly official occasion the tiny Union Jack, usually discreetly furled in its black case, fluttered from the right wing.

"Oh good, H.E. will be back early. I shall have to go and see him," Richard said. A little later—"Goodness! There's the Monsignor, in Dorothée's car," he exclaimed. "What on earth is *he* hiving into Lisbon for, do you suppose? Father Antal must be gone by now; one would have expected Subercaseaux to be sleeping it off."

Mr. Waller laughed. But the sight of Mgr Subercaseaux had aroused another train of thought in his mind; he looked earnestly at his companion.

"Richard, please forgive my asking this, but are you going to become a Catholic when you marry?"

This time Richard did not laugh at the question, as he had done on an earlier occasion.

"Townsend, I don't think so; not at once, anyhow. I don't suppose they'd have me, come to that—I'm not at all religious."

"Oh, they'll have anyone! And they'll *condition* you so that you get religious!" the Unitarian said bitterly. "Almost everyone that marries a Catholic ends up by becoming a Catholic themselves! Don't, *please*, do that, Richard."

"Townsend, it's too soon to promise anything," the Englishman said. "Every marriage calls for endless adjustments, and I suppose one makes them as they come along." Suddenly he felt irritated by this pressure; he spoke almost harshly. "If you were to marry her what would *you* do, if she wanted you to become a Catholic? You'd be wax in her hands, and you know it!"

"Not wax to that extent, Richard—no. But let's not quarrel about it. I'm sorry."

The Monsignor, half-asleep in Countess Páloczy's Rolls-Royce, was going to Lisbon, most reluctantly, to bring back Countess Páloczy's daughter. He had warned Miss Probyn at the reception that Dorothée was insisting on this, and that resourceful young woman had contrived to put through a call from back regions overflowing with caterers' men to poor Hetta, warning her to pack and be ready; the palace telephone was working again. "Oh yes, I shall not make him wait; he will be tired," Hetta said. "Is it a nice wedding?"

"Yes, lovely—the greatest fun; Princess Maxine looks entrancing. The Comte de Bretagne has been asking after you, and the Archduke too; he's frightfully disappointed that you aren't here! If I don't see you before you leave I'll come out tomorrow," Julia added. "Did Father A. get off all right? Good."

Hence there was no delay for the Monsignor when he called for Hetta; she was waiting in the hall, Elidio carried out her single suit-case, and they were off. The Monsignor asked if Father Antal were safely gone?

"Yes. I went with him to the plane; Major Torrens was so kind. But you must be quite exhausted, Monsignor; do not trouble to talk with me. Could you not sleep a little, even in the car?"

Subercaseaux glanced at her in surprise.

"Yes, my child, I will. I am in fact very tired." He studied her face. "You are a good girl; you will do your Richard credit." He leaned back and closed his eyes.

Up to the day before Hetta had been dreading her return to the Castelo-Imperial. She hated hotel life anyhow; and her mother, to her never a congenial or pleasant person, would not only be angry with her, but would be reinforced by the detestable presence of Mme de Vermeil, her rival with Richard. The high-bred ease and pleasantness of life as it was led at Gralheira had, even in those two days, increased her reluctance and distaste. But *now,* everything was altered; she was engaged, secure; she need fear nobody, since Richard stood behind her.

Esperanza took her at once to her mother's room. Dorothée was on her bed, the lowered sun-blinds only admitting a dim light; she had taken several aspirins to counteract the royal champagne and lay somnolent, triumphant, but more than a little cross.

"So *there* you are! Well later on you can tell me *what* you've been up to, and where—but now I really have to rest. The wedding was *marvellous,* but these big functions are quite exhausting."

"I am so glad you enjoyed it, Mama. You got my note?"

"Yes of course, but we must talk about all that later on. I really am too tired now."

Hetta was hurt, with good reason, that this should be her mother's sole reaction to the engagement of her only child. A sharp sentence came into her mind; she bit it back, remembering Father Antal's words—"Be kind, be kind," and bent over the bed to give her difficult parent a kiss.

"Naturally, Mama. Rest well; I am sure you need it." As she stood up Esperanza came in.

"A Senhor from the British Embassy asks for the Menina on the telephone. Shall I put the call through here?"

"Yes, yes!" Dorothy Páloczy said irritably. "Here, of course." Esperanza went out, and Hetta eagerly lifted the receiver of the bedside telephone; in a moment she heard Richard's voice, to her full of reassurance.

"Darling! Are you all right? I rang up the old holy, and found that he'd carted you back."

"Yes, quite all right," Hetta said.

"The Major tells me that your private holy got away according to plan, and that you saw him off. I'm so glad."

"Yes; he was *very* kind to arrange this."

"Well I'm sure that has made you feel rather sad, sweetheart, and I'm having a quite hideous time here, trying to clear off my back-log of work. I suggest that presently we both call it a day, and cheer ourselves up by going out to have supper at the Guincho. What do you say?"

"This is where I swam?"

"Yes, my love, you did indeed!"

"And the cooking was *so* good! Yes, Richard; I will come."

"Excellent. I'll call for you soon after seven. Till then, dearest Hetti."

The girl put down the receiver and addressed the rather collapsed figure on the bed.

"Mama, that was Richard. He asked me to dine with him this evening. I have said Yes."

"Well really, I should have thought that tonight, at least, you might have dinner with me, and explain everything," the Countess said crossly. "Anyhow I don't want you to do any more running around with young men, after this week's escapade. You'd better call him back and say No."

Hetta was silent for a moment.

"I cannot do that," she said then, quite gently—"at least, I shall not. Tonight, dear Mama, I dine with my *Verlobte*." (In the stress of this first moment of deliberate independence she could not remember the English word for "betrothed.") She stooped down and gave her mother a second kiss. "Rest well. Why not have something to eat in bed? You must be so tired." She went out closing the door as gently as she had spoken. Alone in the darkened room Countess Páloczy burst into angry tears, interrupted by hiccoughs—in five minutes she was asleep.

Chapter Nineteen

BEFORE driving out to Estoril to take Hetta to dine Mr. Atherley carried out his intention of going to see the Ambassador; as he left the Chancery he was accosted by Tomlinson.

"May I offer my congratulations, Sir? I understand that you are engaged to be married."

Richard was highly entertained—oh the delightful diplomatic grapevine! Who would know about his engagement sooner than the messenger and the telephonist?

"Thank you very much, Tomlinson," he said, holding out his hand. "I may say that my wife-to-be, like yours, is a very good cook!"

"Yes Sir; so I understand. She cooked for quite some time for this Hungarian agent who was flown out today, didn't she?"

Richard shouted with laughter.

"Tomlinson, I believe you're employed by Colonel Marques on the side!" He went out through the walnut-wood and wrought-iron doors, while Tomlinson slipped into the telephone-room to report the Head of Chancery's latest crack to his wife. "Mr. Atherley looks ever so happy."

"He's nice—I hope she is," Mrs. Tomlinson replied. "*Esta?*" she said into the mouthpiece of her head-phones, and went on with her work.

Richard was looking more thoughtful than happy as he set out on that short up-and-downhill walk from the Chancery to the Embassy, through the cheerful inconsequent architecture of the Lapa quarter, brilliantly pink and white in the rich sunshine of late afternoon. During the night—and the day as well, for the few moments when his mind had been disengaged—he had been suffering from the back-thoughts inevitable to sensitive people after they become engaged. For Atherley these doubts were rather more acute than is usually the case, since he was perfectly well aware of the attitude of the Office towards foreign marriages; and while he was not inordinately ambitious, he did care a great deal about his work, and his career in connection with it. And he was not only marrying a foreigner, but one who had just come from behind the Iron Curtain; the vitriol press would undoubtedly seize on this, barely disguising malice as romance or sensation—there would be references to Burgess and Maclean. As he turned the last corner into the steep street leading down to the Embassy (in whose lower reaches washing, propped out on cords from the windows, flapped with a pleasant domesticity in the river-breeze blowing in from the Tagus) he threw up his head and drew a deep breath of the soft salty air that ruffled his bare head. Hetta was worth it, whatever happened!—and anyhow he could always retire to farm and shoot on his mother's place in Herefordshire if the Office got really bloody-minded, and tried to send him to Bogotá.

The Ambassador always kept open house for his staff at the end of the day, with a choice of Scotch or Irish whisky, in a big downstairs room whose windows gave onto the Rua Arriaga, known as his study; he greeted Richard there. "It's so warm, shall we go up and sit in the garden?"

They sat in that small paved courtyard where Hetta had read out the Latin inscriptions and armigerous mottoes of former envoys to the Duke of Ericeira. Richard realised that Sir Henry had suggested this arrangement in order that they should not be interrupted; down in the study the most junior of secretaries, under this accessible chief, could pop in through the Arriaga entrance un-announced, but up here in the private apartments permission must be asked. He was rather touched by this thoughtfulness; H.E. really *was* a kind old boy. It was pleasant in the courtyard: the delicate formal foliage of the great pepper-tree overhanging the steps cut a fine tracery against the blue sky, the scent of flowers came down from the beds fostered by Lady Loseley; from a cage outside the glazed passage her doves cooed gently.

"Those doves!" Sir Henry said. "Comical birds—they're very knowing. They laugh, you know, when anything amuses them. I remember in 1938 listening on the wireless to the speech of one of our masters after Munich; it was chilly, so we had the doves indoors, and when he began to talk about 'peace with honour' you should have heard them—'Hoo-hoo-hoo-hoo-hoo!' We had to laugh ourselves, though it was no laughing matter."

"No animals seem to have cared much for that individual," Richard said, delighted by this reminiscence. "Did you ever hear, Sir, about Miss Stark's little alligator, or lizard, that some Sheik had given her, complete with a golden collar and chain? It rather liked music on the wireless, but one evening in Italy when they were listening to him too, the little creature got so furious that it broke its chain and ran away, and they spent two whole days hunting all through Asolo for it before they got it back."

The Ambassador laughed loudly.

"Your story is rather taller than mine, Richard, but I like it."

"What I really came for, Sir, was to thank you for those two extra days' leave," the young man said. This was true, but he felt such confidence in his friendly superior that he was hoping for an opportunity to air his doubts and problems. He was not disappointed.

"It worked out all right, did it? I gather you're engaged."

"Yes. I don't suppose the Office will like it much, but that can't be helped—one really can't marry merely to please the Private Secretaries and the Chief Clerk!" Richard said somewhat acidly.

"Well in the first place, Richard, I congratulate you most warmly. I think your little Countess is a splendid girl—pretty, intelligent, and learned." He threw a glance at the plaques. "*And* a good cook! I think you've done remarkably well for yourself." He cocked an eye at his Head of Chancery. "Now I'm going to make myself unpopular, and give some unasked-for advice."

"Please do."

"Don't patronise her, Richard. Of course she's got a good deal to learn superficially, but I suspect that her real knowledge begins where that of most diplomatic wives leaves off."

"I realise that, I think." Richard spoke slowly; he hesitated, and then said—

"How much do you think this will affect—well, what I do?"

"Anyhow you can obviously never be sent to any Curtain countries!" Sir Henry said cheerfully. "That's an enormous let-off in itself. Think of those poor devils in our Missions in Moscow and Prague and Warsaw —what a life! You'll escape that." He eyed Richard. "Are you worrying about it?"

"Just a little."

"I shouldn't. It may prevent your being sent to Washington, at least for some time; but Washington is so infernally hot, *and* so infernally expensive!—that's really a let-off too. The fact is, my dear Richard, I think your little lady will soon turn into such a winner—if you don't cow her and make her nervous—that she will be a raging success anywhere."

All this was nectar and ambrosia to Atherley, of course.

"How would you like Rome?" the Ambassador asked suddenly.

"Rome? Why, am I being shifted?"

"Not that I know of. But I think they may want someone for Rome quite soon, and I could slip in a word. If, of course, it would suit you to be shifted. I should be exceedingly sorry to lose you," Sir Henry said—"but possibly you might prefer another post, now."

"Really I should be most grateful if you would slip in that word," Atherley said. "In fact 'grateful' is silly; I should hardly know how to thank you—sorry as I shall be to leave. But—well, I think a change might make things easier for Hetta."

"I think so too," the Ambassador said drily. "Very well—I'll do what I can. And now how about telling me that story we hadn't time for the other day?—of the rescue. Didn't you say the Duke's little girl had played some sort of a lone hand? Another whisky?"

While Richard Atherley—keeping a furtive eye on his watch—was telling Sir Henry Loseley, with considerable relish, the full tale of Hetta's rescue in the Embassy courtyard in Lisbon, the news of the engagement reached Gralheira. Mrs. Hathaway was with Nanny and Luzia when Antonio summoned her to the telephone; on her return she said—

"That was Miss Probyn. It seems the wedding was quite splendid; she says she's busy writing up her despatch about it, but they'll all be back tomorrow afternoon, so we shall hear everything then. And Mr. Atherley is engaged to little Countess Páloczy. They settled it yesterday, on the drive down."

"Well, I call that very suitable," Nanny said. "It's time he settled down, and she's a very nice young lady; well-connected, I understand, too, in her own country."

Mrs. Hathaway glanced at Luzia. The girl's strange Celtic-classical face had taken on its Medusa look; it startled the Englishwoman—she watched that face, suddenly, with the sort of anxiety with which a disposal squad might look at an unexploded bomb.

"Hetta is lucky," Luzia said at last—and Mrs. Hathaway let out the breath which, quite unconsciously, she had been holding. "Atherley's wife will be very happy."

"*Mister* Atherley, Luzia," Nanny said mechanically, as so often before. But on this occasion Luzia was recalcitrant.

"Atherley's wife," she repeated; "or *Richard's*. She is lucky," she said again—"and I hope they will both be most happy." She sprang up from her chair and ran out of the room.

Mrs. Hathaway looked questioningly at Nanny.

"Oh, ever since he came to the house to talk to Miss Probyn about the accident to her car, and all this business of the priests began, the child has been quite mad about Mr. Atherley," Nanny said. "I'm sure you know how young girls are, Madam—at about sixteen their heads are full of poetry and beauty, and absolutely nothing else. They're just waiting for love, only they don't know it; and the first man they see they fall for. Well that's rather a vulgar expression," Nanny said apologetically. "These girlish fancies, they're as fine-spun as cobwebs with the dew on them! But they can be very upsetting, all the same."

Mrs. Hathaway was struck by Nanny's percipience, and still more by the manner in which she expressed it. The neat elderly woman in the navy-blue suit and white silk blouse must at some point in her undiscoverable past life have been impressed by the silver gauze, spangled with dewdrops, spread out on autumn pastures in Leicestershire—to the point of using it for a comparison with the lyric love of sixteen, as she had observed it. Or had she experienced it, too? Almost awestruck by this idea, Mrs. Hathaway gazed at her companion. But Nanny soon brought her down to earth.

"Personally, I think the Major much the more attractive of the two," she said. "But, of course, it's been obvious all along that he has no eyes for anyone but Miss Probyn; whereas this business of the Countess and Mr. Atherley has been what you might call short and sharp."

"Ye-es," Mrs. Hathaway said thoughtfully. She had encountered Major Torrens with deep interest, and was still wondering how that affair stood, and whether he was really the person for her beloved Julia. She would have been rather glad to hear Nanny on this point, but could not quite bring herself to ask. Nanny, however, obligingly volunteered her views.

"I don't know, I'm sure, whether Miss Probyn will take him or not. And I find it hard to make up my mind whether she'd be wise to. He's a splendid gentleman, but he's *solid*, and she's so quick—it mightn't work."

"You're very fond of her, aren't you?" Mrs. Hathaway temporised.

"Of course—what's more, I *admire* her. Who wouldn't, that had lived and worked with her?"

Mrs. Hathaway's discretion was melted by this tribute.

"Nanny, you think she—well, might blow him sky-high?"

"She might; or he might pull her down. It wouldn't hurt *him* to be given a bit of a lift, but I should hate to see her wings clipped," Nanny pronounced—and Mrs. Hathaway, deeply agreeing, could have embraced her for those words.

While this conversation was taking place the subjects of it were standing together at the window of the schoolroom in the Ericeira Palace in Lisbon, occupied with the same problem. The round table behind them was strewn with sheets of typescript; when the Major arrived Julia had been busy finishing her account of the wedding, which she intended to take out to Portela by car to catch the late plane for London—Julia was rather good at wheedling pilots or bribing stewards into doing this sort of job for her. Torrens' arrival threatened to upset her time-table, but the moment he entered the room she realised that he was in a state of emotional urgency; she greeted him kindly, looked at her watch, and decided that he could have twenty-five minutes for whatever was eating him. She could guess all too well what it was.

"Well, that job's done," she said easily, after hearing his account of Father Antal's departure.

"Yes, thank God. It has been a teaser, too. And but for you I should have mucked it—they would have nabbed us at the level crossing coming out from Estoril that night. In fact really you've done it all." He looked at her. "The last time our lines crossed on a job you were against me, and you beat me; this time you were on my side. I—I very much prefer it that way."

"Well anyhow bless you, Hugh, for having taken Hetti out to the airport to see him off," Julia said, still lightly and without stress. "That was a real kindness."

"You say 'Bless you' so easily," he said irritably. "But you know quite well that there is only one blessing I really want, and you go on and on withholding it. When are you going to make up your mind?"

The girl continued to stare out of the window onto the garden, where one corner of the lawn was rendered countrified by a coop in which a hen still sat on Nanny's bantam eggs—that good woman had decided against taking the clutch up to Gralheira lest the drive should spoil them. She found it hard to answer the man beside her—moreover, she had a slight sense of guilt on his account. When she had first met him in Tangier, just over a year before, he had seemed determined and masterful, almost aggressive—up to a point that was something she approved of, and she had rather fallen for him. She did still like him very much; physically he could easily stir her. But—oh, what was it? Somehow in this Portuguese context he had shown himself as *less* than he had in Morocco; occasionally he had been at a loss, or out of key. All that was natural enough: he had found himself plunged into a totally strange environment, to her deeply familiar—it was no wonder that he had had to rely on her for a great deal. And to be just to him he freely admitted his debt. But—again—it was no good marrying someone whom you had to be *just* to! Perhaps later on it might all come right; in other circumstances, or elsewhere. She was angry with herself that at this moment there should arise in her mind, quite unbidden, the picture of Hugh sitting in the Land-Rover holding Luzia in his arms: that was irrelevant and unworthy—but having arisen, it stuck like a burr. Well he would have to wait, till she saw her way; no, *felt* her way, in a fashion which would make justice as irrelevant as his merciful care of that exhausted child.

"Hugh, I can't make up my mind now," she said gently. "If I did, it would have to be No—and I don't want that to be the answer, any more than you do. But you must leave it yet-a-while."

Of course he argued, protested.

"No!" she said at last, sharply—"I won't be rushed. If you try that on, it's No for keeps! I expect I've been vague and daffy-ish, and I apologise, if so—but don't try to bounce me. I won't stand for it."

"If you don't want it to be No ultimately, I don't see why you can't make it Yes now," he urged. "What *is* it, Julia?—what's in your mind?"

"I don't know—Portugal, perhaps. But please leave it for now, Hugh."

"I believe you're in love with the Duque!" he said angrily.

"No, I'm not—though I can't think *why* not; he's such a charmer. Of course the person he ought to marry is Mrs. Hathaway," she said. "That would be so marvellous for Luzia." She turned to him. "Hugh, when do you leave?"

"Day after tomorrow."

"Where for?"

"London, in the first place."

"And where's Colin?"

"Back at Gibraltar—I heard this morning. He did that business at Cannes very well."

"May I tell Edina? Discreetly?"

"Yes, I think so. Wait till it breaks in the press, though."

The mention of the press reminded Julia of her despatch; she looked at her watch.

"Hugh, you'll have to go now; at least I shall. I must get this thing off to my paper." She moved to the table as she spoke, and began pushing the sheets of typescript together; then she left them, and turned to him.

"Don't be angry with me, whatever you do. Drop me if you think I'm too much trouble to be worth while; otherwise just forgive me for wanting to be certain." She pulled the velvet strap of the bell. "Goodbye."

"No, damn you, au revoir," he said; and picked up his hat and went out.

The run out to Portela was a relief to Julia after this scene, which left her dissatisfied with herself, sorry for Hugh, but implacably determined not to marry him till her heart and mind should give the word together. The evening air came in at the windows and cooled her flushed cheeks; the horizon over the Tagus was a soft green and rose, and out in the open land the olive-trees detached themselves, dark and shapely, from the green and rosy fields. At the airport she handed over her package of script to one of the air crew, and then drove leisurely back into Lisbon. At this hour, just before nightfall, there was a wonderful quality in the light—the pale tones of the buildings glowed, street lamps burned like great stars through trees whose green had a depth and richness unknown by day; in the blocks of flats the windows were oblongs of soft light. Back at the house, after parking her car in the courtyard she rang up the Castelo-Imperial; but Hetta of course was out, dining with Richard at the Guincho. Oh well, never mind—tomorrow she would recover her car from Colonel Marques and flip out to see the child before driving herself to Gralheira.

She went up to the schoolroom. Her typewriter still stood, open, on the table; mechanically she clipped on the cover and set it in its place on the bookshelf, emptied an ash-tray, patted the faded cushions on the old sofa—there! But still the room, now tidy, was somehow full of poor Hugh and his distress. With an impatient shrug the girl went over to the window and leaned her elbows on the sill. And at once Hugh and his troubles fell away; Portugal and its beauty enfolded her once more. The light was almost gone—the white shapes of the two swans who circled, cold and detached, in the pool on the lawn gleamed in the gathering dusk: she could barely distinguish the humble grey oblong of Nanny's hen-coop. To think of Nanny was to think of Luzia, and her mind lingered on that lovely child—Julia had guessed what Nanny had guessed, and she remained for some time wondering just how hard her pupil would be taking the news of Atherley's engagement. About that engagement itself she had no doubts—Hetta was as tough as Hell, she would learn what she needed to learn, and be the making of Richard, once that old poppet of an Ambassador had pushed him off to Rome. But what a funny, *rapid* business it had all been! The last thing she expected when she came out to cover the wedding for the *Northern Post* was to find herself involved in the escape of a little Hungarian priest and in Hetta Páloczy and her affairs; all the same these episodes, Julia Probyn decided, as she leaned from an upper window in Lisbon, were intrinsically much more important and exciting than the royal marriage which tomorrow would fill the headlines of the world's press.

Tomorrow!—tomorrow would see her back at beloved Gralheira, sunk in the country life of Portugal, with its ageless calm and beauty. As she turned away from the window there came a knock on the door, and Francisco the footman entered.

"*Minha Menina,* the Senhora Condessa desires to know if the Menina is coming down to say the Rosary?"

"*Sim,* Francisco—I come." And twining her black lace mantilla round her golden head, Julia Probyn went down to the Chapel to join her hostess.